ONE TRUE MATE · 5

Shifter's Rogue

LISA LADEW

So many thanks to...

Book cover by The Final Wrap <3

Cover model: Matt Zumwalt. Rowr.

Photographer: Shannon McPeek

Muse by The Blurb Diva, Anette King, (www.theblurbdiva.com/). Many hilarious convos about random Mac mannerisms ensued in the last 7 or 8 months. Made the book harder to write (I had to figure out how to stick all the bits in), but a thousand times more hilarious.

Of course, no book of mine could be finished without the help and influence of Kristine Piiparinen and Amanda Quiles. Thank you both. Amanda really went above and beyond with this book with some great ideas for me. No spoilers. <3 <3

Thanks to my boys (Joe, 14, Broin, 4, and John, 52) for holding down the fort and understanding my quirks and passions.

And then there's the readers. You who love this story, this world, this universe. It loves you back. Big time.

GLOSSARY

Bearen – bear shifters. Almost always work as firefighters.

Citlali – Spiritual leaders of all *Shiften*. They are able to communicate with the deities telepathically, and sometimes bring back prophecies from these communications.

Deae – goddess.

Dragen – dragon shifter. Rare.

Echo – an animal with the same markings of a *shiften*. Usually seen as a harbinger of bad things, but could also be a messenger from the Light.

Felen – big cat shifters. Almost always work as mercenaries. They are also the protectors of Rhen's physical body and a specially-trained group of them can track Khain when he comes into the *Ula*.

Foxen – the *Foxen* were created when Khain forcibly mated with female *wolfen*.

Haven, The – final resting place of all *shiften*. Where The Light resides.

Impot – a *shiften* that cannot shift because of a genetic defect caused by mating too close to their own bloodline. Trent and Troy are not thought to be *impots* because they were born during a *klukwana*.

Khain – also known as the Divided Demon, the Great Destroyer, and the Matchitehew. The hunter of humans and the main nemesis of all *shiften*.

Klukwana – a ceremony where a full-blooded *shiften* who mates another *shiften* does so with both in animal form, then the mother stays in animal form during the entire pregnancy. The young in the litter are always born as their animal. *Wolven* from a *klukwana* always come in at least 4 to 7 young. *Bearen* are always two cubs, and *felen* are unpredictable, sometimes only one. *Shiften* born from a *klukwana* are almost always more powerful, bigger, and stronger than regular *shiften*, but many parents don't try it because of the inherent risks to the mother during the (shorter) pregnancy and the risk that the *shiften* young may choose not to shift into human form. A lesser known possibility is that the *shiften* young will have a harder time learning to shift into human form, especially if no one shifts near them in the first few days after birth.

KSRT – Kilo Special Response Team, or Khain Special Response team. A group of *wolven* police whose primary goal is to hunt down and kill Khain, if that can be done.

Light, The – The creator of the *Ula*, humans, Rhen, Khain, and the angels.

Moonstruck – Insane. *Shiften* who spend too long indoors or too long in human form can become *moonstruck* slowly and not even realize it.

Pravus – Khain's home. A fiery, desolate dimension that sits alongside ours.

Pumaii – a small group of specialized *felen* tasked with tracking Khain when he crosses over into our dimension.

Renqua – a discoloration in a *shiften's* fur which is also seen as a birthmark in human form. Every *renqua* is different. The original *renquas* were pieces of Rhen she put inside the wolves, bears, and big cats to create the *shiften*. Every pure-blooded shifter born since has also had a *renqua*. Half-breeds may or may not have one. Some *foxen* acquired weak *renquas* when they mated with *shiften*. Also called the mark of life.

Rhen – the creator of all *shiften*. A female deity.

Ruhi – the art of speaking telepathically. No humans are known to possess the power to do this. Not all *shiften* are able to do it. It is the preferred form of speaking for the *dragen*.

Shiften – Shifter-kind.

Ula – earth, in the current dimension and time. The home of the *shiften*.

Vahiy – end of the world.

Wolfen – a wolf shifter. Almost always works as a police officer.

Wolven – wolf shifters, plural.

Zyanya – When a *wolfen* dies, the funeral is for the benefit of humans, but the important ceremony is the *zyanya*. The pack mates of the fallen *wolfen* run in wolf form through the forest, heading north to show the spirit the way to the Haven. When they reach a body of water, they all jump in and swim to the other side, then emerge in human form.

CHAPTER 1

*M*acalister Niles, Mac to his friends and enemies, stared at the massive teakwood shelving unit that took up all of one of his walls, trying to determine what was *off* about its contents.

At a glance, everything looked ok. The tiny terrariums he'd found in his favorite cereal, Alpha-Bits, were pointed at the Sesame Street mini-beans, so Big Bird, Grover, and Elmo could see the plants inside. The entire collection of Pokemon collectibles were neatly lined and sorted by color and cuteness. The Darkwing Duck Fanny Pack was perfectly equidistant from the Teenage Mutant Ninja Turtles bowl and the spooky spoons, the light-up spoons, and the dinosaur spoons.

Mac bent and checked a lower shelf, then the next, but the unopened sticker packs were all in place, the rings, whistles, and temporary tattoos all looked perfect, and the mini pinball machines were exactly as he'd left them.

He got down on his knees to examine the shelves that would have been the perfect height for three-year-old Mackenzie, his now long-gone little sister, to comb through. The wacky wall-walkers, monster bike spinners, glow-in-the-dark skeleton pirates, ghost detectors, and monster disguises were all exactly as he'd placed them. Mackenzie would have said they were *adowwable*. She always had liked the strangest shit for a little girl. No Barbies for her. She had only liked it if it had four eyes or simulated entrails... or, of course, if it came out of a cereal box.

Mac stood to eye the unit as a whole, moving around a bit to see it from a different angle. He saw it! The replica of Mackenzie's favorite blanket that lined the back wall of the shelf had shifted off-center on one side, revealing a sliver of the wood behind it. Mac stepped forward and gingerly reached his hand past all the treasures, pulling at the red spiky blanket, trying to get it just right, barely hearing the car pull up in his driveway.

Heavy footfalls sounded on his porch, and Bruin's deep but somehow gentle voice reached him. Talking to himself.

"Is this the place? This has got to be the place."

Spring had not quite arrived, but it was trying hard and the sunshine of the morning had been enough to make Mac leave his security door open, so only the screen door was between him and Bruin. Shit. Instant regret, not only for that, but for inviting Bruin to his house at all. Bruin would be the first person to see the place in... ever?

It had been his family's place, where he'd spent most of his boyhood, but after the females had been killed, his father had pined for his mate and had died young, drank and sorrowed himself to death, leaving Mac even more alone than he'd been. Since his father's wake, had he ever invited anyone over?

Mac's jaw tightened at the memories wanting to flood in on him. He'd had it no worse than anyone else and he wouldn't act like he did. Boohoo had no place inside his head.

He tugged at the blanket one more time, then stepped back to survey his work as Bruin pulled the screen door open gently and stepped inside, making the room seem too small, suddenly, even though Mac wasn't even looking at him. Bruin had that effect on most rooms.

"Mac! I knew this was the place!" Bruin cried, excitement in his voice, like he hadn't seen Mac in months, years maybe, when in fact they'd seen each other less than ten hours ago. Mac grinned and faced him, his grin faltering as Bruin's eyes shot past him and took in the room instead.

Mac knew it was a hot mess, but it was his hot mess, and it made him feel… better, somehow.

Bruin took in the spiky red blankets hung in the center of three of the room's walls, the red upholstered reclining chair, also done in that spiky red fabric that looked like it was rough, but really was surprisingly soft. Faux Fur Fabric Long Pile Monkey Shaggy was the name of that particular fabric, and fire red had been Mackenzie's favorite shade. She'd never gone anywhere without her blanky, burning through so many of the things that their mother had bought an entire forty-eight-foot roll of the fabric to cut and sew the blankets herself, and damned if Mac hadn't continued the tradition, even after both of them were gone. Sometimes he would make a new one, just so he could pretend Mackenzie was waiting anxiously behind him for it, pretend for forty-five minutes or so that she was still alive, that when he pulled the blanket out of the sewing machine, cut and tied the threads, then turned to her with it in his hands, her baby blues would widen and she would rush to him, hugging and kissing him first, then take it from him reverently to rub across her plump cheek. Ba-ba, she'd called the blankets, even after she could say blanket correctly.

Mac let the thoughts and emotions flit through his mind for a mere moment before he pushed them away, manhandled them into some mental dream chest, and slammed the lid. He both loved and hated his memories of Mackenzie, and the conflict tore at him daily. He clenched his fists and reached for the only emotion that could cover it. Pissed-off-ness. Then he summoned his best super power. Snark. Now he was ready to deal with someone else in his home. Bruin was a good start. No matter what he said to Bruin, the male would not get angry, would not turn away from him.

Bruin took in the bits of haphazard red without comment, then his eyes landed on *The Cereal Prize Shrine*. Mac waited for Bruin to laugh, to make fun, for his eyes to widen and maybe for him to back out the door like he'd just entered the den of a freak. But Bruin only raised his eyebrows, pursed his lips, and gave an I-can-dig-it head bob, like maybe he'd even expected it.

The knot inside Mac loosened slightly, but he still glared at the big bear. "Not a word," he warned.

Bruin held up his hands, then mimed locking his lips and throwing away the key. He pushed past Mac, his head still bobbing up and down, to get closer to The Shrine. His thick fingers raised as he prepared to lift a small toy from the shelf.

"Ah!" Mac moved so quickly he expected to hear wind whistle past his ears. He caught Bruin's hand in mid air and pushed him backwards a step. "No touchy, big guy. I've got extras you can play with after your nap, but right now we've got places to be."

Bruin bobbed his head again, his eyes still on the little

toys, his expression saying he wouldn't say no to playing with them, or their extras. "Cool. Do we have time to watch *I Love the 80s?*"

Mac pushed Bruin back another step. It was like pushing a linebacker who didn't want to go. At a couple of inches taller than Mac's six foot three inch frame, and certainly thicker through the chest and shoulders, Bruin was hard for even a brute like Mac to manhandle. "Yeah, you're hilarious. I get it, cuz my decorating reminds you of the era." He pushed again. He'd done it. Another person had been in his house and he hadn't lost it, but emotions he didn't like to examine were perilously close. It was time to go. Time to do anything else. "Keep moving, big and hairy. Time to go to work."

Bruin let himself be pushed. "Can we stop to eat on the way?"

Mac glanced at the time. 10:04 in the morning. "You didn't eat breakfast?"

"I did. I'm hungry again. Besides, there's a place I keep hearing about we gotta try. It's out on Route 41, called the Honeybee Garage or something. The pies there are supposed to be the bee's ankles."

Mac stopped pushing, even though they'd almost reached his front door. He half-grinned and stared at Bruin. "The what?"

"You know, bee's ankles. Better than bee's knees, but not quite as good as the bee's nose."

Mac shook his head and laughed, pushing past Bruin to the door and opening it, waiting as Bruin took one last look around his place. "Actually, Bru, I don't know about bee ankles or noses. I've only ever heard of the bee's knees."

Bruin bobbed his head one last time and followed Mac out onto the porch. "It's just as well. The bee's nose is pretentious. Don't even get me started on the bee's elbows."

Mac could believe they were having the conversation. Bruin was a font of ridiculousness. "Do bees have elbows?"

"Are you kidding? They have six!"

Mac locked his door, shaking his head. Six elbows. Beebows. Got it. He turned to see what Bruin would be driving him to work in, then groaned at the sight of the tiny red Ford Escort with black trim and the ridiculous spoiler on the back. "Bruin, that thing is smaller than the car we had to drive back from California. It's a fucking lunch pail. How many juice boxes can you fit in the trunk?"

Bruin strode to it, his face proud. He patted the hood. "She's a 2003. Gets 32.9 miles to each gallon. I tracked her myself. Name's Peony Honey."

"You're kidding me, right? This is a joke. You've got a truck stashed somewhere." He looked around, hopefully eying the big evergreen in front of his neighbor's place. There could be a truck on the other side of it.

"I never joke about quality wheels, Mac-attack. It's practical. That's what matters in a car."

Mac started forward, then stopped mid-stride and studied Bruin's face. He was telling the fucking truth. Mac would be stuck in this thing until his car was fixed or the insurance company totaled it. "Bruin, come on." He dropped his voice, eying it and shaking his head. "You can't even fuck in the backseat."

Bruin bent and peered in the window, as if to check, then straightened, a frown on his face. "Your car doesn't have a backseat, Mac."

Mac groaned again, louder this time, as he dragged his feet over the concrete to Bruin's sedan. "Maybe not, but at least I look cool in it, not-fucking. This thing is pure woman repellant."

Bruin pulled open the driver's door, bent into the car for a moment, then popped back up again, cheap blues-blocker shades covering his eyes. "Not the right woman, Mac. Remember that."

Mac watched as Bruin climbed into the tiny car and the entire thing settled to the left to accommodate his bulk. Mac hoped a tie rod would snap, then they could walk the twenty-two miles to the police station. That would clear his head. Maybe.

No such luck. With a sigh, Mac pulled open his door. Only good thing, he wasn't thinking about that thing he didn't want to think about, anymore.

Really.

CHAPTER 2

*R*ogue Kendall pushed her cart into the maintenance elevator of the Chicago condo, her cap pulled low over her face, her non-descript blondish-brown hair hidden under it, her athletic but slim build hidden by the bulk she'd strategically placed under the blue coveralls she wore. To anyone further than five or six feet away from her, she would look like a man. But if they got closer, she could be in a bit of trouble, since she'd worn no facial hair or tried in any way to disguise that she was really a woman. Even in the new millennium, not too many women were working maintenance and wearing coveralls.

She pressed the button for the fifth floor and settled back against the wall as the doors to the stinky elevator closed jerkily and the thing lurched upward. She'd disguised herself as a man many times before, successfully. With her height, she could pull it off, wearing a fake goatee and oversized ball cap, unless someone wanted to talk to her. No matter how often she practiced, her man's voice was always lacking, and pretending to be mute attracted more attention than it dissuaded. Acting pissed off and dangerous worked better, but people paid attention to pissed off people. Remembered them. Which was the exact opposite of what she was going for.

She shifted her eyes to the corner of the elevator and fixed her face with a neutral expression. Bored employee, counting the hours until work was over. Women would leave her alone, but men almost always tried to talk to her. Not that she thought she would run into any tenants, and she knew she wouldn't run into any other maintenance employees. She had their schedules memorized.

The elevator reached the floor she wanted without stopping, and, when the doors dinged open, the way was clear. It was the middle of the day, and most people would be at work, even the silly, spoiled mistress she was going to pay a visit to had a spa to visit and a massage to get on Tuesdays.

That morning, Rogue had reached into her bag of tricks to ensure the day security guard to this condo building would not make it in. The night guard who'd been forced to work overtime was currently snoring behind the desk on the first floor. She expected no interruptions, and if there was one, she would handle it. Handling shit was her specialty. One of her specialties.

She pushed her cart to the end of the hallway, eyes swiveling, ears straining to identify every sound. All was normal. When she reached the heavy metal door that led out to the roof, she parked her cart to one side and eyed the control pad there. The standard emergency code would probably get her through the door, but there was no challenge in that, so she would do things the hard way. Maybe someone would almost catch her and she'd have to run, fight, break a sweat, use her brain.

Maybe some cops would show up. Maybe one in particular. Tall, muscles for days, a sharp tongue, not scared of anything...

Rogue came back to herself with a jerk, the sounds and sights of the hallway rushing instantly into her consciousness, along with blistering self-recrimination. What was *wrong* with her? She listened to the hallway closely before turning her head and confirming what she already knew. It was still empty. She'd been doing that... fugue thing more often lately. *Too often.* Drifting off into some private recess of her mind, some private fantasy world where a big—

Rogue cut the thought off relentlessly and bent over her work. She'd figured out what the trigger was two or three times ago, now if she could just keep herself from thinking about it again she could finish this job. She'd wanted a challenge? Try being a cat burglar and paid spy who couldn't think the word cop without losing a few minutes of her life.

That wasn't entirely true. She could think the word, she just couldn't allow herself to feel the emotions and connections that the word brought to her. The strange fantasy that always—

Rogue jerked again, returning to her conscious mind with a small, startled cry this time. She set her tongue between her teeth and bit down, whipped her head around to ensure the hallway was still empty, refused to contemplate how long she'd been out, and faced front to study the keypad on the wall in front of her, pulling off one of her too-big work gloves to reveal the slim, thin gloves underneath. She always covered her hands. Her fingers were too long and thin.

Artist's fingers that marked her almost as much as her height did. They would be remembered, especially by anyone with an artistic bent.

Three days before, she'd been up here in a different maintenance outfit, and dusted the pad. Now she leaned in, looking for the numbers that the dust had been wiped from by repeated use. 2, 3, 6, and 8.

24 permutations. She'd be on the roof in minutes. She started with the most likely one. 2368- but, as soon as she pressed the 2 in 2368, the box beeped and the door buzzed open. What in the hell? She looked around, stared hard at the box, then pushed the door open before it decided to lock again. Shit. That hadn't made any sense at all. Was someone messing with her? No. Some instinct told her no, no one was messing with her. The security box must be... malfunctioning. She always was lucky with shit like that.

Rogue maneuvered her cart through the door, the slight chill of the March morning biting at her cheeks. She pushed her cart across the flat, open, roof area, to the northeast corner of the building, distracted by the view for only a moment. The condo was a red-brick building, very typical Chicago, located in an up-and-coming neighborhood, but since it was only five stories high, the view from the roof barely stirred any excitement in her. She needed at least fourteen floors before her heart beat faster. The higher the better.

She parked her cart against the three-foot wall that ran around the roof, corralling it to keep people and crap from falling off the edge, then knelt and dug through the cargo area under her cart, pulling out her Bosun's chair and rigging, working hard and fast. Just the way she liked it, ha ha. Her lips curled into a bitter line. Yeah, right. She wished she could find someone to give it to her hard and fast, slow and gentle, any way at all. Just one man who wasn't a weenie, that's all she needed. Just one who wouldn't look at her height and her muscles, her sharp tongue, her tendency to throw elbows first and ask questions later, if then. If she could just find that one guy who wouldn't take all of that in and suddenly remember a very pressing appointment to get his dog washed or his tires retreaded. Just one guy who maybe was bigger than her, stronger than her, not scared of her, who could handle her at her worst, because she didn't have a best. She could almost see him, The One from her dreams, knew what his profession would be. And wouldn't that be a bona fide *hoot*, if he really were a cop? How would that even work? She wasn't giving up her *profession*, what she was best at, even if the dick game was strong, even if he called her beautiful…

Rogue jerked and looked up into the streaming almost-spring sunlight, blinking and wondering how much time she had lost. She shook her head sharply and bent back over her work, tongue clamped between her teeth so hard the pain kept her grounded.

Fourteen minutes later, she had it all set up. She threw the Bosun's chair over the side, donned her work belt and harness, tested her rigging, then leaned long ways along the wall, and recklessly dropped her feet into the chair. She grabbed her bucket and squeegee from the top of her cart, attached them to her belt, then wiggled her way into the chair, until her butt was sitting on the canvas seat. She clamped her safety gear on, then lowered herself to the first window, making a good show of cleaning it. Someone was watching her. Make that two someones. She could feel them, both from the building across the street, both on floors lower than her. The eyes on her felt like beacons, pointing out their owners with uncanny precision. Weird, yes; she'd discovered as a child that no one else seemed to have the ability to know when someone was watching them in the way she did, but she certainly appreciated it, weird or not. Growing up in the way she had, it had been a boon, a blessing, a way to survive.

She moved to the next window, cleaning it slower than needed, then dropped down to another. Within just a few minutes, the eyes lost interest, and went about their day. She moved back up the wall, back to the top floor, then decisively went over the side of the balcony there, pulling her chair with her, dropping it onto the floor behind the privacy wall. Anyone looking now would see only her ropes. She would be in and out before any looky-loos thought to call somebody.

Crouching, she scanned the balcony and just inside the door for cameras. Finding none, she quickly stripped off her harness, coveralls, and cap, revealing her black yoga pants and black long-sleeve shirt underneath, loose around the belly and forearms, the better to hide what she had there. Her slim gloves stayed on. She stood and headed for the sliding glass doors, fingering her lock-picking instruments through the leather of the slim black pouch around her waist that looked like a belt. Sometimes she wore it under her shirt, sometimes over, but she almost always wore it. No purses for her.

She didn't need her tools. The door was unlocked, the alarm not even set. Stupid woman. Rogue knew her target would never have left the door unlocked, but when men chose their mistresses for her honey hams and candied yams, sometimes things like brains and the ability to follow simple instructions that didn't have to do with mascara or lip liner got left out of the equation.

Rogue pulled the door open and prowled inside, getting a feel for the place as a whole. She knew exactly where the bag she wanted would be, if it were here, but simple human curiosity occasionally got the better of even her. Pictures lined one wall. Rogue snorted when she realized most of them were selfies of Miss Candy Yam herself, with Rogue's target, Lorenzo Dotti, The Chief of the Chicago PD's Organized Crime Bureau. Her mouth pursed distastefully as she studied them, their brashness. What would Mrs. Dotti think if she saw these pictures? Rogue refereed a brief internal struggle about sending them to her, then decided against it. Mrs. Dotti knew Lorenzo had an outside snuggle bunny. Rogue had discovered, over the last six weeks of surveillance of him, that he spent more nights in this condo than he did at home.

She'd read it in the paper a few times, too, never wanting to believe that someone in such a high position of authority in the city got away with such frequent and public intimations that he was unfaithful to his wife. That may have been why she'd taken this job. Ordinarily, she would never take a job that had to do with the cops, or even someone who wasn't a criminal, but she was pissed at Chief Lorenzo. Had been for a long time. That shit wasn't right.

Rogue headed straight for the tiny alcove off the bedroom that Chief Lorenzo kept as a third office. The words *Chief Lorenzo* tasted bad to her, even in her head. He was good at his job, but crappy at his personal affairs. Why get married if you weren't going to stay faithful? What was even the point? She shook her head and entered the tiny room, more of a closet than an office. When Lorenzo had left work the night before, he'd had the black messenger bag over his shoulder, and when he'd left the condo this morning, he hadn't. Simple logic said that she would find it in here, and if she did, she could put a six-week job to rest.

She grinned as she visually swept the room. When she found that folder, it would make her a quarter of a million dollars richer.

CHAPTER 3

Mac shifted in his seat, but there was no pulling his knees out of his chest, even with the seat back as far as it would go. Bruin looked even more ridiculous than Mac felt. The big bear hulked over the steering wheel so his head wouldn't brush the ceiling. If they crashed, the air bag wouldn't stand a chance; it would pop like a water balloon flung against a brick wall.

"Bru, take a right here. Let's hit Mik Maks instead of that new place." Mac didn't have a lot of hope *that new place* existed. Bruin was famous for his wild goose chases of anything that had the word *honey* associated with it, the more unlikely the better. Just last month, they'd driven four hours north to Langlade Forest in Wisconsin, on a rumor that bees had been seen entering caves in the Bear Haven Wildlife Preserve. Never mind that it was the middle of winter. Never mind that Bear Haven Wildlife Preserve didn't actually contain caves of any decent size. Bruin had rented a full-size van, filled it with climbing and rappelling equipment that made Mac's stomach shrivel into a tiny, painful ball, then dragged Mac with him, regaling Mac with tales of Elvish honey that had been found in a cave in Turkey and routinely sold for $2000 an ounce. According to Bruin, it could cure any disease, including, apparently, tooth decay and something called Foreign Accent Syndrome.

They hadn't found any caves or any honey, and Mac had escaped with only a small bit of frostbite on his pinky toe. Easily cured with a shift. Mac considered himself as getting off lucky, since, if they had found some cave they needed to rappel into, he would have been glad to break his own leg or arm to make sure that didn't happen. Gah, he hated heights of any kind, and even got nauseous on a stepladder.

It had almost been as bad as the time when Wade had forced him to a trust-building exercise in Yosemite with a group of patrol officers, thinking Mac could work on his asshole-tendencies and his fear of heights at the same time. But all Mac had done was ditch the crew and bang some hot-as-lava climber chick as the sun went down…

Still. Mac spoke quickly before Bruin had a chance to think about it. "We'll check out that Honey Garage another time. There's a rut tomorrow night and I'm still in charge of recruiting the females. We need about ten more."

Bruin rubbed his chin, a thoughtful expression on his face, not turning where Mac had indicated. "But Mik Maks is all badge bunnies. If we go to The Honey Shop, maybe there will be regular females there. You don't like badge bunnies, anyway."

Mac grunted. Bruin had him there. "They are generally too… petite for my taste."

Bruin shot him a grin. "You like a woman who looks like she can kick your ass."

Mac shrugged. "Or at least like she might try." He licked his lips and savored the thought of a gorgeous woman who was a match for him in every way. A female he wouldn't have to be gentle with or watch what he said around. He hated trying to filter the bold thoughts in his brain into soft lumps of uselessness that wouldn't offend anyone. Not to mention that trying made his head hurt. The hash tag #nofilter had been invented for his mouth. He knew it. #notgonnachange-whoIam was his, too.

"Here, Bru! Here, turn here. We gotta hit Mik Maks. We'll go to The Honey Spot tomorrow."

"You promise?"

"Yeah, I promise." If it didn't exist, then he wasn't lying.

Bruin turned the wheel, easing the ridiculously tiny car into the lane that would take them to the cop bar on the other side of the park.

"Hey, why don't we leave the car here, cut through the park? We could get some fresh air. Nice day today. Sunshine. Spring and shit."

Bruin threw him a look. "You don't want to be seen getting out of my car."

Mac gave up. He'd tried. If the bear wanted the truth, Mac was honor-bound to give it to him. "Damn skippy I don't, Fozzie, this thing is a disgrace. If you hadn't crashed my car, we could be riding up in style in my Corvette. Park it, sister!"

Bruin pouted, then actually hung his head, almost brushing his cheek on the steering wheel. "Sorry, wolf, I should have told you bears can't resist honeybee nests."

Mac snorted, knowing he was gonna get his way, but unable to resist rubbing it in. He loved his car and she was currently smashed to bits at the mechanic shop. "What if you'd been on your way to a fire, with some other *bearen*? Would all four of your dumb asses driven the fire engine off the road into a tree if you'd seen a bees' nest in it?"

Bruin pulled over and parked the car, shaking his head. "That's what the Dalmatian is for."

Mac smacked himself in the forehead, the crack of skin on skin loud in the confined space. "You are not fucking telling me that firefighters only use Dalmatians in order to keep them away from beehives."

Bruin grinned and bobbed his head, then opened his door and unfolded himself from the lunchbox he called a car. Mac swore he heard Bruin whisper, "Duh. It's the dots. They look like bees," as he climbed out.

Mac ripped open his own door, but Bruin was already striding off into the park, his nose lifted. Mac ran to follow him. He smelled it, too. Strawberry shortcake? Pie? He couldn't tell.

Bruin stopped at a piece of metal art Mac had always found ridiculous and useless. It was high and flat, like a wall, but undulating to give the appearance of flowing, like a humungous metal flag waving in the wind. It was so close to the busy road that it never had problems with graffiti. Until today.

Mac stopped next to Bruin to read it. *The wolves are guarding the sheep, wake up, sheep!* Below it was a black and yellow line-shaded drawing of a wolf that took Mac's breath away, it was that good.

He whistled. "If I could draw like that, I'd draw nothing but naked females."

Bruin didn't even look around. "Wouldn't you have to have seen one first?"

Mac laughed, surprised into it. "Funny, Paddington, I've

seen me with females, you know who I've never seen with a female? You. Never gone to one rut. You scared of vaginas? Do boobies spook you?" But Bruin was already jogging away. He disappeared on the other side of the weird art. Mac shook his head. "Mik Maks is this way!" he shouted, but Bruin was gone.

"What?" Mac snarled to a young boy on a scooter who had stopped on the path to stare alternately at each of them. The boy scooted away and Mac hurried in the direction Bruin had disappeared in, ignoring the fresh air and birds.

He found the big male sitting at the end of a long table lined with people, each with a pie placed in front of them. A man nodded at Bruin, then a pie was set in front of him, too, and a whistle blown. The others at the table dropped their faces into their pies and began eating like their lives depended on them finishing their pies in 3.2 seconds.

Bruin produced a shiny fork from somewhere in the folds of his light jacket and dug in to his pie, his face alight with anticipation. Mac rolled his eyes. "We don't have time for this shit. Did you enter the pie eating contest?"

Bruin delicately chewed and swallowed the bite that he'd brought to his mouth before answering. He motioned at the tin full of crust and sugared berries in front of him and crooked one eyebrow at Mac. "Free pie."

Mac nodded, like everything made sense. "Meet me at Mik Maks when you're done."

Bruin didn't acknowledge him, already intent on his next bite.

***

Twenty minutes later, Bruin finally walked in the door, but Mac was almost done there. He had six new females already. Real party girls. The rut would change them for life, either set them on the path to becoming nuns, or ruin them for single men forever.

He eyed another group of giggling females, testing out opening lines in his head. *Do you like cops?* was used to death and useless in here. They all did, this was a cop bar and they knew it. How about something new? Hmm. *How sensitive is your gag reflex? How long can you hold your breath?* He nodded. The last time he'd used something like the first one on a female, she'd slapped him. He raised a hand to his cheek and rubbed the stubble there, savoring the memory. She'd been a feisty one, all attitude and snark right up until she'd invited him back to her place. He'd gone back for seconds and thirds with her, something he didn't do often.

Bruin passed him without comment and hit the group of girls first. They eyed Bruin up and down, smiling openly at him. Sure, he was tall and muscular. He could think up a good joke every once in a while. But whatever else the females favored in him, Mac couldn't see it. His brown hair was thick and never took a style. He almost had to clip it to his skull to make it not look ridiculous. No matter how often he shaved, he always had a five o'clock shadow, and, in fact, he'd taken to wearing a short-trimmed beard now that he never worked as a firefighter anymore. His nose was bent like it'd been broken a few times and his eyes were the same auburn brown as his hair, plus when he smiled, his dimples were lopsided. Whatever. There was no accounting for female taste. Mac settled back in his chair, watching closely. Bruin didn't talk about females much, and Mac wanted to see if he had any game at all. Mac could still be friends with him if he didn't, he just wouldn't take him out much.

Bruin pulled over a chair and sat down with the females.

Score one for him. But Mac almost fell over in his chair when he heard the first thing Bruin said.

"I live at home with my parents."

Mac's mouth dropped open and he looked around. Had anyone else heard that? He didn't know any of the cops in the bar by name, but he recognized most of them as patrol officers. All of them had their eyes glued to their food. Clowns.

Bruin was at it again. He leaned in close to one brunette and smiled at her, just one stupid dimple appearing. "I have my own pad in the basement, but my mom packs my lunch every day."

Mac shot to his feet while all the females at the table giggled. *School was in session.*

He tapped Bruin on the shoulder, smiling at the women. "Ah, Scorpion, could I talk to you for a sec?" He winked at one female who had raised her eyebrows at the interruption. "Scorpion, that's his nickname." He pulled Bruin to the bar and whispered intently to him. "Bear, be cool, you're gonna ruin everything."

Bruin jerked his head back, his eyebrows drawn tight. "What? Those are my best lines."

Mac shook his head. "Those aren't lines. Those are confessions."

Bruin frowned. "Scorpion's not my nickname. Who told you that?"

Mac's eyes bugged out of his head. "*You* did, you big marshmallow."

Bruin grinned. "Oh yeah, I remember." He leaned in close. "Look, I have a rule. I can only lie to a female five times in our entire relationship. So I like to get them out of the way at the beginning. It doesn't hurt that girls eat the corny stuff up."

Mac stared hard, trying to make sense of any of what Bruin had just said. He looked at the table of females, half of whom were watching them, all still with smiles on their faces, then back to Bruin. "What happens when they find out the first five things you said were a lie?"

Bruin shrugged. "I don't know, I never had one stick around that long."

"What is wrong with you?"

Bruin crossed his arms over his chest. "Right, like you've had long relationships? Lay your longest one on me. What was it? A month? A week? Overnight?"

Mac didn't say a word. He couldn't defend himself.

Bruin raised his hand, palm facing Mac. "I thought so. Talk to the claw."

"That was corny as shit."

Bruin grinned. "Corny is my thing. I thought you knew."

Mac frowned. "So, what about me? Is any of the shit you told me a lie?"

Bruin was already looking back at the table of women, waving at them. His eyebrows jerked as he glanced at Mac for only a second. "I don't know. Read it back to me."

"You big—"

Bruin put his hand on Mac's shoulder to cut him off, leaning close. "Ooh, I got a good one. Watch and learn."

He leaned over the bar and grabbed a lime, then headed back to the table of girls, producing a sharpie from some hidden pocket somewhere, and writing a phone number on the lime. He handed it to the female he'd been sitting next to before. "That's my best pickup lime, just for you."

Mac grabbed a chair and pulled it over, unable to believe he was going to even humor the bear, but the female had already whipped out her phone and texted the number

Bruin had put on the lime, making Bruin's phone chime in his pocket. The rest of them were giggling again.

Mac frowned, trying to think of the stupidest thing he could possibly tell a woman. He would give Bruin's way a try, just so he could rub it in Bruin's face later when the girls all took off.

He had it! He turned to the blonde next to him. "I didn't learn to tie my shoes till I was 12. Velcro was my best friend."

She threw her head back and laughed, then told him her name and touched his forearm lightly, making him shake his head.

Damn stupid bear.

CHAPTER 4

Rogue turned her face to the struggling sun as she walked down the sidewalk, a green messenger bag hanging from her shoulder. After this job, she would disappear somewhere for a few weeks. Somewhere warm with cliffs to jump from. Maybe she would try base jumping or flying a squirrel suit from the top of Angel Falls in Venezuela, her dream jump. Exhilaration stirred her good feelings. She had the file that was worth a small fortune. All that was left was to get it to Soren.

She hooked a right, heading to the parking garage where she'd left one of her cars the night before. As she turned the corner, a cold wind blasted her, lifting her hair and reminding her spring was still only a promise, despite the sunshine. She pulled her light jacket tighter around her, cinched her stocking cap lower, and slouched a bit more. Cold weather was a friend in her business, bulky clothes and caps providing concealment that made her almost invisible. Long sleeves hid the knives strapped to her forearms.

She'd ditched the coveralls and cap back in the mainte-nance closet where she'd gotten them, intending to put them back in the stack, but she hadn't been able to resist a load of wash agitating in the machine deep in the back of the small room. She had stuffed both items in, not reflecting on her luck. She'd always been an extraordinarily lucky criminal.

Halfway up the dusty concrete stairs to the second floor of the parking garage where her car was stashed, her senses pricked up. She slowed her steps and glanced to the ceiling of the stairwell. No one there. She peered over the handrail. No one below her either. But it wasn't *her* being watched, she realized, it was her car. She had no idea how she could know such a thing, but she trusted her instincts implicitly. She kept climbing the steps past the floor she had intended to enter, all the way to the fourth floor, then pushed open the heavy steel door into the echoes and stink of the garage. She strode purposefully across the concrete, her Ugg boots making al-most no noise. Ugg, she hated the boots, but they worked with her college girl ensemble/disguise which also included yoga pants, and a fur-fringed jacket pulled deep over her face.

She *felt* the eyes of her first tail fall on her right away, coming from the roof of the squat building across the street. She faked hurrying to her car in the far corner, out of his view, but his eyes didn't slide off her. His interest didn't go elsewhere. Which meant he'd been warned how good she was, and he would not dismiss her as the unrelated person she was trying to appear to be.

As she walked, shoulders hunched, hands shoved deep in fur-lined pockets, she thought about who was watching her, and why? If it was Soren, it meant he suddenly didn't trust her, and that meant she could be in real trouble. The guy was dangerous. Not to her, never to her, but why would he watch her?

Rogue lowered her head, circled the row of cars, and headed back for the exit, feeling the interest on her double, although she still hadn't placed the second watcher. She reached the exit door, hit it at a run, and shot down the stairs as lightly as she could in the ridiculous boots. They were good for not making any sound, at least. Once on the ground floor, she headed back the way she had come.

To lose herself in a crowd.

Any crowd.

***

Rogue dodged people on the sidewalk, weighing her options. She hadn't been followed the night before or any time recently. These watchers were new, and somehow they'd known which car was hers, a feat which should have been impossible. It had been bought with cash, registered under one of her aliases, and left in storage until she needed it. She couldn't think of one person who knew that alias, although she could think of a dozen who might have reason to follow her.

Her tails were still behind her and there were more now, one on the block to her left and one on the block to her right, keeping time, while more tracked her from behind, coming fast. They didn't have a visual, but she bet they had radio, and they would be on her in moments if she didn't do something quickly.

On impulse, Rogue turned to her right and jogged up the steps of a brownstone, her eyes scouting the lock type, her fingers teasing a curtain pick out of her pack on their own. She only had a few short moments before her tails were close enough to see her. She was an amazingly fast pick, but was anyone that fast?

She reached the door. Her fingers brought out her tool and seated it in the lock as her eyes searched the room beyond the glass. No people. It was a foyer to what looked to be a two-unit building. Perfect. Score one more for her intuition.

Before she had a chance to feel the placement of the levers or turn her pick, a succession of soft clicks told her the levers were sprung.

She frowned. She hadn't even- shit. She turned the knob, pushed open the door, and slipped inside, ensuring the door behind her was locked again, then sprinted up the stairs. A window on the second floor would give her a much better vantage point to see who was following her without them seeing her.

She reached the window just in time. From just to the left of it, she saw her follower on the sidewalk closest to her, and his partner across the street. They were dressed similarly. Work boots, dark pants and shirt and jacket, caps on their heads. They strode forward with purpose, eyes scanning the people in front of them.

That they were Soren's men seemed more likely than ever.

Which made no sense at all. He didn't need to tail her. She was headed to his place next. She'd never given him any reason not to trust her.

She bit her lip and pressed a hand to the glass, craning her neck to watch the backs of the two men disappear down the sidewalk.

Contingencies raced through Rogue's mind. She couldn't let anyone track her, even Soren. Especially Soren. In her business, when the big boss didn't trust you, you turned up dead. She was way too young for that shit.

She'd known she wouldn't be able to do what she did forever, but was it really time to get out so early? Her nest egg, the one that needed to last for the rest of her life, was still half-empty. She frowned. Half-empty. Half-hatched. Whatever. She was a thief and a spy, not a fucking writer.

Rogue began to form a plan. Step one, she would change disguises. No one beat her at her own game. Ever. Step two, she would visit Soren. Feel him out. Only then would she be able to decide what to do next. If he wanted her dead, there was no way it would happen at his house. Or near his house. He didn't operate like that.

Nearest disguise? She pulled out her phone and looked at her private map. The Englewood post office was the closest. She had a post office box there where she mailed herself a box of clothes once a month, as she did many places in Chicago. It was just good sense.

Decision made, Rogue hurried down the stairs and out the door, turning left and walking the opposite way of the two men who'd trailed her, her senses telling her she was unwatched. She had no sense of the two men anymore, which meant they had lost her completely.

Within moments, she was close to the post office, approaching it from the east, the sun shining from almost directly overhead, heating the day to a pleasant temperature, despite the still-chilly wind.

The post office loomed in front of her, all tan brick and harsh lines. The closer she got, the more her teeth clenched. Something about the place set her on edge. Even before she'd heard of Dr. Henry Howard Holmes or Herman Mudgett, which was his real name, she'd hated visiting this post office.

The echoing of her feet on the tiled floor and the closed-in-ness of the square, squat building stirred a dusty fear inside of her that was rare for her to feel. She had only one true fear that she knew of, well, maybe two, because they went hand in hand, and something about this building made her think of them. A certain emptiness beneath her feet as she walked in the building that always made her think the dungeons belonging to America's first serial killer hadn't been fully filled in like everyone claimed they had. She could sense something below the building.

Rogue used her laser focus to control her emotions, walling them off into a tiny square and covering them with the steel discipline she'd perfected as a vulnerable young girl. In and out, she'd be done in no time. No time for fear or indecision.

Rogue walked up the steps as she had dozens of times before… but she immediately noticed something off. A strange pulse called her attention, firing her neurons and making her muscles sing.

Thump. Thump. Thump.

Rogue frowned and looked around. A man pushing out the exit doors to leave didn't seem to notice anything amiss. Her body on autopilot, she walked in the door he held open for her and made a left to head to her box.

Thump. Thump. Thump.

The sound became louder, like a heartbeat, a living, breathing heartbeat that was not her own, but somehow conveyed excitement to her.

Her own heart sped up, and it wasn't a bad feeling. A humming started inside of her, like power, like electricity, wrapping her muscles and bones in energy. Her eyes crawled over the rows of identical numbered post office boxes in front of her, barely seeing them. She felt, suddenly, like she could fry something with a glare or a touch. Power thrummed through her, shaking loose the trepidation the building brought to her, dissolving the negative emotion in heat and light.

Rogue sensed something wanted her. Something huge and brimming with life. She looked down at her hand, surprised to see it looked normal. No light shot out of it. No electricity sparkled from her fingers.

She dropped her hand and let her body do what it did best. Act normal, no matter what was going on inside her, no matter what her thoughts were hiding. Her feet carried her in front of the row of boxes where her post office box was. She knelt and reached to the flat pouch around her waist to dig out her keys.

A voice sounded, making her hand falter. It seemed to come from everywhere, and yet not outside of her. After a moment's contemplation, she realized she placed its origin right at her heart.

Rogue, come. Come to us. We belong with you.

Rogue looked around, eyes blinking rapidly. No one was paying her any attention yet. There weren't many people there. A mom and a baby to her right, four or five people in line. A big guy coming in the door behind her. A few employees. None of them seemed to notice anything out of the ordinary.

The voice had been loud in her ears, with a feminine lilt and tone, but still clear and booming, like whoever had spoken to her did it through a megaphone.

Rogue stayed where she was and turned inward, replaying the statement. She didn't know what had spoken to her, or if she were completely out of her mind, but she could feel the rightness of the statement, they did belong with her. Whatever they were.

Mine? she thought, digging around in her experiences, trying to sort out what was happening.

But no, that wasn't quite right. *They* belonged *with* her, more than they belonged where they were, but they did not belong *to* her.

Sister, sprang to her mind and she clenched her teeth together again. This had nothing to do with Amaranth, or did it?

Dizzy, Rogue leaned against the post office boxes in front of her. Her touch created a cascading waterfall of clicks and all the little metal doors sprung open, revealing mail-filled boxes.

Rogue pulled her hand away, startled and appalled, dropping heavily to her knees.

Rogue, come now. You must come.

Unable to make any sense of what was happening to her, Rogue shot to her feet. Mailboxes flipped open all around her, creating cracks like gunshots as the moving doors slammed into each other. An employee yelled and another called back, their voices filled with confusion. Eyes fell on Rogue. She raised her hands, showing they were open and empty, then backed away from the post office boxes, turning and hurrying out of the building, leaving the confusion of the employees behind her.

Rogue pulled in on herself as soon as she got outside. She turned right at the bottom of the stairs, following the unwavering thumping and humming of power that was in her very blood, calling to her. She turned right again at the end of the building and hurried over the sodden grass, which was smashed flat by the weight of recent winter snow, then more-recent spring showers.

An overpass stood in front of her, cars whizzing by on top of it. She couldn't see them, but she could hear them. She hurried to the side of the concrete overpass, pushing through the overgrown weeds and kicking aside an old smelly blanket to get close to it.

She reached out a hand to touch the wall at eye level, but her attention was called by something at knee level. Etched into the concrete wall of the overpass were three grooves in the concrete that met in a way that made it look like a small door, barely big enough for an adult to squeeze through. It stood no higher than her knees and was the size of a dog door for a rather large dog.

Rogue stared at it, understanding filling her. Oh no, she was *not* going in there. She didn't care how *right* the voice sounded to her, how much power it was filling her with.

Rogue, yes, come. Come to us.

Rogue squeezed her eyes shut. The power hummed through her, and her hands moved of their own accord. They touched the concrete side of the overpass, but the door had no lock, no knob. It didn't matter. As soon as she touched it, she heard levers spring, and the door that looked like concrete swung open, revealing darkness beyond. Rogue took a step backwards, her eyes locked on it.

"No, not underground. I can't." She almost whimpered and she hated herself for the weakness.

You can. We are here.

Oh God, she had to. She squeezed her eyes shut.

No. Choose to do it, or don't do it. You have *to do nothing.*

Rogue squeezed her eyes shut, her fingernails scrabbled into her palms, digging at the skin there.

She chose.

Digging a tiny light from her pack, Rogue stepped

forward, then knelt and shined it into the hole. Only the opening was small, as soon as she got inside, she could stand.

The air that hit her face was stale and old. But she would not tarry. Her decision had been made.

She shimmied into the hole, her eyes crawling over the dank walls and the dirty ground and the downward slope. She could feel that no eyes were on her as she entered, and no one saw the door swing shut behind her.

CHAPTER 5

*M*ac raised his hand to the leaving group of women, then closed the door to the bar and headed back inside. All of them were going to the rut the next night, but the realization gave him no satisfaction. He was over the ruts, and pissed off that he still had to do the leg work for them. Someone else needed to take over, stat. Someone who was still benefitting from them instead of being terminally frustrated by them, like he was.

If he could just scratch that fucking itch... but random females didn't feel right. Jerking off was the only thing that his body was ok with recently, and that was no fucking fun. Fuck! If he had to wait another year or two for his one true mate to show up, he was going to flip his lid. If he got one at all. There was no guarantee...

To his right sat a pissed-off looking male with long hair mostly covered by a black leather do-rag. Not a cop. He'd been eyeing Mac and Bruin for the last hour, seriously putting himself on Mac's radar. Ol' boy snorted as Mac went by. Mac shot him a look. He wasn't fucking, so he might as well fight, and if leather do-rag was a not-cop in a cop bar, that's probably exactly what he was looking for. Wade would have his ass, but Mac could go for some knock-down, drag-out right about now. It would take the edge off.

Mac turned and walked backwards, glaring at leather do-rag, but the guy had turned his attention elsewhere. Just as well. Mac slid into the booth across from Bruin, shaking his head at the male's burger and fries. "Hurry up. We have to be at the station by one. They are going to hypnotize Beckett's girl to get more information on Grey. See if he said anything that might tip us off to where he was living."

The guy in the black do-rag snorted again. Mac cast a look that way, but the male had already looked away. Fucking troublemaker.

"Beckett's lucky," Bruin said, around a mouthful of fries.

Mac snorted. Whatever. "Yeah? How so?"

Bruin shrugged. "You know, he found his…" His voice dropped and he looked around the room before he finished his sentence in a whisper. "His one true mate."

Mac nodded. He knew the feeling of being ready but still having empty arms. It sucked. "You'll find yours. It just might take a little while."

Bruin shook his head and shoveled in a few more fries. "Nah, *bearen* don't get any. Well, one might, but it won't be me."

Mac snuck a fry. "What are you talking about?"

Bruin dropped the last of his fries and pushed his plate away. He'd finally had enough. In Mac's eyes, it was nothing short of a bear-freaking-miracle. A bearacle, Bruin might say.

Mac snorted, but before he could tell Bruin, the big male's eyes looked anywhere but at Mac and he spoke as if reciting something he'd memorized in school, something that pained him terribly.

"The *bearen* have lost their way and now they will pay. Only the Bear of Great Insight can renew them, make them worthy again. Through the strength and purity of his choices and the caring of his one true mate, all *bearen* will be restored to their former glory, able to work as one again."

This time Mac was the one who looked around to see who might be listening. Leather do-rag was facing the other way, but that didn't mean anything. Mac dropped his voice low and leaned over the table, almost talking in Bruin's ear. "Is that a prophecy?"

Black do-rag turned and caught Mac's eye as he sat his ass back in the booth. The male snorted and Mac shot him a dirty look. Mac looked back at Bruin, not liking the sick look on Bru's face.

Bruin licked his lips and leaned forward, mirroring Mac's volume. "Yeah, but our *Citlali* don't get prophecy anymore. That was the last one that came through. Most *bearen* believe none of us will get one true mates until the Bear of Great Insight gets his and redeems us, if even then." He hung his head. "We messed up."

Mac frowned. "I've never heard of this before."

"We are forbidden to speak of it."

Mac leaned back in the booth and nodded heavily, surprised Bruin was telling him. Black do-rag guy snorted again. Mac curled his lip and turned that way, tension making his fists close. "I'm going to have to kick his ass soon."

Bruin looked over. "He's just jealous. You should feel sorry for him."

"I can feel sorry for him and kick his ass at the same time."

Bruin raised an eyebrow. "Can you?"

Black do-rag pushed away from the bar and stood, walking heavily past Mac and Bruin, his work boots thudding on the floor. Mac locked eyes with him, assessing him. Finally, Mac would get to work off some of his tension. His peripheral vision ate the male up, looking for any sign of weapons or weaknesses.

But black do-rag's feet kept going, steadily headed for the bathroom. Just after he passed Mac and Bruin he growled, "This bromance turn homance yet?"

That was it. Mac heaved to his feet, but Bruin grabbed his arm to keep him in place and called after the guy, "It's not a bromance. It's a bearmance."

Mac shook his head and dropped back into the booth, still tight. "What in the hell is a bearmance?"

Bruin leaned forward, his hand on Mac's arm, whispering, "He doesn't know I'm a real bear. He just thinks we are big hairy gay guys."

Mac pulled his arm out of Bruin's reach and smacked himself in the forehead with the palm of his hand, rolling his eyes so hard they hurt.

Bruin snapped his fingers in front of Mac's face and said, "Forget him. No fights today." He looked around the bar. "Let's practice your pick-up lines. You need a ton of work. Pick the hottest girl in the place."

Mac frowned. He'd rather fight, but Bruin was right, he didn't need the hassle. He ran his eyes over all the women in the place. None of them were quite what he was into, but a hottie in the far corner caught his eye. He pointed her out to Bruin and said, "Her."

Bruin nodded, a knowing look in his eyes. "I should've known you'd pick the only girl in the place who's tall enough to walk the runway without heels. Short girls need love, too, you know."

Mac snorted. "I'll save them for you. You only weigh like 400 pounds. How do you not crush them?"

Bruin ran a hand through his thick hair. "We bears are rather delicate lovers."

Mac snorted again and shook his head. Bruin shot him a look.

"You ever heard of tantric sex, Mac?"

Mac nodded, a frown on his face. "Sex without sex."

"Not exactly. Just without moving so much."

"What's the point, then?"

Bruin tapped a finger to his temple. "The mental connection."

Mac leaned back in the booth and folded his arms over his chest. He'd heard enough. "Sex isn't in the mind, Bruin. It's in the body. Are you sure you're not a virgin? Go with me to the rut tomorrow night. I could show you how it's done."

Bruin's eyes narrowed and he leaned forward across the table. "So, you're going then?"

Mac shrugged. He hadn't decided, but he knew where he was leaning. "Maybe not. I'm not feeling it."

Bruin leaned back in his seat and his hands fell to his sides, slipping off the table in a way that made Mac think of a drunkard. Bruin's face went slack and his voice dropped an octave. His eyes stared through Mac and his words made Mac's heart beat faster. "Good, because your mate will be there. And if she sees you with another woman, she'll never accept you. You don't want to get off to a bad start or you might never get another chance. She's not a very forgiving one, your rogue."

Tension shot through Mac's body. His hands curled into involuntary fists and his mouth filled with saliva. "What?" he sputtered, still trying to put together everything Bruin had said.

Bruin shook himself and looked around for a second before he focused on Mac. He looked normal again, just confused. "What?"

Mac's fingers dug into the table. "You just said my mate is going to be at the rut. You got all weird and then you said it."

Bruin's face reddened under his beard and his eyes slid away from Mac's. He stood, his thighs hitting the table and forcing it a few inches towards Mac. His lips worked like he was flustered, and his face reddened more. Mac had never seen him flustered before. Bruin was always as cool as an icebox.

Bruin took a step away from their table. "I'll be right back," he muttered and headed for the bathroom. Mac stared at the spot where Bruin's broad back had been long after it turned the corner of the hallway. His mind raced. His mate would be at the rut? He couldn't think of a worse situation, if it was true. If he recognized her in the act with someone else, he would kill the male, certainly. And her? He sucked in a deep breath, trying to cool the fire in his chest before he thought about that. He'd have to meet all the females at the door. Test them. Touch them. Make sure none of them belonged to him...

His mind took the image and ran with it, leaving him with no peace.

When Bruin finally returned, his sleeves and even his collar were wet, as if he had been splashing copious amounts of water on his face. He couldn't meet Mac's eyes, still seeming flustered, off his game.

Mac couldn't wait for him to get himself together. He had to know. His voice a low growl, he said, "Bruin, man, bear, tell me what the hell is going on. I gotta know."

Bruin pushed a hand through his hair again, then met Mac's eyes. "I've never told you this before, but I do that sometimes. I haven't done it in awhile and I guess I hoped it was over."

"Do what?"

Bruin shrugged. "I guess I see the future."

See the motherfucking future. Mac really was going to meet his one true mate. Hope and something thicker, almost like anxiety, threaded through him. What he was anxious about he couldn't say, but the feeling was unbearable. Distract. Snark it up. Focus on something else. He shot out of his seat and rounded the table to get close to Bruin, pulling at Bruin's shirt. "Holy shit. Are you a *Citlali*? Do you have a star *renqua*?"

Bruin swung an arm around and caught Mac in the chest, making Mac stagger back five steps, catching his lower back against the bar. Mac rubbed his chest, feeling like he'd been hit there with a sledgehammer. He watched Bruin's face. Flustered and pissed. Two new emotions for Bruin. But was he really pissed? He didn't look pissed. Just tired, and a little worried about how Mac would react, his eyes searching Mac's face. Mac bet that Bruin hadn't meant to hit him that hard, he was just strong.

Mac went back to the table and sat down in his seat, not quite able to identify what he was feeling. His face was hot and he couldn't meet Bruin's eyes. He grabbed Bruin's discarded menu and began to tear up one of the corners. "Sorry," he mumbled.

Bruin rubbed a hand up the side of his face. "Remember yourself with your friends."

Friends? Mac had never considered the dickheads he hung out with his friends. More like his acquaintances. Until now, he'd never known anyone he cared enough about to call them friend.

Mac stared at the big male and realized Bruin was right. Bruin was his friend, and Mac needed to figure out how to act right before he fucked that up.

CHAPTER 6

error clawed at Rogue's cheeks and throat with scrabbling fingers she couldn't ignore, slowing her footsteps, making her feet drag in protest, the sound a sick scraping over the ground. She stared at it, the broken concrete pattern that was occasionally overcome by dirt, looking so much like spider webs that it put her teeth on edge.

The concrete path she followed was tall enough to stand, but her shoulders almost brushed each side. Her eyes and her light bounced around the coffin-like tunnel, looking for bugs. Not just any bugs. Spiders. Those roly-poly things that had a million legs. Centipedes clinging on the ceiling, just waiting for the right moment to drop into her hair. Rogue cried out and covered her head with an arm, scraping her elbow painfully on the wall as she did so. She forced herself forward, her arm bent over her head, her tiny light shaking in the fingers of her other hand.

Bugs. There was nothing she hated more than bugs. Nothing she was scared of but bugs. Except maybe being underground where bugs loved to live. So far, she hadn't seen one, but she was only a few feet in. She knew there would be many and she had no idea how she'd forced herself in there.

The voice. It was stronger down here.

No bugs. We have cleared them from your path in preparation for your coming.

Rogue stopped walking, startled, then spoke, her voice small and strange in the enclosed space. "Are you reading my mind?"

No, we are reading your being. We know you, Rogue. We are of you.

The overwhelming smell of oil choked her, forcing her to take tiny little sips of air in through her mouth. At the same time, the comforting presence of whatever had called her filled her, giving her courage, threading it through her bones and flesh. She looked around a little more confidently. She didn't see one bug. Anything that would and could do that for her couldn't be bad, right?

The humming power in her body felt constant and strong. She had no backdrop for what was happening to her, and yet, she somehow knew it was right, natural.

To her right, the faint sound of a noise like a scream caught her attention. It seemed to come from directly inside the concrete wall, maybe fifty feet away if it had been open air? She stared at the rough wall, then dragged her finger across it to make sure it was real, then knocked on it. The sound it made was only in her bones, not in the wall. It was solid concrete. She must have been mistaken, so she pressed forward.

The tunnel twisted, even as it continued its downward

slope, heading back under the doorway, and back in the direction of the post office. Rogue shivered, realizing the tunnel she was now walking in was the source of that yawning openness she'd always felt from inside the building above. The Englewood post office sat on the site of Chicago's most famous "murder castle" from the year 1893.

Rogue didn't believe in ghosts, but she did believe in something, trapped energy maybe. And evil. Anyone who had heard the stories of this place had to believe in evil.

The noise came again, this time from her left. She stared at the seemingly-solid wall, distressed to feel a cold wind buffet her cheeks and lift her hair.

The strong, feminine voice came again.

Ignore them. They cannot hurt you. Even if they could, we are stronger than them. We would never allow it.

Rogue swallowed, hard. "Ignore them?" She was getting her feet under her, and her own voice sounded stronger to her. "What are you?"

She stopped while she waited for an answer, shining her light down a short flight of concrete stairs.

Come and see.

An image of teeth, shiny and white and huge, flashed through her mind. Fangs. They made her think of animals, wolves even. An attractive thought to her. She'd loved wolves since she was a little girl. She shivered again, even though the tunnel was not cold. Some unknown yearning spiked in her midsection, but she boxed it up, pushing it away so she didn't have to deal with it, then started down the steps, making no noise in the almost-dark.

She reached the bottom of the stairs, still not one spider seen, and entered a small room with one chair and one table. She could see at a glance it was empty and apparently bug-free. Nothing moved, nothing creeped, nothing waited to ambush her. On the table sat a lantern, and her eyes were dragged to it like an anchor to the bottom of the ocean. It was what had been calling to her.

A faint glow peeked out through the cracks of the lantern- something inside. She rushed to it and picked it up. As her hands touched it, the bottom clicked and turned, and fell to the ground with a clatter. She flipped the lantern onto its side quickly, so whatever was there would not fall out onto the ground also.

She didn't need her light any longer, so she stuck it in her pocket. An ethereal glow pulsed through the dark cloth the two items there were wrapped in. The light touched her, played over her chest and face. With a steady hand, she reached into the bottom of the lantern for her prize.

Her fingers grazed the cloth and she felt a great evil turn a ragged eye toward her. Rogue sucked in a breath, feeling small and scared, wanting to hide somewhere, and despising the desire. She clamped down on it, negating it, making it not so. She was scared of *nothing*. Nothing with less than eight legs, anyway.

The voice spoke, and although she still felt it in her chest, it also emanated from the bundles at her fingertips.

Do not fear Khain. You were born to defy him.

Rogue felt the truth of the statement in her bones, even though she didn't know what it meant. She bared her small white teeth at the open air, turning in a circle and growling into the empty room. The evil presence slipped away, but she knew she had not made it go. Something had hidden her from it.

Rogue turned her attention back to the small bundles wrapped in cloth. She dropped the lantern to the ground and kicked it aside, putting one bundle softly on the table and focusing on the other. She unwrapped it slowly, holding her breath until the small package inside was revealed.

It was an inch-high pendant on a strong gold chain, with a wolf on one side and an angel on the other, light pulsing in the eyes of the two creatures. Power emanated from it so clearly, she could feel the pulses pushing through her fingers, pumping her blood the wrong way. A quick peek at the other bundle revealed it was a similar pendant.

Mine. She stared at it in awe, running her fingers over it, knowing it meant something to her, something that would explain much of her life. She also knew that it was not quite hers. It was her sister's.

Rogue startled as the thought went through her brain. *Sister?*

As a small part of Rogue's mind worried that thought independently of her being, she stared at the wolf and caressed its smooth cheek, sinking down onto her knees to cradle the pendant in her hands and focus more intently on it. Her cop and the wolf, they were connected somehow. And the angel? Did it mean something?

Her head bowed, she stared and thought, thought and stared, losing herself in a way that would have horrified her if she had realized what was happening.

***

Rogue lifted her head and looked around at the dark room, blinking her eyes, shifting her weight from knee to knee, aches and pains telling her she'd been kneeling for a long time. Her light had begun to dim, telling her the batteries were in danger of dying.

She'd done it again. Damn it!

She looked down at the now silent pendant in her hand. That odd, comforting hum she'd felt in her body was gone.

She squeezed her fingers around the small piece of jewelry. "What now?" Her voice echoed through the small room in a way that made her think of the tunnel outside.

The voice came again, but it was faint, not as urgent as before.

Go about your life. You'll know when the time is right to reveal us.

"Reveal you to who?"

That image of an identity-less, cocky cop came again, making Rogue lose awareness of her own body as her mind went where it wanted, pulling her away from reality.

She drifted to the dirty, but bug-free, floor, lost in a dream she didn't want, but couldn't shake free of.

CHAPTER 7

Mac hit the station door at a fast clip, bouncing it off the back wall, hurrying to get through it. He was ten minutes late for the meeting Wade had called, thanks to Bruin and his limes. At the crash of the door hitting the wall, a few males in the duty room looked up, but none of them said a word, all dropping their heads to their work again. Until Bruin came through the door behind him. Shouts of, "Bru!" and "Hey, bear," rang out.

"Big bad wolves," Bruin said to the room, bowing his head, getting a few thick chuckles back from the patrol officers in the room.

Mac made a face. The bears didn't seem to like Bruin much, but he sure got along with all the wolves. Some greedy part of Mac's brain didn't like that, especially since no one in the room had said a word when he'd walked in. Fuckers. He didn't need them anyway. Mac growled under his breath and walked faster, rounding the corner of the hallway that led to Wade's office.

Sebastian was standing there, leaning against the wall, his attention focused inside Wade's office. No surprise that he wasn't inside. The scary fucker didn't do well with people, especially females. They were almost universally terrified of him.

Mac's attention zeroed in on Sebastian, never wavering from the guy's tattooed face, even as his peripheral vision and his other senses pulled in everything else there was to know about him. He smelled relaxed. Good. But like he had a secret. Bad.

Mac focused hard, readying his muscles for a fight, sucking the swirling hallway air into his nostrils for every bit of information he could gather. You never knew if Sebastian would want to fight or not, and even if he didn't want to fight, his animal always did. Sebastian couldn't always control his shift, and when it happened without his conscious control, it was lightning fast and violent. Mac had mopped up his messes a few times.

From behind him, Bruin rounded the corner. Mac could hear his big bear feet slapping on the concrete. The guy could be unbelievably stealthy when he wanted to be, but now was not one of those times.

Sebastian's head swung their way and his eyes narrowed when he saw Mac, then went positively ice-chip when he looked behind Mac and saw Bruin. Mac tensed further, curling his hands into fists, poking the wildness inside him. *Wake up. We might have trouble.*

His animal took over for just a second, jumping to the forefront to see out Mac's eyes, smell what Mac smelled, focus on what Mac focused on. His animal grinned and licked his lips. Fun fucking times if Sebastian went loco.

Mac allowed his animal leeway for a second, then clamped down hard. Sebastian was the only male on the planet Mac pulled his aggression for. Because if he didn't, they would be reduced to fangs and claws and blood in just seconds, guaran-damn-teed. Sebastian was built that way just as much as Mac was, and since Mac couldn't count on Sebastian to be the bigger male, ever, Mac grudgingly did his best. But he did not like the way Sebastian was eyeing Bruin one bit. Sebastian's hatred for bears was well-known, even if the reason wasn't.

Sebastian spoke, his shoulders tense, his voice deadly tight, his knuckles white as he held onto the doorway, possibly in an attempt to stay where he was. His eyes were on Bruin the whole time. "This is a mother-fucking police station, not a smelly cave."

Mac heard Wade's voice coming from his office, and dimly wondered what Wade would do if he and Sebastian came to bites right there in the hallway. Would he really make good on his promise to ship them both off to the Kalamazoo substation, prophecy or no prophecy? Sebastian was rumored not to be bindable, which Mac had never believed until he'd thrown off his own bind in the very office he was headed to, at the sound of a female's voice on a video.

He almost lost his focus as he remembered the sound of that female's voice. It had been like that first bite of something tart and sweet and unforgettable that makes your salivary glands cramp, it's so good. Rich and strong, but feminine with a hard edge, like a flower with sculpted razor blades for petals. He licked his lips and felt his animal take a new kind of interest in Mac's thoughts. The fighting or the fucking. His animal liked them equally. They both did.

Mac eyed Sebastian with new interest. He hadn't gotten

his fight earlier, maybe he could talk Sebastian into going off with him somewhere. Wade would never know. They could throw the fuck down, using Bruin as referee. The big bear was strong enough to stop them, and he'd never breathe a word to—

Sebastian took his eyes off Bruin long enough to look in the room, his attention focused into a laser sight. Mac heard Crew's voice, and Beckett's sharp intake of breath.

Then Wade spoke up, his voice hard. "You know he's not hurting her, Beckett. Relax, or you're going to take a nap."

Ah, so Cerise was already under. Sebastian would have to wait. Mac's animal and his desires would have to wait, too. Mac wanted to know what Cerise was going to say. Chewing on Sebastian wouldn't be near as satisfying as chewing on Grey and that's what they were after. Information on Grey. A lead. Something.

It had been just over two weeks since Khain had snatched Grey and Cerise's pendant, taking them Rhen-knew-where for God-knew-what. Half of the KSRT were betting Khain still had him, while the rest figured the demon must have killed him by now. Mac himself figured something else entirely. Grey had escaped, was his guess. His fervent hope. Mac wanted to be the one who nailed that fucker to the wall. Who was he kidding? He wanted to be the one who nailed them all. He was the only one he trusted to do it right.

Mac pulled up short of the office and stuck his head in, standing only three feet from Sebastian, whose attention was also pulled inside. He was surprised to see only Wade, Beckett, Cerise, Dahlia, and Crew. Where was the rest of the first fuckup family?

Somewhere close, he was sure. They never went anywhere

without each other anymore. It wasn't safe. Wouldn't be, until Khain was gone. If that ever happened.

Bruin came up behind him, took a look, then leaned against the wall opposite the door, crossing his arms over his chest. His smell went from mellow, to uber-mellow, like he was about to take a nap standing up. Sebastian's smell, on the other hand, ramped up a notch. Defcon 4 to Defcon 3 maybe. Mac wished he could speak *ruhi* to give Bru a warning, but he couldn't. He'd have to be ready enough for both of them.

He turned part of his attention back to the room. Cerise was sitting in a chair next to Wade's desk, her eyes closed, her breathing even. Crew was standing over her, his hand in mid-air, while he stared hard at Beckett, who looked like he wanted to tear Crew's head off. That was a first. Those two were normally as chummy as the big spoon and the little spoon.

Wade held onto Beckett's arm, his eyes narrowed, his irritation palpable, while Dahlia watched from the couch, seeming to try to make herself as small as possible, her eyes bouncing back and forth between the males.

Crew dropped his hand and faced Beckett, his arms dangling at his sides, his face impassive, as the hard smell of Beckett's protectiveness filled the room and drifted out to Mac.

Wade launched another tirade at Beckett, but Crew stopped him. "I get it. I wouldn't want anyone touching Dahlia while she was under, either. Beckett, if I wake her up, will that help?"

Beckett's face lost its hard edges and he nodded, letting Wade pull him away. Crew stared at Cerise hard, then passed a hand in front of her face, then frowned. "She's hard to control. Or maybe I'm not good at controlling humans."

"She's not human," Mac said from the doorway, his mouth operating before his brain had a chance to kick in.

Sebastian, leaning against the other side of the doorway, threw him a look and said to the room, "Ignore Mac, brah, Rhen only gave him half one brain," his pidgin accent thick.

Mac knew the accent was just for show. Sebastian spoke perfect English when he wanted to. He just liked to distance himself from the rest of them and that's why he made a conscious effort to sound like he still lived out in the middle of the ocean somewhere. Mac grabbed his junk through his pants, faced Sebastian and yanked, a nasty snarl on his face. "Maybe, but she made up for it by giving me a twelve-inch dick."

Bruin opened his eyes, pushed off the wall, and took a hand to his own crotchal area, almost curiously. He shifted the goods around, then met Mac's eyes. "She only gave you twelve inches? She gave the rest of us sixteen."

Sebastian snorted. His Defcon level lowered slightly, although Mac could still feel the hate coming off him in waves. Just general hate now, no longer aimed at Bruin like a rifle scope.

Mac shot Bruin a look. "If you've got a sixteen-inch dick, I'll kiss your bare ass."

Bruin bobbed his head and grinned. "You said bear ass." He leaned against the wall again and his eyes drifted shut.

"Enough!" Wade called from in the room. "Shut your mouths, all of you!"

Mac snapped to attention and realized everyone in Wade's office had watched the exchange. Even Cerise who'd woken up at some point. He flapped a hand at them and pressed his lips together. *Get on with it, then.*

Crew turned his attention back to Cerise. "I want you

to think about what happened when Grey found you in the closet. Don't try too hard, just let the memories pass through your mind as if I weren't even here."

Cerise nodded and stared straight ahead. Crew frowned. After a few moments, he spoke. "Are you doing it?"

Cerise nodded, her strawberry-blonde hair bouncing around her shoulders, her eyes meeting Crew's then Beckett's. Beckett knelt next to her chair and put a hand on her leg. "Shh. Don't worry, you're doing great."

Crew shook his head. "Something about your nature makes it hard for me to access your memories. Must be your angel half." He threw a look at Sebastian. "You getting anything from her?"

Mac frowned. He hadn't known Sebastian had that kind of an ability. Any kind of ability, honestly. He was just supposed to be smart. A deep thinker. Someone who figured shit out. But they had to hide him away in the basement like a crazy grandma with a penchant for shooting up the visitors because he was dangerous. To everyone. Which made discovery time hard to come by.

Sebastian spoke. "Try out loud."

Crew nodded and turned back to her. "Tell us exactly what happened. Everything you can remember. Start when you were in the closet. Don't leave out any detail, no matter how small."

Cerise drew a shaky breath, the lines in her face showing the fear she'd been swimming in at the time. Now standing behind her, Beckett pulled a few locks of her hair through his fingers and she closed her eyes, leaning back into him while she spoke. "I covered Lillian with blankets in the back corner of the closet. I didn't know what was going on, but I knew it was bad. I was terrified I was going to lose Beckett, and I wanted so badly to go to him. But Lillian needed me, so I stayed put. I heard footsteps on the stairs. The sound of the footsteps came straight to the closet and I knew he knew I was there. I even knew who he was, somehow."

She stopped, squeezing her eyes shut hard. Beckett dropped his hands to her shoulders, encouraging her. She spoke. "He said something then." Her face relaxed and Mac could see her eyes rolling under her lids as she searched for whatever it was. "He said, 'Come out, come out, wherever you are.' Like it was all some game. He opened the closet and stared down at me and all I could think was that he was on drugs, had to be. His skin was nasty and bloody and his eyes were crazy. He was ten times scarier than I remember him being the last time I saw him."

Sebastian poked his head farther into the room. "Wait," he growled, and Cerise's eyes shot open, watching him warily. He pulled his upper half back out and switched to speaking to Crew. "There was something there. She missed something. Have her go back over it."

Crew nodded. "Yeah, I heard it. Didn't make sense."

"Have her do it anyway."

Mac watched Sebastian, interested that the male was behaving like a normal person for once. Maybe he was seeing a shrink or something. Getting in touch with his feelings. Mac smirked and Sebastian threw him a dark look.

Cerise settled, closed her eyes again, a look of concentration on her face. "He did say something. Mudger, pudger, nudger, or something. I thought I misheard him, or it was a chant of some kind."

Mac watched as both Crew and Sebastian closed their eyes, their faces gaining that same look of deep concentration. "No," Sebastian breathed. His voice changed, sounding so much like Grey that Mac took a step backwards and looked behind him down the still empty hallway. "Mudge. Mudged. Pudge. Nudge. Mudgett!"

Crew's eyes shot open and he and Sebastian shared a look. Mac wondered if they'd ever worked together before today. Crew had never been around much, although he was much easier to find these days. Living out on Farm Fuckup, never more than two feet from Dahlia's side. Crew nodded, then his eyes narrowed. "Mean anything to you?"

Sebastian made a nasty face that could have meant anything, but probably signified 'No, fellow co-worker I'm trying not to rip open because I hate everyone'. He shook his head. "Keep going."

Crew nodded and led Cerise through the rest of the experience, but Mac had already lost interest. He shuffled his weight on his feet and glanced back over his shoulder. How much would Wade crack if he challenged Bruin to a foot race to the end of the hallway? He knew he could beat the big guy. Bruin was strong as shit, but not what anyone would ever call svelte. Which was good. A wolf had to have some sort of an advantage over a bear, well, besides smarts and good looks, of course. Mac leaned his head against the wall and turned in a semi-circle until he was facing Bruin.

Let's race, you big animal, he thought as hard as he could to Bruin. Nothing. Bruin didn't even flinch. His eyes were closed, his meaty forearms crossed over his chest, his legs crossed at the ankles, his face relaxed. He could have been meditating, or even sleeping for all Mac knew.

Mac eyed Bruin's feet. Only one was on the ground, the other one lifted slightly, showing him the sole of Bruin's work boot. If he caught Bruin in the ankle just right with a solid enough kick, down he would go. And then the race would be on. No stupid-ass *ruhi* necessary.

Mac grinned, pushing himself off the wall, about to put his plan into action, when his gaze found Bruin's face again. Big and hairy had one eye open just a bit, but when he saw Mac seeing him, he dropped it closed again, the corners of his lips turning up ever so slightly. The fucker knew exactly what Mac was planning. Was gonna let him do it. Maybe grab him in a bear hug when he got close enough, fall on him or some shit.

Still worth a shot to see Gentle Ben fall on his ass. He could move fast and go in low—

Sebastian spoke, pulling Mac's attention back to the meeting, which seemed to be over. "Nah, that's it. Give me some time. I might have something for you in a few hours." He pushed past Mac, throwing Bruin one more dirty look. "Grr, grr, bitches," he said, then strode down the hallway, turning right into the alcove that led to a door to the tunnels.

Bruin opened his eyes and pushed off the wall, watching Sebastian's back disappear. "He seems nice."

"Yeah, nice as a colonoscopy," Mac said. "Or a snake." He rubbed his chin, thinking. "Or a colonoscopy with a snake."

Bruin bobbed his head. "You're one sick wolf, you know that?"

Wade's noise of frustration made them both turn their heads. "Mac, I hoped we'd have something for you to follow up on, but not yet."

Mac stepped forward. "Chief, you gotta give me something to do. I'm going out of my mind."

Wade's face folded in on itself. "Yeah, ok, I know you gotta stay busy or you get in trouble. Until Khain resurfaces, we are light on tasks right now. Throw on a uniform and help patrol. They're short-handed."

Mac backed away, hands up. "Ah, crap, I'd love to, Chief, but I just remembered. One of my CI's says there's a rumor going around that Rex Brenwyn was spotted in Machesney Park. I gotta go follow up. Plus, you know I'm still looking for that *foxen* from the *pravus*, too. All the rest of you may have forgotten about him, but not me."

Wade nodded slowly, his expression showing he didn't believe a word of it. Mac grabbed Bruin by the arm. "Come on, Bru, we got work to do." He snorted at the rhyme and pulled Bruin down the hallway. "See ya later, Chief, call me when you got something on Grey."

"Cool," Bruin said. "Who's Rex?"

"The *foxen* Khain stole out of prison last month. You remember him. We arrested him out at that farm, the one where they set up the fire around the perimeter and put guns in the water towers?"

Bruin grunted and nodded his head. It was where they'd forged the beginnings of their friendship.

Mac threw another look over his shoulder, then got out of the station as quickly as he could. He didn't mind work, but he very much minded the barking dog calls, domestic violence calls, shoulda-gone-to-therapy-but-instead-I'm-gonna-call-the-cops calls, and the *paperwork* the patrol officers dealt with day in and day out.

He'd done his fair share of shit work. Enough to last a lifetime, even for a person who was way more tolerant than he was.

CHAPTER 8

*B*ruin pulled into Mac's driveway and stopped. Mac opened his door and unfolded himself from the lunchmobile with a disgusted sigh. "You don't have a friend you can borrow a real car from?" he said.

Bruin just grinned. "See you tomorrow. Ten sharp."

Mac headed into his house, thinking for a second he should invite the bear in. Or maybe find out where he lived and go over to his house. Curiosity filled him. Did the guy even live in a house? He had to, right? Not a cave or something. Mac frowned as he glanced at the prize shelf, his mind still far away. That was something he should know about his friend. Where he lived, how he lived.

Friend. The word caught in Mac's brain, like maybe it wasn't an accurate description of whatever was between him and Bruin. But that wasn't right. Even if Mac considered all the wolves he worked with nothing more than acquaintances, the big bear was his friend. Even if he didn't know where the guy lived.

Mac *got* the guy in a way nobody else did. He was a marshmallow, until you got him mad. He'd probably never had a bad thought about anyone, not even Khain. Mac could see Bruin putting an arm around Khain, telling him, "Hey, buddy, let's talk about this. We can work it out, you just can't be quite so evil. Pranks are ok. Killing and kidnapping, not ok. But don't worry, I'll help you through it."

Mac frowned as the thoughts slipped away and his eyes catalogued everything on the shelves, making sure it was all right, his nightly OCD trip. Bruin was a marshmallow, but Mac wasn't. What if his one true mate didn't like him because of... the way he was? He turned the thought over, then rejected it, hard. Nah, maybe he wasn't refined, but he was loyal, strong, and never fake. If she didn't appreciate that, her loss. He could survive without her. He was a master at surviving. Always had been. But it wouldn't happen, because he was a mother-humping catch.

Mac turned away from the shrine, ran a soft hand over the red spiky blanket on the wall, then hit the fridge. A bottle of mayo, an empty box of Corona, two jars of ketchup, and a half-eaten Snickers bar. Solid. He hooked the Snickers bar, tossed it into his mouth, and headed into his bedroom. What in the fuck was he gonna do till morning?

His eyes fell on the notebook that sat on the folding chair in the corner of the room, the only furniture there besides his bed. He picked up the notebook and opened it to the page marked haphazardly with a pen. His notebook... it wasn't a diary. Too girly. It sure as fuck wasn't a journal, only metrosexuals wrote in journals. He might like to look good, put on a suit coat for the ladies every once in a while, shave, shower, make sure his shit was tight, but he was no metrosexual. So he called it his notebook.

He licked the tip of the pen and sat down on the floor, leaning his back against the wall, musing about how something that had started as a punishment had ended up being a… habit. One he almost enjoyed.

Without looking to see what he'd written last time, he started a new entry, bending over the notebook, his nose almost touching the paper.

I hate waiting. Waiting sucks. I wish life happened all at once, in one big fucking glut. Like you're born. You shoot up to full size in a few days, you get shit done, and you get out. That would be a life I could get behind. But all this growing and learning and standing around shit is getting old. Boring. I hate waiting and I hate boring.

Mac waited, but nothing more came to him, so he tossed the pen back in the notebook, closed it, and whipped it across the room. He pushed himself to his feet, then eyed the bed. Motherfuck, he hated sleeping almost as much as he hated waiting. Sleeping was nothing more than waiting you didn't remember.

He hit the switch on the wall and dropped onto the bed, considering kicking his shoes off, but deciding it was too much work. He closed his eyes, and was out, falling into sleep as quickly as the room had plunged into darkness when he'd turned off the light.

***

Mac's eyes snapped open and he jumped out of the bed, glad he had his boots still on. His head swiveled around the dark room, looking for what had woken him.

Ring, ring.

He relaxed only slightly and pulled his phone out of his pocket. "Go," he barked, then walked out of the room to see what time it was. The clock on the never-used stove said 4:02 in the morning.

"Mac, we've got a lead on Grey. I need you to head to Chicago. Take the bear."

"It gonna be dangerous?" Mac said, hoping so.

"Probably not. But you know the drill."

Mac did, but if Wade was sending only two of them, chances were it would be no more dangerous than a one year old's birthday party. Fuck. "Where we heading?"

"The Englewood Post Office. It may be nothing, but it may be something, too. Grey said the nonsense word Mudgett to Cerise, but Sebastian thinks it's a name. A hundred years ago, there was a different building on the land the post office is built on, a hotel owned by a man called Herman Webster Mudgett. He murdered a bunch of people in the hotel and the basement below, and the ground is supposed to be haunted. He was named America's first serial killer, and rumor says his spirit still hangs out around there. Given Grey's recent temperament, Sebastian is thinking maybe Grey's got a place close by, thought he was channeling the man or something."

Mac snorted. "You mean, maybe he was eating cats in the alley and stealing mail from the dumpster, like the looney-toon he is? You gotta say what you mean, Chief."

Wade's voice took a hard edge. "Just go check it out. I'd call Chicago PD but they're already handling round-the-clock surveillance on Rex Brenwyn's brother and not too happy about it. Besides, I want one of my males up there."

"What am I looking for?"

"No clue, Mac. Anything that has to do with Grey."

"How am I supposed to find it."

Wade swore like he knew Mac was taunting him. "Act like a cop, and do some investigating. If you can't manage that, then act like a wolf and follow your nose. You can still do that, can't you?"

Mac grinned. He could. He just liked winding Wade up. It wasn't good for a male to have too many ass-kissers around. He hung up and dialed Bruin's number. The bear's sleep-laden voice came on the line after six or seven rings. "'Lo?"

"Wake up, Goldilocks. It's road trip time."

When Bruin finally spoke, Mac had no idea if he was messing with him or not. Probably. "Who is this?" Bruin said in a slow drawl.

"Just get your hairy ass over here!"

***

Twenty minutes later, Mac was freshly showered and shaved, dressed in work khakis, and waiting on his porch. Bruin finally pulled up in the lunchmobile, still rubbing his eyes and yawning.

Mac dropped into the small car, speaking before he had his door closed. "Haul ass."

Bruin reversed, not even looking behind him. "Where to?"

"The station. We'll get a truck." He watched Bruin appraisingly. "We're heading for Chicago, and I don't need you hobbling around like an old man when we get there cuz you cricked your back all out of whack on the drive over. Look at you, hunched over like what's his name. Quimedado."

"Quasimodo," Bruin said, stretching his neck forward, then dropping his ears to first one shoulder, then the other, his eyes still on the road. "Bears don't get cricks in our necks. We're very bendy."

Mac rolled his eyes. "Yeah, I needed that visual."

Once they arrived at the station, Mac signed out a black diesel truck and they headed out. At least Bruin seemed a little more awake, even though the sun wasn't showing its face over the horizon yet. Mac hit the radio button, dialing until he found a station on satellite radio with his kind of music, hopping onto the freeway at the same time. They'd be in Chicago in no time.

A song came on he liked. He reached forward to blast it, when Bru saw something out the windshield. He leaned forward and pointed at the vehicle in front of them. "Oooh, maybe I should get a minivan. It would be more comfortable for my friends than the lunchmobile."

Mac grinned at that, glad the lunchmobile had caught on. He tsked. "You ain't got no friends, bear, you don't need a mini-van."

Bruin crossed his arms over his chest, not quite pouting. "I have tons of friends."

"The guy at the hot dog stand is not your friend. The lady who called you, 'Sir', at Starbucks when you ordered your Venti Pumpkin Spice Latte with extra foam and a light dusting of vanilla is not your friend. And I know don't none of those bears like you. Do yourself a favor and get a cool car. Like mine."

Bruin became very quiet, his energy folding in on itself. Mac shot him a look, then regretted the quiet pain he saw in his friend's eyes. "Ah shit, Grizz, I didn't mean nothing by it. I'm your friend. You buy that minivan and you can take me anywhere you want to go." He wasn't going to regret that promise, not at all.

Bruin's face softened somewhat, but he didn't loosen the knot of his arms. Mac searched his mind for something else to say, but the only things that popped in there implied Bruin would never lose his questionable virginity if he did indeed buy a minivan, so he kept his mouth shut. *Hell yeah, look at me, being all kinds of mature. I got this friend shit wired.*

He cranked the music up, his knuckles tightening on the steering wheel as he rapped along.

And when I'm finished, it's gonna be a bloodbath
Of cops, dying in L.A
Yo Dre, I got something to say
Fuck Tha Police

Mac repeated the chorus then launched into the next verse, until he realized Bruin was staring at him, dumbfounded.

Mac cranked the music the other way. "What?"

"Mac, you're the police," Bruin whispered, his eyes big.

Mac sprayed laughter. "Yeah, fuck me, too!" Bruin's distress worked its way into Mac's system. "It's just a song, B." But Bruin wouldn't stop staring, so Mac spun the knob, looking for another station. "Ok, fine, what kind of music do you like?"

Bruin leaned over, a self-satisfied smile on his face. "I'll find it."

Mac drove in silence, wondering if he'd been played, not even daring to guess what kind of music he'd soon be listening to. It was still two hours to Chicago...

Bruin finally stopped on a station, deliberately leaving it low so he could sing over the words, his deep baritone sounding out of place with the saccharine sweet sound of the females singing.

There's more than one answer to these questions
pointing me in crooked line

The less I seek my source for some definitive
The closer I am to fine

Mac's turn to drop his jaw to his pecs. "What in the holy hell is this shit?" And how did he get roped into giving up control of the radio again?

"Folk rock. Indigo girls? Give it a chance. It's soothing."

Mac snapped the radio dial to the left so hard it came off in his hand. "Oops. Guess we gotta talk."

Bruin bobbed his head, perpetually down for anything. "Good deal. How 'bout a nice game of Would You Rather?"

"Sounds like a game for drunk frat boys."

Bruin grinned like that was a compliment. "Cool, I'll ask first. Would you rather have sex with a *felen* or a *foxen*?"

Mac laughed. "Sheeit, that's easy. I imagine sex with *foxens* would be as awesome as having a root canal pulled through my ass. *Felen* on the other hand, they're all about sex. Sexy, too. You ever seen Kalista?"

Bruin shook his head. "Your turn."

Mac thought for a moment. "Would you rather fuck a hornet's nest or smack Heather on the ass?"

Bruin's face went contemplative, as if the question required a PhD or some shit. He finally answered. "Hornet's nest. Barbequed bear skin is not a good look for me." He rubbed the skin on his face as if remembering an old injury. "Besides, hornets are just homicidal bees. Me and bees, we have an understanding. I'm sure I could convince the hornets my dick was supposed to be in there for some reason."

CHAPTER 9

*M*ac pulled up in front of the Englewood post office and parked. The sun had risen, but barely, the early-morning yellow glow mostly obscured by the buildings around them. Shadows still occupied much of the landscape.

Mac stretched in his seat. "This place won't be open for a couple of hours. We can go ask some questions around the neighborhood, but we might have better luck if we wait till people have had their coffee."

Bruin looked around. "Ooh, I get to play cop for real? Good thing I brought Presley."

Mac eyed Bruin up and down, not able to see where his holster was hidden. "Don't you dare take that gun out, you hear me? I don't care what happens."

Bruin nodded happily and Mac suspected he'd probably have it out with their first questioning, no matter who it was. Old lady? Eat some lead! Small child? Maybe just flash the grip. The bear was too excited to be doing some actual work, but Mac had to admit he was pretty ants-in-his-pants happy about that himself. Working with the KSRT could be described as interminable boredom most of the time, interspersed with brief moments of extreme terror. He wished the terror part happened more often.

He stuck his hand out, about to demand Bruin turn the gun over, and the handcuffs, too, if he had 'em, when Bruin rolled his window down and an indefinable scent filled the cab of the truck.

Mac's hand drifted to the seat and he raised his nose high, sniffing hard. "What is that?"

Bruin wrinkled his nose and sniffed. "What? The fishy foggy smell? Most of Chicago smells like that."

Mac barely heard the words. He took a huge breath of air in through his nose, the scent almost making his spine collapse. "Not that. It's tangy, but sweet at the same time. Lemony? Some sort of citrus. But sugary."

Bruin frowned and sniffed again. "Is it pie?" His face tried to point all directions at once while he looked for a restaurant.

"No, not pie, galoofus. You don't smell it?"

Bruin shook his head.

Mac hit the door handle and climbed out of the truck, following his nose. The smell was sublime. It made his mouth water and his body tense and his dick jump in his pants. Mac adjusted himself for comfort, too distracted to argue with his biology. He wanted to know what smelled like that too badly to care if he looked like he was smuggling a steel rod in his pocket. The smell was so... lovely, fresh, and good, with a sharp edge that made him pant. A voice shot through his memory. The voice of the female on the video of the *foxen* who had come over to their world from Khain's. The unknown female. Was she here?

The skin on the back of Mac's arms prickled, telling him someone was watching him. He tried to act nonchalant, like he hadn't noticed anything. Tried to eye the buildings and the nearby overpass, the parking lot across the street with only a few lone cars in it. He saw no one who could have been looking at him. The feeling faded.

Bruin got out of the truck and stood on the sidewalk. Mac walked over, trying to locate the source of that delicious smell. It wisped away on the wind, in threads no larger than a human hair. He captured each one that he could, burning the scent into his memory. *Jaysus*, he needed whatever it was so bad his teeth ached.

Ignoring Bruin, he headed down the sidewalk one way, then back the other, then back again. He turned to circle the building, but no matter where he went, the smell did not seem to have a source. It drifted aimlessly on the wind, remnants of something that could have been there hours ago, or maybe it had drifted to him from another location, like flower petals from a county away.

Mac's fists tightened and he walked faster over ground he'd already covered, then broke into a jog, circling the neighborhood, running through the parking lot, casing wider and wider circles.

The bear caught up with him and grabbed his arm. "Mac, take a breather. She's gone."

Mac turned on Bruin and grabbed him by his big dumb shirt, trying to shake him, although the bear was immovable. "What? Who's gone?"

Bruin gently folded his hands over Mac's and peeled his

fingers away. "It's your mate, right? That's what you're smelling? You've been running in circles around the building for half an hour now. If you haven't caught her trail, you're not going to. Not now."

Mac shook his head sharply, then took a deep breath. Shit. Half an hour? He had to get himself under control before they attracted attention. He headed back for the post office, speaking low to Bruin as he did so. "We'll head down this street and see if there's any residences, but first I want to get a feel for the place. It's supposed to be haunted. So you let me know if any ghosts grab your ass."

Bruin nodded, a smirk on his face. "My bear ass. Ghosts love 'em."

They made a once-around, and by the time they got to the far side, Mac had caught that delicious scent again. He followed it, heading toward the overpass. At the base of it, he found tall weeds tramped down in a trail, like someone had been here recently. He followed the trail, whiffs of that smell drifting up to him. She'd been here. Mac closed his eyes and took another few steps, savoring the tangy scent.

From behind him, Bruin said, "That looks like a door."

Mac's eyes popped open and he saw a square shape marked in the concrete at knee level. "Yeah, for leprechauns." He moved to it, crouched, and ran his hands along the grooves, then pressed his body forward to take a big sniff… "She was here. She touched this wall." He dug at the grooves with his fingernails, thinking maybe if he shifted, he could dig his claws in there… He had to get that door open. He knocked on it, hearing only dull thuds of bony flesh on concrete. "If it's a door, why no handle?"

Bruin looked around, then touched Mac on the shoulder. "You want it open?"

Mac stood and backed away. "Yeah."

"Done."

Bruin yanked his shirt over his head, kicked off his boots, and dropped his pants, piling the clothes in the weeds. Mac glanced around but saw no one. Until the businesses opened, this little corner of the city seemed to be a ghost town. Which was good. Naked, Bruin cracked his neck, shook out his arms, then began to shift.

Mac watched the transformation, fascinated. He'd seen Bruin shift before, but never had time to examine it, to think about the differences between a wolf shift and a bear shift. There weren't that many, except a bear was a hell of a lot bigger than a wolf. Mac's animal topped out at just under three hundred pounds, a lean-muscled fighting machine that did best when fighting in a pack, claws and teeth coming from everywhere, the pack instinctually working as a unit.

Bruin, though, his animal was monstrous. Mac bet it weighed a thousand pounds. Shit, it was a good thing the brown behemoth was on his side. Mac would be more scared to fight it than he was Khain. Khain was pure evil, sneaky, favoring fire and illusion and terror to create his messes, but always retreating when faced with Mac's pack. This Kodiak bear in front of him? He could take a small pack of Mac's kind, easily. One swipe with his heavy paws and razor sharp claws and Mac would be on his side, split from ears to tail, waiting to be lunch.

Bruin's shift complete, the monstrous bear, so out of place next to the city overpass, backed up a few paces, then lumbered forward as quickly as his bulk would allow and hit the rectangle in the concrete with his head, the sound a dull thud that made Mac raise a hand to his own noggin and wince.

The bear was already backing up again, then hauling its

bulk forward. Slam! Another back up, another slam. Bruin shook his head, then backed up again, farther this time, and roared to the sky. Mac was too fascinated by the process to even look at the concrete wall. His eyes were on Bruin, but when the bear started forward again Mac looked around. That roar was likely to bring them some attention. Mac would have to head anyone off quickly, or Bruin wouldn't be able to shift back.

A dull, thunking sound split the air and Mac shot his eyes to their target. He'd done it. A nasty dent in the concrete with thick cracks spiraling out from it proved there was hollowness behind. "Shift," he hissed at Bruin, shooting furtive glances all around and behind them. "Before someone comes to see if the circus is in town."

Bruin's shift back was faster, his fur sucking into his body quickly, his mass shrinking almost like a popping. It left him sitting on his ass in the weeds and panting, one hand on his head. Mac scooped up his clothes and dropped them in his lap. "Put these on so we're not caught out here looking like cops gone wild, the gay edition."

When Bruin was finally dressed, Mac breathed a sigh of relief and offered Bruin a hand up. "That's one hard head you got there, brother."

Bruin smiled, one of those genuine ones that made Mac want to squirm, then put his free hand on Mac's shoulder. "I think of you like a brother, too, Mac. The brother I never had and always wanted."

Mac's eyes slid away and he pulled his hand out of Bruin's, stepping to the side to get out from under his hand, too. He faced the concrete wall of the overpass. "Good, yeah, let's get to work on this." He bent and began to dig pieces of concrete out of the wall with his fingers.

Bruin knelt next to him, pulling a screwdriver out of some pocket. Mac flashed it a look, but didn't question it. The bear was a regular Boy Scout. Mac liked that. The tool made short work of the concrete and within a few moments, they were staring inside a dark hole.

Bruin produced a flashlight, the bright beam revealing a kind of tunnel that opened up immediately, and sloped downward for as far as they could see. The concrete framing the hole they had their heads craned inside was several feet thick. No smashing through that.

"I might fit in there," Mac said, "But you have no chance." He wouldn't try at all if that lovely smell he'd been following weren't stronger in here. He'd call in a couple of shorties, let them do the dirty work.

"Didn't I already tell you that bears are very bendy?" Bruin huffed, like he was offended.

Mac pulled his head out of the hole. "You go first then, no way I'm gonna be in there while your big ass gets stuck and blocks the exit."

Bruin raised his eyebrows, handed Mac his flashlight, and wiggled around until his feet were in the hole, his eyes fixed on Mac the whole time, his expression a dry one that said 'Watch this, motherfucker,' or maybe, 'I hope those words taste good cuz you're gonna be eating them in a second.' He pushed himself farther in with his hands.

Mac grinned. "When you get stuck at your shoulders, I'm gonna call you Winnie the Pooh until you die. Or I die. Should I bring you some honey? Make it authentic?"

Bruin stopped what he was doing and lifted his head. "Honey? You have honey?"

"Fuck me," Mac moaned. "No, I don't have any honey. Forget I mentioned it. Just keep going."

Bruin's eyes narrowed. "You holding out on me, wolf? Because that's not nice."

Mac leaned forward and pushed at Bruin's head. "I don't have any honey, but if you focus, I'll buy you a honey pie."

Bruin went limp, watching Mac try to move him, his voice suddenly shrewd. "I don't think there's such thing as a honey pie. You made that up, didn't you?"

Mac gave up and sat on his ass in the prickly weeds, his elbows hanging limp over his knees, wetness seeping into his clothes. "I did. I made it up. Sorry. I'll—I'll take you to the Honey Place, that restaurant you wanted to go to. We'll go today, as soon as we're back in Serenity. I swear it, just get moving! I want to see what's in there."

Bruin grinned and pushed himself farther in, pure happiness lighting up his face. He almost did get stuck at the shoulders, but he popped his arms over his head and wiggled the rest of his body like a snake, until he disappeared.

Shit. Mac was gonna call him Winnie anyway. Or Pooh. He wasn't sure why he hadn't already. He handed Bruin the flashlight. "What's it look like?"

"Not bad. Lots of bugs. It's gonna be a bit of a squeeze but at least I can stand up."

"What's it smell like? Gas or anything dangerous?"

"Maybe some oil, but it's faded. Come on in."

Mac dropped to his knees and pushed himself in feet first like the bear had. When his head passed the threshold, the tangy scent hit him from all directions, strong enough to make his mouth water and his dick pop in his pants again. He was going to have to go to therapy if he started popping a woody every time he smelled oranges. Good thing he didn't live in Florida.

He rested his head on his arms for just a moment and

took a deep breath, his face so close to the ground he would have sucked a spider up his nose if there had been one underneath him at that moment. He didn't care. The scent was so pleasing to him, the smelling of it was practically orgasmic in itself.

The light around him brightened and he pushed himself to his feet, watching his head on the concrete ledge around the doorway, then slumping his shoulders so he could turn toward Bruin in the tiny tunnel, his elbows scraping the concrete on both sides.

Bruin's eyes crawled over his face for just a moment, then he performed his own slump and shuffle maneuver until he was facing kind of forward in the tunnel, and off they went, both of them walking almost sideways, shuffling their feet. Spiders and centipedes ran from Bruin's light but the two big males paid the creepy-crawlies no mind, until one fell on Mac's head. It reminded him of the forest slash and burn they'd had to do a few months ago, when Khain had controlled the spiders somehow. "Shit, smash the spiders, bear."

"What? No. They aren't hurting us. And we're in their home. I wouldn't blame them if they did."

The abject horror in Bruin's voice made Mac roll his eyes. But he didn't have any reason to believe these spiders were anything more than regular spiders, so he didn't try to convince his friend. He just smashed all the ones he could reach with the heel of his hand. Spider guts. Yuck.

Bruin stopped in front of him, and when he spoke his voice echoed. "You feel that?"

"What?"

"Just, something. It's creepy down here. I feel... something."

Mac didn't feel anything but like an anchovy in a tin. "Go."

"There's steps."

"Come on, bear, that's toddler shit. I know your mommy taught you to go down steps a few years ago. One foot in front of the other, you can do it. Slide on your butt if it gets too scary."

Bruin snuffed softly under his breath, then started down the steps and Mac followed, glad when the corridor opened up slightly so he could peek around Bruin's bulk as much as possible. At the bottom, he could see a doorway.

The lovely tart-citrus smell was stronger.

Mac held his breath as a spurt of adrenaline kicked through his system.

She was in there. He knew it. She better g-fucking-d be there of her own free will, or Mac would rip his way into the *pravus* and kill Grey himself. Never mind waiting around to see if Khain had already done it or not.

This was it. He was going to meet her. His body tingled all over and he ran through his best lines in his head.

Nothing but the best for his mate.

CHAPTER 10

*R*ogue stood under the ice spray of her shower, raising her face to it, trying to scrub away the overnight stint she'd just spent *underground*. But true to their word, the pendants had not let any bugs get on her.

She'd woken up only an hour before, in that dark room, her light dead, her cheek pressed to the concrete, her right hand and arm aching, two fingernails torn past the quick, blood seeping from three of her worn and achy fingertips. The pendants had gone dark and no light filtered in from any-where. She'd felt around in a mad scramble for the pendants, finally finding them in the flat pack around her waist, then she'd run shaky hands up and down her skin, rising to her feet and stiff-legging it out of there the way she had come, trying not to whimper. And failing.

When she'd reached the end of the tunnel, she'd pushed

open the concrete door and escaped into the sunlight, checking herself again for bugs, then sprinted across the grass, across the street, away from that place, an uncharacteristic franticness marking her every move. She'd stopped for just one look back from behind the business across the street, seeing a black truck pull up in front of the post office. The two men who had gotten out, although they hadn't been wearing guns that she could see, had obviously been cops, which had made her move even faster. She had no idea why the tunnel existed or who the pendants belonged to. All she knew was, they were hers now. *Not hers, but still hers,* her mind had whispered. Yeah, that made a lot of sense.

She had walked toward downtown, sucking in great lungfuls of chilly morning air, glad when her mind had finally cleared enough for her to decide on a plan of action. She still had Soren's file. She didn't want to imagine the consequences of losing an item of such importance to him, although it might not be as bad for her as it would be for other people. She'd long known he had a thing for her, but he never acted on it, because he respected her, too.

Rogue stuck her head out of the icy shower and peeked at the clothes she'd dropped to the floor, including her pack. The pendants were in there. She'd chosen this bolt hole of the three she owned in Chicago specifically because it had a place to hide them.

Teeth chattering, finally forced from the shower, she stepped out and dried off. She still felt dirty, had never been underground for so long before, was very surprised that she'd even gone down there. The voice hadn't just been convincing, it had charmed her somehow, convincing her to do what she hadn't done on purpose since she'd been five years old.

The voice of the pendant. What a mindfuck that was.

How could an inanimate object have a voice? A brain? Be able to convince anyone of anything?

She shook her head and attended to her right hand, which was bleeding and cramped, barely able to flex or open. If only she could remember what had she been doing with it.

She frowned as she spread some antibacterial ointment on her fingers, finding more scrapes down her forearm to her elbow, and attending to them also. What really was a mind-fuck, if she allowed herself to think about it, was all the locks she had sprung with just her touch. The lock at the brown-stone, the locks of the dozens of boxes in the post office, and then, if she wanted to be precise, she probably should include the jury-rigged lock on the bottom of the lantern that some-one had used like a safe. Oh, hold up there, don't forget the lock on the door at Chief Lorenzo's condo. That was a lock of sorts.

She hadn't had the time to consider all of this before, but now that she'd had a night of crazy 'sleep' on the floor of some nasty underground room, it was time to face reality. And re-ality was looking awfully shaky, right about now.

Fuck. She'd always been a wizard at locks, picking sim-ple ones with paperclips at seven years old. *Two years after Amaranth disappeared,* her mind supplied, even though Rogue didn't need the reminder. She'd only made it look like magic, though. It had never actually been magic before.

Fully ointment-covered and bandaged, Rogue headed for the bedroom to pick out some clothes, her mind on the pendants she was leaving behind her. She *would* deal with them. When she was ready. She picked out an under-outfit, all black, then an over-outfit, more colorful but not her, then rooted around in her dresser drawer for accessories, dressed quickly, then headed back to the bathroom.

The clothes she had been wearing, she shoved into the tiny bathroom trash can, holsters, she'd strapped on her forearms, frowning at the one she'd placed on her right arm. The knife was missing. It was a solid blade, expensive, and she couldn't imagine how she had lost it, but she had. She would get another. After. Her pack, she checked for dirt or tears. Finding none, she re-wrapped it around her waist, unzipped it, and pulled out the two pendants that were back in their cloth coverings.

Holding one in each hand, feeling the core of cold metal warm her palms somehow, she stalked through the one room of the small apartment, sending out all her feelers. No one was peeking in a window or surveilling her in any way. It was safe to do what she was about to do. She swerved right, away from the five-canvas picture of the wolf on the wall above the fireplace. Her safe was behind the largest canvas, with a satisfactory amount of money and jewels stashed in it, plus the only things she had left of her sister's. Money she didn't care about, the money and jewels were only a lure in case someone broke in, they'd think they found all the good stuff. The other two items? No thief would take them. They had only sentimental value.

She rounded the corner, entered her bedroom, then stopped in front of a piece of decorative molding in the wall. She dropped to her knees first, then her belly, took out a pick from her pack and lowered her chin to the floor to pick the lock of her main safe, the one she'd created herself by digging out the hole in the wood and plaster, pushing the safe back there, rebuilding everything, and fashioning a hidden door and lock. A thought struck her and she dropped the pick to the floor with a plink, then reached out her bare fingers, settling them onto the wood that hid the lock.

A soft snick rose from the molding and the hidden door swung open.

Damnit. What in the hell was going on?

***

Rogue tried hard to keep her focus as she strode down the sidewalk, approaching Soren's four-million-dollar digs in Lincoln Park from the north, the way she came from when she wanted to stop at Bradford's house. No one was watching her, but someone was watching Soren's place. That someone was across the street, holed up on the roof deck above the garage. His focus swung to her and she pulled into her persona. Young librarian. Sensible skirt with tights underneath. Clunky shoes. Hair twisted into a bun. Thick glasses hiding her face. Purple messenger bag draped over one shoulder. The someone watched her legs move under her skirt for a few minutes, then flicked his attention back to Soren's house. *Great.* Cops. She always felt so conflicted about cops, loving them and hating them at the same time. It was the same way she felt about Chicago. The same way she felt about her profession. Confliction seemed built into her being.

She sensed two more of them in other yards across the street. Soren paid off most of his neighbors with lavish gifts and sometimes outright bribes, but apparently it didn't always take.

How was she going to convince Soren that she hadn't been the one to tip them off? Or maybe she had been. No one caught her stealing the file from Chief Lorenzo's place, and she'd taken several files, not just the one, but that didn't mean they hadn't connected the burglary to Soren because of what had been taken.

She didn't want to be seen entering his place if it was under surveillance. So she would have to tell Soren she was coming in from the back. But not yet. First she would do a bit of her own surveillance.

She turned right and headed up the stairs to the porch of the neighboring custom-built brick home and hit the doorbell, smoothing her skirt and hair, then turning her face to the camera. No one answered. She pulled out her key. Bradford wasn't home and that was exactly what she'd been hoping for. He was the lead developer of nanotechnology at Intel and worked long hours, but he was happy to share his home with her on the off-chance she'd be there when he got home occasionally. Which she was. Occasionally. He was much older than her, but handsome and sweet.

She opened the door to his palatial home and slipped inside, quickly punching in the code to the alarm, not bothering to admire the stark whiteness of everything. The floors, the walls, the balustrade, the stairs, all of it was white. It was an impressive look, but not one she would replicate when she bought her own mansion. She craved something... more. Coziness, maybe.

"Rosita, it's just me," she called, knowing the maid wasn't in, the house was empty, but still playing along.

She climbed the gleaming stairs, letting the heels of her shoes make tiny echoing clips on the marble. When Bradford watched the video later she wanted to look normal. Like she belonged there.

Inside his monster-sized bedroom, she dropped her bag on his bed, then kicked out of the horrible shoes and went straight to her drawer in his dresser and pulled out the book she had in there, and one other item. She settled on the seat in the reading nook in front of the window, made a show of reading for a few minutes, even though she knew there were no cameras in here, then she shifted her position, pulled open the drapes, and glanced out the window lazily, like her mind was drifting.

Tree limbs were in her way, the buds of springtime popping like crazy. She propped a pillow under her butt, then another, then twisted until she could see right in Soren's house, his library completely open to her. But her gaze didn't stay there. It followed the open door into the hallway, then landed on the ornate mirror she'd given him, even telling him exactly where she thought it would look best.

Through its reflection, she could see into Soren's office. The door was open, like always. He disliked feeling shut in, even to a room as large as his library. She knew he'd spent a little time in jail, maybe that was why.

Soren was there, sitting behind his desk, but he wasn't alone. A large man with the build of a natural athlete who'd let himself go sat in the leather chair opposite him, speaking with vehemence, thick movements of his hands punctuating his every thought. Rogue frowned and stuck a tiny earbud in her ear, then flipped on the receiver in her hand, holding her breath to see if either man reacted. When they didn't, she huffed out her breath, glad she was right in thinking her bug was too far away for his constant all-in-one detector, that sat in the middle of his office, to notice.

The two men looked vaguely alike, had the same shoulder-length hair, but Soren's was silver while the other man still had blonde threading through his. Soren was tall and lean with wiry muscle and a thick silver moustache and dark eyebrows, a combination Rogue had always liked, while the other man was bigger, but with more fat around his midsection. He had a full goatee instead of a mustache.

Soren regularly scanned his office for bugs, but a bug had to be turned on for it to be found. This was the first time she had ever turned hers on. A woman working alone in this business needed to be even more cunning than anyone else, but she'd never felt she needed to go this far before. Until she'd been followed, she never would have. Now to find out if Soren was the one who'd had her followed. She turned the sound all the way up and pressed the bud into her ear.

The man was still talking, his voice a low growl that sounded a lot like Soren's. "She could be useful."

Soren shook his head. "She already is useful. But not to you."

Rogue frowned, wondering if they were talking about her.

The other man shook his head as if he didn't like that answer, then relented. "Fine. Back to our little party. The one today is just for show. It won't blow more than a hole in the wall if it does go off, but it won't. You know the chief has done what he was supposed to do and the SPD already has that intel. You'll get confirmation as soon as your girl shows up with your file. They'll do their search, find the medium banger, assume that was it, and drop their guard. In a few days, we'll plant the big banger, the real one, and blammo, goodbye Wade Lombard, goodbye KSRT. Score one for the big boss."

Soren didn't say anything for a long time. When he finally spoke, his voice was strange. Rogue had to listen for a long time before she realized he was terrified. Normally, he was as unflappable as she was.

He looked around his office, strategically located in the center of the house with no windows or outside walls. "Can he hear us right now?"

The other man, who sounded like Soren with a hard edge, snorted. "I think he could show up right there if he wanted." He flicked a finger toward the center of the room. "But we'd see him come. He has to rip a kind of hole to get over here. And a smell like fire precedes him. The *felen* can feel him come, but they can't feel me."

Rogue frowned. Just what in the fuck did *that* mean?

Soren dropped his gaze to the center of his desk. "I wish you never would have come to me with this, Rex. I don't want to be involved. I might not be on the wolf side of the law, but I don't want to kill people."

Rex snorted. "Don't pull that bullshit on me. I know exactly how many people you've killed."

Soren's head raised and his eyes blazed. "Only for good reason. I'm not looking to eradicate an entire species."

Rex shook his head and stood up, kicking Soren's expensive leather chair over on its side while Soren watched impassively. "Fuck that. You telling me that some part of you doesn't burn to get back at all the *wolfen*, those fanged assholes who think they are so much better than you and me?"

Rogue wrapped her arms around herself, not sure why she was trembling.

Soren spoke softly. "I'm telling you exactly that. They are cops, I'm a criminal. They are just doing their job. They don't have anything against *foxen*, and I don't have anything against them."

Rex leaned over his desk. "Then let me tell you this, brother of mine. All your money and all your power will mean exactly dick when The Father takes over. When that happens, our lives will be measured by his mercy, and that cannot be bought, it can only be earned."

Rogue suddenly knew exactly who this guy was, Rex

Brenwyn, Soren's brother. She didn't know why she hadn't put it together before now, except she'd thought he was in prison for life. She chewed on his words, especially *the father*. Not my father or our father, but *the father*. Boe had said those exact words so many times when she'd first come across him, clothed in rags and wandering around the park next to her home in Serenity, blabbering endlessly about things that made no sense. Except the wolves. That part made sense, or at least she wanted it to. *Foxen* was another word she'd heard before, but wasn't completely certain what it meant.

Rex stood tall and thumped a fist on his chest. "You have no choice, Soren, but to join me." He dropped his hands to the desk again and practically hissed at Soren, while Soren's face took on a green pallor Rogue could see even from the next house. "You will have everything you've ever wanted. Ten times the money and power you have now. You'll be a ruler of the world, not just some shitty crime lord in one district of Chicago. No one will tell you no. And whether you hate them or not, I promise you that all those wolves—"

Rogue sucked in a breath at the word.

"—they hate you. They think they are better than you. And they will be destroyed for it!" He pushed off the desk in one great heave and whirled around, disappearing from Rogue's sight for a moment, then he came back close where she could see him from the side. "Look at this!" He ripped up his shirt to his chin. Rogue studied him for only a second until she realized she couldn't see the skin of his chest or his belly—his angle was wrong, so then her gaze shot to Soren's face.

Soren's eyes were huge in his head and his mouth was working like he was trying very hard to speak but had no words, only a guttural response that could not be translated.

"Who wants a *renqua*? This thing gives you power, makes you a monster among males," Rex shouted, his voice full of passion and insanity. Rogue frowned at his words, at everything he'd said, feeling like she'd fallen down Alice's rabbit hole to a place where nothing made sense.

Soren's handsome, normally placid face folded in on itself in disgust and something more, maybe a sick sort of interest? Rex turned directly toward Rogue's line of sight and strode toward the mirror in the hallway, the one she was viewing the scene through, his eyes fiery.

She threw herself off of the window seat onto the floor in one smooth motion, knowing how unlikely it was that he had been looking at anything but his own reflection as he approached the mirror, his face twisted, his hand yanking his shirt up, baring the awful mark that looked like a clawed handprint three times as large as a human hand that had been branded into his skin.

But she swore his eyes had met hers.

CHAPTER 11

ruin reached the bottom step of the stairs in the tunnel and Mac grabbed his shoulder, holding him back. He needed to be the first one in the room. Bruin acquiesced easily, standing sideways so Mac could push past him.

The room was small and bare, and Mac knew immediately that it was empty. A crushing disappointment dropped into his spine and he sagged with the weight of it as Bruin's light played around the room, revealing absolutely nothing but a chair and a small table.

Bruin sucked in a breath, making Mac take a closer look, trying to concentrate even as the lovely citrus smell pushed in at him from all sides, pulling his attention, demanding it.

Bruin gave a low whistle. "It's like a cave painting."

Mac's eyes searched the walls, but then he realized Bruin's face was pointed to the floor. Mac stepped back, but when he realized he couldn't avoid stepping on the designs without leaving the room, he walked right over the top of them, stepping gently, wishing he had more light.

Every inch of the floor he could see was covered with curlicued, intricate circular designs that seemed to radiate out from one starting position, where they'd been black, but the farther they circled out, the lighter they got, until they where white, like instead of color being added to the floor, concrete had been scraped away with a tool. Mac crossed the room to stare right at the central design, the one that everything else flowed from.

It was a startlingly detailed and beautiful rendition of a wolf, done with black lines, the wolf itself howling toward the stairs they'd just come from, it's graceful neck stretched long, one lower canine visible, the one eye he could see open and shrewd, the hair on its muzzle and around its ears detailed and fine-looking. It spoke to him, called to him. It reminded him of the wolf from the park next to Mik Maks.

He dropped to one knee to examine it, only then noticing the words hidden in the curlicues closest to the wolf. He twisted his neck to read them.

The wolf calls to me. I cannot resist him. I run to him, even though it costs me everything.

Mac touched a finger to the words, frowning, then lowering himself further on the dirty floor, dropping his face right to the cement and smelling. She'd been here. Her skin had been pressed against the floor. Assuming Bruin was right and the scent was of his mate, then his mate was the one who had drawn this wolf and written these words.

Mac took a deep breath and pushed to his feet, strange emotions pulsing around in his head that he couldn't define, it had been so long since he'd even cared what they meant.

His chest ached and his muscles felt strangely weak, while his eyes kept returning to the words over and over.

Bruin held something up. "This is how she did it."

Mac wrestled with the strange feeling in his chest, trying to push it away, but it wouldn't go. He pulled at his loose shirt collar, trying to get relief from a shirt that suddenly felt too small. No relief came, so he gave up, instead crossing the room to Bruin and snatching whatever it was out of his hands.

It was actually two items. The first, a Sharpie marker, the cap discarded, the marker part completely gone, the plastic scraped away halfway down the side. The other one was a knife-handle, the blade scraped away to nothing.

Mac tried to imagine creating this work of art with a sharpie and a knife, scraping for what must have been hours, and he couldn't do it. His chest tightened further, making him swallow and try to suck some air into his lungs.

Bruin walked around the room, shining his light in broad arcs. "I dunno, Mac. If your mate did this, I gotta say, I'm kind of worried about her."

Worry! That's what he was feeling.

Shit.

CHAPTER 12

*R*ogue lay stretched out on the floor, her heart hammering in her chest, as she waited to hear something-anything through her earpiece. Had she been discovered?

When Rex finally spoke, his tone had not changed, nor had his subject, so, unless he was just that good, no, she hadn't been discovered. She rested her face on Bradford's thick cream carpet and allowed her breathing to return to normal, as the image of that clawed handprint played through her mind, leaving her only a bit of consciousness to listen to the conversation still playing out in Soren's office.

Rex seemed to be done with Soren. For now. He growled at his brother, and Rogue could imagine him leaning over the desk, elbows locked, gazes meeting. "You need to make a decision, and I pray you make the right one. The Father will not take kindly to you wanting to *stay out of it*. You might be targeted before the *wolven*, if that is the course you decide on. *Brother.*"

There was no goodbye. No shuffle of feet through the house, no opening or closing of doors. Only a gasp from Soren. Then silence.

Rogue pushed over onto her back, thinking of the time she'd seen that exact same clawed handprint. Boe had one on his chest.

She shook her head at the ceiling, feeling like she'd fallen into an episode of the Twilight Zone. All this *father* mumbo jumbo, talking jewelry, and her popping open locks without touching them. She touched a hand to her head, waiting for it all to make sense. When it didn't, she pushed to her feet and began setting Bradford's bedroom back to how it had been when she'd arrived. The future was a mystery, as always, but some piece of intuition told her she'd never be back in this home. Whether that might be or not, her only choice was to keep moving.

Rogue left the way she had come, ducked into the bathroom of the closest coffee shop, did an easy prest-o change-o that had her looking more like herself than the shy librarian Bradford knew her as, except for the oversized sunglasses and the pink ball cap, then headed around the block in the other direction. She jogged into an alley, then vaulted over a neighbor's fence, pausing behind a tree long enough to text Soren to pick up his dry cleaning after five. He knew that meant she was coming in the back way.

He didn't respond, just pressed his finger to the screen long enough for her to see it.

She broke cover and walked to his back gate, punching in the code that would gain her entry, glad when it didn't just pop open, feeling no eyes on her. Which was silly. Incomplete surveillance. But once she was in his yard, she felt someone watching her from a rooftop, two houses down. Crap. But again, she had the strangest premonition that she would never be in this house again. That, indeed, her life in Chicago might be over. She accepted that. She'd always known it would come sooner or later. That's why she worked so hard. Retirement would come early for her.

As long as he didn't get raided while she was inside the house, she would be ok. She could lose any ancillary tails the cops placed on her easily. She'd never been arrested. No reason for her fingerprints to be in the system. The only wild card was in the bag she had on her hip. So she would get rid of it. Now.

Soren's back door was opened by a hulking bodyguard. She lifted her chin at him, ignoring the yawn of empty space she felt under the house, not her business, then wound through the house to Soren's office. His handsome face, lined with the harsh wisdom of a man much older than she, broke into a wide smile when he saw her. He half stood, and for just a moment she was afraid he would come around the desk and hug her. That would not be good.

But he didn't. He bowed at the waist minutely, then dropped back into his chair, his eyes on her bag. "Ah, Rogue, you never fail me," he said, his voice a rough purr.

"I never fail," she said simply, then sat in the leather chair where Rex had been just a few moments before. The seat was still warm, making her grimace in distaste. "There's eyes on the house."

He nodded. "We know. Two across the street."

"Three. And another two houses down on this side." She gestured away from Bradford's house, keeping herself from casting a look at the mirror in the hallway that announced her as someone else that couldn't be trusted.

He frowned. "Good to know. They are looking for my-" He waved a hand. "It's not important. My file, please?"

Rogue raised an eyebrow as she watched him and fished it out of the bag.

He smiled. "Your fee is already in your account."

Rogue took out her phone and pressed two buttons, entered a code, then put it away. It certainly was. Good.

Soren's already-off mood shifted, pulling in on itself, like he was gathering his courage. Rogue let her eyes drift over the plaques and trophies, mementoes of appreciative sponsored local sports teams, on the shelves behind and to the side of him, knowing what was coming. Fuck. She really was going to have to get out of the business. Once she refused him, their relationship would never be the same. He was a businessman, first and foremost, and no matter how much he *liked* her, she wouldn't be allowed to stay once she said no. Not unless she took up with one of his rivals. Fat chance. She didn't mind working for people she didn't like, but she had to be able to trust them at least a smidgen. Looked like she was back to being a free agent.

His silence pulled her eyes to his. When their gazes locked, he said it. "I want you to work only for me."

Rogue only stared. He knew what her answer was and she resented him for making her say it out loud. Finally, she spoke. "You know I work for myself." Fucking motherfucker. Never, ever, ever would she work for a man, the way he wanted her to work for him. Never would she be that reliant on another person, *especially* a man.

"I'll double your fee. Monthly."

Rogue did the math quickly, the balance-sheet queen in her head unable not to. That would put her to where she was trying to get twice as quickly as she was headed now. Ultimate freedom was her goal, and a crap-ton of money was the only fail-safe way to get there, in her eyes. The ability to live in any country she wanted, bribe anyone she needed to, hire any person or business she desired…

But no. She would never subject herself to the whims of another like that.

She shook her head slowly, drawing out each motion, her eyes locked on his. "No, Soren. Final answer."

His face gave away nothing. She admired that. But not enough to give him the answer he wanted. She changed the subject. "How's your mother?"

Now Soren reacted, his eyes hooding slightly. "She's-"

A fiery smell reached both of them at the same time. Rogue looked up quickly, sighting the smoke alarms in the room. Neither was responding. She rose to her feet, but Soren only seemed to collapse into his chair. Before she could move, Rex stepped out from around the corner that led to the alcove where the pool table was, a smirk on his face. Rogue swore he hadn't been in the room a moment ago.

Rogue stayed on her feet, turning to face Rex fully, waiting for him to speak first. His smirk grew wider. "Ah, so this is the lovely Rogue I've heard so much about. Your name fits your face, sweetheart, and your reputation. Tell me, how did you get it?"

Rogue stayed silent, flexing her forearms to better feel the knives there, ready for anything.

Rex watched her not respond, his hand playing over a wooden trophy on the bookshelf he stood next to, his fingernails running over the corners of it, picking at them. Rogue could hear the soft scratch sound they made every time he plucked a finger hard enough to bend the nail.

He spoke. "When someone lobs you a ball, you really

should catch it or hit it back, you know. It's just polite." He picked up the trophy and threw it to her underhand. She caught it by the golden body of the boy throwing a pitch, a real screamer, only to keep it from hitting her in the face. She put it down on Soren's desk, throwing him a hard glance.

He stood. "Rogue, this is my brother, Rex. Rex, back the fuck off."

Rogue nodded once, face a pissed-off mask. Politeness was not in her job description.

Rex's eyes narrowed for a moment, then he walked through the room, carefully picking his way around Soren's wooden mahogany fox statues, the hand-carved wooden stool with the sleeping fox for a seat, and the strategically-placed wooden tables, all with carved foxes somewhere in the art of the creation. Her favorite was the one that they were hidden in the curlicues of the lattice covering the table legs. You had to search for them, but once you saw them, they were everywhere. Cavorting, leaping, sleeping, hunting. Rogue turned her body to follow Rex through the room.

He stopped near the door. Blocking her? "I have a job for you."

She nodded her head, like something had just come to her. "Rex Brenwyn… weren't you in jail?"

He flicked her an impatient smile. "I got out on good behavior." The lie slipped through the air, and he covered it with a fast follow up. "The job is in Serenity. It's a very simple job. Won't take an expert like you more than a few days. I need you to get something back for me. Something very important that was stolen from me."

Rogue flicked her eyes toward Soren, wanting his take on it. This was the perfect kind of job for her. What she was best at. But Soren would not give his approval if he thought it was a bad job. He looked defeated, but did not give her a yay or a nay. Did not even look at her.

She turned her attention back to Rex. A few days. Serenity. He was speaking her language. She loved Serenity, and took every chance possible to get to the city.

Rex sat down and put his feet up on Soren's fox table. Rogue's favorite. She restrained an impulse to kick them to the floor.

He spoke as if bored, not even looking at her. "I'll double your fee."

That got her eyebrows moving north. "You know my fee?"

He yawned. "Of course I do. Or we wouldn't be speaking. My brother assures me you are worth every penny."

"Let's hear it," Rogue said.

Rex laid out the details, never once gauging her reaction. Barely even looking at her.

She couldn't see any reason not to do it. It was way too much money for something so simple, but that was the best kind of job, wasn't it? She'd once beat the shit out of a guy in an alley outside of a bar with a dildo for almost as much. He'd been the one to pay her to do it. People with too much money were different than normal people, and she'd learned not to question it.

"Who is this guy?"

Rex shrugged. "Drug dealer with a penchant for his own product."

"Half now, half on completion," she said, knowing if he didn't balk at that, she would take the job.

He nodded once.

And she was on her way.

CHAPTER 13

Almost four hours later, Rogue took the last exit to Serenity, her destination, the Honey Depot, the Serenity restaurant that was her starting place for looking for the guy Rex wanted her to find. She would go there before she headed home, so she wouldn't have to leave the house again that evening. Serenity was the only place she considered a real home. The only place she would keep if she had to leave Illinois. She hoped someday to retire in this town.

She'd had to stop to see Father Macleese, but that had gone quickly. He'd asked her to fix his toaster, which she'd happily and easily done. She'd been fixing stuff for him since she was young, a definite sinner on the streets of Chicago, hiding out from a controlling uncle and a doormat aunt, both of whom, when they could catch her, would demand things from her that she knew were wrong, but that she was good at. Picking pockets. Sneaking into houses. Hotwiring cars. She'd been doing that one since she was nine, what, like it was hard? Not. Just looking at the wires had told her which had done what and what simple twist would make the car run.

Father Macleese had fed her often, so she only had to go home once a day, if that, only had to deal with her 'family' when she had nowhere else to go. She'd never gone to school, but Father Macleese let her attend all the Sunday school services at St. Joseph's, insisting the teachers help her learn to read but ask her no questions. He was old-school, Father Macleese, a man she'd watched grow more wrinkled and bent with every passing year, even as his heart had grown kinder. And now he was nervous that he was going to lose St. Joseph's. She'd grown up in Chicago, moving all over the city when her uncle had decided they needed to go, but she'd always found her way to St. Joseph's as often as possible. She hated the thought of Chicago without Father Macleese to make it a more livable place. The bishop wanted him to retire, the bishop thought his parish couldn't support the shelter for women and children he wanted to build. The bishop this and the bishop that. The bishop could go fuck himself. Father Macleese did more to help people who needed it than the bishop had ever done in his life, and when Rogue's life calmed down, she would figure out a way to help him.

She rolled onto the main drag of Serenity, heading left and out of town immediately. Her mind went to the pendants, left in Chicago, and for the twenty or thirtieth time since she'd left the city, she told herself she'd made the right decision. She wanted them with her. Wanted them at her house in Serenity. But Boe was at her house in Serenity. And he was a complete enigma. Something told her the pendants had a lot to do with the mystery that she didn't understand but that she was smack-dab in the middle of.

She already knew Boe was part of the mystery, the one that she used to think she was on the outside of looking in, but now she was realizing that she might be a key player in it, with someone else pulling the strings. There wasn't much more she hated than feeling like someone else was in control of her life. Maybe being ignored, but that was it.

As she drove, her mind ran over what she did know.

One. Almost six months ago, on her 25th birthday, she'd begun having… images come to her. Images and emotions and… knowings, that she didn't understand. The mind-pictures had become more intense with each passing week, and the ones she'd had recently had made her do some sort of a blackout-drunk routine. She would think of cops, or wolves, and then lose herself completely. Sometimes for almost an hour. Once she'd "woken up" in her garage here in Serenity, painting a wolf onto a wooden sign she must have made herself. Another time she'd found herself standing in front of that stupid art sculpture in the park downtown, a can of yellow spray paint in her hand, graffiti scrawled on the metal thing that looked like a flag or a blanket in front of her. It had said, *The wolves are guarding the sheep, wake up, sheep!* What did that even *mean*?

Two. She'd realized that she'd started to believe in werewolves, and she wasn't sure when or how. Like one day she was all, *werewolves? Yeah, right,* if she thought of them at all. And the next day she was all, *werewolves? Where? What did they look like?*

Three. Boe had come into her life. She'd been out on one of her *excursions* one evening, waking up in Sinissipi Park at almost four in the morning, graffiti all over the playground, but something else had drawn her attention, making her pocket the Sharpie she'd been using on the side of the building and whirl around in the dark, trying to pick out whoever was watching her do what she'd been doing.

He'd been hiding in the trees far enough away that she knew he couldn't see her face, but still, he might be able to ID her well enough for a cop to arrest her for vandalism. Her heart had sunk at the thought of being arrested in Serenity, for the first time ever, her fingerprints finally on file, and for something so *stupid*! She didn't understand the graffiti. Didn't get her sudden compulsion, her inability to discipline her own mind like she'd done all her life. She'd stood there, hating the underground obsession that drove her to do it for whatever reason, wondering if it was some sort of guilt about her profession manifesting in this silly midnight need, maybe a desire to get caught so she would have the opportunity to admit all her other crimes.

But no, that didn't make sense. She didn't feel guilty about what she did. She only stole from people who had too much, only took jobs after researching them first. She'd already looked up the guy Rex wanted her to find and confirmed what he'd said was true. The target was a small-time drug dealer, liked to hook kids early and bleed them dry. Been arrested for a multitude of other equally nasty things. She had no problem feeding one criminal to another criminal, no problem hooking back property that had already been stolen once.

What about stealing the file from the cops? Rogue shrugged in her car, with no one there to see it. Soren had already known what was in that file, he'd said, and he just wanted it out of their hands. She'd peeked at it, and it was exactly as he'd said. Pictures of his place, speculation about whether or not his brother would go there, and some personal details that hadn't seemed to make a lot of sense. Besides, the cops had to have copies of that shit, didn't they? She knew that and she knew Soren knew that, so what she had finally decided was that the stealing of the file was for a message. A kind of 'fuck you' to Chief Lorenzo. A big slap in the face that said, *you're not as smart or as good as you think you are.*

Rogue didn't mind being part of something like that at all. As much as she loved cops, she hated them, too. She loved them for their big bodies, their I'm-the-shit attitudes, and their total lack of a problem with knocking someone on their ass if that someone was asking for it. She hated them because you couldn't be in her business and not hate someone who had the authority and the balls to take everything away from you with one arrest.

But the only man she'd ever gotten off with had been a cop. Most men she slept with knew her as someone she wasn't, like Bradford, who thought she was a sweet, shy librarian and so he had sweet, shy librarian sex with her. Always missionary position with 42 pumps per minute, and 52.2 seconds of cuddling afterwards. She liked the closeness, didn't mind the sex, but always had to finish herself in the bathroom after. Except for that one guy...

He'd been a cop, a big one, he'd had no idea that she was a criminal, and he probably wouldn't have cared. He saw her free-climbing in Yosemite, on her own, and had broken off from his group of friends to spot her. He'd never once told her she shouldn't be out there alone and she could see his admiration for her every time she looked down at him. He'd been digging her hard. He hadn't spoken much, but the one time she had fallen not-on-purpose, she'd been glad he was there to lead her to the pad. That evening, as the sun had been setting, she'd dropped to the ground, exhausted, and said three words to him. "You a cop?" His haircut and clothes telling her it was that or military, his cocksure attitude and the shit on his belt leaning toward cop.

He'd nodded, and she'd flashed him a slow, predatory smile, one that said, *good for you, if you're gonna do it, do it now. I'm waiting.*

He'd done it, pushing her against the rock she'd been climbing, taking her hard and fast and standing up, and she'd screamed out her pleasure with the light of the setting sun in her eyes.

If he'd said no, he was military, she might have gotten his name and number. Instead, they'd walked out in silence and gone their separate ways, but she always remembered him when she thought about her *werewolf problem*, as she liked to call it. In fact, it was sometimes his face that flashed in her head just before the images began to play. His handsome, rough-hewn face and cocky smile that turned on the mind-movie, frequently spitting her into a darkness she couldn't control.

She shook her head in her sedan. Fuck! What had she been thinking about before she'd gone on the world's longest trip down memory lane. Her mind was shot and she hated it, but she never lingered on shit like that. Get up, brush yourself off, rail and bail and leave no trail. In other words, action, not words.

But still, she had to drag herself back to reality. There was no action to be done, which was her strong point, but plenty of thinking to be done, which she didn't enjoy near as much. But no one else would take over the job. She was the only one available to try to worry the mystery she was wrapped up in into the light of day.

Oh yeah, she'd been thinking of Boe and the night she'd found him.

Ok, starting over. Three. She'd been doing her own version of *the dirty* in the park, felt someone watching her, but instead of taking off, she'd sought him out. Found a grown man of about sixty, thin skin, bruises everywhere, terrified expression and mannerisms, cowering in the woods, his clothes drenched through. She could see the outline of his ribs under the ratty t-shirt he wore. He'd had no shoes on his feet.

Rogue walked silently into the forest on the path, her ability leading her right to the man who was watching her every move. He was no threat, every sense in her body told her that. She stepped off the trail and found him cowering at the bottom of a large evergreen, pushed up against the trunk. He'd been trying to gather leaves to use as a blanket for his bare feet and the dirt was showing through in large circular patches. Snow hadn't flown yet, but the chill in the air said it could be any night. Tonight, even.

"Hey," Rogue said, softly, not wanting to startle him. "There's a homeless shelter about two miles from here."

His eyes flew from the ground to her face, like he'd been hoping she wouldn't talk to him, but when she did, everything had changed for him. "Homeless... shelter?" he'd said, like he had no idea what such a thing would even be.

"Yeah, you can warm up there, they'll feed you. Maybe even let you sleep there. Give you some shoes."

He looked from her face to his bare feet, then back again. "Will there be, ah, lawmen at the establishment?"

His voice was as small as his body, and he spoke with rigidness and an accent she couldn't place. "Lawmen?"

The small man cleared his throat, looking around

furtively, and Rogue's heart went out to him. No one should have to sleep in the woods on a cold night.

"Yes, well, that is to say, a Sheriff. Will there be a sheriff at the establishment?"

Ah, so he'd broken some law and didn't want to get caught. She took him in from head to toe, unable to decide what exactly he might have done. He looked weak as a kitten and half-starved. "No, probably not, unless there's a fight or something."

He'd tried to smile then, and bow at the waist, even though he was sitting down. "Thank you, Mistress, for your kindness. I shall go directly."

Rogue pursed her lips. He was lying to her. And she was about to do something stupid. But she would never forgive herself if she didn't. Besides, something about the man called to her, spoke directly to her, like a voice of a trusted friend whispering in her ear. Her need to know his story eclipsed anything else. "Look, I've got a change of clothes that will fit you at my place. And some leftover pizza. Why don't you come home with me? It's just gonna get colder tonight."

"Oh no, Mistress. That is perfectly alright. I'll be fine." *But his voice broke when he said it, and when she looked closer, the bottoms of his feet were torn up, the skin curled and weeping around open sores, like he'd been walking over sharp rocks for hours.*

She bent and hoisted him under his elbow. "Sorry, Pops, but I'm not leaving you out here to get turned into a pops-icle. Let's go, alley-oop. All I've got is cold deep-dish and Pepsi, but the place is warm and you'll be off your feet."

He'd cried then, but she hadn't let it sway her. He'd cried again after she fed him and clothed him, but she could understand that, especially if he'd been homeless as long as he looked like he had.

Things hadn't gotten too weird for a few weeks.

CHAPTER 14

*B*ack in Serenity, speeding down the rural route in the work truck he'd signed out, sunshine spreading across the fields that surrounded them, Mac huffed out a breath so Bruin would know he was irritated, while Bruin craned his neck theatrically, so Mac would know he hadn't given up hope of finding The Honey Grounds. They'd left Chicago a few hours before, traveled the entire way in silence, and Mac wasn't any closer to deciding how he felt about what they'd found.

If he concentrated, he could still recall the tangy scent of the female who already had his heart. If her personality and her looks were anything like her citrus-y smell and her lovely sharp voice, he would be a goner.

He gritted his teeth. He was so over ready to be a goner for his mate. So why couldn't he find her? The close calls were starting to eat at him, making his body a live wire, a tense block of muscles and tissue that wanted direction, purpose. Wanted a warm female body to point toward, to press into.

Bruin rolled his window down and stuck his head out, looking so much like a dog excited to be going for a ride that Mac had to laugh. Bruin pulled his head back in, his expression excited. "I smell it."

"You smell what? All I see is trees and farmhouses."

"Honey. I smell honey."

"Just cuz the place is called The Honey House doesn't mean it smells like honey."

Bruin stuck his head back out the window, then back in again, not deterred at all. "We're getting close, I know it."

Mac nodded dryly. "Ok, Detective Shnoz, I'll take your—" But on their right, a clearing opened up showing a gravel parking area and a quaint red building, the large sign with letters big enough to read from the road declaring it to be, *The Honey Depot.*

Mac swung in immediately. "Well, what do you know. I'm not going to starve to death after all."

A wide smile crossed Bruin's face as he scrabbled for his door handle, not even waiting for the truck to stop before he jumped out, hitting the ground at a roll, then popping up and brushing the gravel out of his hair like he meant to do that.

"Motherfuck," Mac muttered, pulling into a stall and jumping out himself, running to catch up with the goofy bear.

The parking lot was mostly empty, only three other cars. Mac wondered how they got any business at all this far out from Serenity, unless it came from the farmers and the neighboring towns.

A woman stood off to the right of the restaurant, trying to drape a tarp over a sign that looked just like the one on the restaurant, but this one said *The Beehive.* Every time she pulled on one corner of the tarp, it slid off the other corner because it was so long. Bruin ran over to help her. Mac rolled his eyes and followed.

The woman looked to be in her fifties, dressed like a hippie straight out of some Woodstock picture. White, poofy shirt, long brown skirt, macramé hair band around her forehead, long brown hair parted down the middle. Mac threw a look over his shoulder at the front door, wondering if it was a theme restaurant.

Bruin grabbed the tarp on one end and tucked it around the sign, while Mac hovered over the middle of the long piece of heavy wood. If she wanted it wrapped all the way around, he would lift.

The woman stood straight and wiped her hands on her skirt, then favored them each with a smile. "Thank you, boys, it's good to see young men willing to lend a hand. Wrap it tight if you don't mind. My daughter changes the name of the restaurant so often, I never know if she'll want to go back to an old version, so I keep them all wrapped and stacked right here."

Mac nodded, then took charge, telling Bruin what to do and how to do it. Bruin ran around the sign, following Mac's orders like an Australian Shepherd puppy learning to herd cattle, thrilled to be put to good use. Within a few moments, they had the sign wrapped up tight and leaning against the other ones, all the creases facing down so rain wouldn't get in.

The woman watched them, hands on her hips, then nodded once and held out her hand to each of them. "Right good job there. I'm Lucinda, this here's half my place, and the other half belongs to my daughter. You boys single?"

Mac snorted out a laugh and shook his head no, surprising himself. "Nah, I'm not, but the big guy here is."

Lucinda had already shaken Mac's hand and was working on Bruin's, so she pulled him in close and looked him up and down. At one point, Mac swore she even smelled him. She stood on her tiptoes, putting her hands on Bruin's shoulders to pull him down to her, then whispered something in his ear.

Bruin looked at her, surprised, then shook his head. "No ma'am, I'm not."

Lucinda stepped away and pouted. "That's too bad. Willow would love you. You're just her type." She shook it off. "You boys come to eat?"

Bruin nodded emphatically.

"You tell the waitress, Pam's her name, that I said you could have free desert. Anything you want. The blueberry pie is the best."

"Thank you!" Bruin practically sprinted up the stairs to the wide porch that surrounded the building.

Mac nodded his thanks and followed his friend, grabbing the door that Bruin yanked open, allowing the scents of buttered eggs, salty bacon, and something sweeter to spill out.

Mac gave the place the once over and grudgingly approved. Neat as a pin, lots of rusty red checkerboard patterns, some farm-type accessories on the walls like antique plows and tools, flowers everywhere, and an open, airy layout. Pleasant. Good enough for brunch, certainly.

Until he ran into Bruin's back with a thud. He bounced off and circled past the male, who had stopped dead in the middle of the restaurant, his nose pointed up. Mac edged past a withered old couple who were only picking at their lunches at the closest table, and got in front of Bruin, giving him the once-over. "What in the hell, B?" he asked. "We eating or wh-?"

He cut off when he heard the noise coming from Bruin's

chest, like a rough-idling chainsaw engine. Mac frowned and smacked his friend a good one on the arm. "Quit it."

Bruin ignored him, turning in a circle, his eyes everywhere, his nostrils flaring. When he faced Mac again, Mac stepped in a little closer, trying to figure out what that fucking noise was. And then he knew.

"You're purring. Aww, isn't that cute." His voice turned hard. "You big pussy—"

The woman at the table next to him swatted him with her pocketbook. Mac jumped and shielded himself with his arms. "Pussycat, lady! Geez!" He grabbed his friend by the elbow and hauled him across the room, muttering, "Perv," at Mother Nature behind him, who was still yielding her pocketbook like a shield.

Bruin moved, although not as fast as Mac wanted him to, dragging his feet, still looking everywhere at once. The door opened and a few more people spilled into the restaurant. Mac pulled Bruin to the far side where there was a bar, with cheery stools in front of it.

He pushed Bruin into the stool closest to a retaining wall, shaking his head at the purring still coming from his chest. "Sit, kitty, shut that stupid noise off and I'll order you a saucer of milk."

Bruin sat obediently and Mac shoved a menu at him, waiting for the purring to stop. It didn't. Bruin took the menu, but swiveled in his chair, not paying Mac any attention.

Mac sat next to him, then snapped his fingers in front of Bruin's face. "What is going on, Garfield? Don't make me start calling you cat names, that's just gonna piss me off."

Bruin finally looked at him, the lawnmower still racing in his chest. "I don't know, I can't help it, I just—" He looked around one more time, then leaned in close. "Do you smell that?"

"Yeah, I smell a lot of things. Greasy spoon shit. We're in a freaking restaurant."

Bruin raised his head again and took a big sniff. "No, the honey smell. It's like sunflower honey from the driest, hottest summer imaginable, when the bees had to fly no more than thirty feet to get it, the first rows of combs, when the nectar was the sweetest."

Mac frowned. "Sunflower honey? Never heard of it."

Bruin took another big sniff, then thumped his hand on his chest, his voice reverent. "It's so pure. Nothing gets into the nectar because no one uses pesticides on sunflowers, and the long stem traps soil pollutants." He took another monster sniff, the noise from his chest now so loud that a man walking by gave them a funny look. Bruin lowered his head and leaned in close to Mac. "I can't stop it."

Mac frowned. He was hungry. But damned if he'd have an appetite with Colonel Purr turned up to high next to him. "Is this... normal?"

Bruin shook his head. "I don't know. I've never heard any *bearen* do it before." His face darkened with a realization, while his chest kept vibrating. "Except for the cubs. They do it when they nurse, or so I've heard. But it's been so long since I've seen a cub—"

Mac cut off that line of conversation before his sensitive friend could go all sad on him. "Lemme try something." He made a fist and punched Bruin hard in the chest, only interrupting the noise for a moment. "Hey, it almost worked." He punched him again, harder, then stood up so he could get a better angle, really wailing on Bruin. The noise stopped.

Mac sat back down. Nice. Smart idea he'd had. He looked at Bruin waiting for Bruin to compliment him, but the male was only running his hands over his face.

"You still smell it?" Mac said.

Bruin nodded stiffly, his nostrils waving like flags in a stiff breeze.

A waitress came out from the kitchen carrying three plates. She took them to a table, then came back to Mac and Bruin, her pen poised over her pad, her sharp face swinging back and forth between them. "What'll you boys have?"

"What's good?" Mac asked.

"Reuben sandwich is our signature. All our breakfast is amazing. Most of the pies are great."

Mac looked up and down the menu. "Gimme two Reubens and…" he ran his finger down the desert menu. He looked up. "The skillet chocolate chip cookie."

The waitress opened her eyes wide and shook her head an inch to the right, then left, her eyes speaking volumes while she said nothing at all.

"That good, huh? Ok, give me a slice of pie instead, any kind. Bring it with the food."

She wrote it down and turned to Bruin. He closed his menu. "I'll have a blueberry pie."

"One slice blueberry," she said, writing in her notebook. "Anything else?"

"Not a slice. The whole pie."

The waitress raised her eyebrows and assessed him before deciding he meant it. "Ok, then." She disappeared.

Mac looked behind him at the jingle of the bell over the door ringing again. The lunch crowd was filling the place up. Lucinda came in behind them and headed for the kitchen. Mac leaned over to talk softly to B. "What did Lucinda ask you outside?"

"She wanted to know if I was an angel."

Mac frowned. What a strange question. But then, she

seemed like a strange lady. He turned in his chair to people-watch. "Why were you purring?"

Bruin rubbed his chest like it hurt. "No clue," he said, and Mac checked him out. He seemed off.

Their food came and they dug in. The waitress had been right. Reuben had been a good choice, but, for some reason, there was a tin of honey on the side, like for dipping. He ignored it, till he felt Bruin's eyes on it, so he handed it over.

Bruin took it to his nose, sniffing delicately. "Basswood honey. Great choice." He poured it over his pie, using his fork to assist.

Mac couldn't watch. He focused on his own food, getting most of the way through the first sandwich before his phone went off. He left it in his pocket for a second, but then another text came in, and another and another. Not a good sign. He fished it out, read the messages that were still streaming in like a live news feed, then hit Bruin on the shoulder. "We gotta haul ass. There's a bomb threat at the station."

Bruin stood up, cradling his pie, shoving the last few bites in his mouth and swallowing whole, while Mac threw some bills on the counter. Good thing they'd gotten to eat. Who knew when they'd get another chance.

Damn shame the rut was scheduled for that evening at the Watson building. Unless this thing was cleared up fast, there would be a bunch of unhappy females milling around the big space with nothing to do but each other.

CHAPTER 15

Still musing about the small quiet man who'd become such a strange fixture in her life, Rogue turned into the parking garage where she had another car, making the switch automatically, her senses telling her there was no need, no one was following her, but habit pushing her forward.

After about three days of solid sleep in her guestroom, the old guy had been a new man, although he had already looked older. She learned his name was Boeson, which she'd shortened to Boe. She'd invited him to stay for a week, just till he'd gotten back on his feet, and he'd agreed shyly. She'd had to show him how to use everything, the toilet, the fridge, the TV—which he'd backed away from like he was seeing a ghost—the stove, which she barely knew how to use herself, and even simple things, like books, had seemed to amaze him. He spent hours in her library every day, reading book after book after book. Old Westerns were his favorite. Horror, he wouldn't even touch after reading a chapter or two. Rogue wasn't a reader, but her sister had loved books from an early age, so Rogue kept the library stocked for her, you know, just in case she ever returned to Serenity.

Rogue had a habit of stopping at Serenity garage sales, buying every box of books they had, then bringing them to her home and arranging them by color and size. Boe had taken three days and rearranged them by type after asking if it was ok, whistling and humming to himself the entire time. They didn't look like art anymore when he was done, but as she stared at the packed shelves built into the walls, she realized Amaranth would probably like them better this way. Their haphazard peaks and valleys from bigger to smaller book, their colors scattered like rainbows playing over the carpet from a crystal on a string in front of a window, set to swinging and twirling by a child.

Boe's quiet, unobtrusive, non-judgmental companionship pleased both of them, and a week had somehow turned into however long he wanted to stay.

But the weird part about Boe, and the part that was pertinent to her *werewolf problem*, was when he'd started having nightmares.

Rogue sat straight up in bed. What had woken her?

It came again. A shrieking, sobbing cry from somewhere else in the house. "I've forgotten how! My animal has deserted me! The Father has taken my very nature and now I am bereft."

Rogue shot out of bed and ran down the hall in her sleep clothes, booty shorts and a tank top. She found Boe standing near the bathroom in his pajamas, one hand on the wall, seeming to convulse. She tried to speak to him, but he ignored her, then fell on the floor and moved forward a bit, as if he were trying to crawl, or, more eerily, trying to walk on all fours and not being able to.

"No," he huffed out, then collapsed on his side.

Rogue dropped to her knees next to him. "Boe. Boe, you're ok. Talk to me."

He had, the words coming in a streaming rush, his eyes still closed. "I am not ok. I am lost. Swirling down the noth-ingness. Half a foxen."

She frowned at the word, but it was not the first strange thing he'd said that she didn't understand.

He went on. "I might as well throw myself on the mercy of the wolves. They may kill me, but any knowledge they can glean from my hide could redeem me in some small manner."

At the word 'wolves', her body had jerked forward. She lowered her face close to his, speaking softly, not wanting to startle him or wake him or lose the moment. "Werewolves?"

He rubbed a gnarled hand over his face, his eyelids flut-tering. "They are not werewolves. The moon does not control their shift into wolf or human form."

Rogue's entire body had jerked again at the admis-sion, like she was the one convulsing. Wolves. Wolves who could look like men. Or be men. The idea filled her with an emotion she couldn't identify, and, as a response, her mind clamped down on it, controlling it, denying it ad-mission. Forcing it into a small box she always kept the lid on. Emotions were dangerous. Anything that dimmed your thinking mind and your ability to make decisions was not to be trusted. Especially anything as strong as that feeling was.

Her *werewolf problem* had started before Boe came into her life, but once he'd said those words? It had become a *werewolf obsession.* She should have considered him crazy. A real piece of work. But somehow she knew he wasn't.

He wouldn't say anymore that evening, pulling into a ball and refusing to speak at all, and when she'd approached the subject the next day, he'd looked positively stricken that he'd said anything. She'd had to go to Chicago that afternoon for a job, and had stayed away for almost a month, leaving him at her house alone, not for the first time, but it was the first time she'd been gone for so long.

She trusted him, though. He was close-mouthed about his life, but she learned that he'd once had a wife and kids but had outlived all of them. The way he talked about them made it seem as if he'd had to make some sort of a choice a long time ago, a choice that left them safe, but had changed his life forever. If she tried to question him about other aspects of life, like his past jobs, or where he used to live, he became distressed to the point of getting sick and trying to leave her home. So she never pushed him. He loved to read and to listen to the radio. He preferred classical music, couldn't stand hip hop or rap, was indifferent about most of the rest of it. He still read for hours every day (sometimes reading cookbooks like they were fiction, from page one to the end, all in one sitting), he cleaned her house from top to bottom weekly, and had even begun to cook food for her. He didn't drive or leave, ever, but she had groceries delivered and was amazed at some of the dishes he was creating. In short, she liked having him around, the whole weird, part-of-the-mystery thing notwithstanding.

When she'd returned from the job in Chicago after his first nightmare, she'd done a bit of pushing here and there, until she'd finally triggered something in him so scary that she'd never tried again.

Rogue stood and carried her dinner dishes to the sink. She hadn't eaten a meal like that in… ever. Boe had barely eaten any of his, instead preferring to watch her eat, and smile at every noise of pleasure she'd made. At the sink, her back to Boe, she'd decided it was time and said, almost casually, "Tell me about the foxen. Tell me about that mark on your chest that you take great pains to hide from me."

She could feel Boe stiffen behind her as the atmosphere in the room chilled to freezing. He normally washed the dishes, but she picked up the sponge and ran it over her plate in a distracted manner, waiting for him to say anything, hoping not looking at him would make it easier for him to talk, like it did her. When he didn't, she tried again. "Or The Father. You could tell me about The Father. I know you need to talk about it. Your dreams of him are killing you."

When he still didn't speak, she tried one more time, being sure not to look at him, not to see his distress, because it would make her stop. "Or the wolves, Boe. You could tell me about the wolves. I hear you moan about them at night sometimes. You say things like, 'the wolves will know who I am, and they will make me stand trial for my sins of multitude.'"

A scritch-scratch sound made her turn around. Boe had gone stiff in his chair, his eyes glazed and staring at nothing, his fingers scrabbling on the table like a giant spider. And then he'd spoken, a mish-mash of words that came out of his mouth so quickly she couldn't pick out a one. The color drained from his face, leaving him looking pinched and drawn, and even older. A man in his seventies, now, even though he was warm and well-fed.

He heaved a great breath and another glut of words began to flow, like one great big word. Rogue scrambled for her phone and began to take video, even though the tone of the message made her skin crawl.

LISA LADEW

*"Theselandswillbeourstoreignoveraslordsandourfem-
aleswillberestoredtousourprogenywillfloodthesoilIamthevan-
quisherof…"*

*"Stop!" she cried, because her stomach was turning, a
queasiness making her mouth water. She didn't want to hear
anymore. "Tell me about the wolves. I only want to know about
the werewolves."*

*Boe looked at her, but still his eyes were dead. "There are
no werewolves."*

*Rogue swallowed hard, fighting her nausea with her every
breath. "That's not what you said before."*

*"Werewolves are made up. Make believe. What we are
facing is much more dangerous than a werewolf." His voice lowered, as if he were telling a great secret. "The wolves that live in
Serenity, indeed, in the entire world, are not tied to the moon
in the manner of story. They run by it, mate by it, but they do
not worship it or change only when it is fat."*

*Rogue held her breath, her nausea easing somewhat. This
was what she wanted to hear. "Go on."*

*Boe's head turned an inch and looked at the wall behind
her again. "Ohhearmethycunningandcrimson—"*

"No!"

Rogue's mouth flooded with saliva just at the memory.
Seeing Boe in that trance had made her a bit scared of him
for the first time, and she normally wasn't scared of anything,
not even death. She was on earth, alive, and she was doing her
best at it, but when it was time for her to go, she might just
be happy about that.

She'd stopped the video and apologized, still having to
shake Boe by the shoulder for a few minutes until he'd come
back to himself.

And she'd never asked him about *foxen*, or The Father, or

the wolves again. Never heard the words again until earlier that day.

Rogue drove out of the parking garage, again checking her senses. No one was watching her.

Ah, that was the fourth part of the puzzle, if she really wanted to be honest with herself. She was different, wasn't she?

So she had one—the movies in her mind that were getting worse and worse, sometimes making her black out, making her obsess over wolves and cops, cops and wolves. Two—her absolute belief that werewolves, men who could shift into wolves and back, existed. Three—the seeming coincidence that Boe had been dropped into *her* lap. Four—the fact that she was different, always had been. Other people weren't able to tell when someone was watching them. Other people couldn't pinpoint a hidden person's location by the feeling of their eyes on them.

Oh, and let's not forget that now she had a five! Five, she'd just spent a day of freaky strangeness, somehow popping locks with her touch... or her mind, and then been coerced into an underground tunnel by a disembodied voice that seemed to come from a necklace.

Shit. Suddenly she fiercely wanted those pendants with her, if only to prove that she wasn't the crazy one.

Rogue turned on the farm road, frowning slightly, rubbing a hand to her temple, fearing she was in fact crazy, and having the pendants in her hand would prove absolutely nothing.

CHAPTER 16

Checking again to be sure no one's attention was on her, Rogue turned down the farm road that lead to The Honey Depot as a large black truck took the corner too fast and sped past her going the other way. She had to swerve onto the shoulder to avoid them. She flipped the truck the bird and eased back into her lane, finding the restaurant easily. For a split second, she felt like someone was watching her, but the feeling eased quickly.

She parked, then pulled a guy's picture out of her bag, memorizing his features. Denton Smith was his name. He was hiding out in Serenity, and the only intel on him was that he liked this restaurant, eating here a few times a week. So if she was lucky enough to catch him here, she'd follow him home. Otherwise, she'd ask a few questions, see if anyone knew anything about him.

She strode up the steps, watching through the windows

before she even got inside. It looked busy, but no, so far she didn't see him. She pulled open the door and—

What was that smell? Something harsh in all the right ways greeted her, making her falter just inside the door. Some part of her mind registered the Please Seat Yourself sign and she headed for a table in the corner where she could check out the entire place, then changed her mind on impulse, hitting the bar instead. It struck her that she was following the scent. It wasn't food, although she smelled plenty of that, too. No, it was strong and deep, like a man's cologne, but it was like no cologne she'd ever smelled. It was more like... an aura, or an attitude. Strong masculine attitude and roughened denim, and it wasn't diminishing. She drifted to the second chair in from the retaining wall and more fell into it than sat in it, taking a deep breath, all thoughts of why she was supposed to be there falling right out of her head as she breathed through her nose and—

"Miss, miss! Are you ok?"

Rogue jerked as her conscious mind slammed back into her head. What had she been—?"

"Great," the waitress next to her mumbled. "I'm gonna get Willow. I don't get paid enough to do this shit."

Rogue raised her hand. "No, I'm fine. Sorry. Don't get... Willow." Whoever Willow was. "Sorry about that. I've—ah, I've got a lot on my mind."

The waitress put on an mm-hmm face and held up her pad and pen. "You ready to order?"

Rogue had no idea what they were serving but she didn't want to make any more of a spectacle of herself. "Yeah, bring me a water and whatever the special is."

The waitress, whose nametag read 'Pam', scribbled down the order and left. Rogue took a deep breath and gave herself a few moments to regain her composure.

When she had, she realized the smell she'd been so capti-vated by had dissipated quite a bit. She frowned, really hating what was happening to her. Maybe she should see a doctor? Wouldn't it be a kick in the head if her *werewolf problem* was nothing more than a tumor pressing on her brain stem. Maybe Boe was nothing more than a figment of her imagi-nation. The pendants, too.

Shit. Too depressing to contemplate. She didn't want to leave this world tied to a hospital bed. She wouldn't, either. If that's what it came down to, she'd find something high to jump off of—

Crap! She was spacing again, sure as if she'd thought of the cop. That smell had done something to her brain, scrambled her circuits, reminded her of that time in Yosemite—

No. Not doing this again. She rallied her brain, brass-knuckled it into behaving, and turned slightly on the barstool so she could survey the other patrons. Smith wasn't among them. No problem, she'd ask Pam about him when she got a chance. Linger over dessert if she had to. Come back tonight or tomorrow. Never were jobs that easy anyway.

She sat forward in her seat, letting the conversations in the restaurant wash over her, turning slightly every time she heard the bell over the door jingle, accepting her Rueben sandwich with honey for dipping with a confused smile, then trying it. It was good. Strange, but good.

From her vantage point at the bar, she could also hear all the conversations in the kitchen. A back door slammed. "Willow!" someone called, and a few more hellos were mur-mured. A soft female voice, so darn soft and sweet that it set Rogue's teeth on edge spoke. "Hello, Bart. Hi, Mom, Pam, I'm so glad to see you today."

Rogue raised her eyes to look through the long and

narrow window into the kitchen, wanting to see the owner of that voice. It sounded too sweet and nice to be real. But when she saw the person who had been speaking, she figured it probably wasn't an act. Some people were really that sweet, she knew, and this woman looked to be one of them.

Her hair was long and a honey-colored brown that shone in the overhead lights. Her skin was flawless and her eyes big enough and kind enough to belong to a Disney princess from the early years, back before they were badasses. Her cheeks were colored with a blush that looked to be permanent, from healthy eating and perpetual excitement, probably. Shit. Rogue knew that kind of girl. Everyone's friend, always the person you went to when you were feeling down or sad, she would talk to anyone, lend out her last dollar, until some nutjob stalked her into hiding. Rogue didn't like many women, but she found herself drawn to this one. She looked too sweet to dislike.

As if she felt someone looking at her, Willow turned and made eye contact with Rogue through the window. Rogue lifted her eyebrows and her chin. *Hi.* Then looked back down at her food.

But the door to the kitchen opened and Rogue looked up again. Willow was there, her pink cheeks and open stare pointed right at Rogue. She stood right in front of Rogue on the other side of the bar. "Do I know you?"

Rogue shook her head.

Willow came around the bar toward her. "I'm Willow."

Rogue wiped her hands on her napkin, but before she could stick one out, Willow was putting her arms around her. Rogue turned her wrists inward to be sure Willow didn't inadvertently feel the knives strapped to the inside of her arms.

She chewed quietly and waited for the hug to be over. Anyone else would have gotten a push to the chest or maybe a backhand to the face, but not this woman. That would have been like kicking a puppy who licked your boot. Rogue could feel Willow's gentleness seeping out.

Willow backed up and looked down. "Sorry, ah, I'm a hugger." She blushed, her cheeks pinking up prettily. "I usually have more manners, I apologize."

Rogue waved a hand. Whatever. Chew. Chew. Swallow.

Willow sat down next to her and stared hard at her. "It's just that... well, I feel like I know you. Or like I want to know you."

Rogue looked Willow up and down, her mind quiet. She didn't mind being rude when someone got up in her grill, but she wouldn't be with Willow. She understood exactly what Willow meant, was feeling a bit of it herself. "I'm Rogue." Fuck, shouldn't have given the real name. She was slipping.

"Rogue. Lovely. What a wonderful name, although it doesn't describe you in the slightest. You're gorgeous. You should be named fancy and beautiful, like Elizabeth, or Bronwyn or... or..." Willow snapped her fingers and pointed at Rogue. "Seraphina!"

Rogue laughed, surprised into it, then surprised that she'd done it. There wasn't a lot of levity in her life and suddenly she couldn't remember the last time she'd laughed. She shook her head. "Sometimes it's better not to stand out."

Willow nodded like she knew the truth in that statement, then twisted her body on the bar stool like a small girl who'd been forced to sit still for too long. "How's your sandwich?"

Rogue held up the half in her hand. "Surprisingly good.

I wouldn't have thought honey would go with a Rueben, but I like it."

Willow clapped her hands together and something in the mannerism made Rogue think of her sister as a young girl. Although Amaranth had been more like Rogue, hard, suspicious, grown up way too young. So why would Rogue think of her now?

Willow smiled. "Oh yay! I'm so glad you like it. You absolutely have to try my skillet cookie. I make it with coconut flour, cricket flour, and yacon syrup, so, not only is it tasty, it's super good for you, too. Full of protein."

Rogue had been about to say yes until she'd heard cricket flour. Absolutely not. And yacon syrup? Wasn't that an ingredient in dog food? She put her sandwich down and stared at it. "There's no cricket flour in that, is there?"

"No, no, just my cookies. The farmers love them."

Rogue shook her head. "Good thing you tell people first. Mess around and feed people crickets without their knowing and someone might get upset."

Willow laughed, a tinkling, melodic sound, that soothed Rogue, almost made her feel better about the bug cookies. She stood up, then touched Rogue on the shoulder. "Sorry to bother you, I just wanted to say hi."

Rogue didn't want her to go. She shelved the thought, pushing aside the emotion in her expert manner. She had a purpose here, one that did not include making a new friend. Willow waved one last time and disappeared.

Rogue finished her sandwich. Dessert? Only if there was something bug-free. She waved down Pam, but instead of ordering anything else, she spoke the words that popped into her head. "Hey, you ever seen a guy named Denton Smith here?"

Pam's eyes narrowed. "Yeah."

Rogue launched into her lie smoothly, without premeditation. "We ah, we kind of had a thing last summer and I was hoping to get back together with him, at least see what he was up to."

She left it there, pasting an innocent, hopeful expression on her face, thinking Pam would tell her when the guy was most likely to be there. But instead, she hit pay dirt.

Pam's face smoothed out and she looked Rogue up and down. "Oh. Yeah, well, I heard he's caretaking the Watson building. Moved in upstairs of the warehouse. You know, free place to live and all that."

Rogue nodded and smiled, a big fake one. "Totally, that sounds just like him." She knew exactly where the Watson warehouse was. Historic building, sometimes used for weddings or graduations or reunions, but almost always empty until late spring. She could check it out that evening. If it was empty, she'd be in and out in no time at all. If the job really was going to be that easy, she almost would feel bad taking Rex's money. Almost.

She paid, and headed out the door, faltering for just a moment when she felt eyes hard on her. A quick scan of the parking lot told her it was no one there. She knew it wasn't coming from behind her. She strode forward, blinking against the setting sun, walking directly for whoever was watching her. If they had a weapon trained on her, her senses would tell her that, but they didn't. She held up a hand to block the glare, and tried to see past the rays so strong they were like a physical thing, but the feeling was already gone. No one was watching her anymore.

She strode to where she'd felt the gaze on her, past it, then turned around so she could see with the sun at her back.

Whoever had been watching her had been inside a large shed off to one side of the parking lot, a small window set in the middle of it.

Just an employee. She got in her car and left, headed toward downtown.

CHAPTER 17

Mac watched through binoculars as the robot, situated on a platform like painters used, lifted the bomb out of the hole they'd drilled in the concrete wall of the now-empty police station, right into the crawlspace above the duty room. The bomb looked small, barely big enough to do much damage, but what did he know? He wasn't a bomb expert.

The robot lowered the silver box onto the platform. Mac held his breath when it hit the wood, but nothing exploded. He hurried over to the robot handler and watched what the male saw through the camera, looking over the shoulders of the federal agents in front of him.

Two tense hours later, the thing was unarmed, lying in a messy pile on the platform.

Mac had a dozen questions about how it was placed, who would have done it, and how they found out it was there, but it wasn't his case, wasn't his department, and, unless someone assigned him something to do, it wasn't his business. There were sixteen ATF agents circled around the platform, all of them salivating at the thought of ordering around the Serenity PD for the next few weeks. Fuck that. He was out.

He found a distracted Wade in the crowd of blue talking to an ATF agent. When the agent jogged away, Mac got in Wade's line of sight. "Anything I should know, Chief?"

Wade sighed and pushed a hand through his graying head of hair. "Yeah. Rex Brenwyn did this."

"Shit."

"Yeah, shit. That lead in Machesney Park turn up anything?"

Mac looked around at the crowd, measuring who might overhear them, then stepped in close. "They say he's in Chicago, which we already knew, but they are also saying he suddenly has the ability to disappear into thin air." He snapped a finger. "Poof."

Wade considered, then shook his head. "I heard that, too."

"Right. You think it's possible? You think a *foxen* could have the ability to move in and out of the *Pravus* like Khain?"

Wade rubbed his eyes and looked over at the gaggle of ATF agents. "Might explain how a bomb got in our building." He looked back at Mac, a hard edge in his eyes. "It's not good news, if it's true."

Mac cocked his head to the side. "Gotta say what you mean, Chief. I told you that. If it's true, we're fucked."

"Yeah," Wade said, looking down at the ground. "We are."

Mac nodded, lifting his head, looking for Bruin, who had

disappeared when the fire truck had shown up. He spoke to Wade, eyes still searching the crowd for the big male. "So what now?"

"Normal operations, till I say otherwise."

Mac bobbed his head. "So the rut is on?"

Wade sighed. "Yeah, of course. Just keep your phone on you." He locked eyes with Mac one more time. "I'm surprised you're even going, after what you told me about your female. She's close. Your paths will cross soon... I didn't expect you to come home from Chicago once you called and said she'd been there."

Mac shrugged. With nothing to go on but a smell, he could wander around a city the size of Chicago for decades and still not find her. Coming home had felt... right, like fate was bringing them together, and if he didn't continue his normal routine, he would fuck that up.

Besides, he had his ace in the hole, didn't he? Bruin had said she would be at the rut. "If I weren't in charge, I wouldn't be going. I'll be around, make sure the males have what they need, but I won't be partaking." He wondered for a moment if he should share what Bruin had said about his mate being there, but decided against it. He didn't think Bruin wanted anyone to know about his... prophetic nature, something that normally only *citlali* would have. Besides, he had his plan all worked out. He'd segregate the males and the females at first, then as soon as he saw her, he'd be grabbing her by the elbow and getting her out of there. There was no way anyone was getting their hands on her. Bruin could take over. Everyone in the department had accepted Bruin like he was a *wolfen*, even Wade, so none of them would object to Bruin being in charge, especially once they knew another one true mate had been found.

Mac would leave to spend the night *getting to know* his female.

He spotted Bruin in the crowd and raised an arm to the guy. "Gotta go, Chief. Rut starts in an hour."

He didn't wait around for an answer.

***

Rogue drove past the Watson building, a former warehouse now turned events hall, eyeing the thick hedges that hid eight- foot-tall security fences with barbed wire on top. Everything was open, though, the gate at the front flung wide, the parking lot already filling with cars. There was an event there that evening. Perfect. The other cars and people in and out gave her cover.

She drove in the gate and around to the back. No cars back here. Her notes from Rex had said Smith drove a beat-to-shit dark-colored Camaro, and it wasn't around. She eyeballed the back of the building, counting six bays where trucks used to drive up to unload cargo. Now the doors themselves were all showing signs of misuse, rusting and collapsing, but she bet the retaining wall they'd built on the inside to cover the open doors looked great. Situated directly above three of the bays on the flat roof, like a square afterthought, was the caretaker's apartment, probably situated up there since much of his job was clearing snow off the roof in the winter. Rogue leaned forward in her seat, trying to figure out how to get into the apartment. She let the car drift forward twenty feet until she found what she was looking for. A stairwell, winding around the side of the building, straight to the apartment. Perfect. She'd take a look-see, maybe get inside and poke around. Maybe find what she was looking for that evening and be done with the whole mess, and just a little bit closer to that fabled retirement at 30.

She drove around the building again, eyes scanning the security for possible exits if she needed one. She never went in on any sort of a job, even a simple one like this, without multiple points of escape lined up. Which was one reason she'd never been caught yet.

A person-sized gate to the left of the building caught her attention. Good. She glanced up at the apartment on top of the warehouse. No, actually, it wouldn't do. There was a door out of the warehouse itself that led right to this gate, but nothing from above. She eyed the roofline. Unless she hung from that ledge, swung herself to that window, then dropped the twelve feet to the ground. Easy.

She drove out of the parking lot, eyeballed the building next to the one she would be going into, made her escape plan, then parked her car about a half mile down, hiding it in a restaurant parking lot, heading back on foot.

She felt eyes on her a few times, but nothing threatening. By the time she was back at the warehouse, she was ready for the night to be over. Ready to get to her cozy home and take some actual time off.

She headed past the warehouse, casting an interested eye at the people heading in the front door. Lots of women in skimpy outfits, some of them obvious working girls. Lots of burly men who moved and dressed like cops, but couldn't possibly be. Maybe it was a Chippendale's type of thing. A bachelorette party? She kept outside the farthest row of cars, her eyes down, until she heard a low growl. She picked her head up and stared as one of the men cut one of the women off from the pack she'd been traveling in. He lowered his head to her neck and pressed her into a nearby car with his body.

Her startled squeak and subsequent laughter turned into a sensual moan as he put his lips on her collarbone, his hips gyrating against her lower half.

Eyes wide, Rogue edged past the car they were writhing against. The man finally pulled away from the woman. "Inside," he ordered her, smacking her on the ass as she hurried to comply. Her skirt was short enough that Rogue could see her bare flesh jiggle. What in the hell was going on inside there? Curiosity ate at her, but she clamped down on it and hurried to the back of the warehouse. She was here for a job, and nothing more.

She rounded the building, stopping long enough to pop the lock on the gate that led into the next lot, no picks needed still, then started up the stairs, acting like she belonged there. At the top, she had a fantastic view of this portion of the city. She took just a moment to admire it, ignoring more female laughter that drifted up from the front parking lot, then hurried along the walkway to the apartment.

She knocked on the door. For a split second, she felt eyes on her, from inside the building, but it was so short, she almost felt like she must have imagined it. No answer, so she knocked again, peering in the window of the door, but she couldn't see as much as she would have liked because of the sun glaring behind her. It was almost down, but again the rays were foiling her vision. All she could see was that the inside was an alcove of sorts, leading to the main house, a mud room filled with shelves and tools and all manner of crap stacked everywhere, leaving only a bit of bare floor. No cameras in the high corners. No sounds or signs of life. Rogue slipped on her gloves and put her hand on the knob. It opened easily, and she stepped inside, took a few steps through the junk, then raised her hand to knock on the inner door.

Inside, on the floor of the kitchen area that she could see, was a body. Rogue knew at once it was a body because of the awkward way that it lay and the pool of congealing blood around its head.

Denton Smith? It could be. Of course it was. Great, a fucking set up. She didn't stop to figure out who was being set up, she was out of there and would figure it out later. She'd call for help anonymously once she was back at her car. She stepped away from the door, when a fiery smell hit her nose. One she recognized.

She whirled around, only a bit surprised to see Rex standing inside the tiny alcove, barring her exit to the door, his messy hair even messier, his blondish-grey beard and moustache sticking every which way. The door hadn't opened, and he had not been there a moment before. Fuck, that appearing-in-the-smell-of-smoke shit was creepy and she wanted no part of it. Did not want to add it to her list of items that made up her *werewolf problem*, although she probably should.

She shot him a dirty look. "You're still paying me, dickhead."

He threw back his head and laughed. "Such a feisty human. Don't worry. You won't need money where you're going."

Rogue kept her face a mask of hatred. Human? She shook her head. "Where is that? Jail? Did you really kill this poor guy just to send me to jail? What did I ever do to you?"

Rex shot a look over her shoulder, into the house. "Oh, but I didn't kill him..."

Rogue looked, too, she couldn't help it, seeing exactly where this was going all of a sudden. Sure enough, next to the man's head was a trophy with a wooden base and a boy throwing a pitch on top. A real screamer right to home plate.

The one she'd caught in Soren's office, putting her finger-prints on it.

"Why?" she spit at him. Bad guys liked to talk about how smart they were. Evil guys downright insisted on it. She pegged Rex as evil and knew he would spill something she could use against him. It wasn't the first time she'd had to beat a blackmailer at his own game, and the time before that she'd done it, she'd ended up better off than when she started. Life just worked out like that for her.

He shrugged, then eyed the nail beds on his right hand, telling her it was his choice to talk or not. But then he talk-ed. "My brother is taken with you. He won't do anything he thinks you wouldn't approve of. You either need to be out of the picture completely, or you need to be something I can bargain with, not something that's working against me."

Rogue let boredom play over her face. "Really? This is all a family squabble? You could have just asked me nicely to bow out."

Rex's eyes turned hard. "I'm not playing a fucking game here, missy, this shit is for keeps. My brother has made a lot of stupid decisions in his life, but he's about to make one of the stupidest, and something tells me you are part of the reason. You've made him soft."

Rogue didn't let her confusion show. Sure, Soren liked her, but he knew there would never be anything between them. But soft? Soren was the exact opposite. Maybe Rex was confusing soft with smart. Smarter than Rex, obvs. Ok, she'd given her last fuck to this asshole, and it was time to let him know he didn't have her like he thought he did.

She eyed the evil Jeff Bridges, as she was beginning to think of him, running through her options. He crossed his arms over his chest, smiling an- oh, what do you know? An *evil* smile at her, letting her think, putting on a show like this was all a game and he had it in the bag. Guaranteed Smith was dead, so there was no time element to worry about. If she removed the murder weapon, or at least wiped it off, that would take her away from the scene. Rex was a convicted criminal, she'd never been arrested. She could disappear from the area for a long time, which she'd known it would come to eventually. No one gets away with a life of crime forever.

But then a sound caught her attention.

Rex lifted his head and held a finger up. "Ah, you hear that? That's the sound of the batter rounding the bases, bringing in all the runs."

Rogue bit her lip from the inside without moving her face, so he couldn't see her dismay, because he was right. He had her.

The noise was police sirens.

CHAPTER 18

Mac counted heads one more time. Forty-two women. He'd smelled every one of them, made them all say something for him.

She wasn't here.

He ground his teeth together, as someone pounded on the door to the room he had them all sequestered in. Bruin had been wrong.

Or not. More women would show up. He would stand at the front door, examine them as they came in.

"Mac, what the fuck?" came the cry from outside. The males were getting restless, pissed off that the party hadn't started yet. A particularly heavy slam against the door and it let out a noise like the splintering of wood. Fuck, he wasn't going to get his deposit back on this place if they broke the damn door down.

"Hold your fucking horses," Mac snarled over his shoulder. "Break that door and I break your face!"

But the pounding kept coming. Mac nodded at the women. "You're done, you can go."

Some looked scared, nervous, the newbies who didn't know what to expect, but the ones who had been there before? They crowded around the door until someone was able to open it, their scents eager, their murmured words excited.

Lance, a patrol officer, was the first one at the door. "Ladies," he said, extending his hands like he was asking them to dance. Mac guessed he was. The females filtered out and Mac left, too, heading for the front door, not sparing the room a glance.

He didn't care what was going on. He only cared about his one true mate. When was she going to show up?

If Bruin had been wrong, Mac was gonna kick his ass up around his ears for him.

***

Rogue curled her hands into fists and bent her knees. She would take Rex on if she had to, but she didn't want to. Fighting a man was never a guaranteed win, no matter what she knew about joint-manipulation fighting styles and open-hand control tactics. Rex was big, with a bit of a belly starting to protrude from his middle, but the rest of him was all hard muscle.

She shook her head instead, stepping to her right, eying the window in the other direction, even considering going into the house to find a back escape route. "You think I'm caught, but there's one thing you don't know about me."

She pulled on a shelf full of power tools, finding its

tipping point, ready to put it between her and Rex, as soon as she decided on her exit point. "I've never been caught, and I never will be."

She was planning to go right through the door behind her, but only if that fucker popped open the way the other ones had. Her new secret weapon. She heaved on the bookshelf and tipped it toward the middle of the room, getting her weight behind it to send it on a caddy-wumpus fall onto Rex, when she caught sight of something behind it. Split second decision time. Continue on with the original plan? Or take this one. The waist high, two-feet by two-feet crawl space that probably led to the heating and cooling system for the warehouse would fit her easily. Rex, however? Not so much. His belly would make it a tight squeeze. It would mean she left the murder weapon with her prints on it behind. But it would give her a better chance of actually escaping.

Crawl space. Decision made. Time for a snappy one-liner. "Bases might be loaded," she said, heaving the shelf one last time. "But the catcher's got the ball." Fuck if it was stupid, it was still baseball.

As the heavy shelf fell onto Rex, tools spilling out and booming onto the floor, she didn't stop to see what he would do about it. She pried her fingers under the white grate that covered the crawl space and pulled it off, adding the noise of it clattering to the floor to the sudden cacophony in the small, closed area, then jumped into the crawl space, head first.

Faith. It was all she had at the moment. Faith, and fearlessness, and she worked them both to her advantage.

The metal tube she was in held her weight easily, the tunnel of sorts leading straight ahead for ten feet, then T-ing. It would have to go down at some point, and she hoped like hell the slope was gradual.

She scrambled on her hands and knees, glad the opening was big enough for that. When she reached the T, she looked back. Empty. She couldn't even hear the sounds of the sirens anymore.

Which way? The slope to the space on the right was less gradual, so she chose that one. No idea where this would lead, but ending up back on the roof wouldn't help her. She needed to get down in the warehouse. Hopefully somewhere quiet. A furnace room would be perfect. If she could find the exit that she'd seen earlier, the one that faced the gate she'd popped the lock on, she was golden. If she hurried.

Rogue continued to crawl through the space, heading down, down, down, relying on her marginal sense of direction to get her closer to the exit she was seeking, and not farther away.

When the crawl space ended and an air duct system opened up in front of her, she didn't even hesitate. She would have to get through it to get to the ground. Sounds of a party filtered up to her. The high trills of women laughing, accompanied by lower grunts of satisfaction from men. She almost stopped when she realized some of the noises almost sounded... sexual. But no, what she'd seen in the parking lot was messing with her head.

Inside the metal air duct, she had to low-crawl on her elbows, shimmying herself along like a snake. "Now I know what a TV dinner feels like," she said, quoting Bruce Willis, grinning that she had the chance to use the line once in her life. He was her all-time favorite action hero, because almost half the shit he did in the movies could actually happen. Crawling through a ventilation system? Totally.

She had a moment to worry that Rex would point out where she was to the cops when they arrived, but then she realized it didn't matter. He was probably long gone but the cops would figure it out themselves. All she had to do was get out before they had the presence of mind to lock the building down. So time was not on her side.

She crawled faster, glad for the thump of the music to cover the metallic sound of her moving through the shaft.

But then she reached a dead end.

She'd taken a wrong turn somewhere, and now the only options were back the way she had come, or pop out the grate below her and drop in to the party. *Drop in*, hardy har har. Total Bruce line if she ever heard one.

Grinning slightly, she stuck her eye to the slats. It looked like less than ten feet to the floor, and no one was directly below her. Good deal. The closeness of a wall suggested she was in a bit of a nook. Even better. She could hit the ground, orient herself, and push through the crowd before anyone knew what was happening. She put her ear to the grate, but couldn't hear much over the music. Certainly no sirens.

With the flat of her hand, she hit the grate a dozen times at the screw sites until it popped open, then she got moving.

***

Mac watched the shadows of the evening play over the cars in the parking lot, shifting from foot to foot, until he couldn't take it anymore. He turned to Bruin and popped the bear on the shoulder, harder than he'd meant, but his frustration was making him edgy. "Were you playing with me, Bruin? Cuz that shit ain't cool."

"What?"

"You said she was coming. So where in the fuck is she?"

Bruin frowned, his brown eyes losing their near-constant

good humor, as dismay filled them instead. He couldn't even look at Mac, his eyes rolling instead, looking at everything but. "Mac, I don't know. I don't—"

He cut off, staring at something only he could see through the glass in the door. "She's inside."

"Oh my fuck," Mac growled. "I am going to murder someone."

He yanked the door open, slamming it back against the wall, hurrying inside, looking at everything, but not really seeing anyone. He didn't care if the male had no way of knowing. He didn't care if things hadn't even gotten started yet. Anyone who had a finger on his mate was going to pay for it. He didn't know what his mate looked like, but he knew what she smelled like. Too bad he could smell nothing but sex and booze—

***

Rogue's first thought when she hit the ground was that she had stumbled onto the set of a porno. The room was large, big enough for a wedding reception, and placed in rows, like tables would have been, were couches. Couch after couch, each with at least one couple, some with more, with free love in full action, women and men alike, moving with the music, no shame or upset at the other bodies close to them, doing the exact same thing.

As someone who prided herself on her poker face, she knew when her mouth popped open, but the fact that she wasn't able to close it bothered her the most. That, and the fact that there were no cameras anywhere. Not a porno. So... what?

She thought no one had noticed her yet, but was proved

wrong when the man closest to her spoke to her, like he wasn't pile-driving the female in front of him at the same time. He was big and naked and broad through the chest. Pleasing. His dick looked monstrous, too, what she could see of it. She shot a look to the ceiling. Maybe the cameras were hidden?

"Quite an entrance," the man said, a mischievous look on his face. "Come on over here and I'll show you what I thought of it. Lose the coveralls."

Rogue realized her hat was gone, probably had been for a while. She edged past the man, trying to recover herself long enough to spot the exit door. She found the front doors to her left, and bingo, there was the exit straight ahead, exactly where it should be. Time to make like Houdini.

"You look a little busy," she told the man, "but, ah, thanks for the offer. Maybe some other time?"

He winked at her! Actually winked, and the hard planes of his face let him pull it off. She blinked and looked around. Was this candid camera? He spoke again. "We'll be back here next month. Night of the full moon. But I'm never too busy for someone as beautiful as you." His hips kept time with the music and the blonde beauty he was pleasuring made eye contact with Rogue, too. Something in her stare told her she was into Rogue being a third.

Rogue startled, then fought to get herself under her usual steely control, remembering something Boe had said.

"The wolves that live in Serenity, indeed, in the entire world, are not tied to the moon in the manner of story. They run by it, mate by it, but they do not worship it or change only when it is fat."

Mate by it? Fuck, this was all getting too weird. She had to get out of here. Over the music, she heard the sound of the police sirens swell, then wane. They were in the parking lot, driving to the rear of the building. That was her cue. She moved quickly, patting the man on his massive bare shoulder as she went. "You practice. Maybe I'll think about it."

She ignored his low chuckle and wound her way around couches, moving fast, keeping her eyes down, heading for the door with the single-mindedness she was known for. The room was so *wide*. She broke into a jog, ignoring anyone else who tried to speak to her.

She got within twenty feet, having to move quickly to pivot around a naked man in her path, almost there, when the front doors shot open and a pile of cops streamed inside.

Rogue almost wanted to stop, to see what was going to happen to the orgy so ungraciously interrupted but she knew she couldn't. Once they spotted her, the chase would be on. She should have shed the man's overalls... she wouldn't even stand out if she had. Too late, just get out while she still could-

Someone grabbed her elbow from behind, a grip she couldn't pull free of. A man's grip.

Fuck that.

No way she was getting caught here.

CHAPTER 19

*R*ogue took a step back, turned her body, stepping toward the guy who had her, grabbing his wrist with her other hand at the same time as she twisted her elbow hard, out of the slot that his closed fingers were trying to clamp down on. Her arm pulled free and she twisted around the man, coming up behind him, pulling his arm with her, tweaking it at both joints so he would be sure to feel the creak of his own tendons as she threatened to dislocate shoulder or elbow, whichever one she wanted. Maybe both if he was a shithead.

As she moved, her hands did their own work, knowing their moves exactly without any input from her brain. She had practiced this move hundreds of times, almost always on men bigger than her, so this was no problem for her. Except for the sudden feelings that were swimming through her. Contentment. Happiness. Motherfucking joy? What in the hell was going on? Rogue clamped down on the feelings, hard, reversing the momentary relaxation they'd spread through her muscles. Fuck them. She had shit to do. Buildings to escape from. Guys bigger than her to subdue.

With a practiced slide of her hand, she released one of her knives from its holster along the side of her forearm and pulled it out, holding it up to the man's throat, so everyone could see it. "I've got a knife at your throat," she hissed in the man's ear. "Cooperate and it will stay outside your body. Make one wrong move and you'll know what a loaf of bread feels like." As she spoke, she moved them both backwards, her eyes crawling over the cops in uniform, most of whom had noticed her, one who was already getting out his gun. Good thing the fucker who'd had the poor judgment to grab her was big. She was almost completely hidden behind him. Big. Broad. Just the way she liked them, when she wasn't about to be arrested.

Another cop saw her. Rogue couldn't hear what he said over the music, but it looked like an, "Oh, fuck," rolling off his tongue to her. A woman near him screamed and pulled away from the guy who was still trying to do her, seemingly uncaring about the cops in their midst.

Surreal, and the thumping beat of the bass made it more so. Someone should stop the music. Everyone should stop the fucking. Rogue tried to move another step backwards, towards the exit door, surprised the guy she had ahold of wasn't howling in pain as she cranked harder on his arm to get him to move. In fact, he was sagging against her, moving into her hold not away from it, his massive weight throwing off her balance. She checked his face as much as she could from behind him. His eyes were open, but they almost seemed to be rolled back in his head. Like he was enjoying himself.

What in the fuck kind of freak show had she *dropped in* on? "Hey, Sleeping Beauty, wake up, unless you want to be sliced and diced. Move with me here." She cranked on his arm again, expecting him to do anything to lessen the pain. A few more steps backward were what she needed.

He didn't, though. He didn't even acknowledge the pain. He seemed to wake up a bit at least, and took more of his weight back on his own two feet. She noticed he smelled amazing and she tried not to breathe, not to notice more. "Your name," he rasped out. "I have to know your name."

"Rapunzel," she said. "You're getting shanked by a fuck-ing Disney princess. Now *move*." She pulled him backwards, trying to decide how much injury she was willing to inflict on him. He could be a cop, but he could also be in the wrong place at the wrong time, playing the hero. Fuck, why did everyone have to do that shit? Even if he was a cop, she didn't want to hurt him if she didn't have to, but if it couldn't be avoided… she would do what she had to do. Teach him a little lesson about sticking his nose where it didn't belong. Nothing a doctor couldn't fix.

He was trying to turn around. She shook him by his trapped arm, pressing the knife farther into his neck. "Don't make me hurt you," she said.

"H-have to see you," he panted, still trying to turn, paying her almost no mind at all. Like she wasn't even there. Nothing pissed her off more than being ignored.

She pulled back, cranking on his arm and wrist at the same time, adding some finger action in there, fully expecting him to howl in pain, but he must have been on drugs or something. He kept trying to turn toward her, his single-minded obsession making her have to move with him, until they were moving farther away from the exit door instead of toward it.

Time to get serious. "Stop!" she hissed right in his ear again, then pressed her body into the back of him, standing on her tiptoes, prepared to twist out from under him and make a run for it if he thrust his weight backwards with the intention of throwing her off her feet.

She pushed the knife tip into his skin, deliberately slicing him. Pain would get his attention. "Fucking listen to me, asshole, or you're going to have a new hole in your neck. One you can't breathe out of." He stilled finally and she got him to move back a few steps, trying to ignore the bright red blood she saw dripping down his neck. She'd only had to use a knife one other time in her life, and she'd hated it then, too. They were more tools, or for show, or emergencies.

But still, he wasn't paying attention to her. He put his free arm up and shouted at the cops who were all coming toward them now, all of them with their guns out, pointed at them as they carefully wound their way through the couches and people on the floor. Absurdly, she noticed their trigger discipline, all of them with their index fingers outside the trigger guard.

Her guy shouted at them. "Put the fucking guns away!"

Rogue felt like looking around questioningly, like pinching herself to see if she was even there.

He shouted again. "I said, put them away, or I'll have all your fucking badges!" He tried to lunge forward but she kept him against her with another crank on his arm.

One of the uniforms spoke. "What should we do, Mac? Just let her stab you?"

"Yes, goddamit, any one of you so much as puts a scratch on her and I'll kill you!"

Rogue's hold loosened in shock. She almost let him go

completely, unable to believe it when all the officers returned their guns to their holsters, and a few of them even started to back away.

But then her ass end hit the door. She disappeared her knife and leaned into the metal behind her, bringing up her foot, planting it in the guy's ass, kicking off as hard as she could as she let go of his arm, then ducked out the door, ignoring the blaring alarm as it opened.

She was out.

Time to disappear.

***

Mac stumbled forward, falling over his own feet, catching himself on his good arm, rolling, ending up on his feet again, his left arm dangling loosely at his side.

"I never even saw her face!" he bellowed as he shot toward the door. "What did she look like?" He hit the door with the one arm that would listen to him, wondering for just a moment if his other one was dislocated. He'd known he was in pain, but in the ecstasy of his mate's touch, he barely felt it. Now his arm was like a lead weight attached to his body. It wouldn't obey a one of his commands.

Movement on his chest caught his eye and he looked down. He was bleeding. Lovely.

Bruin pushed past two patrol officers, and Mac could tell by the look on his face he'd held back out of respect for Mac, and hadn't seen much of what had happened. He didn't know what she looked like either.

"Was that... your mate?" one of the patrol officers asked haltingly.

"Yes," Mac grated. "What in the hell did she look like?"

A few of the officers exchanged glances. "She was hot," one of them said.

"Real fucking helpful," Mac growled. "Half of you out the front door and surround the building, the rest of you with me. Anyone finds her, you tell me. No one touches her. No one points a gun at her. I don't care what she's doing. No one touches her but me."

Mac grabbed a radio off a patrol officer's belt, threw Bruin a look that said follow-me, and headed out the door his mate had disappeared out of, still working one handed.

Shit was finally getting interesting.

CHAPTER 20

*M*ac rubbed his eyes, staring at the computer screen he, Blake, and Bruin were gathered around. They'd been out all night, but hadn't found a trace of his mate. He'd caught her deliciously tangy scent several times, but not one more glimpse of her. He hadn't even known where to look! They'd worked their way out from the warehouse in a circle, but hadn't found one trace of her. Not even when they searched through the large air vent she'd popped out of. No fingerprints. No stray hairs, nothing.

Blake yawned, collapsing into his chair. "My vision is blurry, Mac, we've already looked at over a thousand mug shots. He pointed to the clock on the wall. "We've been here for hours. I can't do this all day, I gotta work tonight."

"You're done when I say you're done," Mac growled. The dead body they'd found in the apartment upstairs with the fingerprints on the blunt and bloody trophy next to him that didn't match any they had in their system rankled him. Officers were already whispering that his mate was a murderer, but that shit didn't sit right with Mac. She'd been protecting herself, or she'd been set up, something. He'd gotten a sense of who she was when they'd touched, and she was hard, she was tough, but she wasn't a murderer.

He had to find her, before anyone else did.

Wade came in the duty room, and by the look on his face, Mac knew he'd been filled in on everything by someone.

Wade walked over. "Blake, you're dismissed. Mac, I want you to go home."

Blake disappeared quickly, avoiding Mac's glare as he ran for the exit. Mac stood and faced Wade. "Not yet. I want to listen to the 911 call again." He gestured to the computer. "Plus there's thousands of mug shots we haven't gone through yet. I need someone who saw her face—"

Wade cut him off. "They all left. They're all home sleeping. Go home. If I see you back here before five hours have elapsed, you're gonna regret it."

Mac looked to the side, not trusting himself to answer. Wade didn't have a whole lot to hold over his head, but Mac still needed Wade's protection and approval, especially if his mate was in some sort of trouble.

Wade looked him right in the eye. "I mean it. Home. You don't have anything to go on, so all you can do at this point is get some rest."

Mac swore but stepped off. Shit. More waiting, more sleeping. Without his mate. "Bruin, I'm gonna take the truck home. I'll see you tonight."

Bruin nodded, heaving himself out of his chair, his entire body drooping with tiredness. "Meet you here at sunset? I need at least six hours of shut-eye, or I'm a mess."

Mac stalked off, not looking at Wade, barely looking at Bruin. "I'll call you."

***

Rogue drove slowly, putting way too much of a gap between her and the guy she was following, but he was a cop, he had to be, and if she tailed too close, he would spot her for sure.

Luckily, he was in a huge black truck that was easy to see, even from blocks away. She frowned, wondering if it was the same one that had pulled up outside of the Englewood Post Office, just as she had been leaving, the wolf and angel pendants in her hands.

It would have been too much of a coincidence for her to even think about believing, except her life seemed to be nothing but a series of coincidences and craziness lately. Ever since her 25th birthday.

One of the police officers had called her guy 'Mac'. She frowned, trying to remember Mac's exact words to her and to the other cops. He'd wanted to see her face, wanted to know her name, then freaked right the fuck out when his brothers in blue had taken their guns out, even though she'd had a knife to his neck, maybe even had stabbed him a little bit.

She rubbed her temples, feeling bad about that. Had it been unavoidable? Even if it hadn't, was that really an acceptable excuse? She'd always prided herself on not hurting anyone, not stealing from anyone who didn't deserve it. Criminals stealing from criminals was her domain, and one she rarely strayed from, at least not since she'd been in charge of her own crimes.

The truck turned left, then right, heading out of town.

Rogue followed single-mindedly. She had to know who this guy was, and why he was so interested in her. The one thing she knew he couldn't be, was a werewolf. Right? There's no way a werewolf could be a cop. The rest of them would have figured out something was strange about him.

What if he was her cop? The one that she thought about so obsessively it made her stupid? She hadn't gotten a good look at him, but the guy who starred in her mind movies didn't usually have a face, anyway. He certainly was big enough, brash enough, badass enough. And the way he smelled... Ugh, Rogue had to stop her eyes from rolling back in her head. He smelled good enough to eat, literally. Like if he were ever on the menu, she wouldn't be able to stop herself from taking a long, leisurely trip through his pants.

Fuck. Just what she needed. A crush. Or worse, an obsession. What she really should be doing was getting the hell out of Dodge, but here she was, still in Serenity, hadn't even been home yet, following some cop just to see what his connection was to her. Not her smartest moment.

But she couldn't help herself.

After several more miles, he turned right down a farm road, pulling into one of the newer subdivisions that had been built around old farmhouses, then right again, disappearing from her sight. Rogue had put even more distance between the two of them, because traffic was light out here. For a brief moment, she wondered if he knew she was following him, and if he was doing a quick U-turn to get into position to turn the tables on her. The thought of him confronting her made her heart speed up, but, as she pulled level with the road he'd turned down, she saw his truck parked in front of an ordinary looking house, no one inside.

She cruised past, checking out houses on the next street

until she found an obviously empty home. Real estate sign out front. Grass a little too long. Lock box on the front door. No trash, no cars, no signs of life. Rogue parked her car a block down, grabbed a bag from the back, walked as quickly as she could to the house, straight up the front walk like she belonged there, put her hand on the door knob, and clunk, she was inside with a mental twist of the lock. She shook her head as she went in. If she wasn't meant to be a criminal, why did her biology make it so damn easy? Even if she had to get out her picks, she would have been inside in less than thirty seconds, but the ability to spring a lock with only a touch? It suited her.

She prowled through the empty house, straight to the back porch, which was off the kitchen on the second floor. Perfect.

She fished a pair of binoculars out of her bag and trained them on the house Mac's truck was parked in front of. It was one level, and all the windows she could see in showed nothing but empty rooms: part of a dining room, a sparse kitchen, and a bedroom.

Wait, there he was. He stalked into the bedroom, his face almost sad, his shoulders lowered like he was defeated. She frowned, wanting to know what made him feel that way, then frowned again because something about him was so familiar it almost hurt, like she just had to figure it out. He stopped in front of the bed and stared at it like he hated it, head drooping. She took the time to trace his face with minute movements of her head, the binoculars making it jump into stark focus. His jaw was chiseled, his eyes hard as diamonds, thick stubble giving him a harsh look. His almost-light hair was cut short, just the way she liked it, and his body, from what she could see of it, was broadly perfect. Thick arms, wide torso, slim hips, muscles filling out his shirt in a delectable way. She licked her lips, caught herself doing it, stopped, and trained the binocs on his neck, wanting to see how bad the slice was that she'd made.

There was only smooth, unbroken skin.

Rogue let the binocs fall for a second, perplexed, then picked them up again, focusing harder. Mac turned away from the bed and looked out the window, away from her, his expression still sorrowful, but contemplative. His shoulders twitched and he shook his head slightly, giving her the feeling he wasn't comfortable with the contemplation. He looked like more of a man of action.

She could see all of his neck now, and there was no injury. Impossible! She could see the blood on his shirt that had dripped down from a slice in his neck that was no longer there!

Rogue dropped the binoculars, her mind spinning furiously. No one healed that fast. No one. It had been... she counted back, not even ten hours since she'd cut him. He should have something there!

She wanted to go outside, scale the fence between the yards, then press her face up against his window, but she wouldn't. She wouldn't even go into his yard. She got the feeling he would... smell her or something.

Rogue's hands shook. She tightened her fingers on the binoculars, but they fell out of her hand anyway, the sound of their impact on the hardwood floor shocking in the empty house.

Get ahold of yourself. It doesn't mean anything. She tried to bend to grab the binoculars and ended up falling on her ass, instead. She'd seen Twilight, mostly to see what all the fuss was about. The werewolves in that movie had healed lightning fast.

Did her *werewolf obsession* really hold water? Was she not crazy? Not pushing through life because that was the only thing left to do? Because sitting at home doing nothing because you thought you were insane was so gauche as to be stupid?

Unable to gather her will, Rogue let the shaking go, let it move right through her until it dissipated, since she was unable to do anything else, then, when she was still again, she stood, certain Mac would no longer be visible in the window. Certain she had fucked up somehow.

But he was there, sitting on the bed, a pen in his hand, as he wrote furiously in a notebook on his lap.

She watched until he filled a page, then held the book to his chest like a life preserver as he laid on his back and stared at the ceiling. Only when his eyes slipped closed did she move from the room, leave the house, and head out into the real world, trying to figure out what she could possibly do now.

CHAPTER 21

*R*ogue drove home on high alert, her homecoming much different than it would have been if she had gone directly home the day before. Now she was suspicious, scared, nervous that she was going home at all. She had some decisions to make about the rest of her life. She'd always thought she would retire in Serenity, at least some of the time. Expand her house, get some horses, find someone to share her life with. Maybe by then she would have found her sister. They could have been a part of each other's lives.

Was that all ruined now? Maybe. She knew she hadn't killed that guy, but if she were ever caught, ever fingerprinted for any reason, she'd be the main suspect in the murder of that man.

She couldn't leave it like that. Even if she disappeared, she had to implicate Rex somehow.

That cop will help you. He would protect you with his life, even from the other cops.

Rogue frowned at the thought. Really? She didn't know him, had no idea who he was or why he'd acted so strangely. And there was no way she was going to him for help.

Her home come into view and suddenly exhaustion weighed on her. She could shake it off long enough to get into bed. She watched her country home as she drove up to it, still admiring it even through her tiredness. The trees in the yard were still bare, but buds protruded from each branch. Past them, the two-story limestone-exterior sat solidly in the middle of its plot of land, beckoning her.

Rogue pulled her car around the back of the house, walked once around the perimeter to ensure all the bug traps were in place, and that none of them were too full to work, then stepped up the back steps.

Once inside, the slight smell of peppermint greeted her. She smiled, knowing Boe had been following her instructions in her absence. That was one of the best things about having Boe around, he kept up her war on bugs while she wasn't around. No spider or fly would dare show its face in her house.

She found Boe in the library, of course, sitting in the window seat, a cup of tea beside him, a book in his hand, a look of quiet enjoyment on his face.

Oh, but he looked old! Like he'd aged another ten years in the few weeks she'd been gone. The lines on his forehead and around his mouth and eyes had turned into grooves, and even more of his hair had fallen out, leaving him only a horseshoe around his ears and the back of his head. He looked like a man on the tail end of his eighties. Which made no sense.

He noticed her and scrambled to his feet, still able to move around well. "Mistress!" he cried and hurried across the room to her. She bent and accepted the arms that went around her waist.

"Hi, Boe, good to see you."

"And you, Mistress. I had hoped to see you soon."

Something in his tone made her look closer at his face, and she wondered suddenly if he was dying. She pressed her lips together. "Oh? Do you need to tell me something?"

"No, no, it just gets lonely in this big house all alone. I missed you."

That was something she could understand, although she did not get lonely too often, and she did love her space.

He held her at arm's length. "You look tired."

She nodded. "I haven't slept all night."

"Oh! Will you be sleeping now?"

"Yeah."

She headed into the hallway, knowing he would follow her. It was his way. "Wake me up when it gets dark?" she asked. He nodded. "And tell me if anyone pulls into the drive-way or down the street, anyone at all, even…" She hesitated to say a word, but she had to. "Even the police."

His eyes got big, but he nodded and didn't ask any questions. "Your linens are clean. I turned them down last night, but made your bed this morning. Please, let me." He pushed past her to get into her room. When she got there, he had the blanket and sheet stripped to the foot of the bed, checking for spiders as he knew she always did, then he pulled them back and folded a corner over for her.

"Thank you, Boe."

"Of course, Mistress."

She changed her clothes, took care of her face and teeth

and hair, then crawled into bed, tired in her very bones. But it was a long time before she was able to fall asleep.

The faceless fearless cop was no longer faceless, and she couldn't stop thinking about him.

***

After Boe woke Rogue, she had quickly put away the dinner he'd made for her, calling it breakfast, then left the house, a nearby destination in mind.

She had some very serious thinking to do, and only one place seemed right to do it in.

The sun had set an hour before, and the night was chilly already, the stars high in the sky. She parked her car on the side of the road in front of Sinissipi Park and walked in, taking a well-maintained path through the ten acres of forest that bordered one side of it, breathing deeply through her nose to catch the forest scent. As she walked, her mind worried out one of the reasons she always returned to Serenity, and she tried to decide if she was there at that park to say goodbye. Was it time to give up? Leave and never come back, giving up her hopes of retirement there? Maybe, if her hopes were based on nothing more than the desire for something that might never happen. Seeing her sister again.

As she walked down the quiet path, hearing the whispers of small night animals over and under the leaves on the ground around her, she imagined the laughter of that day at this very park, the last time she'd seen her sister.

Amaranth Kendall, or Amara, as Rogue liked to call her, had been missing for twenty years now. Since the day after that lovely day on the playground that was burned into her memory. Her uncle, may-the-devil-spit-on-his-soul had done... something that five-year-old Rogue hadn't understood, and Rogue had never seen her sister again. As an adult, she realized he'd probably sold her, and Rogue prayed that it had been to a good family who wasn't able to have children of their own, someone who would have treated Amara right. Rogue knew the reality was probably the exact opposite, but that didn't stop her from hoping... from getting down on her knees and praying every night, even though she didn't quite believe in God, which she'd never admitted to anyone, especially Father Macleese. She still prayed because, well, what if she was wrong about the whole God thing?

Amara would be an adult now, no longer a child who could be kept in someone's home like an animal if they so chose, but still Rogue prayed. Prayed her sister was well and happy and that Rogue would meet her again someday. Prayed Amara would remember Serenity as well as Rogue did, and maybe someday return here, looking for her sister.

The path branched in front of her, and she took the right branch, recalling how her five-year-old feet had pounded in the opposite direction as she had run from her sister and the other girl they'd been playing hide and seek with. The afternoon had been warm, their aunt and uncle hadn't been fighting for once, and she'd been happy. If it was the last time she could remember being happy in her life, well, that was her business, wasn't it.

The next morning, when she'd woken up, her sister hadn't been there. Her uncle had ignored Rogue's frantic questions, and her aunt would only say, "She's on a vacation, having fun. You don't have to worry about her." Rogue barely knew what a vacation was, and since they didn't live in Serenity, were only there visiting some of her uncle's 'old war buddies', her aunt and uncle sleeping on a twin mattress in the corner of a filthy spare room in one of the buddy's houses, while Rogue and Amara slept on the floor, and then only Rogue slept on the floor, Rogue couldn't imagine how Amara had gone on vacation from there, but the more she insisted on going to find her sister, the more irritated her uncle and aunt had become. Her aunt mostly only hit with wooden spoons, her swats easily avoided, but her uncle, if he got ahold of you, he was more likely to shake you until you thought your brains were going to leak out your ears, or maybe your brain was going to bruise in your skull, swelling until you couldn't speak or see. Rogue always made it a point to disappear when he got angry.

That day, when they were supposed to head back to Chicago, and she planted her feet in the driveway and refused to get back in the car, when she'd seen the look on his face that said she would be sorry, she'd run. Ran right down the road, into a culvert, across a ditch that she and Amara had played in, following it until she was sure she had lost her uncle, thinking she would sleep in caves and eat crawdads if she had to, yelling for her sister because her sister was the only thing she had in the whole world. "Amara!" she'd called, thinking if maybe she yelled loud enough, Amara would be able to hear her, even if she was across town.

Rogue cut the memory off mercilessly. She hadn't found her sister that day and she never let herself think about what really had happened.

Rogue heard voices, young male voices, and she lifted her head. She'd reached the end of the path and was about to be spilled out into the moonlight flooding the open field, of which the large wooden playground sat right in the middle.

She let her eyes adjust as she watched the movement she could see at the top of the playground. Three boys, probably in their mid teens, bent over something at a turret at the very top. It took a few minutes before she realized one was spraying spray paint across the beams in wide, white strokes, while the other two were sawing the turret off at its support posts.

Shit. She should leave. Call it in anonymously. The cops could roust them. But if she did that, she might not have a chance to come back. Might not have a chance to say goodbye, if that's what she was doing. Fuck that.

She strode forward, waiting for them to notice her, walking right up to the base of the turret they were destroying. They didn't see her, not until she picked up a small rock and beaned one of them in the head, the biggest one. He was wearing a leather jacket and had his hair slightly long and curled around his head, getting in his eyes, but she could tell it was styled that way. In fact, all their hair was styled that way, and they had heavy eye makeup on. My Chemical Romance, juvenile edition.

"Hey!" he yelled, his voice whispered, but outraged.

She spoke at a normal volume, her voice hard and harsh, like her mood. "Get out of here, boys, and maybe I won't tell your mommas you're juvenile delinquents who need to go to military school."

"Fuck you," one of them whisper-yelled.

"Good one," she said, putting her hands on her hips. "Wholly original. You should write comebacks for TV."

The three boys looked at each other and she could almost see them sharing out their one brain cell. "We should kick her ass," leather jacket said to the one with a platinum blonde helmet of hair.

"Totally."

Not My Chemical Romance. Beavis and Butthead with a hanger-on. Fun. Not.

"That would be a very stupid move, boys."

But leather jacket cast one more look at her, one that said he might do more than just a little ass kicking if he thought he could get away with it, and then the three of them were beelining for the stairs. Leather jacket stopped on the shaky bridge and ordered one of them back the other way. "We can surround her."

Rogue shook her head and waited for them, knowing exactly how they would come at her. In fits and starts, none of them ever been in a fight before that didn't end up with him on the ground, trying not to cry.

And she was right. Once around her, the three of them circled her warily, especially once she put her hands up loosely, turning in a tight circle, waiting for them to make the first move.

"Better move fast, emo," she said, eyes on leather jacket. His expression was still hungry, but his was the only one. She jerked her thumb to his friends, both of whom looked like they were starting to seriously doubt the intelligence of their actions. "Your friends are about to bolt." She was dressed in dark, tight clothing, plus steel-toed boots, and knew she looked like every inch the experienced cat burglar she was, while they looked every inch the frightened little boys they were. She considered telling them she was wanted for murder, but decided against it. Not smart.

"Get her!" leather jacket screamed, and ran for her, telegraphing his attempted clothesline with his eyes and the way he lifted his arm at the shoulder. She ducked the arm and stepped into him with a good, old-fashioned jab to the button of his chin. He was on the ground, unconscious, before his friends even took a step forward.

"Shit," one of them said, staring at him laid out on the ground.

Rogue took a few steps back. "Don't bolt without him," she advised. "And don't come back, no matter how good of an idea it might seem when I'm not in front of you anymore. You'll regret it."

Leather jacket's friends grabbed him up under the arm-pits and, in just a few moments, she had the park to herself.

She climbed slowly up onto the playground, wanting to see what they had done. But more than that, she realized, she did need to say goodbye. Rex had spoiled Serenity for her, turned it from her haven to another place where she needed to constantly look over her shoulder, wonder if the cops were on her trail.

She didn't know where she would go. Or what would happen to her house. Or Boe. But none of that was more important than staying out of jail.

CHAPTER 22

*M*ac drove on autopilot, barely seeing the road in front of him. He had his window down, and was driving around the city in concentric, hopeless circles. He hadn't even talked to Bruin yet because he didn't want the male to see how despondent he was. His one true mate hadn't responded to him *at all*. To her, he'd been just anyone, a meat shield, a... *hostage* to use to get herself out of the building, and all the other cops thought she was a murderer.

He'd barely slept, eking out maybe three hours of fitful slumber, and he'd been in the truck driving around since before the sun went down, but he didn't know where to go from here. Fate had turned him over a barrel and fucked him hard, and if his mate really was a murderer, she was most likely gone already. He'd never see her again. Unless they caught her, and then she'd go to jail.

Fuck that. He shook his head. She wasn't. She just *wasn't*. When she'd touched him, he'd felt the steely strength of her, exactly how he'd known she'd be, but he also had gotten a soul-ful of her goodness. Maybe it was down-deep goodness, hidden under a few layers, but it was in there. She was not a murderer, cold-blooded, premeditated, or otherwise. Someone had set her up. He felt it in his bones, in his blood, in the deepest part of him that was more animal than human, more instinct than reason.

His phone rang and he ignored it. Bruin had tried to call a few times, but Mac had let it go to voicemail over and over again. That was the one thing he didn't know if he could handle, if he saw it in the bear's face that he thought Mac's female was a murderer. All the rest of them could go to hell. But Bruin? That would hurt.

So he drove. And ignored.

The wind hummed through the open windows of the truck, plucking at his short hair and his scruff he hadn't bothered shaving off, until he couldn't stand the lonely noise of it anymore.

But he couldn't close the windows.

He snapped on the police radio just to break the constant pull of that hum. Gentle chatter greeted him. Lots going on, but most of it attended to. No one yelling, no one even excited. Good, quiet nights were always best. Unless they meant you were driving around in a fucking shambles, with nowhere to go and nothing to do.

"Argh!" Mac voiced a guttural yell to the sky as he dropped his head back for just a moment and tightened his hands on the steering wheel until he felt it bend under the strain. He eased up.

A dispatcher's voice came over the radio. "Central to 634, report of vandalism and graffiti at Sinissipi Park."

No one answered. Of course no one did. 634 was a ghost unit. The unit they called when everyone was busy, but they wanted to make it seem like someone was heading to a simple call like vandalism of a public place. Unlikely anyone would get hurt, more likely that the perpetrators would get scared away, if they had a scanner on them.

Mac ignored the call, the tires of the truck eating up the miles underneath him, until he realized he was in front of Sinissipi Park. He glanced over, unable to see much of the park from the road. It covered almost forty acres, much of that bike and exercise paths, part of it a large, sprawling playground, one of the best in the city. He knew the park intimately, because it divided two forests; one they'd trained in when he was a teen in the war camps, and the other had been the home of the volleyball camp his first teenage crush had attended. He'd snuck out repeatedly, just for a glimpse of her, most of the time taking the underground tunnel—

Mac's thoughts ground to a gravelly halt as one word stood out in his mind like a neon sign. *Graffiti.* He remembered the wolf in that room under the post office in Chicago, the one with all the curlicues, and the words scrawled beneath it. *Graffiti.* He remembered the wolf drawn on the art in the park near Mik Maks. Images of pictures of more wolves drawn at various places around the city, almost always with a cryptic message painted nearby flashed into his consciousness, along with the one true mate prophesy. He didn't have it memorized, or he didn't think he did, but the first part of it played through his mind as easily as if he'd written it himself.

In twenty-five years, half-angel, half-human mates will be discovered living among you.

This is how you will rebuild.

Warriors, all, with names like flora.

Save them from themselves, for they will not know their foreordination.

They will not be bound by shiften law, but their destinies entwine so strongly with their fated mates, that any not mated by their 30th year will be moonstruck. Those who are lost may be dangerous.

A pledged female will have free will that shiften know not. Never forget this or it will cause grave trouble.

Mac stopped the truck dead in the middle of the quiet road, his mind racing over a few of the lines again and again.

Save them from themselves. Not bound by shiften law. Destinies entwined with their fated mates. Moonstruck. Dangerous. Free will.

Motherfuck. His mate didn't know who or what she was, didn't have any reason to trust Mac, even if she had felt the same things he had. It wasn't her fault, none of it. And it *wasn't* a rejection of him.

A weight rolled off of him and he pulled the truck to the side of the road so fast his tires squealed.

He picked up the mic. "Central, this is SRT-436. I'm heading into Sinissipi Park, will make checks."

"Roger."

"No backup needed."

"10-4."

Mac practically jumped out of the truck, his heart light, his steps fast. She was here. He knew it. He could sense it, as surely as if she were a magnet and he a big piece of metal. And he knew why she was there. She was crazy. But that was cool. As soon as they got together, it would stop. She would have him. He would ground her, level her, plug that hole in her being that she didn't know was there.

Mac grinned. His night was about to turn on a dime.

He stuck his nose in the air, not scenting her yet, but he would.

He would use every bit of charm he had to convince her that he was the one for her. Only after she came to him smiling, arms open, would he spill all the rest of that crap.

He wanted to give them both the chance to choose each other because they were right for each other, before she ever knew anything about who they were to each other.

Free will, and all that.

***

Rogue examined the damage the boys had done with a sour bitterness in her heart. The circular turret that covered one of the main parts of the playground was cut almost all the way through at two support beams. This park would have to be shut down until someone could fix it. She knew Serenity didn't have unlimited funds for that kind of thing. Shit. Maybe the community could get together and do the work, pitch in the money to fix the playground.

She couldn't stand the thought of the playground being closed for any length of time. She knew all too well how, in some children's life, places like this were the only opportunities for joy they had. Sometimes home was too... loud, too violent—

Rogue crouched in the dark and quiet as a knowing grabbed her by the back of the neck and forced her down. Someone was... what? Not watching her. There were no eyes on her. But someone was in the park... looking for her specifically.

Squatting, she felt outwards, and found the someone, coming in from the main street, walking quickly. She was dressed all in dark clothing, and would be hard to see, but her face and her hands were visible and would give her away. She had only a moment to get down off the playground and melt into the forest.

She didn't take it. Something held her right where she was, until the minute had passed, and the someone came into view.

A man. Her hostage. Why was she not surprised to see him out here? He looked good enough to eat, wearing work khakis, heavy work boots, a dark long-sleeved shirt that covered him like a second skin, showing the muscles of his abs and torso as he moved. His big arms swung as he walked. He hadn't shaved, and that scruff on his cheeks and chin made him look like a Greek god come to life. Pure attraction to him licked through her insides, heating her from the inside out, making her think of both the faceless cop that played in her mind movies, and the one from Yosemite four years ago.

Her eyes narrowed as she wondered if all three were the same man. Could such a thing even be possible? And what would it say about him if it were? A single word pounded through her brain, making her frown in the darkness. *Destiny.*

Fuck that. She had a life. She had a plan. Destiny didn't exist.

She wasn't losing herself, though, that was good, even though she was thinking about cops. Should she test it and think about wolves, too? No, she couldn't afford to pass out here, or whatever she did when she lost it.

But before she was even done making that decision, he stopped on the path, his hands curling into fists, and raised his head to the sky. The moon wasn't completely overhead yet, but a soft yellow light above the path illuminated his face just enough that she could see his nostrils flaring. He was smelling the air. He moved forward a few steps, out of the circle of light, then stopped again.

His eyes glowed a freakish yellow that both soothed her and scared her and she pushed herself backwards, until her ass hit the wooden posts behind her. *Wolf!* her mind screamed. The yellow faded, and his face turned toward her, and she instantly wondered if she'd imagined it.

There were no lights over her. He shouldn't be able to see her.

"I know you're here," he said, his voice a low, sexy rumble that made Rogue weak and pissed at the same time. She hated how insanely attracted to him she was.

She didn't say a word, just in case he was bluffing.

He stood still on the path, but his eyes slid off of the place where she was hiding, to the forest beyond the playground. Ah, he might know she was there but he couldn't see her, mostly hidden behind the posts, in the dark. Either that, or he was playing with her. The thought that he might be playing with her sent new thrills of emotion through her body, and her very core swelled with wanting. Fuck. That. This guy was dangerous, and not cuz he was a cop, or bigger than her, but because she wanted him, plain and simple. She had to get out of there.

And still, she stayed put.

Then he said something that changed everything.

"I know you didn't do it. I won't let anyone arrest you."

Holy shit. His actions in that crazy orgy came back to her with stunning clarity. *Put the guns away, or I'll have all your fucking badges!*

Rogue always thought her attraction to cops had been a bit of a taboo thing, her being a criminal practically since she was old enough to walk, her uncle filling her head with propaganda about how cops were all lying, corrupt assholes who stole and lied just as much as anyone else. But now that she was an adult, she'd realized that could apply to some cops, but certainly not all of them, not even most of them. But shit, the way he looked? All muscles and clothes that said he was here to kick ass and take names but he didn't give a fuck what your name was. And the overt authority he exuded. He made naughty images play through her mind of him giving orders, sensual orders, and her scrambling to obey them. She'd never had such a thought in her life! And the way she just knew he wouldn't be scared of her, even a little bit. She scared men, she knew she did, with her height and her muscles and her own attitude, and she didn't mind doing it, but she would never, ever do a man she scared.

Rogue stayed quiet, conflict raging inside her.

He spoke again, his voice softer. "I want to help you."

Rogue stood up. His eyes went to her almost lazily. He had known where she was. Eye contact with him made her brain scorch. "Why?"

He smiled and Rogue wanted to fall to her knees at the simple masculine beauty of him.

"Hi," he said on an outbreath, almost a whisper that barely carried through the chilly, moonlit air.

Rogue ignored her feelings, her desires, every single thing her body was telling her. She crossed her arms over her chest and cocked out a hip. "Why do you want to help me?"

"You're just as beautiful as I knew you would be." His voice was firmer now, but still airy, like he wasn't even talking to her.

She scowled at him. "So that's what this is about? Sex? You help criminals stay out of jail so they'll fuck you?" The words stirred something primal in her and suddenly that was all she could think about. Getting fucked by this man. Him bending her over every piece of furniture in her home, in his home, maybe the desks at the police station, shit, right here on this very playground, with the moonlight in her eyes.

No! He was playing her, and she would not let her body invite him to do it. She wanted to know what his game was.

He frowned, genuinely perplexed by her words, but then he recovered himself, and his face became all smooth charm, as if he knew exactly how he looked to her and was willing to use it to his advantage. "Not at all. I want to help you because I know you didn't take out that guy, and because I know you are... special. But it's not about sex." He began walking toward her, his body moving like something big and deadly would move over its home trail in the forest, knowing it owned everything it saw. His voice dropped an octave as he came closer, intimacy dripping from it. "Unless you want it to be about sex. I'm down with anything you want from me."

Rogue tried to concentrate on his earlier words. Special? What? But her mind kept playing over what he'd just said. *Unless you want it to be about sex. Anything you want from me.* Fuck, she couldn't even keep a thought in her head! And he was closer. Coming up to the stairs on the wooden structure that would lead him to her.

"Stop," she cried out, grabbing the railing behind her to keep from spinning off into space. He didn't stop. He kept walking. She could feel the vibrations his body made in the structure as he placed each heavy foot on the steps.

"I'm not going to hurt you," he practically purred. "I'm Mac, by the way. I never did get your name."

Rogue gripped the railing behind her tighter. "That's because I didn't tell you what it was."

"You should."

I shouldn't! Oh man, but she wanted to. She wanted to spill her full name, hear how it sounded coming from his lips. Her thighs quivered as he came closer and closer and she thought about his mouth... on her. She looked to her left. He was big, but she was fast. She could outrun him.

But she didn't. She believed him when he said he wouldn't let anyone arrest her, and she had to think that meant him, too. She wanted to see what he would do when he reached her, God help her, she did.

He crossed the wooden bridge, his eyes locked on hers. And then he was there. One more step and he was in her space. She stared up at him, putting him at six foot three inches, easy, maybe six foot four. At six foot even, there weren't many men she could look up to, and she relished doing so. He leaned forward, placing his hands on the railing outside hers, locking her in the cage of his arms.

"Hi," he said again, his lips curling up slightly, his body so close she could smell him. Denim, attitude, a whole lot of clean man. She wanted her lips on him. Wanted his lips on her. Heat poured off of him, driving away the chill in the air. She couldn't form a thought in her head that didn't have to do with this man taking her in his arms, doing things to her that would relieve the sudden throbbing in her core.

And she fucking hated it. Hated him for making her feel this way, for being so perfectly the kind of man she'd always wanted but never had. Hated that she found him completely and totally irresistible.

Fuck. That.

CHAPTER 23

This was more like it. Mac leaned in close, as his mate's scent flared in the open air, that tang turning sweet as Minneola tangerines, picked fresh from the tree. His mouth watered and he leaned in. She wasn't running, wasn't fighting, she wanted him as much as he wanted her, it was in the lines of her body, the way she trembled as he got closer. He'd seen her glance to her left, known she'd thought about bailing, but she'd decided against it. Decided to stay with him.

She was beautiful, more beautiful than he'd ever dared hope, her eyes a warm hazel, her cheekbones high and her skin smooth, her hair so soft even the slightest breeze could pick it up and blow it against his face.

Her scent flickered suddenly, going harsh, then smoothing out. "You're him," she said flatly, her voice changed somehow.

"I'm anyone you want me to be, baby," he said, leaning in to her neck, about to graze her flesh with his lips.

A sharp point at his abs stopped him. What the fuck? He looked down, and, sure enough, she had a knife teasing his gut, not bearing down enough to cut through cloth or skin, but the threat was obvious. "Seriously?" he growled. "We doing this again? You didn't slice me up enough yesterday?"

Her eyes found his neck and he knew she was seeing unbroken skin there. Oops. *First sign you are dealing with something you don't quite understand, sweetheart?*

"Don't call me baby," she growled right back at him.

"Got it. No baby. Now put the knife away."

"Not if you paid me," she spit out.

Mac raised his eyebrows, but didn't respond. Instead, he leaned into her knife, just enough that he felt his skin pucker, then pop, then warmth spread as a bit of his blood flowed where it shouldn't be. He caught her eyes and held them, but she was good. She didn't let any emotion out of her cold stare.

Neither of them spoke, until he couldn't stand it anymore. "I could take that knife from you in a half a second."

She almost smiled. "I know you think you could, but you're wrong."

Something in her stare, her posture, and the way her eyes didn't quite look at him, but instead stayed loose, taking in his body even as they maintained eye contact, told him she might be good enough to counter any move he could throw at her. He licked his lips, and, Rhen help him, he popped a motherfucking boner at the thought. He would almost be willing to let her slice him up a little bit to see what she could do.

He smiled in gracious defeat and took a step back, but when she felt him going, she sliced out wide with her wrist, but just barely forward, just enough that his shirt split open in a gaping mouth. His skin didn't even well any blood, except in the spot where he'd pressed up against her blade. The slice had been nothing more than a warning that she really was that good.

She kept eye contact with him, cleaned her knife on her black pants, then tucked it back inside her left sleeve. He watched her do it, then checked her other sleeve. Yep, she had one there, too.

"You don't tell me your name, and I'ma have to call you something. Blade, maybe." He cocked his head questioningly but she didn't respond. "No, ok, how about Hard-ass?" She still just stared at him. "Not Hard-ass." He put a hand on his chin. "Ok, ok," he grinned, knowing she would hate it. "No Blade, no Baby, no Hard-ass. I know, I'm gonna call you pumpkin."

Her eyes narrowed and he almost laughed. He had her fucking number and he loved that she hated it. Loved that she looked like she wanted to murder him. Fuck, what she must be like in bed! A wildcat. A feminine version of him. A full lifetime of scorching hot sex stretched out before him like a promise and he was ready for it. They could start tonight.

He caged her again with his arms, leaning in close, taking deep breaths through his nose. His lips touched her neck and he couldn't resist nipping her with his teeth. She shuddered and he smiled against her flesh. Oh yeah, this was going exactly where he wanted it to. She raised her arms and put them on his shoulders, holding him in place so she could whisper in his ear.

Her voice was soft, her breath hot against the shell of his ear. "You can call me pumpkin, but every time you do, I'm going to call you princess."

He captured one of her hands from his shoulders and

pulled it down the front of him, placing it on his cock, which strained at his pants. Not his classiest move, but she'd started it. "Let me show you my crown," he murmured to her, then groaned as her fingers curled around him, moving from base to tip through the fabric, like she was testing his size. She melted against him for just a moment and he celebrated, curling one hand against the nape of her neck to hold her closer to him, to maneuver her head in for their first kiss—

She was gone. A twist in his arms and she'd ducked under. He blinked, then turned to find her standing behind him.

Ah shit, he hoped he didn't make too much of a fool of himself, chasing her like some love-sick puppy. He'd try to keep his shit tight, but he wanted her so bad he could taste it.

He advanced on her.

***

Rogue held up a hand, glad to see him stop dead in his tracks, like he still had some control over himself. She barely had any left herself, but if this... thing between them went any farther she was going to let him do all kinds of dirty, delectable shit to her, right out here in the open, cop or not, criminal or not, all-sorts-of-weird-shit-between-them or not.

She did the only thing she could think of to throw water on the situation. "You fuck me once and disappear and you really think I'm going to let you do it again?"

That did it. He blinked and stammered and lost every ounce of cool he'd had, and he'd had way too much of it to be good for her, if she wanted to keep her pants on.

Finally, his mouth managed to work. "Fucked you... once?" His face went hard. "Don't tell me you have me confused with someone else."

She rolled her eyes. "You don't even remember me. Great, even better. Just what a girl wants to hear. Is four years so far out of your man-whore cycle that you can't remember anyone from that long ago?"

His eyes narrowed, then widened and she could see very well the moment when the knowledge of who she was slammed into him. He half pointed at her, then wiped his mouth, then pointed at her again. "You're her. From Yosemite." His voice was barely a whisper.

She nodded briskly. "Nice job, cop. I mean princess. Great memory you got there. You'll excuse me if I don't want a repeat."

She turned and headed away from him, across the walk-way of the playground, catching the steps lightly, reaching the ground, a fierce kind of satisfaction filling her that she'd thrown him such a mean right hook, even as her body screamed at her that she did want a repeat, that he'd been the only satisfying sex she'd ever had, that she should let him back her up against a tree the way he'd backed her against that rock. She could use another orgasm that made her think she was going to die. Since that one time, she'd almost decided that was the only kind of orgasm worth having.

Behind her, he must have finally came to his senses, because his heavy footfalls sounded, crossing the walkway, then down the steps, she turned around, walking backwards, and held up her hand again, the cool air whistling past her ears as she went. "Seriously. I'm done here. You really want to help me, just let me go."

He shook his head, looking all deadly again as he followed. "I can't do that."

"You said you weren't going to let anyone arrest me."

"I'm not."

"Not even you?"

"Not even me." But he didn't stop coming.

Rogue pressed her lips together and looked around. She couldn't outrun him fast enough to get into her car and start it, but there was no way she was sticking around. He was too dangerous for her.

... Unless she went home with him. Just one night. Fucked him into a stupor, then slipped out while he slept. She already knew it would be the best sex of her life.

Crap. But it would also be dangerous as shit. A guy like that, you let him into your life just a little bit, then all of a sudden you feel like you can't live without him. You do stupid shit. You never leave. Become his girlfriend. Give up all your dreams and desires and your own self for whatever the two of you make together. Then he asks you to marry him and you say yes because it's a promise of him loving you for the rest of your life, feeding you orgasms like candy every single night until you don't care about anything but getting home to him, making sure he still loves you as much as he used to, as much as he promised he always would.

Still walking backwards, still being stalked by Cop Danger, Rogue barely restrained herself from pulling at her own hair in frustration. She didn't want him to know how conflicted she was, didn't want him to see anything but belligerence in her stare. If he knew how much she wanted him back, he would never give up until he was balls-deep inside her. Then he probably could take her or leave her.

True, after their tryst in Yosemite, he'd wanted her name, wanted her number, but she hadn't given it to him, so she'd never known if he would have called her or not. Never known if they could have had something then. But she sure as shit knew they didn't have anything now.

She had to get out of there.

***

Mac followed where she led, his brain scrambled. He'd known her before! He'd had sex with her! He'd been 31, and she must have been 21. She believed he'd forgotten her because she hadn't meant anything to him, but, truth be told, he'd been fascinated with her from the moment he saw her clinging to that rock alone. Fascinated because she was hot, with a tall, athletic body that was exactly his favorite kind, fascinated because she was alone, fascinated because she was fearless, but there had been no glimmer of her being his mate then. She'd even smelled different to him. He'd liked her, sure, but had never realized, never even dreamed…

He raised his eyes to meet hers, trying to collect his thoughts. "I wanted your name, I wanted your number, you were the one who said it would be a better fantasy if we never knew each other's names."

She shrugged. "I guess it didn't mean that much to me either. You *were* kind of forgettable."

Mac's heart stung in his chest and his steps faltered. But, no, he remembered her breathy gasps in his ear, the way her nails had dug into his skin as she came, the way she'd screamed, then blushed when her orgasm was over, looking around to see if anyone had heard them. He remembered her hot pussy clenching at his cock as she drenched him. She was lying now, but her body had told the truth then.

He pressed forward, matching her step for step. She threw a glance over her shoulder to keep herself on the path, then glared hotly at him.

He glared back. "You came so hard you forgot your own

name, *pumpkin*. I'm not sure why you're lying to me now, but you can take this to the bank. I *know* you're lying. I know I rocked your world."

Her lips curled and he thought she would slow down. But no. "Arrogant, much?" she told him, then turned on a dime and sprinted away from him.

"Fuck," he growled, breaking into a run. She really was going to make him work for it.

The moon shone down on them as if to say it was a good night for a chase.

He agreed.

CHAPTER 24

*R*ogue laughed as she ran, stepping off the path, racing not the man behind her, but the moonlight as it dipped and spattered between the trees. She knew she couldn't outrun him forever, but she could wear him the fuck out, until she decided what to do next.

One night of pure, animal sex was looking better every moment, if only it wasn't laden with everything that would come after. No, it was better this way. Something would happen that would give her a chance to slip away. The second she did, she would go straight home, pack what little she wanted to take with her, and get the hell out of Serenity. Chicago, too. She'd head out there, grab the pendants, split the state, maybe the country, and decide what to do about her house and Boe and her sister later.

But, for now, she ran, the simple childhood joy of moving

warring with the hot anticipation of being caught. If he caught her, would she let him kiss her? Maybe. Maybe she would jam his thick hand between her legs and rock on him until she came, stealing enough satiating pleasure to let her think clearly, get over this obsession with him.

Werewolf, man, it didn't matter what he was. She would regret leaving him, but she would regret staying with him more.

She zigged and zagged between evergreen trees, her hair streaming out behind her like a flag, her boots landing evenly on the ground. She could sense him behind her, keeping the same distance between them, just keeping pace with her so he didn't lose her, looking for his opportunity to turn on the speed and catch her around the waist, throw her to the ground and fall on her. Take her, fuck her. She groaned as she ran, wanting it badly, trying to tear her imagination away from the images. How fucking hot would it be?

Her lungs burned in her chest and she pulled ahead a little, then stopped dead and held out her hand, turning to face him. "Stop!" she cried. "Let's make this interesting."

He skidded to a stop and looked at her, hands on hips, and she was dismayed to see that she might be just a bit more out of breath than he was. Fucker was in phenomenal shape. Which only made her want him more. Oh, and what do you know, his dick was still hard.

"I'm listening," he said.

"I tell you what. If you can catch me, I'll give you what you want. If I can elude you for ten more minutes, you let me go."

He shook his head and said it again. "I can't do that."

She frowned. "Can't do what? Let me go?"

He nodded, panting only a little, his shirt flapping where

she'd cut it, revealing his hard abs. "Can't let you go. Can't ever let you go."

She turned in a little circle, breathing heavily, encouraging the anger that flared up at that statement. She would need it. "You aren't going to arrest me, you already said that. So I don't get what you fucking mean, you can't let me go. What are you planning on doing, kidnapping me? Holding me hostage somewhere?"

He shook his head. "No. But you and me, we're together now. You just got to… understand." He held his hands out, his words still coming in huffs. "Look, I can see how this is confusing for you, but believe me, you are going to want to stick with me. We've got some shit to talk about."

Rogue's heart pounded, and she knew suddenly that the answer to her *werewolf problem* was hers for the taking. All she had to do was talk to Mac.

But she didn't want to know. Didn't want her life as she knew it destroyed with a few words. Didn't want to be put in this fucking situation!

Anger spilled through her and she whirled, using it to her advantage, taking off at a dead run, sensing she'd gained a few precious seconds on him.

She *would* get away from him.

***

Mac cursed in the moonlight as his mate pulled away from him, widening the distance between them. He put on a burst of speed, half-tempted to shift and corner her, but that would scare the shit out of her, so he wouldn't do it, not unless he absolutely had to, but there was no way he was letting her out of his sight. Like the knowledge had been dropped on him from above, he finally understood Trevor, Crew, Graeme, and Beckett all choosing to live on the same plot of land. There was safety in numbers, and when you managed to mate a female this… phenomenal, one that a demon would give his left nut to get ahold of, you didn't leave anything to chance. You didn't let her out of your sight for a second. Even if she was strong, and sharp, and deadly, like his mate obviously was.

Now if only she would stop running and realize that she belonged with him.

His need for air drove all conscious thought from his brain as he tracked her movements and tried to avoid tripping over anything. She never once looked back over her shoulder to see if he was gaining on her, or even still chasing her. She turned suddenly, left past a tree, and he skidded right past where she'd disappeared, widening her lead on him. If he only knew her name he would yell it out, scream it, but he didn't know it, and he needed his breath, anyway.

A thud and then a curse told him she'd hit the ground. He put on a burst of speed, saw her up and trying to run, but not quite standing, and he caught her, throwing one arm around her waist, twisting his body so he came down on the ground hard on his back, with her on top of him.

She didn't struggle, just let him pull her until their bodies were snuggled in next to each other. He loosened his hold on her, just a bit, enough that she could push herself up, her legs on either side of his torso, her ass dangerously close to his erection.

"I caught you," he told her, panting, and trying not to show it.

"Only because I fell." Her voice was tight like she was pissed. At him? Or herself?

"Still counts."

She didn't say anything for a few moments as she caught her own breath, but her fingers on his stomach were coming dangerously close to caressing his skin through the hole in his shirt. He held her tight around her hips, so she wouldn't think of running again. He stared at her, soaking in the feeling of her on top of him.

"Ok," she bit out. "You caught me. So what do you want?"

Mac could see in her face what she expected him to say. But he wasn't going there. When he kissed her, when he took her, she wouldn't be doing it grudgingly. She would be completely there with him, wanting it as much as he did.

"I want to know your name."

She licked her lips, then wiped sweat off her forehead. Her hair fell down around her face, and her small breasts bobbed with the great rolling breaths she pulled in. His hands itched to touch her there, so he clamped down harder on her hips.

She bit her bottom lip as if she was deciding what to tell him and he braced himself for a lie. It wouldn't mean anything, if she lied to him, just that she had her own stuff going on. He could understand that. She didn't know him, had no reason to trust him.

Her fingers spread, moving over his stomach and he bit back a groan. Her touch burned him, spread lust over his skin, made his cock jump in his pants. *Fuck.*

She wiggled backwards a bit, until her ass came in contact with his erection, then she gave him a sly smile. "You sure you don't want something else? A kiss maybe? Or…?"

He smiled back. "I'm sure."

Her smile disappeared. She appraised him with sharp eyes, then lifted her hips and moved towards his feet, then settled back down on him, the hottest part of her now in direct contact with his dick. Fuck him, he didn't know if he could take it. The desire to get her under him, to get inside her was killing him.

His eyes drifted closed and his hips punched upward, lifting her, pressing their bodies together where they were joined. He groaned at the friction they were creating, groaned at the tightness in his balls, the pure need that had ahold of him.

When he opened his eyes, the sly look on her face told him she knew exactly what she was doing to him. Ah shit, he could give as good as he got, and he wanted to see her as desperate as he was.

In one move, he rolled her over onto the forest floor, the scent of dirt and leaves hovering for just a moment, then replaced by her clean, sweet tang. He parted her thighs with his knees and got all up in there, then pressed himself against her, watching her face so he knew when he hit the right spot. She didn't give up much, but she pressed back against him, her breath tearing in and out of her mouth with a new rhythm, one that told him she wanted him, that she would happily exchange sex instead of giving up her name.

He gritted his teeth, then stopped himself. "Your name," he growled. "I want it."

She arched under him, pressing against him, opening her legs for him. "That's not all you want."

He ground against her again, running a hand up her arm and shoulder, fisting his fingers in her hair and pulling lightly. "It's not, but if I can only have one, I choose your name."

Her eyes closed and her head went back with his hand, a small whimper escaping her throat. Her smooth, creamy neck called to him, and he bent, pressing his lips to her throat.

"Fucking first," she whispered, as her hands found his head and pulled him harder against her. "Name after."

Fuuuuuuuck. She did not just say that. She was going to kill him. He hardened his resolve, realizing with a blinding force that threatened to knock him on his ass that she had no intention of giving him her name. She was willing to give him her body, but not her name. If only he could make her...

He moved deliberately to the side, pulling away from her, then pressing his hands into the sweet juncture of her thighs where it was hot enough to burn him. "Name first," he growled into her ear. "Then kissing, then fucking." He pressed down on her softness, feeling her response, knowing when he'd found the right spot by the soft gasp and the punch of her hips.

He worked it. She didn't respond at first, and he didn't care, pressing, caressing, gliding, until she moaned and arced into his hand. She was close. He was going to make her come, and come hard, all over—

Mac stopped. Pulled his hand away with a force of will he hadn't had to exert over himself in twenty years. Just... done.

He stared at her, waiting for her to open her eyes. When she did, he could see how much she wanted him to go on, but that determination was there, too. She wouldn't lie to him, wouldn't give him a fake name, but she wasn't going to tell him, either. Fuck, he was halfway to in love with her already.

But he would keep trying. "You want to keep doing this here? In the dirt? Or should we head to my place?" he said. "You can not tell me your name in my bed."

She didn't answer for a long time, and he could see the calculation in her eyes. When she spoke, he had to bite his lip to keep from laughing. "How about you keep doing what you were doing, and I'll tell you your own name in another minute or two."

He grinned. "Oh yeah? I might consider it, just to hear you scream it out." He looked around in the stillness, the darkness. "You can make sure the whole forest knows my name."

A car door slammed, catching his attention. He looked up, unable to see anything through the forest, even though he could tell they were close to the road. Shit, dispatch had probably sent someone to check on him.

A young male voice came, eagerness making it sound younger than it probably was. "If she's still here, she's mine first. I'll hit her with this, you two hold her down, then we'll switch."

Another young male voice. "Ah, Joel, I don't really want to—"

The first voice spoke again. "She fucking knocked me out, Dean! You let her! You think she should get away with that?"

"But... you said we were just gonna fuck with her a little bit."

The boys continued to argue, and rage built inside of Mac. "Motherfuck," he swore, then looked at his mate. "Who are they talking about?"

Her eyes were narrowed. "Me."

"You have got to be fucking kidding me!"

She shook her head. "We had a little talk before you showed up. They were cutting the top off the playground. I taught one of them a painful lesson."

Mac got to his feet, rage filling him so completely he couldn't think of anything but getting to those boys. "Stay here," he told her.

He headed straight out of the forest, stepping over

downed trees and drooping plants, honing in on the boys, pulling his handcuffs out of his pocket as he went.

Nobody talked about his mate like that.

CHAPTER 25

Rogue parked her car in the parking lot of a vet's office, then jogged down a dark sidewalk, night vision binoculars in hand, until she found a spot behind a dumpster with a direct line of sight to the park she'd been in.

She saw Mac, standing over the top of the three males, all of whom were on their bellies in the dirt, their hands cuffed behind them. Mac's face was twisted in anger as he lectured them.

Rogue smiled, unable to hear him, but she could imagine what he was saying. He was unbearably sexy to look at, so she trained her binocs on the faces of the boys, instead. A blur crossed her vision and she pulled the binocs away from her face.

A patrol car was rolling up. As soon as a uniformed officer got out, Mac said a few words to him, and then he sprinted back into the forest.

Rogue winced when she thought she heard his bellow of frustration at finding her gone, even though she was more than a half mile away.

She turned and jogged back to her car, knowing she only had a few minutes to leave the area, before he had people looking for her.

He hadn't really thought she was going to stick around, had he?

No way. She was heading home for a few hours of sleep, then she would grab a few things and then she was gone. She wouldn't tell Boe, the house was in a trust that could never be traced back to her, and she'd leave it as it was, let her lawyers watch over it, maybe come back someday? Or not. Then back to Chicago to close up all her homes there, grab what little she wanted to take with her. Her tools, a few pieces of clothing, some cash, her financial accounts, the two things she had that had belonged to her sister… and the pendants. Shit, what to do with them? Figure that out later.

And then she was gone. Where to? She had no idea. Let four wheels or some wings take her and see what happened. Mexico, Hawaii, Florida, Alaska, Canada. Probably Hawaii or Florida. More work for her there. Or maybe she would make a full break and head out of the Americas altogether. Australia. Eastern Europe.

She could live anywhere she wanted.

Anywhere, but Serenity.

Rogue sighed. If Amara hadn't come back here yet to find Rogue, she never would.

So there was nothing keeping her here.

Nothing at all.

***

Mac blinked against the early morning sunshine, parked the truck in the P.D. parking lot, and dragged his worn-out ass into the station.

She'd disappeared. No trace. Not even a scent on the wind. He'd been driving around for hours, but he'd finally given up.

He couldn't believe it. He'd met his mate twice, no, three times, and she'd bailed on him every single time.

He strode through the duty room, throwing anyone who looked at him a dirty glare, pulling out his phone as he went. He texted Bruin.

I need you. Meet me at the station, asap.

A voice text came back in no time. "Almost there."

Mac headed straight for Wade's office, barging in. As soon as Wade saw him, he leaned back in his chair and raised his eyebrows.

Mac slammed the door behind him. "I met her before."

"What?"

Mac stopped on the other side of Wade's desk and leaned over it. "I fucking knew her, chief." He got closer to the old male. "We had sex before, but I didn't know she was my mate. There was no sign at all. No smell, no pull, no weirdness when I touched her. Fuck, I didn't even recognize her at first."

Wade rubbed his eyes and asked his question with his hands over his face, his voice weary. "How long ago?"

"Four years."

Wade dropped his hands to the desk. "That makes sense, I guess. The prophecy said they would come of age at 25. And until they were as matured as their father intended them to be, you wouldn't recognize her as your mate, but you could easily still be attracted to her, and she to you, once she was an adult."

Something about what Wade said reverberated in Mac's

mind. *Adult.* Why did that make his brain twist and bend, like there was something more for him to remember?

Wade spoke again. "Where is she?"

Mac couldn't respond. He was reaching, trying to figure out what else there was for him to remember. He couldn't quite grasp it...

"Mac?"

"Shit!" Mac pounded his hands on the desk. He placed his palms flat, still leaning forward. "She's gone. She took off. I don't even know her fucking name, still."

Wade's eyes narrowed. "But you saw her again?"

"Yeah, at Sinissipi Park, last night. She was there. We... we had a thing."

Wade nodded. "But you didn't tell her."

Mac stood and ran a hand through his hair, then over the day's worth of growth on his face. "It's not that simple. She-she's strong-willed. I don't know if she would believe me, no matter what I said."

Wade's eyes flicked down to Mac's skin that was showing through the hole in his shirt. "She do that?"

Mac grabbed the flap of shirt and yanked at it till it separated more, hanging lower. "Yeah, she did. She pulled a goddamn knife on me, Chief! Again!"

Wade looked downward and moved his hands in front of his face, but not before Mac saw him smile.

"You think that's fucking funny?"

Wade didn't bother trying to hide his smile as he met Mac's eyes. "Not funny. Just... fitting. Don't you think?"

"What are you talking about?"

"Come on, Mac, you've been a pain in everyone's ass around here since you were a teenager. Did you really think your mate was going to be any different?"

Mac pulled himself up to his full height. "You calling my mate a pain in the ass?"

Wade threw back his head and laughed. "She's got your panties in a full-on twist, doesn't she? I gotta tell you, Mac, I really didn't expect anything less. I've been nervous about your mate for months, knowing when she finally showed up, shit was gonna hit the fan. I'm with you, I don't believe she murdered Denton Smith, but I do think you are going to have your hands full with her. She's not going to *come quietly*, as the phrase goes." He eyed Mac up and down. "I never saw you with someone nurturing like Ella, or quirky like Heather, or creative like Dahlia, or innocent like Cerise. Did you?"

Mac's eyes narrowed. "If she's none of those things, then what is she?"

Wade leveled his gaze, then looked hard into Mac's face, like he was trying to figure out if he really wanted to know or not. "Dangerous. Independent."

Mac took a deep breath, then collapsed into the chair behind him, covering his face with his hands. He didn't speak for a long time, then forced himself to say what was on his mind, his eyes closed behind his fingers. "What if I can't get her to stick around?"

Wade came around the desk and laid a hand on Mac's shoulder. "You will, Mac, I know you will. The fact that she is the way she is, that she's giving you such a hard time, tells me with absolute certainty that you are the only male who can handle her. The only one who has a chance of winning her heart. I hesitate to repeat a cliché under the circumstances, but… you were made for each other."

A knock sound at the door, and they could both tell by the *shave and a haircut, two bits* riff, that it was Bruin.

Mac scrubbed his face and Wade gave him a moment,

then leaned over and spoke softly. "Tell your bearfriend to get you home. You need at least a few hours of sleep or your mate is going to run the other way after one look at your face." He straightened. "Come in."

Bruin pushed the door open. "Come on, Mac, I got the lunchmobile outside, ready to take you home." He looked at Wade, eyebrows raised. "And it's bearmance, Chief, bear*mance*."

***

Mac let Bruin push him up onto his porch. He really was exhausted after another night without sleep. But his mate was more important than sleep, and no matter what Wade said, Mac knew in his heart that if he didn't find her soon, he wouldn't have a chance to win her over. She would convince herself that she would be better off somewhere else, and she'd be gone. He'd never see her again. Which would kill him, leave him a miserable shell.

"Come on, big guy," Bruin said, pulling at Mac, taking his keys and unlocking the door, then pushing him inside. He waved a hand toward The Cereal Shrine. "Bitty-bit toys all fine." They kept going and Bruin waved another hand at the kitchen. "No food in the kitchen, that's ok, we can eat when we're dead." He pushed Mac right into the bedroom.

Bruin snorted, presumably at the lack of decorating and the spiky red throw on the bed. "Let's go, Mac, out of those clothes."

Mac fell face first onto the bed. "Fuck you," he said, not unkindly, maneuvering his body so his boots could stay on but not touch the blanket.

But Bruin wouldn't let him leave them on.

Mac fell asleep before Bruin was even done unlacing them.

***

He woke up with a memory playing out like a dream. He flipped over on his back and stared at the ceiling, grasping at it. The tunnels. The girl. It had been so long ago…

His notebook! Mac whipsawed off the bed and landed on the floor in a heap, grabbing his notebook and flipping it to the front to check out the date of the first entry. This one started six years ago. Not long enough. He crawled to his closet and pawed through the detritus of his life piled on the bottom, until he found a stack of notebooks, picking the very bottom one.

He'd been forced to start writing in his notebook by someone he still hated, but he'd discovered he kind of enjoyed putting his thoughts about his day down on paper. He hadn't written consistently since the day he'd won the battle with his War Camp Training Instructor, sometimes skipping as long as a year here or there, but when he had something he felt strongly about, it always went in the notebook.

He flipped back to the beginning, skipping over all the shit about how he was being forced to do it, then finding his first entry about Sandra, skimming over it, then flipping to the next page.

And there it was.

Shit. I fucking hate bureaucracy. I hate that we are all fucking helpless until we are big enough to get a job and beat someone's ass if they try to force us to do something. I found a lost little girl in the tunnels today, when I was skipping class to go see Sandra, and of course I didn't have any options but to turn her over to the camps. I know they'll dynamite the tunnels closed now, but that doesn't matter at all. What's worse is that the little girl had to go home, had to go back with her aunt and her uncle who were absolute shits to her. Why couldn't anyone else see it? Fuck. Life is just not fair sometimes.

He'd drawn a crappy pen doodle next, but he didn't even look that over. All he cared about was the next part, where he'd spelled out what had happened. He kept reading, his eyes taking in each word like the secret to eternal life was hidden within the meaning.

Sandra said she'd meet me by the boat dock, but she could only wait till midnight. BFD was determined to stay awake and catch me sneaking out, so I snuck some laxatives into his coffee and hit the tunnel while he was stuck in the bathroom. It's always worth getting punched around to see Sandra.

But I didn't see her. I was about halfway there, running hard, when something made me stop. A noise in the tunnel. I followed it, and eventually I figured out it was someone crying. It sounded like a little girl who was scared out of her mind. I called out to her, and she got really quiet, like she was scared of me, but then I didn't need to hear her to find her. I could smell her clearly, a biting, pungent smell that I eventually realized was absolute terror.

I rounded a corner and found her, holed up in the very center of a small room off the main tunnel. She had no light, and my light was off, so it was pitch black, and I could more smell her than see her, knew she was curled up in a little ball, her hands around her knees, rocking back and forth as she talked to herself. "It's ok, Rogue," she said. "You can do it. Just try again. The spiders can't hurt you. They are little and you are big. You can smash them. You'll find your way out this time. You just have to get up and walk."

I dropped to my knees so I wouldn't scare her, but when I spoke, she let out a squeak anyway. I said, "Hey, are you lost?"

She shot to her feet and backed away from me, but when her back hit the dirt wall behind her, she screamed and bounced off it, then cut her scream off with a hand over her own mouth, her eyes looking right at me, even though I knew she couldn't see me. No human down there could have seen anything.

"I'm going to turn on a light," I told her and snapped on my flashlight, covering it with my hand. She squeezed her eyes shut anyway, then covered them with her hands, like the light hurt. "How long have you been down here?" I asked.

She didn't say a word, just stood there, trembling, her hands over her eyes. "How old are you?" I asked, keeping my tone soft, which was something I didn't have a lot of practice with.

Her hands finally came down from her face and she blinked repeatedly. I could see tear and dirt tracks all over her face, and her hair was matted with dirt on one side, like she'd slept on the ground.

"Five," she whispered to me, her face so sad.

Motherfucking five. That was some bullshit. I'm fifteen and I wouldn't have been able to sleep in those tunnels. They were spooky as shit, and worms and bugs always fell on me when I ran through them. If BFD hadn't been on my ass so much, I would have been able to go through the forest, but not with him posting sentries every ten feet, trying to catch me.

"Hey," I said, but I didn't say anything else, because I wanted her to feel better, and I couldn't think of anything that would make that happen. But then I did. "I can get you out of here," I said. "I know where the exit is."

She looked at me then, really stared hard at my face. I didn't know what she was seeing, or trying to see, but she screwed up her courage, I could practically see her doing it, and said, "Did you see any other little girls? One who looks a little bit like me, maybe? Me and my sister found this tunnel a while ago. I wouldn't go in it, but she wanted to. She called me a baby, but I still wouldn't go in. She's gone now and I can't find her."

I shook my head. "You're the only girl I've seen. But I'll help you get out of here."

In my head I was already trying to figure out how to get her home, and still make it to see Sandra before midnight. But it wasn't going to be that easy.

She came closer to me, and her hands kept running over her shoulders and her hair, until she yelped and hit at her shoulder, almost falling over in some sort of fit.

"What?" I yelled.

"It's a spider, it bit me!" She was hitting at her shoulder and kind of falling around the room, so I grabbed her and turned her, shining my light on the place she was smacking. I grabbed her hand to stop her. "It's not, it's just some dirt," I said.

She started crying then, and I didn't want to feel bad for her, but I did. I imagine that she was probably a lot like Mackenzie would have been if she had—

Mac frowned, turning the page, then turning it back. The entry had just stopped. There were a few tear marks lined with ink in the lower right corner, like he had torn the pen through the paper in anger or frustration, but there was nothing more to the memory. Mac dropped his head down to the floor, realizing it didn't matter. He could remember it now. She'd been so fierce and brave, but so scared at the same time. They'd walked out together, and at some point she'd put her hand in his, and he'd been glad the tunnel was dark, because it could have been his little sister with her hand in his, and oh god, he missed Mackenzie so badly, she'd been a complete and total innocent and never should have died, she'd been so sweet, so beautiful, so fun and funny.

Mac pressed his hand to the floor, determined not to do what he had done that day, which was break down and cry. It had been the first time he'd done it over his sis since he'd been a pup. But after he had, he'd felt better. A little. Cleaned out some, the grief that had piled up in the decade since she and his mother had gone washed away a bit.

And here he was, twenty years later, still feeling like crying. He pushed himself up onto his hands and knees, wondering if the little girl from that night in the tunnels could really be his mate. She would have been the right age. Five, now twenty-five. But, if so, that would mean that he hadn't only been brought together one time before with his mate, unknown to him, but twice.

He'd taken her to the administrative office of the camp, told his story, and thankfully, BFD had still been on the shitter, so a Sergeant had been called over from the police department. They hadn't even needed to question Rogue to find out who she was, she'd been reported missing the day before by her aunt and uncle. Mac had been allowed to stay there with her until the two came to get her, mostly because she'd clung to him and only cried when anyone else had tried to talk to her. He'd hated them on sight, especially the way they seemed more concerned with what she'd said to the police than with how she was or what she'd been through.

His memory slid over the long walk out of the dark tunnel, when he'd asked her why she was named Rogue. She hadn't spoken for a long time, but then in her small, but somehow still-fierce voice, she'd said, "I hate my real name." He'd made a joke about Rogue, the villain turned X-man and she hadn't said a word. Oh.

But he knew her full name, didn't he? Rogue Kendall, and he even remembered her aunt and uncle's names. Brenda and Kevin.

And he remembered the last thing she'd said to him before her aunt had peeled her out of his arms and carried her to the car.

Mac, I don't want to go home with them. Can I live with you?

CHAPTER 26

*O*h, this is very generous," Father Macleese said, squinting over his wire frames at her, his hand creasing her check. "So generous, Mrs... I'm sorry, I lost your name again." He frowned. "I'm getting old. You really should be talking to one of my deacons."

It was the next day. Rogue had made it out of Serenity, and only had this and one more thing to do before she could leave Illinois for good. She was paying her debts, closing her accounts, shutting down this life, and it was almost done.

Rogue dipped her head. She knew Father Macleese couldn't see well, even with the glasses, but his stare still made her nervous, like he suspected something. When she spoke, she kept her voice soft and high. "It's perfectly fine, Father. Miss Shedd. I never married."

"Right, right. Shedd. I should remember that. It's such an unusual surname."

She smiled tightly, bowing her head a little to hide behind the scarf that covered her old-lady wig, knowing the thick glasses and makeup were doing their job, hiding her identity. She pulled a contract out of her purse and handed it over. "I've had my lawyer draw this up. If your Bishop accepts that check, it can only be used here in this parish. And it can only be used to fund your church if he gives approval for the Beds of Hope shelter you've been planning."

The old priest sighed, took off his glasses and rubbed his eyes. "How did you learn about this?"

Rogue slid the contract onto his desk. "There's been word on the street, Father. Someone came to me, asked for my help. How could I say no to such a worthy cause?" This was why she had to come herself. To make sure he was going to take it to his Bishop. To make sure he knew this was for him and his project, and not for anything else the Bishop might convince him was more important.

He peered at her again, without his glasses. "Do you attend services at my church?"

She shook her head. "I only live here in the spring, but I did grow up here, as did my sister. This parish will always be important to me. It needs what you have planned for it."

Her stomach growled loudly and she coughed to cover the noise. Damn. She just had to convince him, then she could grab something to eat, visit her last place to get the only things she couldn't replace, and then she would be done.

She'd decided on where she was going. Australia. At least for a little while. She'd visited her lawyer that morning, put all her money except a small travel fund into this trust she was turning over to Father Macleese, and then she'd be driving out of the state to catch a plane in Indiana.

Australia was literally on the other side of the world from Chicago.

And that was as far away from Mac as she could get.

This truly was goodbye and she'd decided on the drive from Serenity to Chicago that when she got to Australia, she was turning over a new leaf. Changing. Maybe handing over all her money to a man of God for the simple reason of helping people could erase her past in some way. Then she could just do something simple.

Something normal that had nothing to do with cops, criminals, angels, or wolves.

She could always find a job as a locksmith.

***

"Yeah, thanks." Not. People in Chicago were so damn closed-mouthed. Mac let the old lady slam the door in his face. He turned to Bruin, who was coming down the steps. "Anything?"

"Nah, they say nobody under the age of fifty lives in this building, certainly no twenty-five year old woman. And they never heard of the name."

"Yeah, that's the same answer I got. Shit." He rubbed a hand over his face. It was like chasing a ghost. Someone who might or might not exist.

He'd run all the Kendall names through both Serenity and Chicago computers and gotten nothing on Rogue since that time she'd been reported as a missing child and Mac had found her in the tunnels. Which was shocking, because both her aunt and uncle had been arrested multiple times in the years before and after, mostly for petty crimes like pick-pocketing, theft, passing bad checks, and forgery.

Some of the notes had mentioned there had been reports of a young girl with them occasionally, sometimes even part of the crime, but she'd always gotten away, and Brenda and Kevin had always insisted there was no girl. Chicago PD had never cross-checked files with Serenity PD, so the fact that Rogue existed had escaped notice, until she was almost a legend. Then Kevin had died and Brenda had disappeared, and no whisper of Rogue had ever been heard again.

Rogue. He'd been saying the name under his breath all morning, loving it more and more each time. He knew it was a nickname, but it was sexy as shit. He rubbed a hand over his face, wishing he'd taken the time to shave. The scruff was making him itch. But no, they hadn't even eaten. He had to find her quickly, before she disappeared for good.

Knowing her name hadn't helped him at all. Rogue Kendall had never been arrested, never been in the military, never asked for government assistance, never filed taxes, never been recorded in any way that he had access to. There were 266 Kendalls in the phone book, probably half of them female, and he could have searched through them to find a first name *like flora*, but simple cop instinct told him that was a stupid move. He wouldn't find her that way.

The first entry he'd read that made mention of her had been three years after he'd found her in the tunnels, so that would have made her eight. Chicago PD had a rash of pickpocketing cases, literally fifty and sixty people being pick-pocketed a day in the same three-mile radius. No matter what they did, they couldn't catch who was doing it. They would set out undercover cops and cameras where the pattern specialist said would be the next hotspot, also leaving some at the last few hot spots, but the pick-pocketer was always one step ahead of them. The victims had never noticed anyone, or been suspicious of anyone in particular, except a few had noticed a pretty young girl, a few had even talked to her. But none had wanted to believe she could have been the one who had taken their stuff.

Just by chance, Kevin Kendall had been pulled over on something completely unrelated, and found with a trash bag full of wallets in the back of his car. He'd eventually confessed to being the South Side picker, even though all of the cops and even the judge were skeptical, because he didn't seem particularly smart or smooth. But he knew where and when the stuff had been taken, and he had the wallets. He also had enough money to hire a good lawyer, and he was let out of jail in eight months, during which the crimes had stopped completely.

Mac and Bruin had spent the morning reading every file they could find on Kevin and Brenda Kendall, especially the arrest notes. They'd compiled a quick mock up of the addresses the pair had given over the years, especially taking note of any mention of a young girl with the pair. It hadn't been particularly helpful. Then they'd tried cross-referencing with any crimes during the time period where a young girl was suspected or caught.

Mac had been itchy, unable to do a complete investigation, feeling the pull to get on the road as soon as they had something, anything, to go on. Bruin had driven to Chicago, with Mac in the passenger seat, still reading.

But then the dead end. Kevin had been shot and died, unknown assailant. Brenda had disappeared, never been arrested in Chicago again. Rogue never was mentioned at all. She would have been 14.

Mac had wanted to give up in frustration, but his stubbornness wouldn't let him. The only alternative was driving around, hoping to catch her scent again, and he knew he wouldn't be that lucky twice, even if fate did seem to be trying to put them together. Fate helps those who do the shitwork. He knew that.

So he went back to the computer. Tens of thousands of crimes went unsolved in Chicago every year. Obviously, Rogue was still operating out of Chicago and/or Serenity, and it made sense that she was still a criminal. It was what she knew, what she was good at. She'd never gone to school, a quick check of the computer records told him that, at least not with the last name Kendall.

The fingerprints found on the trophy that had been used to murder Denton Smith weren't on file, which meant she'd never been caught, never been arrested, if they were hers. So they'd started checking unsolved crimes. And finally found something that they could work with.

There'd been a cat burglar operating in Chicago for, as far as they could tell, the last seven years. Never caught. Somehow never even caught on camera, unless it was a shadowy or grainy shot that didn't tell the investigating officers anything. The assumption, of course, was that the cat burglar was a man, but a few of the detectives had decided that, no, the cat burglar must be a woman, and they'd started calling her the pussycat burglar. Not officially, of course.

Mac had read through all the notes and decided it was bullshit, they had nothing concrete to go on that would say the cat burglar was a woman, except for good old intuition, and the fact that they'd never caught him/her yet. The things the burglar did were unusual, sure, but they didn't point to a woman over a man, in his opinion.

One: The burglar only broke into homes and offices of

criminals. Most criminals didn't report when their shit got stolen, but sometimes they did. Insured art, that kind of thing.

Two: Six times over the last seven years, the FBI or the Chicago PD had received a neat little package in the mail, a damning package that implicated a criminal in some activity they had tried to hide from the cops. One time, it had been a video taken of a contract hit, with a note of where it had been found and that there were more where that came from. When the police had entered the home on a warrant, the suspect had been surprised as hell that the video was even gone from his safe. *It must have been stolen*, were his outraged words. Another time, the FBI had received an email from a suspect's computer that included a complete image of the hard drive, saying, "Hi, I'm a fucking dirty pig, and I need to be arrested." Mac didn't even want to think about what they'd found when they'd gotten into the hard drive.

Three: The times the burglar had been sighted on security cameras had all seemed to be deliberate, like the burglar had known right where the camera was and turned in such a way to show only what he or she wanted to be seen. It always looked like a man, normally dressed in work clothes or maintenance clothes, with a cap on his head and gloves on his hands, but there was one picture that had been magnified and Mac had stared at for way too long as the road to Chicago whipped by, Bruin humming folk rock in the driver seat. The image showed the person walking away from the camera. Just his back, but the coveralls he had been wearing had been just a bit too short for him. The picture had been zoomed in on the ankles, where dark purple leggings showed over the top of slim socks.

That was one fact that Mac could agree with the other officers on. Men did not generally wear purple leggings.

But knowing that fact had done nothing to help him find Rogue. Until he found one detective's notes. If those few facts the guy had compiled helped Mac find Rogue, he didn't owe that guy a beer, he owed him a car or some shit.

The guy was a computer nerd. Liked to write programs that solved crimes using data and correlations a human eye couldn't find. The courts didn't allow much of it yet, so his Lieutenant didn't encourage the behavior, but the guy still did it, for whatever reason. Maybe for fun. Some people were weird as shit. He'd written a couple of programs that cross-referenced major financial crimes with large monetary deposits all over the world. All U.S. banks and most banks of countries that were U.S. allies reported all deposits over a certain amount, or many smaller deposits by the same person across multiple banks in the same time period.

The code-happy detective had written a smaller program to compare the cat burglar's reported crimes with all financial deposits that they knew of, around the world. The program had spit out one name, a name of a person who only seemed to exist in the IRS's files, except she'd once gotten mail in this building. To an apartment that didn't exist.

Angel Shedd.

Mac crumpled the piece of paper in his pocket that had the name on it with his fist. He'd written it down. Brought the paper with him, even though nothing could make him forget that name.

She was screaming to be found, and she probably didn't even know it.

Angel. Because she was half angel. Shedd, like the Shedd Aquarium, which placed her firmly in Chicago.

Mac wasn't a big thinker. Never a philosopher. But the one true mate prophecy was starting to become more interesting to him every day, and not just because he was the one in the thick of it at that very moment. Not just because he'd first met his mate when she was five years old, then connected with her again at twenty-one, then just happened to plan the rut at a place she dropped into that night? That angel had wound who these women really were into their very beings. Or fate had done that. Something more than coincidence had to be at work.

Graeme believed that Rhen and Khain weren't predicting the future, but rather that they were somehow creating it, spinning it like yarn between two needles, into the blanket of the *shiften's* lives.

Mac was starting to believe that also, and he didn't know if he liked it or not. If they were being steered, how were they being steered, and why? Were they really nothing more than pawns, given enough needs and desires to think they were important, that they had free will and a purpose, then set loose on a board of play, to be turned occasionally by some cosmic hand like a young boy would turn a bug with a toothpick?

Mac raised a hand to his head. His temples were pounding. "Shit," he said to no one in particular, even though Bruin was right in front of him. "We lost her. We fucking lost her."

Bruin shook his head. "No way. We just need to reconnoiter. Food will clear our heads."

Mac let himself be led out of the building, hoping Bruin was getting a little of that cosmic help right about now.

Because otherwise, he'd been dealt a blow he wasn't going to recover from.

CHAPTER 27

*B*ruin was ahead of Mac on the sidewalk, following his nose. Ordinarily, Mac would have given him shit, called him a name, asked him if he was on his way to the virgin convention and wanted to be first in line. Today, he didn't have the energy to fuck with the guy. He didn't feel like eating, either. Kind of felt a little like sitting in a corner and counting the cracks in the sidewalk, but whatever. He could put one foot in front of the other.

He slowed down even more, not looking where he was going. People streamed past him in both directions, one of them bumping his elbow. Whatever. Shit. He just knew she was gone already. He would never find her if she didn't want to be found. It wasn't like him to say die, to give up, to feel hopeless, but something about Rogue had him twisted up inside.

Bruin grabbed him by the arm. "Here, Mac, let's eat lunch here."

"Yeah, sure," Mac said, not even looking up to see where here was. How many people lived in Chicago? Almost three million? That was a lot of humans to sort through. It seemed impossible—

"Mac, come on. Inside." Bruin steered him by the elbow and Mac had just enough time to read the sign on the door, Best Slice Pie Company, before he was pushed inside. Pies. Great. Exactly what he fucking wanted for lunch—

The sweet smell of citrus flooded his nostrils and he picked his head up, looking around carefully, grabbing at Bruin to stop him from walking to the register. The place was big for a pie shop. Twenty tables or so, more room than he would have thought, but most of them were empty. His gaze played over the people in the room as he elbowed Bruin, hard. "She's here."

"Who?"

Mac rolled his eyes, his spirit back. "The motherfucking pie fairy."

He elbowed Bruin again before he could start going off about 'Is there really a pie fairy? Why haven't you told me before?' and whispered, "Rogue."

"Oh. Sweet." Bruin stopped for a beat, then said, "You sure?" as he looked around.

Mac shook his head. He didn't see a tall, athletic female with dark blonde hair either. But she was here. Her scent was strong and steady. He looked everyone over again. No, on the couple at the table next to them. Not any of the young men behind the counter. No on the man sitting in the corner. Not the elderly lady bent over her walker near the register, with the bright scarf covering her hair. Shit. What was he missing? He walked forward slowly, following the scent, until it took him right to the register, right next to the woman who was standing there. If he had to give an initial assessment of her age, based solely on the way her back was bent and the hump at the base of her neck, covered by her sweater and her scarf, plus the age and style of the clothes she wore, the smartness of her black pocketbook, he would have said in her eighties. But her stockinged ankles were slim and shapely, and the hand she was using to drop the change into a pocket in her tan sweater had age spots, but no thinness of skin.

Her back tensed and she turned away from him, to go back out through the line, instead of the way most people who were done with their transaction would go. She knew he was there. Somehow.

He took a large step to come up close to her. "Hungry?" he whispered, bending down toward her, his hand reaching into his pocket so when she started screaming, he could flash his badge and shut everybody up.

But she didn't scream. She kept up the charade, acting like he didn't exist, until he went around the other way and got in front of her. Still he couldn't see her face, because she was bent over the walker, and her scarf was pulled low over her forehead.

But it was her.

He stepped in her path, and his heart soared when she lifted her eyes to his, even though hers were narrowed in anger and… not hate. Please not hate.

She stood up straight and looked him in the eye. "Your mother ever teach you it's not polite to follow people?"

He grinned. "Why don't we sit down and talk about it."

***

Rogue couldn't believe he'd found her. She was slipping.

She had to have done something wrong, for him to track her this well. Now she just had to find out what he knew, and then figure out how to get rid of him.

Her flight to Australia wasn't leaving till three the next afternoon. She had plenty of time to give him the slip. She just couldn't let him get under her skin. Sex was definitely off the table, no matter how much one look at him made her want to climb right on the table and flip over onto her back.

But she knew when she was caught. She made her way to a table near the wall, walking normally, folding up her walker as she went. She sat down with her back to the wall, stuffed the walker between the chair and the wall, took off her scarf and her glasses, then started to wipe the makeup off her face and hands, fishing a wet-nap out of her purse to help.

He sat down across from her, a smile beaming on his face. She shot him a dirty look, then realized that he wasn't the only person watching her. A guy at the door. Bigger than Mac by a few inches and some bulk. Handsome, in a sweet kind of way. Not a cop, for sure, but he was staring at her so hard he was obviously with Mac. "Who's that?" she said, lifting her chin at the big guy. A few jabs played through her mind. *Your lesbian life partner?* Nah, insulting to lesbians. *Your sandbox playmate?* No, that didn't even make sense. *Your big, hairy sidekick?* Closer. Ah, she had it. "Your domestic partner? The P.D. let you carry him on your healthcare?"

Mac scowled at her and she hid a grin. He turned around to speak to his friend. "Bruin, get some pie, stay close."

Rogue spoke loud enough that everyone in the place could hear her. "Yeah, stay close, Bruin, just in case Mac can't handle me. Two guys on one little girl. That's fair."

"Keep your voice down," Mac told her.

She laughed. "Or what? I would ask are you gonna spank me, but I know how hot you are for me, and I wouldn't want to give you the wrong idea."

His mouth dropped open. Rogue leaned back in her chair and opened her bag of food, getting out her spinach quiche, trying not to smile. No reason not to get eating out of the way while she was dealing with his stubborn ass.

He leaned forward over the table, practically hissing at her. "There were two of us in those woods. I know you were into it, too. You can't fake something like that."

She raised an eyebrow. "Oh no? You ever seen *When Harry Met Sally*?"

He shook his head, and looked almost hurt. Oh well. He couldn't, under any circumstances, know how much he affected her. She'd let too much out already. Much more than was good for her. His hurt seemed a small price to pay for her freedom, so she hardened her heart against caring about how he felt.

She cocked her head to the left and eyed him. "You look a little like that guy that starred in it... what was his name? Ah, never mind. He's forgettable."

She looked away, not wanting to see him when she said what else she had to say.

"Just like you."

***

Mac ran a hand through his hair, then itched his damn scratchy beard. He couldn't wait to shave the motherfucker off, and he would as soon as he had a spare second. This woman was confounding him, and he didn't know if he hated it or loved it. Fuck! He wanted to stand up and pace, burn off some energy, but he couldn't let her see how much she got to him.

He knew women like this, had slept with as many as he could get to respond to him. They turned up their noses at the first sign of weakness… until they had fallen for you, then you got a bit of a pass. But she hadn't fallen for him yet. According to her, she never would. She found him forgettable, and presumably, not attractive. Fuck, if that wasn't a kick in the balls, he didn't know what was.

She leaned back in her seat, staring at him, her eyes flashing, flaming, burning holes in him. A bit of stage makeup was smudged on her left temple and he had to physically hold himself back from wiping it away. He wanted to touch her so bad it hurt, but she wasn't about to allow it. He knew the only way he was going to put his hands on her without her trying to break one of his wrists was if he arrested her. Even then, she still might try to pop one of his joints. Fuck, he needed to move around.

She stuck her long legs out from under the table and crossed them at the ankle. He couldn't help but follow the movement, starting at granny-skirt and ending at blocky, granny-shoes, but everything in between, shit, it was exquisite, the curve of her calf beckoning to him.

When he looked up from her legs, her eyes were narrowed. "So what are we doing here?" she asked, her voice tired. "You swore you weren't going to arrest me. Were you lying?"

He shifted in his chair, knowing damn good and well he wasn't going to let her get away from him again. If he had to arrest her to get her home with him, he would. And then what? Throw her in jail? Keep her at his house? Force her to love him? He wasn't a big winning-over kind of guy. Women either loved him or hated him, and there wasn't much he was capable of doing to change that. He threw a look at Bruin who was three tables over, but the guy was ankle deep in a pie and absolutely no help.

"I don't want to arrest you," he said softly.

Her eyebrows raised, and she sat up straighter in her chair, her ankles disappearing under the table. Damnit. She looked around theatrically, then put her hand to her eyebrows, as if she was shielding her eyes from the sun and looking for something. Finally, she dropped her hand and gave him a hard glare. "I don't see the guy holding the gun to your head. If you don't want to arrest me, then don't. Let me go."

"I can't."

She nodded briskly. "Right, you said that already. Here we fucking go again. You gonna tell me why?" She held up a hand. "No, don't. I just know it's gonna be some story that ends up with me being in great danger if I don't come back to your bedroom, *right now*, and play into your secret fantasy. You're the hero of this story, right? And I'm the damsel in distress?" She leaned forward, and the enmity in her expression made him shudder. "Let me fill you in on something, *princess*, I'm good. I don't need your protection."

Mac thought his heart was going to stop in his chest. He'd never felt so much emotional pain in his life. Being rejected by his mate was a whole new kind of hell, one he'd never been able to imagine before.

She stood, her chair scraping loudly on the tile floor. He stood also, but slowly, all his fight gone again. She stole it without even trying. She held up a hand. "I just gotta pee. I'll be right back. Look, I'll leave my purse." She tossed it on the table and turned toward the sign marked restroom, which led down a small hallway. Mac sank back into his chair and watched her go, making sure she didn't head out the back way.

She didn't. He sighed and put his hands behind his head. The way she'd pre-empted his truth left him with few options. He hadn't wanted to tell her what was going on until they'd gotten together, but that was a complete bust. At this point, he'd settle for her just being nice to him, one time. But that wasn't going to happen, either. And if he tried to explain it now? She was either going to think he was a lunatic, or he was making it all up. She'd as much as said so.

He pinched the bridge of his nose and tried to think of a way to proceed that didn't make him look like an asshole. He'd never cared much what people thought about him, but he cared very much what she thought about him, and he also didn't want to have to go back to Serenity with his mate handcuffed in the back of a patrol car to keep her from bolting. He would never hear the end of it.

Mac glanced over at Bruin, then back at the bathroom door, then half stood as a suspicion came over him. He stared hard at the door, trying to calculate how long she'd been in there. He grabbed her purse off the table and ripped the mouth of it open wide. Nothing in there but a few wet-naps and some tissue paper.

Motherfuck. "Bruin," he said urgently, getting the big male's attention and heading to the bathroom door. He knocked on it as Bruin came close. "Hey," he called, "You in there?" She didn't know he knew her name yet, and this wasn't how he wanted her to find out. No answer, though. Frantic, he tried the knob. Locked. Shit. Find a key? No time.

"B, I need this door open, now."

Bruin nodded, got opposite of it, and slammed his bulk

into it. The flimsy lock gave way easily and the door slammed off the back wall.

The bathroom was empty, the small window leading to a back alley open, as if it were laughing at him.

CHAPTER 28

$\mathcal{M}$ ac and Bruin ran, full speed, back the way they had come. When they reached the apartment they'd already been at, Mac laid on every buzzer until someone answered. "Police, open up," he said, holding his badge up in case anyone was looking, still pressing buttons until the door buzzed.

"What are we doing here?" Bruin puffed inside the foyer. "Didn't we already check this place?"

"Yeah, start again, but this time we're looking for an older lady, tall if she weren't so bent over, who likes colorful scarves and walks with a walker."

"Ohhh," Bruin breathed, but to his credit, he headed straight up the stairs.

Mac knocked on the first door in the foyer, the last one he'd hit up the first time they'd been there. The same lady answered, her face suspicious. But he charmed her better this time, and in just a few moments, he was standing in front of an apartment that had seemed empty the last time, no one answering the door. He called Bruin down to him, eyeing the heavy locks on the door. This was no restaurant bathroom.

"You think you can get in this one?" he asked. He could do it himself, but it had to be quick, in just one hit, and, shit, he knew the bear liked to be useful. He would call a locksmith, but if Rogue had gotten in from the outside, she might be in there right now. They didn't have time.

Bruin nodded and backed up, leading with his foot this time, hitting the door square, splintering the lock area.

They were in. A quick check of the small rooms told him Rogue wasn't there. He lingered over her black bedspread, his eyes tracing the pictures on the wall. There weren't many, and they all seemed generic, like maybe they hadn't been picked so much for what they were, but rather what they said. Normal. Nothing out of the ordinary here.

This wasn't a place she thought of as home, and although it did carry her scent, it wasn't strong enough to say different.

Feeling like a complete asshole, he started going through her things. The hair ties on the nightstand, the pile of clothes on the floor. Bruin stood in the doorway and watched, but didn't try to help, and didn't say a word. Good. Mac opened the drawer in the nightstand next to the bed, not surprised to find a gun. He shut it and opened the second drawer, then slammed it shut again.

Mac stood up, and turned around to look at Bruin. "Hey, ah, buddy, could you go out in the kitchen. Look through the drawers out there, tell me if you find anything of a personal nature. Numbers, notes, anything like that."

"Got it."

Mac turned slowly back to the nightstand and pulled the

drawer open again, then reached his hand in and touched the purple vibrator that lay there with one finger. She wouldn't come back for this. You could buy one of these anywhere, but he was suddenly certain she was coming back all the same. She would be here, he just had to wait around for her to show up. And this time, she wouldn't get away from him. He would cuff her to him if he had to, whether it pissed her off or not.

He couldn't afford to play games anymore.

He pulled the thing out of the drawer, mentally comparing its size to his own. He had it beat easily, so he had that going for him. She would never need one of these again. He made to toss it away, but had a better idea, his spirits still high.

He crept out into the kitchen until he found Bruin, back to him, hard at work going through the drawers there. Easy job, they were all practically empty. She didn't even need a kitchen, just a card table and some silverware in case the takeout place didn't provide chopsticks.

Mac turned the vibrator up high, then touched Bruin on the back of the ear with it. "Bees!" he yelled.

Bruin jerked away, slapping at his ear as he went. His expression said he wasn't surprised at what it really was. "You should never joke about bees, Mac."

Mac smirked, then hid the vibrator behind his back. "My mistake," he said, then disappeared, returning the toy where he'd found it, ignoring Bruin's whispered, "Blast him," from the other room.

Ol' Winnie couldn't even swear right.

***

Two hours later, Mac leaned his head back against Rogue's

couch, where he was sitting next to Bruin. It was either that, or sit on the floor. Her tiny apartment didn't have any other furniture. They'd found a safe behind one painting, but there hadn't been anything of value in it, just some cash, a small, worn Swiss Army knife- like a child's first knife, and a book. He'd flipped through the book, but found only a single word written in it. The word *Amaranth* printed on the cover in childish block letters, like a name.

Nothing in the place was her. Nothing told him any sort of story. Except maybe the vibrator, and if that story was that she didn't have a boyfriend, it was one he wanted to hear.

Mac frowned, starting to worry that he'd been wrong when he decided she was coming back here. For what? Not her battery operated boyfriend. She could live without the five grand in the safe. If she was really as good of a thief as she seemed to be, she would have much more than that stashed away somewhere. The knife and the book? They seemed to be personal mementos, so maybe.

She certainly wouldn't be coming back for him.

He spoke, even though he hadn't had any intention of doing so. "My mate's a criminal," he said, his voice sounding exactly as miserable as he felt.

"A *good* criminal," Bruin countered, as if that made it better. "Does it bother you?"

Mac thought for a long time before he spoke. "I don't think so. It's all she knows." The room was silent for a long time before he finally was able to say what he was thinking. "But what now? Assuming we ever find her. Assuming I can get her to come back with me, what then? Am I gonna have to tell everyone to hold on to their wallets while she's around?"

Bruin snorted. "That would be hilarious. Imagine if she just stole shit from people. Like your chief."

Mac smiled. "Maybe." The smile dissolved. "But they won't trust her."

Bruin sat up straighter and twisted in his seat to look Mac in the eye. "I'll trust her."

"Why?"

"Everyone has some good in them. No matter what."

Mac shook his head slowly. "She does. She really does. I can sense it. Smell it. Feel it when I touch her."

Bruin bobbed his head. "See? It doesn't matter what she's done."

Mac felt the stranglehold on his heart tighten, not loosen. "But it does. What if she has to go to jail?"

"Come on, Mac, she's part of a battle for humanity. No one's going to let that happen."

Mac clutched at the couch cushion beneath him. He could see that. If she'd really only stolen from criminals, no one was going to be in any hurry to make her pay for it. "But what if she won't stop?"

Bruin didn't even sound worried. "She will. She just needs a good reason. You're her reason."

The door that no longer locked slammed open and Rogue strode into the apartment, eyes locked on Mac, her face an angry mask, her hands balled into fists, her shoulders and hips tight. She stopped two feet in front of him, and he imagined he could see steam coming from her ears, like in a cartoon. The old lady outfit was gone, and she was dressed all in black. Long black leggings, a black long-sleeved shirt that hugged her curves, and simple black boots. Her hair was loose around her shoulders, the ends curling around her face. Fuck, she looked good, even when she was angry. His cop brain took in the slight bulges at her inner forearms and the slim black pack around her waist, like something a jogger would wear, barely big enough to hold a phone and some keys.

Mac scrambled to his feet, so damn glad to see her he had the impulse to drop to his knees and hug her around the waist. But she wouldn't have it. Wouldn't have him. Instead, he waited for her to start chewing on him. He would take every bit of it, gladly.

Bruin stood up, too, slowly edging away from Rogue. "Ah, Mac, I'm going to head out for a little bit. You, ah… good luck with your handful." He edged farther away. Mac kept his eyes on Rogue, who was staring at him like she wanted-ed to mow him over, maybe throw him out a window. Bruin cleared his throat. "You need any help with bad guys with guns, or flamethrowers, or bombs, or whatever, you just yell." Mac nodded, his eyes still on Rogue.

Rogue finally noticed Bruin. She turned her anger on him and Mac could see him shrink from his peripheral vision. She mocked taking a step at him, shouting "Boo!"

The look on Bruin's face was classic, and at any other time, Mac would have laughed. He had six or seven inches on Rogue, at least a hundred and fifty pounds, but he knew damn well it wouldn't help him with her.

Bruin hugged the wall. "Ok, just call me, you've got my number." And out the door he went. Mac didn't blame him. It was easy to face off with a man. You yell a little, maybe you fight. You kick ass or you get your ass kicked, and then it was over. But with a woman? They stored mean shit up like acorns, always knowing exactly what to say at exactly the time it would hurt the worst. And even if they hit you, you didn't hit them back. Even when they were tough or deserved it. You never won a fight with a woman, so the smart males didn't even try. They stood there and took whatever the lady wanted to dish out, or they ran.

Once Bruin was gone, Rogue didn't even look around her place, giving Mac the suspicion that she already knew exactly what they had done there. Like she'd been watching them from somewhere. Watched them break in the door, go through her stuff, call the locksmith to open her safe.

"How dare you?" she shouted, her scent a flat, harsh orange-yellow. "You had no right."

Mac pulled his badge out of his pocket, knowing it was a stupid thing to do, but it was better than not saying anything. He held it out. "This gives me the—"

She hit the back of his hand with the palm of hers, sending the badge flying across the room. "I'm not talking about you as a cop. I'm talking about you as someone I had a-a." Her expression clamped down even harder, and she whirled on her back foot, moving away from him, pacing around the room.

"A what?"

She stopped and exploded at him, hands raised up to shoulder level as she gestured at him. "A connection! That's what. How dare you come into my house and go through my shit when you've done nothing but try to tell me there should be something between us! It doesn't work that way." She stepped right back up in his face, dropping one more word between them. *"Princess."*

She was hurt? So she was trying to hurt him? Shit, he still couldn't keep his big mouth from popping off. "A connection? Is that why you left me in the woods? Refused to tell me your name? Snuck out the bathroom window? Is that why you've got a car full of your stuff somewhere close by and you're about to take off and I'm never going to see you again?"

She didn't say anything, but the way her face went all cool and smooth gave him all the answer he needed. "Yeah, that's what I thought. Put that in your *connection* pipe and smoke it." Lame-ass thing to say. He blamed all the time spent with the fucking bear, talking about bee's elbows.

His brain was mush-ifying, and someone had to be to blame.

CHAPTER 29

*R*ogue had had enough. Enough of this asshole and his hairy friend. Enough of men in general. Enough of… all off it.

She stuck a finger in his face. "I'm not playing any more games with you, dickhead. Tell me what you want from me and let me go on my way. I was wrong. There's no connection here. If you aren't going to arrest me, then get the hell out of my house. And if you are going to arrest me, maybe you should call someone else in to do it. You don't have issues, you've got whole damn subscriptions, and frankly, I'm sick of that magazine."

Mac sank down on the couch, his face crumpling. He put his fingers in his scruff that was quickly turning to beard and scratched, his eyes sorrowful. "I wish things were different between us."

The yearning in his voice got her attention in a way

nothing else would have been able to and she felt some of the anger leak out of her body. She kept her guard up. The only reason she was here was for the pendants hidden behind the drywall in her bathroom, and the two things in her safe. Once she got them, she would figure out another way to get away from him.

They're his, you know, a voice in her head told her. No way. They weren't his. But she was supposed to *reveal* them to him. Knew he was the cop from her visions. Fuck, if she hadn't been having those fucking fugues and fantasies, would things be different right now? Maybe. Maybe she wouldn't be so on guard with him.

He tried to catch her eye. "You really need to know some things."

She held up a hand, staring down at him. "I don't want to hear it."

"I know you don't. But you've got to."

Rogue shot him a nasty look, then stuck her fingers in her ears, pulling them out, then stuffing them in again. She popped them out. "Only if you hold me down while you force-tell me." She knew she was being childish but she couldn't help it. Something about him brought it out of her. He wasn't speaking, so she quit it.

He sighed. "I really wish we could do the whole normal thing."

She sank down on the couch next to him, half wanting to hear what he was going to say. "Yeah, what would that look like?"

Something hopeful came into his face. He leaned closer to her, probably unconsciously. "What's your favorite thing to do?"

That was easy. "Jump out of stuff. Jump off of stuff."

He went absolutely green. "You're kidding."

She hid a smile behind her hand. She was still pissed at him. Had never been more pissed at a guy in her life. But she liked to see him off balance. "Nah. I've been doing it since I was little. The higher the better." She'd been doing somersaults and rolls off park structures in the city since long before parkour was cool.

He nodded slowly. "You were amazing on that rock in Yosemite. Got a lot of finger and arm strength."

She eyed him. "If you don't like heights, why were you there?"

His eyes narrowed. "How do you know I don't like heights?"

She pointed at his face, drawing a circle around it in the air. "It's all written right there."

"Oh." He took a deep breath and leaned back. "My boss made me go. He was mostly fucking with me, I think." He looked back at her. "But I'm glad I was there. I'm glad I met you. I still think about you all the time."

Reaaallllly? Lie, or truth? She made a face. "Like I believe that."

His expression became earnest. "Seriously. I remember everything about it. You were wearing tight shorts and that pack around your waist. Something in it poked me one time when you came down. I remember thinking that I should tell you to take it off, but I didn't because you were the one who knew what you were doing. You also had on a purple paisley sports bra. The muscles in your back would flex when you moved from hold to hold and I remember wishing you didn't have it on so I could see all of your back. You were like... a model up there. Someone people would pay to take pictures of."

Rogue felt a blush stain her cheeks. She clamped down hard on her emotions, knowing that probably made her cheeks redder.

He kept talking. "I also remember thinking that you weren't ever gonna fall and I wasn't ever going to get to touch you. When you finally did, there was just a moment when I thought you'd done it on purpose. Like maybe you wanted me to touch you. But I know you were just that good. All your falls were that controlled."

Rogue felt more heat blast into her cheeks. She had fallen on purpose. Every time but once.

He looked down at her boots. "How's your ankle?"

Oh, right. She'd scraped it on an outcropping the one time she'd fallen for real, and lost a long stripe of skin. She pulled her pants up to show him. "That was a long time ago, so it's fine. Just a bit of a scar." He frowned when he saw it, like he didn't like that she'd been hurt. She remembered how distressed he'd been. He'd taken off his shirt and cut a huge slice out of it to wrap tight around her ankle and stop the bleeding, and hadn't wanted her to get back up on the rock.

She had to stop thinking about that. She jumped up. "That's not even my best scar." She pulled up her shirt, showing him the twisted one that looked like a river along her side, courtesy of misjudging a leap from a building and landing on a fence. He winced. "And one here." She pulled up her sleeve, showing the back of her wrist and being careful not to reveal the knife on the other side of her arm, even though she'd seen him notice it already. That scar was shorter, but wide, the injury had been a real gouge all the way to the bone. A fight with a guy who'd thrown a hunk of scrap metal at her when she was sixteen and living on the streets, after Uncle Kevin had died and before she'd gotten her shit together.

Mac reached out and touched the scar with one finger, a pained frown on his face. His hand looked strong, veiny, and his finger was warm and soft. She tore her eyes away, snatched her arm away, then sat back down, as far away from him as she could get. "What about you? Let's see 'em."

He shook his head, confused.

She rolled her eyes. "Your scars. Come on, you're older than me. I know you don't jump off of stuff, but you're a cop. You've gotta have some bullet wounds hidden somewhere, or some knife slices…?" Shit. She'd sliced him up and the very next day there had been no scar. Her friendly reminder that she was smack in the middle of some weird shit. He was looking at her intently, and he opened his mouth, about to say something but she shook her head and plugged her ears. "Sorry. Forget I asked. I really don't want to know." She waited for all the emotions to cross his face. Irritation. Frustration. Acceptance. He leaned back against the couch and put his hands behind his head, waiting for her to take her fingers out of her ears.

When she did, he shook his head, as if to say he wasn't going to tell her what she didn't want to know. "Ok, then that's what we'd do. If that's what you like to do, we'd go climb something, or you could jump off something. Maybe I'd pack a picnic lunch. Sandwiches. Drinks for when you were done. We could eat next to a lake where the air was sweet and the ground soft. We could talk about… stuff. Stuff you like to talk about. Music. Movies. Knives. Fights. You could tell me what it's like when you jump off of something and fly through the air."

Rogue could almost see it. She could almost want it.

Mac turned toward her, his expression full of something dangerous.

She jumped to her feet again. "But that won't ever happen. Don't forget you're not here in my apartment because I want you to be here. Things aren't different between us. They are what they are, so let's get on with whatever comes next, mkay?"

CHAPTER 30

*R*ogue tested the door handle in the back of the truck they were in, then rolled her eyes when it wouldn't open. No wonder they'd made her sit in the back. Window? Nope, she couldn't get it to lower, either. She bet she wasn't getting any bathroom breaks anytime soon, either. But at least she had her stuff. She'd managed to sweet talk Mac into letting her go into her bedroom alone, but only after she'd showed him that the window in it was nailed shut.

She had the pendants, she had her sister's Swiss Army knife, and her book, the knife and pendants stowed in the flat pack around her waist, the book shoved in her back pocket. She had the cash from the safe, and she had her phone, and that was it. When she got away from Mac, she'd be leaving straight from Serenity, fuck going back to Chicago. It would be hard to do without any I.D., which she'd left in her car, which was sitting in a paid parking lot in Chicago, but she would figure something out. She probably wouldn't be making it to Australia anytime soon, but if she could just get out of Illinois…

The two men in the front seat were tense, Bruin especially. She eyed the back of his earlobe and considered flicking it just for something to do, but decided against it.

She leaned forward. "Fuck, we really gotta drive back? You cops don't have a helicopter stashed somewhere?"

Mac shook his head. "No way am I ever getting on a helicopter again." He looked at Bruin. "We rode into Ella and Trevor's wedding in one. It was awful. Way worse than a plane."

He flashed a look over his shoulder at her. "Trevor is my boss at the Serenity PD. He met Ella last fall. They—"

Rogue cut him off. "What are you telling me for? I'm not your friend. And I'm not interested."

Bruin winced and looked out the passenger window. Mac shut his mouth and ground his teeth together so hard she could hear his molars squeak. Good one.

But then Mac pulled over. Right there on the side of the highway, into the breakdown lane, making them all swerve in their seats. He slammed on the brakes, threw the truck in park, got out, and ripped her door open, staring at her, his eyes accusing. "You don't want to go with me, fine! We'll go where *you* want to go. Anywhere. I'll even leave the b—Bruin behind. If that's what you want. You and me, against the world, Rogue. I'm game. I'll defy my boss, my upbringing, everything I know, and I'll go with you. You won't let me tell you why I have to do this, but I'll be damned if I let you make me feel like I'm doing something wrong anymore. This sucks that I have to do this to you, but if you weren't so goddamned stubborn, you would be with me willingly."

Her heartbeat slowed down and the rest of the world fell away, the cars whizzing by them at 70 mph nothing more than an insignificant buzzing. When she spoke, she almost didn't recognize her own voice. "You know my name."

"I do."

He didn't tell her how he knew and she didn't ask, even though she burned to know if he knew what she was. What she did. And if he still wanted her anyway.

She took in a breath and let it out before she spoke again, never breaking eye contact with him. "What if I say I'll never willingly take you with me? Not even to the grocery store."

He made a face, like she couldn't have hurt him worse, but his eyes were still harsh. "Then we're both doomed."

He slammed the door shut and went back to the driver's seat, pulling out his phone and calling someone as he put on his seatbelt and looked for a break to get back into traffic.

Someone answered on the other end of the phone, and Mac spoke, his voice tight and flat, his answers to the other person's questions clipped short.

"We're coming back."

"She's with me."

"No."

"My house. I need you to have someone board up the windows from the outside."

"Yeah, all of them. Bruin and I can watch the exits, but she's sneaky as fuck."

"No."

"Because she won't listen."

"Yeah. Ok. Tell them not to get close."

"No, he's fine. It hasn't bothered me yet."

"I don't know, maybe because he's a—because of who he is."

He sighed. "I have no fucking idea."

"Yeah, bye."

Mac hung up. For Rogue, the silence in the cab of the truck in the aftermath of that phone call was almost as painful as him calling her *sneaky as fuck*.

***

Mac pulled up in front of his house. Rogue recognized it from the day she'd followed him here. She closed her eyes, not even sure how many days ago that had been. Three? Four? Less?

Mac got out and opened her door. For a brief moment, she contemplated making him pull her out. Just complete and total disobedience on her part, but rejected it. She was pissed off at him, but if he put his hands on her, she would like it, no matter how or why it was done. She slid out and stood there, refusing to look at him.

He grabbed her elbow and steered her to the house. Fuck. His hand on her arm was warm, the connection making her hyper-aware of his big body next to hers. She almost wanted to—

No. *No!*

Up on the porch, in the front door, all three of them, and then the door locked behind them. Mac flipped on the lights right away, because, like he'd asked for, all the windows were boarded over with plywood like a hurricane was coming. Hurricane Sneaky-as-fuck.

Mac spoke, and his voice was strange, dead, like it had been in the truck when he'd been on the phone. "Like you said, you're a prisoner here, so act like it. Behave and I won't take you to jail. This will be much more comfortable."

She couldn't help herself. "Oh, so your promise is no fucking good now? Now I only get to stay out of jail if I don't try to run from you? This is fucked up, you know," she said, dropping her voice and hissing at him. "If you weren't the fucking cops, I would call the fucking cops." She shook her head and repeated herself. "This is fucked up."

"I know," he said, and he headed away from her, his shoulders tight, his being defeated.

Good. She took a look around, interested in spite of herself to see the inside of his house. It wasn't at all what she'd expected. The house itself was ordinary enough. Open living area, connected dining and kitchen area just past where she was, hallway leading, presumably, to a bedroom. Stairs leading to a basement.

But the decorating? That was completely off the wall. A large, expensive shelving unit covered most of one side of the room, it's back covered with a horribly ugly, red, spiky fabric that made her eyes hurt. On each shelf was a hodge-podge of toys, cheap toys, with not even an inch between each one. On each of the other walls of the room was more of that fabric, each cut baby-blanket size and hung on a point, diamond-shaped. She'd never seen anything like it in her life. No pictures on the walls. No other decorations. Nothing. It was like the place was a temple for ugly shit, instead of a home. It did remind her of one thing.

She walked slowly through the living area, nodding her head like it made sense, then peeked around an entry wall, then looked at Bruin, since she didn't want to look at Mac. They were both sitting at the kitchen table, like it had been a rough day and they were exhausted. "Is it in here?" she asked, pointing down the hallway.

"Is what in there?" Mac answered.

Still looking at Bruin, she answered him. "You know, the casket for the dead 80s groupie who obviously decorated this house." She frowned, then sniffed the air. "What is that? Hairspray? Is someone gonna scream through here and do a guitar solo?"

Bruin snorted, then clapped Mac on the back, almost forcing him face-first onto the table. "See!" he said, chuckling.

Rogue didn't wait for an answer or an invite. She took a slow tour through the house. Bedroom, yes, she'd already seen it from the house across the way. Another bedroom over here, completely empty. Not even a spare bed. Kitchen clean, but- yep, she opened the fridge and there wasn't a thing inside it but two bottles of ketchup, a jar of mayo, and an empty Corona box. Stellar. If they got together, their babies would starve, since neither one of them could cook and cold pizza, beer, and French fries aren't good for babies. Only adults got to poison themselves with that shit.

She froze, hand on the fridge handle. Babies? What in the actual fuck, Rogue? He's your captor, not your fucking boyfriend. At the very least, he's your arresting officer, whether he's actually arrested you or not. Close the fridge. Keep walking. Down the steps. Basement has a couch and a TV. No decorations down here, except for one picture on a spindly little end table, but it was faced toward the wall.

Mom-gorgeous, Dad-hot and obviously related to Mac, big bro about five, little sis about three. Was she looking at Mac as a child? He had been a total towhead, and absolutely adorable. And the arm he had slung around his little sis's shoulders said they'd been the best of friends. She put the picture down carefully, not wanting to know anything about him.

She looked around. What now? She didn't know exactly what Mac's plan was. Maybe keep her here until she had a change of heart? Yeah, right, she wasn't big on Stockholm Syndrome. She had to imagine there was an investigation underway in the murder of Denton Smith, even though no one had asked her about it yet. Maybe that's why she was here.

She checked the windows, but none of them were big enough to crawl out of, so no wonder she hadn't been followed by one of the men. She was about to head upstairs when she heard them talking.

"What do you *think* she would like?" Mac was whispering to Bruin.

"I don't know, what do you think? She's *your* mate."

Rogue swallowed hard at that word. She shook her head and looked around, panic setting in. She had to *get out* of here. Before she found out what that word meant. Before she bought into all of it.

But there was no way out down here unless she could tunnel through concrete.

Upstairs, Mac was speaking again. "Let's just get one of everything. One pizza. Some Chinese, one of everything on the menu, subs, Italian. What else?"

"Ooh, how about three pizzas, everything else you said, plus Thai food, burgers, and a couple of things from the Mediterranean place."

"Yeah, sounds good. She'll have to like something."

Rogue was hungry, and slightly touched that they seemed to care what she would like.

Mac spoke again and Rogue frowned at the vulnerability she heard in his voice. It sounded so out of place from what she knew of the man. "Ah, are you ok with staying here to-night? I need someone with me, but I don't trust anyone else."

Bruin sounded like he was smiling. "I'm here as long as you need me."

"Thanks, B, you really are a good friend."

Rogue couldn't resist. She bounded up the stairs, hoping they would be hugging. They weren't, but Bruin had his arm on Mac's shoulder. Good enough.

"Ah shit," she said, holding her hands up and backing down the stairs slowly. "Did I interrupt something? You two need to hang a tie on the railing or something next time. Try not to be too loud, ok? I'll take a nap or something until you're done."

She disappeared, laughing softly to herself. She was 100% for people loving whoever they wanted to, as long as everyone was a consenting adult, but she also would take any opportunity to slam Mac.

She leaned softly against the wall at the bottom of the stairs, one ear cocked to the two men above her.

Neither of them said a word for so long, she lost interest. She sat on the couch and looked around the basement.

What now?

CHAPTER 31

wo hours later, tummy full, following the men up the stairs, she watched Bruin and Mac maneuver the couch from the basement up into the living room, faces red and sweaty. They'd already brought up the TV and TV stand, and even moved that strange shelf with all the cheap little toys on it into the empty bedroom. Mac had been strange when he'd done it, tight-lipped and edgy, making her wonder what those toys were to him. They'd made her follow them around so she didn't disappear out the front door. Fun times.

"A little to the left," she told them. "No, right. Now lift it over your heads, now drop it. That's it, right on the ol' noggins."

They lowered the couch in front of the only exit left in the house. Rogue stood and walked over to them, hands on hips. "Now that just won't do. You've got every window boarded over, even the doors going to the back patio, and now you've got the couch in front of the front door? What if there's a fire? We're all gonna flash fry in here. I'm gonna call the fucking fire inspector. Or your boss. Who is your boss, anyway? How do I even know that this shit is kosher? People who are actually working within the boundaries of the law don't bring other people to their house and then board up the windows and put couches in front of the door." She looked around, exaggerating her movements. "This is really the beginnings of some fucked up cult, isn't it. You got Jim Jones stashed somewhere? Is that what's next? Am I gonna get a lecture on the benefits of cyanide mixed in with my Kool-Aid?" She rounded on him, bitch face on. "Fuck you, Princess."

Mac gave her a long-suffering look. "Why don't you go back to not talking to me?"

Oh no, he did not. Rogue let him have it. Both fucking barrels. "Seriously? You just said that shit to me when I'm locked in your fucking house like some plaything? This isn't legal, you know. Or ethical. But hey, my commentary's not welcome, so why don't you just let me go? You don't even have to take me back to Chicago. Just let me walk out the door. I won't say a fucking word. You'll never see me again. Oh? You don't want to do that? Then you're going to hear every. Thought. That. Pops. Into. My. Head. Especially if you won't like it."

She stalked off, knocking an open container of kung pao chicken off the table just cuz she felt like it, then headed back to the only bedroom with a fucking bed in it. "This is my room, and nobody better come in here or I'll slice their fucking balls off." She slammed the door.

But boredom drove her back out into the living room an hour later. She was tired, but not tired enough to let her *kidnappers* get some rest. Sure, she'd come with them willingly, in order to save her own hide, but she still didn't want to be here. She'd stay up till they let her go if she had to. Time to stir up some shit.

She found them both sitting on the couch watching something apparently called *Cake Apprentice*. All the teams had to do a scene from Rapunzel, and two had pretty decent fondant towers with flowing blond hair going, while the third team was eating spilled cake off the floor in between defeated whispers to the camera.

She found the remote next to the TV and snatched it up, then planted her butt right between the two men. Fucked if she was gonna sit on the floor. "Screw this," she said. "Let's see what else is on." She flipped through the channels, landing on Paw Patrol, then threw a look at the big guy. "This is your kind of show, isn't it, Bruno?" He bobbed his head and she snorted. "Figures." A couple more clicks and Keeping up with the Kardashians was on. Kim's face filled the screen. Rogue glanced over at Mac. "You'd do her, wouldn't you, you sick fucker, tell the truth now." Before he could respond she clicked off of it. She felt a look pass between the two men behind her head. Nice. What next?

"Ahh, Nightmare on Elm Street. I didn't know they were doing a remake." She dropped the remote onto her lap and curled her legs under her, then settled in to watch.

"Popcorn," she said, snapping her fingers at Mac, not taking her eyes off the movie.

"What?"

"Popcorn, I want popcorn."

Another look between the two men. "I don't have any popcorn."

"Then go get me some leftovers. Wontons. Something crunchy."

Mac didn't move, but before she could rip into him, Bruin shifted on the other side of the couch. When Rogue looked at him, he had his face covered and was peeking between two of his fingers at the TV. It wasn't even a super-bloody part. She looked at Mac incredulously, popping her thumb out to point at Bruin. "Is he for real?"

Mac leaned forward slightly to look at him, then settled back in his seat. "He purrs, you know."

Rogue smiled. Gossip. She could do gossip. As long as Bruin told her something about Mac at some point. "Purrs?"

"Yeah, we went to the Honey Depot, this restaurant out on 41, and as soon as we walked in, he started purring. Sounded like a lawnmower on high idle."

"Weird as shit."

Rogue turned the volume up, screams filling the room, causing Bruin's hands to tighten over his face.

She snapped her fingers at Mac again. "Food, you were getting me food."

"Turn the TV down."

"Ha, make me."

He looked at her then, strangely, pointedly, and she couldn't keep herself from glancing at him to see the exact expression on his face. It was clear as the clothes on his body. Lust. He *wanted* to make her. And he wanted her to want him to make her.

Oh shit. Her core swelled at the naughty images that flitted through her brain, blood rushing to her clit until sex was all she could think of. Not just any sex. Sex with Mac. Hard. Hot. Sweaty. Fucked up against the wall until you screamed kind of sex. She couldn't tear her eyes away from him, especially when she saw her own thoughts reflected in his gaze. He bit his lower lip, then licked his top one, their stares locked together.

He reached for her hand that was holding the remote, grabbing her by the wrist and wrenching the thing out of her hand, then turned the volume down.

Then dismissed her.

He stared at the TV as he spoke, flipping through the channels. "We're watching Cake Apprentice. It's Bruin's favorite show and he's missing it. You want food, get it yourself."

Ah fuck. Beat at her own game. Rogue clenched her legs together and squirmed in her seat, unable to think of anything but Mac, naked, holding her wrists above her head, using her body.

***

Mac hadn't heard a word the people on the show had said. His dick was pounding in his pants and all he could think about was relieving the pressure, somehow, before he did something stupid and tried to kiss Rogue. Or talk to her. Fuck, she was mean.

Don't forget the sexiest woman he'd ever met. Even mean, she did it for him. Everything about her, even her fuck-you attitude. He was a sick fucker because everything she said, even the mean shit, maybe especially the mean shit, made him want to press her up against the wall and rip her clothes off her. When she'd turned on Paw Patrol and asked Bruin if it was his favorite show? Rhen help him, he'd barely been able to keep from pulling her back to his room caveman-style.

And she was so close to him! Her normally sharp, clean scent was condensed somehow, sweeter, thick like syrup, filling his nostrils, making him too aware of her next to him. One reach and he could have a hand on her leg. One slide and that hand could be on her pussy. Even if she pulled one of those knives out of the holsters strapped on her forearms and buried it in his arm, it would still be worth it. He hadn't taken them from her, and he wouldn't, because, shit, that wasn't something you did to your mate.

He gritted his teeth and stuck his hands under his thighs. *Keep control of yourself, Mac. You have to keep control.*

But what in the hell? The cushion his leg was half on shifted slightly as she leaned over to him. *Fuck, don't pant, whatever you do, don't pant.*

Her breast brushed his arm and his eyes rolled back in his head. "I really want you to get me some food," she whispered, her face and voice soft.

He would. He would get her any of it. Carry the fridge right over here next to the couch so she could pick what she wanted without moving. He couldn't cook worth a damn, but he'd take a course. Hire a chef. Anything she wanted.

Mac shook his head. She was playing him. And he was about as playable as they came when it came to her. Fuck. How to keep himself from giving in? He still had hope in his heart that they were gonna end up together, or she wouldn't even be here, and he wanted to get her food, he really did, but not while she was playing him. And that's all she was doing. She didn't want him.

She leaned in closer, her soft skin yielding against his arm. She didn't have a bra on! He swallowed, hearing the dry click in his throat. Had she taken it off? Was it lying on his bedroom floor right now? Or had she not had one on earlier? He remembered watching her boobs move while he'd been sitting on her couch and her standing over him, but he hadn't realized she might not be wearing a bra. He licked his lips.

She leaned in closer to him. "If you don't get me some food, I'm going to ask Bruin to get me some, and if he does,

I'll be ever so grateful to him. He's handsome you know, big. I really dig that strong silent type."

Mac lost it, just fucking lost it right there. A savage growl ripped from his throat and he took Rogue's wrists in both hands, standing and yanking her up with him. He pointed at Bruin. "You get her food and I'll kick your ass, I don't give a shit how big you are."

Bruin didn't even look surprised. He held up his hands, palms out. "Food? No way. I don't even know what 'food' is."

Fuck! Mac pulled Rogue into the kitchen, trying to ignore her nearness, praying for the words to make himself clear, his hand still clamped around her wrist. "Look, Roe, you can't do that. You just can't. I know what you're doing, and I know why you're doing it, but that shit ain't smart and if you'd just listen—"

She cut him off, a finger over his lips. He clamped his tongue between his teeth to keep it in his mouth.

"My name is *Rogue*, not Roe."

Her scent was flaring so strongly, it made his eyes water. So sweet, he needed some milk. It smelled so good he had to fight from pushing her against the counter and taking her lips with his mouth, tasting her, mother-fucking *consuming* her.

He nodded. "No Roe. Fine." He narrowed his eyes and looked at her sideways. "So, what's your real name? Poppy? Begonia? Zinnia?" Anything to get him back on firm footing.

She frowned.

He tried again, ignoring the pounding in his dick. "Chrysanthemum? Basil? Blossom?"

Her face drained of its color, shock and dismay in her expression, more every time he tried again, and it was the most emotion he'd seen out of her yet that wasn't anger. He smiled just a little. "You wondering how I know it's a plant name? I'll tell you. All you have to do is ask. Or at least act like you want to know."

She pulled her wrists free from his grip. "Fuck this. And fuck you." She stalked out of the kitchen, turning back to look at him long enough to say, "I'm going to bed. Call me if you ever decide kidnapping is a bad look for you." She went down the hall, then yelled, "Oh, I forgot, it's not kidnapping when you're a cop. Cops get to do whatever the hell they please."

His bedroom door slammed.

Mac returned to the couch and plopped down heavily. This wasn't going any better now that he had her in his home. Nope. It was ten times worse.

CHAPTER 32

*H*e muted the TV and rubbed his face with his hands. "I give up, Bru. I'm gonna let her go. Maybe she's safer without me. If Khain never connects her to me, to us, maybe she won't be in danger. It'll never work between us, no matter what. She hates me."

"Nah, wolf, she likes you."

"What? Are you even here? Did you hear what she said to me? Do you see how she looks at me?"

Bruin leaned back against the couch and gave Mac an appraising look. "I've never dated a woman like Rogue." He shuddered. "But it seems to me, like that would be foreplay for her."

Mac considered. But no, she *was* more extreme than any woman he'd ever met.

Bruin went on. "You've dated women like her. Do they just fall into bed with you?"

Mac rubbed his hand over his stupid new-beard again. He still hadn't shaved that thing. "No, they like to fight first, or tease. Some of them make you excited just trying to get you to slam them around a little bit, maybe choke them."

Bruin's eyes popped open wide and so did his mouth.

Mac had to chuckle. "You've never choked a woman during sex?"

Bruin shook his head. "God, no, do they like that?"

Mac shrugged. "Some do. Some definitely don't. That's not something a male should initiate most times, but if she takes your hand and puts it on her neck, go for it. Follow her lead. Just don't do it for too long."

The look on Bruin's face told him the bear would never try it. Or probably never be with a woman who liked it.

Bruin leaned forward. "What if you accidentally kill her? How would she explain that to The Light and the angels?"

"Shit, B, I don't do it that hard!"

Bruin considered. "Mac, you know I'd help you bury a body, but not your mate's. So I don't think you should choke her anymore."

Mac slapped himself on the forehead, feeling almost normal, wondering for just a split second if the bear was playing up his innocence for Mac's benefit. Nah. "Look, bear, I haven't even kissed her. I don't know if she likes that shit or not, but I can promise you if she does, I'll never go overboard."

Bruin rubbed his own beard, mollified somewhat.

Mac looked around, then whispered, "But if she wants her ass spanked, you can bet I'm gonna do that." And fuck, his damn dick was throbbing again. At least he didn't feel like throwing himself off the roof anymore.

Bruin rolled his eyes. "Everybody's got daddy issues. I swear, Mac, why can't you have sex like normal people?"

Mac snorted. "What, normal people like you? This coming from the Build-A-Bear virgin kit."

Bruin grinned and tried not to laugh, and Mac felt damned grateful the bear was there with him. He wouldn't have been able to do this alone. Half of him was screaming that he was wrong for making her be with him if she didn't want to be, but the other half was screaming just as loud that she was in danger and he could never let her go, would die if something happened to her. And it would all be his fault, wouldn't it?

Bruin lifted his chin. "Back to Rogue. Hasn't she given you any sign at all that she likes you? Like something she can't control. We know she's got her emotions on lock-down, but can't you just *tell*?"

Mac frowned. Ordinarily he would be able to, but all Rogue's *yes* signals were immediately covered with five or six or ten *no* signals. Like, maybe she did want him a little bit, but not enough to give in to him in any way. Like maybe he wasn't quite her normal type, but she was hard up or something and she could be convinced. He frowned. He didn't want to convince her. He wanted her naked and writhing and panting underneath him, and fucking begging for it. Like she'd been in Yosemite.

But not just sex. He wanted her to look at him with admiration in her eyes. He wanted to see a smile on her face that didn't signify his balls were about to be roasted. He wanted sweetness and love. Fuck, he wanted it all, but she wouldn't even let him in a little bit.

If only her moods matched her scent, he would be golden.

Shit. Her scent. He turned to Bruin. "She... I can kind of tell how she's feeling by her scent. It changes. When she's normal, it's level and tangy, like fresh citrus trees in a field. When she's pissed, it gets strong and flat and harsh, like straight up orange oil, so concentrated you're scared to get it on your skin. But there's something else… sometimes it goes sweet and mild, like candied lemon slices." His cock swelled in his pants and he frowned at it, then looked around to see if she'd come in the room. She hadn't.

Bruin bobbed his head. "That's it. That's your indicator when she's hiding something from you. And I bet it's your key to knowing how she feels about you. You should call one of your friends. Ask them about it."

"One of my friends? Who? Trevor? Graeme? Fucking Beckett?" He could call Graeme maybe, though. They got along ok. And Crew. He and Crew had never had any major issues.

Bruin gave him a stern look. "Yes. Your friends. Treat them like your friends, like their opinions and experiences matter to you, and you might be surprised at what happens. Everyone needs help sometimes, Mac."

Mac stood and paced around the living room. "Fuck," he muttered and pulled out his phone. He dialed Graeme, but got no answer. "Shit." So he tried Crew. Still nothing. He held the phone down by his side, then jerked it to his face and dialed Trevor. They'd managed to bury their hatchet months ago. No answer. He swore. "Good thing I'm not in trouble here." He paced a bit more, then pulled up Beckett's number and hit send.

Beckett's guarded tone said he knew exactly who was calling, but he didn't know why. "What."

A smart ass comment sprang to Mac's lips but he bit it back. Calling Beckett biscuit-head would not get him any closer to where he wanted to be. "Hey, ah, Beck. How is everyone out there at Camp Fucksalot? Anybody else turn up pregnant yet?" He grimaced at Bruin and held up his hands, knowing he was messing up already.

Bruin flapped his hands in Mac's direction and nodded. *Keep going, you're doing great.*

Mac shook his head and mouthed, *I'm sucking ass.*

No, no, no, you're rocking it. Best friend ever, Bruin mouthed, shaking then nodding his head, his most serious look on his face, his eyebrows quirked together.

Mac turned away to keep from laughing. Beckett still hadn't said anything yet. "Ah, Beck? You there?"

"Do you know what time it is, Mac?"

Mac looked around. No, he absolutely did not. Hadn't even thought about it and his windows were boarded. "Ah, is it late?"

"Yeah, it's late. What the hell do you want?"

"Um, well. Can I ask you a question about your m— about Cerise?"

Beckett's tone turned hard. "What fucking question?"

"What does she smell like?"

Beckett's growl sliced through the miles between them, so strong, it made their connection go static-y.

Mac yelled to be heard over it. "Jiminy Christmas, corn-br—, I mean, ah, Beckett. I don't want your female. Look, I know you'll take a bite out of my ass if I even look at her. I got that! Can you cool it with the warning long enough to help me out. I've got a situation here."

The growl stopped, slowly, but Beckett's tone left no room for wondering if he was still pissed. "What situation?"

Mac let out a breath. He didn't want anyone to know any of this. Didn't want to admit his mate didn't want him. The guys would never let him hear the end of it. Shit.

But Beckett already knew. His tone softened a little bit. "She still giving you a hard time?"

Mac couldn't say it. Couldn't say it. But then he did. "Yeah."

"That sucks," Beckett said, and what do you know? His tone was genuine. He wasn't making fun at all.

"It does suck," Mac said, feeling the hole in his heart throb. "And, well, Bruin thinks maybe she's, well, I think that there's a chance that she's… Shit. I'm not good at this. But she smells good, you know what I mean? All tangy and sharp and clean and sweet, and I can tell when her moods are changing by her scent but her words, they just don't match her smell. So—shit. I just need to know if you know what I'm talking about."

"I do." Beckett's tone was thoughtful now. "Cerise has an underlying scent that is different than anything I can pick up from anyone else. Like it's meant just for me."

Mac nodded, knowing exactly what he was talking about. No one's scent had ever been as strong for him as his mate's was. Or as perfectly mouthwatering. "So, what does it mean when her scent goes sweet?" He thought he knew. Damn, he hoped he was right. It would change everything.

Beckett laughed and the sound grew tinny, like his phone wasn't up by his face anymore. Mac could imagine him throwing his head back. A real belly buster. Whatever. He could take it. Beckett put the phone back to his face. "I don't think you're in as much trouble with her as you think you are, Mac. If it goes sweet, that means it's time to get her in the bedroom."

"Shit. I fucking knew it. Thanks, Beck."

Hang up. A moment of thought.

And then Mac went to find his female.

CHAPTER 33

*R*ogue sat on Mac's bed, her head in her hands, her mind racing. He hadn't discovered her real name, but fuck, he would figure it out if he kept trying.

She pressed her hands against her temples, hard. She'd known for days, months maybe, that there was some kind of freak show going on here, even before she saw a man appear from nowhere. Before she'd been framed for murder. Before she'd even met Mac, this time.

Time to stop pretending she didn't know what was going on. She wasn't crazy. Werewolves existed, two of them were in the house right now, and one of them thought she was his mate. Good lord, the word made her tighten her fingers in her hair. Mate. It wasn't a word used about humans a lot, but it still conjured up images she was better off not thinking about. Mate meaning partner. Mate meaning one of a pair, mate meaning to be connected to. And let's not forget the meaning of the word that was making her heart pound. Mate meaning sex.

Urgggh. Rogue threw herself back on Mac's king-size bed, sitting alone in the corner, no headboard, just shoved against the wall, the horrible red blanket covering it. She couldn't do the whole partner, pair, marriage thing, but God knew she could fuck him. Wanted to badly. Wanted him to pull so she could push, wanted to resist so he could insist, wanted that friction that would be so explosive with him they would set the fucking house on fire.

And then all burn to death since the exits were all blocked. Hardy har har.

Heavy footsteps sounded in the hallway and she scrambled to her feet. She looked around, then grabbed the window frame and pulled herself up onto the windowsill. She'd pulled the screen out earlier, bent it, and flung it against the wall, more to piss Mac off than anything, but if he was coming in, she wanted to look like she was actively trying to get away.

She got up there just in time. The door slammed open. She froze, then held onto the wall to turn herself around, mustering up all of her anger and sexual frustration into a cold stare she could level him with.

He looked so good. Fucker was big. Handsome. Just the right bit of attitude in his face. She liked his clean-shaven face, but this scruffy, almost-beard? Made her want to stick her tongue down his throat. And he looked pissed, too, which she liked. She held back a smile.

He strode toward her, then pointed at the floor. "Down, now," he said, voice hard.

Rogue laughed, then kicked out with her foot, aiming straight for his nose. She hated to mar such a perfect face, but, man, nobody talked to her like that. She pulled the kick just a bit, not wanting to black his eyes, too. Shit, that was a mistake.

Mac caught her foot two inches before it hit his face, twisted his body, and, before she knew it, she was in the air, yanked by her leg into his arms, then slammed unceremoniously on the bed on her belly. He fell on top of her, a hot, heavy weight that scrambled her brains. He pushed her right ear into the mattress, maneuvering her head so he could whisper into her left ear.

"If I didn't like you, I would have broken your knee. Bring it, as hard as you want. I can take anything you've got. Don't forget what I am."

Fuck, double entendre much? She didn't know if he meant cop or werewolf, but her entire body was throbbing with absolute want for him. Which was going to make it that much harder to kick his ass. Damn sexy fucker.

He rolled off her, and, just before he went, she realized an erection the size of a tree trunk was pressed against her ass. Talk about unfair! Her mouth watered and he chuckled behind her like he knew exactly what she was thinking.

Rogue pushed herself off the bed and whirled to face him. She was pissed now. "I won't forget what you are, *Princess*, but don't forget that you don't know shit about me," she said, circling away from the bed. He was too big and strong to fight, and she knew he'd trained to counter any move she could make. So how to fight smarter?

"You get bored butt-fucking your buddy?" she said from a fighting stance, just searching for something, anything that would get a rise out of him. "Did you decide it's time to make me pay for my room and board with my body? Maybe I'm a little easier to hold down?"

Mac came in slowly, more controlled than she thought

he would be. No rage on his face, only a thick determination. He stepped right in the half-circle of her arms and pressed up against her until she had to take a step back. Shit. Her ass was against the wall, and he just kept coming, till every inch of him was against every inch of her, his face bent, his mouth open slightly. She could smell wintergreen on his breath, like maybe he'd brushed his teeth before he came in.

His voice was low, controlled, deadly. A sexy rasp that made her want to say yes to everything. Just hand herself over to him. But she never would. She'd die fighting. She had to force herself to listen to his words, not just watch his lips move, watch that slick tongue work in his mouth. "I've never forced a woman, and I never will. Never had sex with a male, but if I were going to, Bruin might be my first choice. He's a good guy. You could stand to be a little more sensitive, you know, but I won't hold that against you. My mouth gets away from me sometimes, too."

Rogue took a deep breath, made her decision, and put her arms around him without a word.

***

Mac smelled her scent flare sweet, then tangy, then sweet, then flat, then sweeter than he'd ever smelled it. He just knew if he got his fingers inside her, she'd be drenched. Fuuuuck, he wanted her more than he'd ever wanted anything in his life. Wanted inside that hot, grasping pussy. He would give her anything she wanted, if she would just admit she wanted him, too. Just give him the smallest sign. Just give a little. Sigh, smile, offer up her neck or her lips for a kiss. Anything.

Her arms went around him and he relaxed slightly… until he heard the snick of her blade out of its holster and felt cold steel press against the opening of his ear. He could see the pulse point at her neck, beating fast, belying the deadly control she had over her voice and her muscles. Fuck, she was stubborn. Fuck, he liked it way more than was good for him.

He pressed in closer to her, until his mouth was less than a half inch from hers. "Go ahead, because another hole in my head is the only thing that's going to convince me that you don't want me as much as I want you." The knife pressed in farther, penetrating cartilage, but her scent was so sweet and strong he knew he had her. He moved his mouth just a quarter inch closer to hers, then licked his lips. The underside of his tongue grazed her bottom lip no heavier than a butterfly kiss. "Slice me up, baby. I'll be a MacKebab for you anytime you need it." He pressed his erection against her. "And then I'm going to fuck you like you need. Hold you down, like you want. Slam into you again and again and again. Make you come until you think you're going to die from pleasure. How long's it been since a male did that for you? I bet I know. Four years, am I right?"

Her eyes were lidded, heavy, and her breath was coming fast. The knife at his ear wavered. He slid his hands onto her waist, then onto her hips, holding her in place like he'd done in the forest. Time to press his advantage. "You remember what it's like, being with me, don't you? Hot, right? All slide and glide and pawing at each other. Screaming, panting. You bite. I like to be bitten. Just one sign, Rogue, that's all you need to give me. Just a nod of your head. Or one kiss on my lips. It can be as rough and fuck-all as you want it. I'm down with all of that. But you have to tell me yes."

His words hung in the air in the closed-up room. The room he'd never considered as more than a place to sleep, but if she would just give him that yes, the place would forever be sacred to him. The room where he connected with his mate. He would decorate it in gold, or however she wanted. From the other room, what seemed like miles away, he could hear the laugh track of some sitcom play while his dick throbbed so hard in his pants he felt like the head would blow clean off if she ever put her hands on it.

The knife left his ear. Her face didn't give up anything, her expression didn't change, but her scent flared one time, like a lightning strike. She was going to say yes. She wanted to. He could tell—

Her knife sliced down the side of his face and neck, cutting a flap of skin open, while she stared coldly into his eyes. A shallow slice, so neat it was almost painless, but a slice, nonetheless. She dropped the knife to the floor, where it clattered harmlessly, his blood probably dripping off it.

He took a step back, separating his body from hers, and began to take off his clothes.

He wasn't giving up on her.

***

Rogue left her hand in the air, fingers splayed open, staring defiantly at Mac. God, she wanted him, but she didn't know how to say yes. She couldn't do it. Not when so much was at stake. She didn't know exactly what was at stake, but it had to be everything.

He stepped backwards, his face not angry, not upset, not even disappointed in her. For the first time she noticed how blue his eyes were, like the ocean on a sunny day.

He pulled his shirt over his head in one motion and her gaze went to his chest. Greek-god worthy, certainly, but not going to convince her. The spiky tattoos that climbed up his left arm and chest, winding their way up his body? Shit, just don't look at them. Damn sexy fucker. But she could resist.

She smirked. If that's what he was reduced to, she'd won, and if she wanted to fuck him later, she still could, because she'd won this battle. *If* she wanted to. Yeah, right.

But then he kicked off his boots and undid his pants and pushed them down. Nothing sexy about it. A very utilitarian act. Practical. He wasn't taking his clothes off to show her his body. Fear built in her midsection. Blood dripped down his neck onto his chest, and guilt hit her, too, along with the fear.

His erection sprang free as he dropped his underwear, stepping out of everything, kicking the clothes behind him. He took his cock in his hand and moved it out of the way so he could bend down without it poking him in the belly, the movement, again, completely utilitarian, but Rogue couldn't tear her eyes away. God, if only he would stroke it. She would pay money to watch that.

But it wasn't to be. He let go of it, then dropped to all fours, hiding all of his body but his back from her. She opened her mouth to say something smart, but his body was already rippling, his back so rigid that she could see the outline of every muscle.

Then he... changed. His back slimmed and elongated and his hips and arms slanted in a different direction, as white fur erupted from his back, covering his skin and hair completely. Rogue gasped for breath and tried to back up, only succeeding in pushing her ass against the wall, her feet sliding against the carpet.

A huge white wolf stood where Mac had been. It raised its head and made eye contact with her, yellow eyes burning. She could see Mac in its face, its attitude, its expression, even in the fiery black sword on its shoulder.

Scrambling sounded in the hall. Bruin. "Hey, Mac, why are you shifted? Is everything ok in there?"

The wolf flicked its eyes to the door and gave one deep baying bark, kind of.

"Blast, I hope that's a yes," Bruin muttered and Rogue heard his feet move away from the door.

The wolf dropped its head, and the process happened again, but in reverse. The fur sucked into the body until only flawless skin was left, his head rounded, his paws becoming arms and legs again. He stood, still naked, and stared at her and, holy fuck, the slice she'd made down his face and neck was gone. She swallowed hard, but realized she actually wasn't surprised at all.

Mac spoke. "That wasn't a yes, *pumpkin*, but I won't hold it against you. I did ask for it."

He shifted his weight and took just one step forward. "Let's try this again. We can do this all night. I fucking love this. But I need to know that you love it, too. So if you won't give me a yes, how about a no? All you have to do is say, no. One time. Say that word. I know your mouth works. Say no, and I walk away. I'll never try to kiss you again. Never try to fuck you again. Never try to make you mine again. I'll talk to my chief about letting you go about your way, see if it's possible. It will kill me dead, make me a walking shell of a man, a ghost here on Earth, but I'm not going to force myself on you, ever. Say the word, Rogue, and I'm gone. I'll leave tonight. Bruin can watch over you until I get to talk to my chief."

Rogue licked her lips. She didn't want to say it. She had to say it. She couldn't say it. She couldn't not say it. Fuck, why did he have to do this to her? But shit, here was her one chance.

She opened her mouth. Closed it. Opened it. Closed it.

Don't say it. You can do it. Tell him yes, instead. You don't always have to be strong.

Opened it. "No." Her heart screamed in her chest and her body tried to rebel, tried to spill her to the floor. She kept herself upright by sheer force of will.

Utter defeat entered his eyes but he kept his face strong. He nodded his head to her once. "Be well," he whispered, then bent and gathered his clothes.

He no longer had an erection.

CHAPTER 34

Mac pulled open the door, the whisper of it swinging on its hinges weighing a thousand pounds in his hand and his ears. What now? His life was over. His mate didn't want him. He hadn't lied when he'd said he would be a shell of a man. Because he loved her. Loved every stubborn, defiant inch of her. Loved how she smelled, how she looked, how she moved, what and who she was. But she didn't want him.

The hallway swam in front of his eyes as he plodded through it, trying to imagine what his life would be like from now on.

"Mac!" One word, and then Rogue came barreling out of the room. She launched herself onto his back, wrapped her hands around his throat and her long legs around his waist. "I didn't mean it. I take it back."

Mac backed her against the wall of the hallway, dropping

his clothes, and twisting in her grip until he was facing her. "Fuck, yeah, you didn't mean it, don't you ever do that to me again," he rasped, then covered her mouth with his, a burning, slaking thirst for her taste filling him, making him desperate. Tears spilled over his lower lids, mixing with the tears on her cheeks, as they pawed at each other. He ripped her sleeves up as his mouth covered hers and she bit and sucked at him. He tore away one knife holster, then the other, dropping them to the ground.

Her legs wrapped harder around his waist and her hips bucked underneath him. His cock hardened and pulsed, its bare skin against her clothes.

"Ah, guys, I can hear you." Bruin said from the living room.

Mac put his arms under Rogue's ass and carried her back into the bedroom, then kicked the door shut behind him. He lurched across the room and slammed his mate into the wall, still holding her under her generous ass.

"Fuck, woman, you're gonna kill me," he told her, as she clawed at his back and his head like she couldn't get enough of him, couldn't get him close enough to her.

"Maybe," she said, then slammed her mouth against his again, as they kissed like they were dying.

He set her down. "Pants off," he panted.

"You take them off," she told him, latching onto his neck with her teeth. "Mr. Big Bad Sexy-ass Wolf. You can manage that, can't you?"

"Fuuccckkk," he groaned into her mouth. "I'm gonna paddle your ass, make you nicer."

She smiled against his mouth and opened her eyes, her nails scratching his back and shoulders until she held his cheeks in her palms. "This is as nice as I get. But you could still try." Her lips met his and the kiss told him everything he needed to know.

Mac popped a claw, feeling his fangs grow in his mouth, while he kept a tight lid on his shift. Just a bit was all he needed. He pulled back from her long enough to slit her pants from waist to ankle, then grabbed her black panties at the crotch and slit them on both sides, too. He ripped them away and flung them to the floor. Now he wanted to make her scream.

"Those were expensive panties," she panted into his mouth, grabbing him by the ears and grinding his face against hers.

"From now on, you don't wear any."

"Yeah, we'll see about that."

He kissed her more, desperate to feel the slide of her tongue, the scrape of her teeth, before he could respond. "We will see about that. I know you won't listen to me, but that's good. I'll tear those fuckers off you every minute of every day if I see them on you again."

"You're buying them, then."

"Deal."

He picked her up under her ass again and leaned her into the wall, his fingers delving into her hottest spot. "Good god, Rogue, you're as wet as I knew you would be. Fuck, that's hot. I want to eat you."

She panted, her head swiveling against the wall. "No way, fuck me first. Like you did in Yosemite. Hold me up against the wall. That was the best orgasm I've ever had."

Mac grinned, feeling like the cock of the fucking walk at her admission. See? He knew his mate. He was good for her. "I can do that all fucking day." He lowered her down slightly, wishing her shirt was off, so he could get his mouth on her breasts, or even just see them, but he only had two hands. The head of his cock touched her and she squirmed, then reached between them and grabbed it, making him groan. She fed it inside her, and Mac uncurled his biceps, letting her fall fully onto it. Her head fell back against the wall. Her eyes were closed, her lips slightly parted, her hair a mess all over her face. Mac took a mental picture of his mate at her most beautiful. Now he wanted to see her screaming.

Shit, she was tight. She squirmed on him, her hands on his shoulders, pushing at him.

"Shirt," he bit out.

She whipped it over her head and dropped it, and then he had her as blessedly naked as he wanted her. If all their time could be like this, he would die a happy male.

He slid himself inside her just a bit more and she let out a moan, so he dropped her farther, until he was seated fully inside that hot sheath. "Fuck, yeah, Rogue, I've been wanting you like this since you held that knife to my neck at the rut."

Her eyes shot open and fixed on him, her stare deadly. "Did you fuck someone there?"

He grinned. "No, baby. It's just you for me, from now on. From the moment I saw you that night."

She smiled a little. "Don't call me baby. And you should have told me you were a werewolf."

He withdrew and thrust, making her moan, making himself moan, she felt so fucking good. "I'm not a werewolf. There's no such thing."

She scoffed, holding his shoulders, her nails biting into his skin. "Yeah, like I'm gonna believe anything you say. I'll talk to Bruin when we're done."

Mac growled, low and deep in his throat. "Don't play with

me, beautiful. You know that's dangerous, right?" He withdrew and thrust again, building up a rhythm.

She frowned, or tried to, but every time his cock rammed all the way into her, she had to let it go and breathe out his name, instead. "Dangerous for me?"

Faster. He used his arms, curling and lowering, to give the mind-scrambling slip, slide, and slam of each thrust more velocity. Rogue's head banged against the wall. "No, Roe, dangerous for him. So far, it's been ok, probably just because of who he is, but we're not mated yet, and I won't be safe with you around other males until we are."

She swore and her face tightened. "We *so* need to have this conversation. But I want you to make me come first. Fuck me harder."

"Shit, woman, you got a mouth on you." But he did as she asked, slamming her down on him, meeting each slam with a thrust, until a low moan started in the back of her throat, and her breathing told him she was getting close. Her head fell back on the wall, the noise a dull smack, and her fingers gripped him hard enough he knew she was breaking the skin. He leaned into her, sucking on her neck, her collarbone, taking in her scent. "That's it, Roe, come for me. Fuck yeah, come all over me. I want to watch you."

The spasms started deep inside her, clutching at him, and he gritted his teeth, giving her everything he had, staying himself. Her pleasure first. Her pleasure first. Her hips shot forward, and her elbows locked, pinning him in place, locking them together. He set his feet wider, so he could get up underneath her, continue to slam into her.

Her mouth opened and she screamed, the same scream he imagined she would make if she were kicking someone's ass. Her pussy clenched at him and he couldn't resist its pull.

He moaned and threw back his own head, holding on to her ass as her body jerked around him and his cock spilled inside her.

Spent, she went limp in his arms.

Gently, Mac walked his mate to the bed and placed her on it, then pulled out of her, and lay down next to her, trying to catch his breath, trying to believe it had actually happened.

From utter heartbreak to complete ecstasy.

He had a feeling that was only a tiny preview of what life with Rogue would be like.

CHAPTER 35

Rogue grimaced at the wetness seeping out of her. Good fucking thing she had an IUD. He hadn't even asked her. Which reminded her, she was still pissed at him. She just wasn't pretending she didn't want to fuck him anymore. Damn sexy werewolf. "Ew," she said, shifting her hips. Mac jumped up and disappeared into the bathroom, coming back with a washcloth.

He cleaned her up, smiling gently as he did so and she felt something inside her melt just a little bit. He got rid of the washcloth, then came back to lie next to her, running his fingers over the curve of her hip, his eyes drinking in her body.

She squirmed a little under his gaze. It was nice, but scary, too. She'd never had a man pay her the kind of attention he did. But then, she'd never been with a man who really knew her, either. Every man before him had known whatever persona she'd put on, not her real self.

LISA LADEW

She was touched, but she didn't know how much more she was ready for. She'd given him her body, but not her heart.

His fingers brushed her breast, then palmed it, then he leaned in for a kiss. She grabbed him by the ear and twisted it. "Talk first. Fun later."

"Ow!" He rubbed his ear. "Damn Roe, those aren't handles, you know."

"Hmph. Spill on that mated bullshit."

"It's not bullshit." He flopped over on his back. "Where to start?" he said, then was silent for a few minutes. Then he launched right into it. "Your father's an angel."

Well, that was a kick in the head. "A what? I know he's dead, but he's no angel. In fact, he would have gone in the other direction."

Mac shook his head. "No, a real angel. Like never was on Earth. Wings and everything." He lifted his hands to the ceiling, and Rogue couldn't help tracing the veins on his forearms and the tattoos on his bicep with her eyes. Damn sexy fucker. "You know. God. Heaven. All that good stuff."

She glared at him. "I don't believe in God."

He laughed. "That doesn't matter. Your father was still an angel."

"My father was a drunk and an asshole who hit my mother when I was a baby. She took off and he got arrested, so we ended up living with my aunt and uncle while my father choked on his own vomit in jail."

Mac pushed himself up on one elbow and faced her. "That wasn't your father. Either your mom thought he was or she told him he was, but your real father is a real angel who came down out of The Haven, ah, Heaven, and impregnated a ton of human women."

Rogue pursed her lips. She wanted to tell him he was a

284

crack-block with no hope, a looney-tune, a 5150, a cuckoo, a wackadoodle, but then, she'd seen him turn into a wolf before her eyes. If he was insane, so was she. "Why would an angel do that?"

He rubbed the back of his head, then pulled on his scruff. "Shit, I gotta shave this off," he said absently, rubbing his hand over it.

"Don't," she said, putting her hand on his elbow. "I like it."

His eyes lit up. "Beard it is, then. Tell me when it's too long. Ok. Why would an angel do that? It's a long story."

Fifteen minutes later, when she'd heard it all, she almost felt like she'd known it already. It hadn't seemed that strange at all. Except for the demon part. And the killing of all their females, including Mac's mother and baby sister. Damn, now she kinda understood the weird toys in the other room a little bit. He'd glossed over that part, spoken a bit like a robot, and she could tell it was a weight he still carried.

Mac ran a hand down her hip again, his eyes roving over her body. "Look. Your sisters, supposedly there's hundreds of them, or thousands, we don't know how busy your father got, but I know four of them personally. They live over at Camp Fucksalot with my packmates."

She snorted. "Camp Fucksalot? We should name this room that."

He grinned and pulled her closer to her. "So far it's only Camp Fucksonce, but we can change that real quick. But I'll need a new name for the freak-farm."

She thought for a minute. "How about Village Fucktastic."

"Sheeeit, girl, that's perfect."

She grinned at the compliment. "I know."

"So, anyway, your sisters, they all have powers that prove

they are angels. You've got something, too, I'll bet. Can you do anything… supernatural."

She twirled a bit of hair around her finger. "Well, I've been told I suck a mean dick."

"Shit, woman, don't tell me that!" But his cock stiffened in front of her eyes.

She clamped her teeth on her tongue and grinned. "Why? You don't strike me as the type who wants his women to be blushing virgins?"

He considered. "That's true. Ok, then, just don't tell me how many."

"You're safe. As long as you don't tell me how many vaginal fields you've plowed."

He shook his head no and scratched at his beard solemnly, his eyes lowered. "Not many. Not many."

She laughed and pinched his nipple. "Liar."

He nodded his head yes. "No, not me."

Rogue relaxed onto Mac's bed and let him pull her into his arms, both dismayed and delighted by how comfortable she was with him. By how perfectly they fit together.

Mac ticked out one finger. "So that's the whole story. One—you're half-angel. Two—I'm *wolfen*. Three—You were made for m—"

Rogue launched herself out of bed and stared at him, all her good feelings gone. "Wait. Wait a minute. Are you telling me that I'm a-a babymaker? That I was 'made' to give you babies?"

She wanted to pace, hit something, but she had to see his face when he answered her.

He'd gone pale. "Yes. No. Shit, I don't know." He reached out for her but she ducked away from him. "Rogue, sure we need babies, but it's about more than that. We need companionship. Love. Someone to hold."

She nodded, then turned and strode in a circle, naked and not caring. "Yeah, right. And someone to fuck until you fill her belly full of babies for the fight." She rounded on him, hands on hips. "I don't want babies."

He shrugged. "Me neither."

"Ever?"

His expression was sick. "Maybe not ever. I don't know."

Yep. She fucking knew it. "What happens if I reject this little plan, just walk away, say I don't want anything to do with it?"

His voice was soft. "To you or to me?"

"Me."

He shrugged, the most miserable movement she'd ever seen a person make. "I don't know."

"You."

He shrugged again, weaker this time, and even though the torment on his face hurt her, she didn't do anything to soothe it. He might not have thought up the baby-maker plan, but he sure as shit had gone along with it, no problem. And now he expected her to just roll over and accept what she supposedly was, like a good little girl. So convenient that there was a big, bad demon ready to snatch up all the mates if they dared to live their own lives, away from the *shiften*. Fuck, did he expect her to cook and clean, too?

She flopped on the bed and kicked him off of it with her feet. "I need some sleep. I've barely had any in days."

Mac rolled off, then stood next to the bed, like he wanted to touch her, or climb back in.

"I sleep alone," she mumbled, then turned over, facing away from him, showing him her back, scooching over and stretching out until there was no room for him.

He didn't say a word.

Neither did she.

CHAPTER 36

*M*ac woke up all at once, pushing himself off the floor, checking his bed. She was in it. She hadn't somehow disappeared in the middle of the night.

He walked over to her, quietly. She was still naked, sleeping on her right side, lovely sideboob showing under her left arm, snuggled into his pillow. In her sleep, her scent had gone quiet. Still there, but muted, hovering close to her like a blanket, instead of furling out into the room like it did when she moved, talked, teased, yelled, fucked. He could almost see it, a shimmery, light aura, holding tight to her body, keeping everything that was Rogue close to her flesh.

He longed to touch her skin. Lay a hand in her hair. But he didn't know how light of a sleeper she was, and he was loathe to wake her. He didn't blame her for her anger the night before, he just hoped they could get past it.

If she didn't want pups, they wouldn't have pups. That was no problem. The two of them would have asshole pups, anyway. They'd be the ones pushing down the human kids on the playground, stealing their candy and toys, calling them names that would make their parents huff and exclaim and talk about it for weeks.

Mac grinned at the thought, seeing a little girl, tall for her age, with an athletic build and long, soft hair, chasing the boys, rubbing their faces in mud, then flipping off any adults who tried to stop it. But then his heart clenched and he frowned, turning away from the bed, padding softly out of his room on bare feet.

He opened the door, stepped through it, then closed it quickly, because Bruin was sawing logs in his living room. The big bear sounded like he was dying. All snorrrrrk, snorrrrrt, hrrrrk, urrrkkk, both on inbreaths and outbreaths. Mac found him sitting up on the couch, remote in his hand, HGTV on the TV on mute, head straight back on the cushions, mouth open, eyes closed.

Mac kicked his feet. "Bruin, wake up."

The noise stopped at once, then Bru opened his eyes, then he picked his head up slowly and looked around. He smiled when he saw Mac. "I told you she liked you!"

"Don't celebrate yet. She's pretty pissed still."

"But-but I heard you two having sex."

Mac sunk down onto the couch. "That part was great. It was what came after. She doesn't want pups."

Bruin nodded. "Ah, and she didn't like finding out that's what she's going to be expected to do."

"Yeah."

Bruin crossed his arms over his chest. "I don't blame her. She's only twenty-five. She's got this exciting life. Been on her own since she was fourteen, it seems. You gotta give her some time to get used to the idea."

Mac tried not to sound as miserable as he felt. "I know. I'm just afraid she's gonna disappear before she gives it a chance. You didn't see her face."

"She won't go anywhere. She doesn't have to have your pups to want to be your mate. Just don't push her. You're both young. You don't need to start having pups for another fifteen years. Who knows, maybe since she's half-angel, she can have them later than most people. Everybody changes over the course of fifteen years, Mac. She may wake up to you one day and be excited about it all of a sudden."

Mac stared at the TV for a long time, not seeing the colorful pictures on it. After what seemed like a minute, but was probably much longer than that, he turned to Bruin. "You're right, bear. How'd you get to be so smart?"

Bruin grinned, showing all his teeth. "Bears think more than wolves, Mac. We're philosophers. We *get* life on a very deep level."

"Whatever, Bearistotle."

***

Rogue was up, pacing in Mac's room, feeling cranky as shit, and pissed that she was still there, even though she'd had a good orgasm and finally caught up on some sleep. So Mac was a wolf, and a cop, and he could fuck good. So what? That crap about her being *made* for him? Fuck that. No way. Not gonna happen. She was no one's oven, never would be. Kids were ok as long as they could walk and talk and reason. Babies? Shit no, not in a million years. She'd rather have a tapeworm inside her than a baby.

She had to get *out* of here. Being with Mac was cool, she liked him a lot. Especially liked how into her he was, but she needed to do it on her own terms. Somehow. She looked around at the boarded up windows and felt claustrophobia push in on her a little bit, even though that wasn't something she generally had a problem with. She would figure a way out of here, today. Her flight to Australia would be leaving without her, but that was ok. She didn't feel the need to flee the country anymore. Mac was cool, really cool, but that babymaker shit would be all the brakes she needed to keep him at arm's length. Maybe she could move to another city and he could visit sometimes. Fuck her into a stupor, then leave. Hell, yeah, the perfect long-distance relationship.

She knew exactly how she would do it, too. Talk about fucking into a stupor. She'd play all nice-nice with him, sex him up until he couldn't think, until he thought she had given in, until he passed out in the way that only a well-fucked man will, and then she'd sneak out. Somehow.

The doorbell rang and she froze, then pulled on her clothes as quickly as possible, including her flat pack around her waist, but she left the knives on the floor of the room. She made it out to the living room just as Mac was closing the door, four pizza boxes piled high in his hands.

She smiled at him, making it not too big of a smile, not too small, then flopped down on the couch they'd moved away from the door so they could get the pizza. *Yeah, I'm not that pissed at you anymore. You can trust me. No need to move this couch back.*

Mac smiled back and it was a big one. "Hi," he said.

"Hi, stud." Shit, too much, too soon. He was gonna know something was up. But no, his smile widened till it split his stupid-sexy face, his eyes going heavy. Good. That went well. *Men.*

Bruin came out of the bathroom on the other side of the house, spotted her on the couch, and headed for the table where Mac was taking the pizza. "Morning, Rogue," he said, not looking at her, carefully taking the long way around the table to be as far from her as possible.

"Morning."

Mac brought her a plate of pizza, his face still all smile-y, but his tone was careful, like she wasn't going to like what he was saying. "My chief is coming over today to ask you some questions about Denton Smith. He needs a statement from you. Nothing big."

Rogue raised her eyebrows. "Your chief? That seems a little excessive. Why can't you do it?"

"Because I'm too close to you, wouldn't be right."

Rogue raised her chin toward Bruin. "What about him?"

"He's not a cop."

She knew it. She eyed him critically. "So what are you big guy, a wrestler? A lumberjack?"

"I'm a firefighter."

"Oh." She didn't even have a smart comment for that one. Cool job.

The doorbell rang again. Mac went to answer it, a slice of deep-dish in each hand. He had to stack them on top of each other to turn the knob. Rogue held her breath. Meeting his chief made her nervous. How much did any of them really know about her? Not too much, she hoped. She'd never been arrested for anything, but she knew the Chicago Police Department had connected several of her crimes, knew they were calling her the pussycat burglar, knew most of them thought she was a woman and not a man, which meant she might be close to being caught. What she didn't know was how much the Chicago P.D. talked to the Serenity P.D. and if these officers had any suspicions about her.

The chief came in the room, looking around like he'd never been in the house before. He was tall, big like Mac and Bruin, broad through the chest, with silvering hair. It looked good on him. She would have put him at about 60, but Mac had said he was older because he still had a mate, and being happily mated let the *shiften* live longer lives than humans. When he saw her, he gave her a kind smile, but one that said he knew way more about her than she wanted him to. Super. At least it didn't look like he had any sort of a fingerprint kit with him.

"Rogue, this is Chief Lombard." Rogue frowned. Where had she heard that name before? And recently.

He stopped in front of her and she shoved pizza in her mouth, so she could appraise him without saying much, without shaking hands, without giving up anything to him. He didn't try to force the issue, his eyes shrewd.

He grabbed a chair from the kitchen table, brought it in front of her, and sat down, waiting until she was done chewing.

Fuck this. She wasn't gonna enjoy being *questioned*. She would give an interview instead. "Rex Brenwyn killed Denton Smith."

All the male eyebrows in the room raised as the three guys exchanged glances. She raised hers, too, just to be good company. When the chief was done making sure everyone else had their eyebrows raised, she snapped her fingers at him. "Oh, and he can disappear and reappear like that. Like really disappear and appear from nowhere. No Houdini-fake shit. Just poof and he's gone or there, but no smoke, just a really bad smell." More eyebrows. Another look. Her fucks to give were dwindling fast.

The chief looked back at her. "Why were you at his house?"

Crap. "I sell vacuums door to door in the summer to pay my way through college."

Mac disappeared into the kitchen and she heard a noise float out of there that sounded suspiciously like a muffled laugh. The chief sighed, like he'd already had enough of her shit. But he'd only just met her. Usually it took more time.

She went on the offensive. "You a werewolf, too?"

Eyebrow raise. Look around. Shit, she should start taking bets on how often they were gonna do that. Finally an answer. "Yes."

"I want to see you shift."

His voice was tight. "No you don't."

"Yeah, I do."

He ignored her. She hated that, but before she could get something out of her mouth, he spoke. "Let's get off Denton Smith for a second. There's something else you can tell us about. Last fall, a video was released onto the Internet that shows an older male, named Boeson, being prompted to talk about werewolves, which he does a little, but then he starts talking about something else, something super fast that didn't seem to make a lot of sense. Smaller guy. Thinning hair. You know anything about that?"

Crap. Boe. She hadn't even thought of him in a few days, but she knew these wolves wanted him, would put him in jail. She found herself suddenly thrown off her game, totally flustered at the sudden change of subject she hadn't expected. She would have rather he punched her in the face.

She dropped her plate on the couch and stood, knowing

she was about to get arrested, but not caring. Time for the wolves to show their true colors, their cop colors. "Never heard of it." She edged past him and stormed down the hall, waiting for someone to follow her.

Mac did, but when he caught her in the doorway to his room he didn't yell at her, didn't twist her arms around her back and handcuff her. Instead, he pulled her to him and held her softly. "Hey, are you ok?"

She didn't respond.

"It's cool, you don't have to answer any more questions. Chief's leaving."

Rogue pulled back and looked at him, really stared at him hard. "You're lying."

He shook his head then pulled her close again. "I'm not, Rogue. He believes you about Rex. And if you don't want to tell us about Boeson, he's not going to try to force you. We've waited this long to find out what happened to that guy, we can wait a little longer. He wants to know. We all want to know, but no one is going to force you to do anything you don't want to do."

Rogue felt herself tremble, and she hated it. "Then why am I still here?"

He didn't have an answer for that, but she could feel his body react, like she'd kicked him in the gut instead of asking a simple question.

Pressed up against him, his masculine scent was strong in her nose and she took a deep breath of it, steeling herself for what she had to say. "This will never work for us, Mac. This thing you want to have between us? It will never happen. You're the good guy, the hero. I'm…" She couldn't say it.

"Chicago's pussycat burglar?"

She froze, and her heart stopped. Her eyes opened wide and she stared at his chest. "You know?"

"Yeah. I suspected."

"Does your chief know?"

"Yeah. He doesn't care. Someone who steals from criminals is not high on our list of bad guys. In fact, if the data we have is right about you, you're more good guy than bad guy."

Ah, but she'd broken her own rule, stolen from a cop, and did it all for the money. Money she didn't even have anymore. When he found out... "Do you care?" she asked in a small voice.

"Me? Not at all. I think it's hot."

She laughed a little against his chest. "You think everything's hot."

He hugged her tighter. "With you, yeah, I do. And it's not like it has to be that big of a deal. You gotta stop, sure, you can't be with me and be doing shit like that, but—"

Rogue pulled out of his arms and peered up at him, her voice hard. "You telling me what to do already? I gotta stop? What makes you think I even want to be with you?"

"Roe—"

She cut him off and pushed him out of the doorway, slamming the door in his face and locking it. "I hate Roe!" she yelled. "My name is *Rogue*."

He didn't say a word on the other side of the door, but she could imagine him standing there, wanting to say something kind, so accepting of her stupid-baby temper tantrums. Fuck. She turned around and looked for something to kick. A stack of notebooks against one wall, near the closet. Perfect. She hauled off and kicked them hard, sending a few of them flying into the bathroom. She wanted to get back at him. Hurt him the way he kept hurting her, even if it wasn't him meaning to hurt her, but more the fucked-up circumstances that had been created around them.

One notebook landed near her, open, and as she looked down at it, she realized what it was. Perfect. She snatched it up, then turned back to the door. "I'm reading your diary!"

He didn't say a word, but the sound of his footsteps told her he was heading back down the hallway. She waited to see if he was going to run back and kick the door in but he didn't, so she dropped to the floor and pulled the notebook onto her lap.

Perfect.

CHAPTER 37

*R*ogue stared at the words on the page, not reading yet, trying to get herself under control,
dismayed at how much she really wanted to
read what he'd written. She remembered him leaning over
the book when she'd watched him from the nearby house,
peeked in on him like a peeping tom. She'd wanted to know
then what he'd written, and she wanted to know now if it had
been about her.

She shouldn't. But she would. He'd as much as given her
permission to do so.

She turned to the very last page and noted the date. Yes,
this was the right one. His handwriting was messy, more of a
scrawl, but then so was hers. She could read it well enough.

*I met her last night. I don't know her name, didn't
get a look at her face, but it doesn't even matter what she
looks like. She pulled a knife on me, but I'm sure that can*

be explained. She's perfect. She's strong. She's brash. She's quick-witted. She's tall and got a body like a runway model. But she ran from me. Fuck. I have to find her. Chief made me come home. Rest. I'll be back out in three hours. I don't know anything about her yet, and something tells me she's not a Sunday school teacher, but we'll figure all that out. If I can just find her, I'll do anything to win her, whatever it takes, and then I'll spend my life being exactly what and who she needs. She's worth it.

Oh, and it's time to straighten up. Bruin's trying to help me learn to be a better friend, and I'm going to try my damndest to listen if I'm to be mated. I'm kind of an asshole to people sometimes, and that was ok when I was young, but not anymore. I'm sure my mate will want to be friends with her sisters and their mates, and I can't have them all hating me like they do now. No more bullshit. My mate deserves a good male.

Rogue stared at the last few words for a few seconds, then read the entire passage all over again. Then again. Her chest was tight and her throat closed up strangely. She had a hard time sucking air in.

Shit.

She sat there for a few more minutes, then paged back through the notebook. It had just been started fresh, only two earlier entries, so she crawled over to the wall and grabbed another notebook. She leaned up against the wall and opened it up, starting at the very first page, staring at the entry date and did the math in her head. If he was 35 now, he would have been 15 when he wrote it.

March 12th

BFD said I have to start this diary because hitting me doesn't change anything, and running me into the ground doesn't change anything. Fuck him if he thinks I need to change. He's the big fucking dick, not me. He can't force me to show more emotion. Here's all the emotion I got. Pissed off. Hate. Hate. Hate. Hate. Fucker.

The next entry was only one word repeated fifty times.

Hate. Hate. Hate. Hate. Hate. …

The next few entries were just repeats on the theme, except every once in a while the word fucker was thrown in to switch things up.

Fucker. Fucker. Fucker. Fucker. …

Rogue frowned, wondering why, as an adult, Mac still did something that had started off so badly for him. And who was BFD. A teacher at some messed-up military school?

March 23

I shaved 0.2 seconds off my shifting time. Another fifth of a second, and I'll be the fastest one here. Danger helps. I got sliced up pretty good, but it worked.

Shit. No wonder he'd never flinched when she cut him. Guilt flooded her, whispering how bad of a person she was.

March 24

Whatever. Whatever. Whatever. Whatever. …

March 25.

BFD read this POS journal and beat my ass, but he called it 'taking me to task' like he always does. I swear on my life that I will never, ever do that. I'll always say what I mean, no matter what other people think. I hate you, you stupid cat fucker. You do the stupidest shit I ever heard in my life. You say I didn't learn anything, but you sure did, didn't you? You learned I can't be cowed. I'll never let you get to me.

Rogue frowned deeper. He'd been beaten? In school?

March 26 through April 14 were all repeats of the word *hate* repeated fifty times.

April 15.

BFD hasn't checked this journal in three weeks. I guess we know who won that round. Moo, motherfucker.

April 20

BFD has turned me into a fucking leper. Anyone who talks to me gets extra work, extra pushups, extra discipline. Everyone's scared to even look at me. Babies. Brown-nosers. I don't need any friends anyway. I do just fucking fine by myself.

April 24

I figured out what gets BFD's goat the most. He hates being called nicknames. I slipped up, called him BFD to his face, and he lost it. Punched me right in the head. Knocked me out and everything. He got in trouble for it. They can work us over in the chest and gut, but no face shots. Fuck that. If I can get him to hit me one more time, he's out. Fired, I hope. I got that from the head of the war camps himself. Gotta think of what might bother him the most. Girls' names, maybe. Princess. Mi'Lady. Chicken-head. Cat-lover. Meow mix. I'll think of something.

Rogue stared at the word Princess. He'd never reacted once when she'd called him that. He was smooth. And he'd seen all her shit before. Done it.

The next second had her sucking in a breath.

May 2

I met a girl today.

I found some tunnels under the camp that should probably be closed off, they're old and unused, maze-like, and maybe forgotten, but I figured I'd follow them anyway. If I could get off-camp without BFD knowing how, that'd really piss him off. I ended up in another part of the forest, at a beach volleyball camp, probably about two miles away.

Her name is Sandra. She's as tall as me, maybe an inch taller. And those legs, shit, they were three miles long. Went on forever. Even her braces were hot. I mean, all the girls there were hot, but she was easily the hottest. I told her I lost my number, could I have hers? She scowled at me and hit her volleyball at my head. But she kept looking at me. I even got a smile and her name out of her. Fuck, I gotta see her again.

May 5

Finally got away from BFD. The fucker is watching me 24/7. I swear he'd climb into my cot at night while I slept if he could.

Saw Sandra. I told her she was so beautiful she made me forget my pickup line. She giggled and let me play volleyball with her. Gotta think of better lines.

Rogue kept reading, fascinated by teenage Mac and his first crush, and a little scared to see where it ended up. Obviously they weren't still together, but had he loved her?

May 6

Ok, I heard someone else say this one worked for him so I gave it a try on Sandra when I got out there last night. Did you read Dr. Seuss as a kid? Because green eggs and—damn! I've got better ones but thought I'd try it. It worked. She let me sneak a kiss. Fuck me, it was hot. I think I'm in love.

May 9

Shit. I fucking hate bureaucracy. I hate that we are all fucking helpless until we are big enough to get a job and beat someone's ass if they try to force us to do something. I found a lost little girl in the tunnels today, when I was skipping class to go see Sandra, and of course I didn't have any options but to turn her over to the camps. I know they'll dynamite the tunnels closed now, but that doesn't matter at all. What's worse is that the little girl had to go home, had to go back with her aunt and her uncle who were absolute shits to her. Why couldn't anyone else see it? Fuck. Life is just not fair sometimes.

Rogue froze. Absolutely froze, her skin prickling, her hair standing on end. Even the long hairs on her head. A memory, long-buried, long-denied, rose in her mind. One of the most traumatic events in her life, especially when she used to lay in the dark and imagine her sister lost in the tunnel, with spiders crawling all over her. That's why she'd gone down there in the first place. Looking for Amara. That was the only thing that could have dragged her underground.

No way. No fucking way. It could not be. Could it? She kept reading, her eyes skipping over the doodle that covered most of the rest of the page, right to the next words.

Sandra said she'd meet me by the boat dock, but she could only wait till midnight. BFD was determined to stay awake and catch me sneaking out, so I snuck some laxatives into his coffee and hit the tunnel while he was stuck in the bathroom. It's always worth getting punched around to see Sandra. Especially if he hits me in the face.

But I didn't see her. I was about halfway there, running hard, when something made me stop. A noise in the tunnel. I followed it, and eventually I figured out it was someone crying. It sounded like a little girl who was scared out of her mind. I called out to her, and she got really quiet, like she was scared of me, but then I didn't need to hear her to find her. I could smell her clearly, a biting, pungent smell that I eventually realized was absolute terror.

I rounded a corner and found her, holed up in the very cen- ter of a small room off the main tunnel. She had no light, and my light was off, so it was pitch black, and I could more smell her than see her, knew she was curled up in a little ball, her hands around her knees, rocking back and forth as she talked to herself. "It's ok, Rogue," she said. "You can do it. Just try again. The spiders can't hurt you. They are little and you are big. You can smash them. You'll find your way out this time. You just have to get up and walk."

Rogue scrambled to her feet, walking around the room in tight little circles, her skin crawling, her spine tingling. She might have died in that tunnel if Mac hadn't found her.

Mac. Found her. When she was five. Saved her. Shit. Shit! There really was more at work here than she knew or had been able to admit, but if she didn't face that now, she was stupid. It seemed like her life *had* been leading her to this male, even if it had taken a roundabout way to get there.

She lifted her head and stared at the closed door that separated her from Mac. Soul mate? Mate? Destiny? She didn't believe in that, but should she? Was it time to change, at least a little?

Her mind crawled over that experience, underground in the tunnel, spiders everywhere, examining it fully for the first time in almost two decades.

Shit.

CHAPTER 38

$\mathcal{M}$ ac sat on the couch, scratching the stupid, itchy beard. Rogue liked it, so he'd never shave the damn thing off unless she wanted him to, but damn, could it just stop itching already?

Bruin offered him another slice of pizza from across the room. Mac shook his head. All he could do was wonder what Roe was thinking back there. In his room, reading his notebooks. He couldn't even remember everything that he'd written in them. He hoped it wasn't too much about other women. But she wanted to read them, and he had nothing to hide from her. Never would. Bruin said he allowed himself five lies in a relationship, but Mac swore he would never, ever lie to Rogue. No matter what. The only way he had even a chance with her was if he was the best possible mate he could be. No slip-ups. No fuck-ups.

His bedroom door opened, and Mac froze. Shit, was he

about to get reamed? He looked wildly at Bruin then waited for his mate to come to him. Waited to hear what she was pissed off about now.

But when she appeared in front of him, her face was soft. She climbed right into his lap, straddling him, then cradled his face in her hands, a soft smile on her face as she stared at him. "Is that how you knew my name? Because you remembered me, then looked it up in your diary?"

He nodded, holding his breath. She shook her head, just a little, from side to side. "I'm glad you came for me that day. I was terrified until you showed up. I really hate being underground."

His fingers crept to her hips and he grasped her to him, his cock swelling in his pants at her nearness. Mindless idiot. But she didn't seem to mind. She shifted to get closer to him. "I just wish I could have done more for you," he said.

She lifted one shoulder. "You were just a kid, too. Not your fault."

She leaned in and kissed him, but this time it wasn't the frenzied, frantic kiss they'd shared before. It was soft, sweet, half-promise, half-statement. A gentle meeting of lips and tongues that said, *This thing between us, maybe it could work, let's give it a shot.*

Her arms crept around his head and she held him closer, snuggling into him, sighing into him, pouring herself into the kiss.

"Awwww," Bruin said from the dining area. "I knew you two would work it out. You're meant for each other."

Rogue stiffened slightly and Mac broke the kiss to stare into her eyes. "I was wrong before. You weren't made for me. I was made for you. If you'll just give us a chance, Rogue, I'll spend my life proving it to you. And no babies. Not unless you want them."

Her lips curled. "Who knew the big bad wolf could be so romantic."

She hadn't agreed, but when she kissed him again, he didn't care. Her mouth became more greedy, and her hips shifted over the top of him. He didn't need a written invitation. He lunged forward on the couch, bringing her with him, wrestling himself to standing with one arm underneath her ass, then both arms. He carried her down the hallway as she made him promises with her lips.

He slammed the door, and lowered his mate gently to the bed, staring in her eyes as he slipped off her pants. No panties. That got a smile out of him. She pulled her shirt over her head, then propped her heels up on the bed and waited for him to come to her. Her knife holsters weren't on her arms, either, and neither was that pack she wore around her waist. She wasn't going anywhere.

"Let me just look at you for a minute," he growled, rubbing his hands ever so lightly down her legs. Her inner thighs jumped and her hands curled into fists, but she didn't stop him. Her hair was haloed out around her head and he thought she'd never looked so beautiful. Naked and in his bed was her best look. "You're so beautiful," he rasped.

"More beautiful than Sandra?"

He nodded. "A hundred times more beautiful than her."

"What happened to her?"

He cocked a brow at her as he continued to rub his hands along the soft skin of her legs, making her flesh break out into goosebumps.

She shrugged. "I stopped reading after the tunnels. I-I felt different about reading your stuff then. Wrong."

"The next time I made it back, the camp was over. She

was gone. I never did get her number. All I knew was that she lived in Connecticut. I never saw her again."

Rogue pursed her lips, seeming half-glad, half-sad that she'd made him miss out on meeting Sandra that day. "My fault."

"Make it up to me," he growled, kneeling in front of her. "Let me make you come."

Her hands fell onto the blankets on either side of her hips. He grabbed both of them, pinning her in place with his hands, then lowering his head to her core, where she was already dripping wet, her sweet scent filling the room.

"I'm not gentle when I do this, so make sure you tell me if it's too much. I want to learn your way, how you like it."

Her hips bucked. "Not gentle sounds about right."

He latched onto her clit, creating an immediate suction he knew had to be a little bit painful, but his Rogue, she didn't seem to mind flirting with pain here and there. She screamed and her hips bucked again, making him smile, which made him lose his suction. Damn. He kissed and licked around her sweet pussy a few times, getting all up in there, imagining he could see her clit throb. Fuck, yeah, time for lunch.

He set upon her, sucking at her like she was a damn lollipop. She tasted good enough to be one, her swollen flesh slick around his mouth. With more gentle suction this time, he flicked his tongue against her, again, again, then flattened it and rubbed it up and down while she moaned and writhed. Her right hand almost got out of his grip, so he choked up on her wrists, tightening his hold on her.

"Fuck, Mac," she breathed. "You're gonna kill me."

"Maybe," he growled, then went back at it, his only goal wringing as much pleasure from her as possible. He found his rhythm, one that made her pant and make little noises that were sexy as anything he could imagine. His cock throbbed in his pants and he ignored the shit out of that fucker.

She moved her hips under his mouth, creating her own rhythm, and he countered it. Her legs clamped around his ears, her muscles tightening, as her little noises came quicker, her panting faster.

He kept his pace, never hurrying, not pushing, not rushing, trying to see her face over the planes of her body. She threw her head back against his bed, and a scream built in her throat, starting loud, getting ear-splitting, as she came all over his face. Good lord, his mate was a screamer, and he fucking loved it. He'd hand out schedules so the neighbors could clear out when he was gonna go to town on her.

Her orgasm went on and on, as Mac kept his rhythm, watching the sex-blush spread out from her belly to her breasts, up to her face, making her look even more lovely.

She collapsed, her muscles soft, her wrists limp in his grip, and he moved away from her enough that she wouldn't push him away, still breathing on her. Give her a minute to recover, then he would be right back at it.

But no, she had other plans. When his lips found her again, she wrestled one hand out of his grip and tried to grab him by the hair but it was too short, so she found an ear again and pulled him up to her mouth, her kiss just as sweet as it had been in the living room. "Take your clothes off," she panted, kissing the remnants of her desire off his face.

Shit. He was naked in 1.2 seconds, and just as quickly, she had him by the stiff cock, feeding him inside her. "I want you to fuck me," she said. "Make me come again."

"I love it when you order me around."

She smiled a little at that. *Good*, the smile said, and when her hand was out from between them and he was fully seated inside her, he took her wrists again, pushing them up over her head, holding her just above her elbows, as he went to work on her breasts, giving them the attention they hadn't gotten from him yet. He pumped into her, loving the glide of her slick flesh against his, sucking first one nipple, then the other, into his mouth, as heat spilled off both of them, coming together the same way they were coming together.

He found his rhythm again, slow, steady, wanting to stay that way so he could focus on her breasts, little more than apple size, but perfect, pert, firm, and all in his face.

"What happened to BFD?" she panted.

He frowned, letting go of her arms and propping himself up, his energy turning hard, so he pumped faster, then harder as he told her. "I got him fired. He went up to Alaska to guard a substation up there from the moose."

"He was a real shit, wasn't he?"

"Yeah," he said, frowning more, thrusting into his mate, aggression spilling inside him at the memories he hadn't thought about in years. Her eyes closed and her head lolled on the mattress, as she yelped with each of his thrusts. He dropped over her body again, staring at her. She liked it this way. "If you want it rough, Roe, all you gotta do is ask. You don't have to maneuver me," he said, ramming into her harder.

Her eyes opened halfway, the pleasure on her face obvious. "Ok. I want it rough. I want you to fuck me hard. I like it hard."

"Shit, I bet you do," he panted, thrusting, retreating, thrusting again, until she writhed underneath him, panting as hard as he was. He pulled her wrists down so he could pin them in place on one side of her with one hand, then grabbed her hip hard with his other, using his strength to give her that last extra little bit of leverage, forcing himself inside her, making her give up the moans and the noises that drove him out of his mind. Fuck, he was going to need months to figure out what kind of kinky shit she was into, maybe years. He knew he wasn't her first, but something told him he was the first that she let this side of herself show to. She probably didn't even know what she liked, beyond the simple, 'rough' and 'hard'. They could discover it together.

His heart bloomed with simple gratitude that almost floored him. She wasn't running. She was going to give them a chance. He bit his lip, staying the promises that wanted to spill from his mouth, keeping inside the declarations of love and faithfulness that were running through his head. He didn't want to do anything to ruin her quiet acceptance of their situation, didn't want to push or scare her. He would give her what she wanted, not what he needed.

He let go of her then and flipped her over, pulling out only long enough to get her on her belly, then bam, he was back inside her, one hand on her hip, his fingers digging in to the soft flesh there, the other hand gathering a fistful of her hair and pulling her head back by it.

"Oh shit," she breathed, as she came up on hands and knees, trying to ease his hold on her. But she didn't say stop, and her quiet moans thickened, telling him she loved it. Loved all of it hard, wanted to experience it any and every way he did.

He eyed the smooth spot where her neck met her shoulder and his mouth watered, his fangs lengthening. He wanted to bite her, claim her, make her his forever, but he clamped down hard on the desire. There would be plenty of time for that. No way he was going to do anything to jeopardize their current sexy truce.

Fuck, he was in for a good rest of his life.

CHAPTER 39

Mac snuck out to the kitchen naked, grabbed a handful of leftovers, then brought them back to his mate, spreading them out before her on the bed like an offering.

The edge was finally off. He'd given her five orgasms, and he'd had three himself. He could look at her naked body, cross-legged in his bed, and not pop an automatic boner. At least for a bit.

He sat down across from her, his weight on the bed making the food containers tip. She laughed, a relaxed sound that made his heart glad.

She opened a container of chicken fried rice and began to eat perfectly with the chopsticks he'd found. "Lily," she said out of nowhere, then her eyes met his and he saw intense vulnerability there. A vulnerability she'd never shown him before. He wasn't sure what kind of an admission lily was, but he was going to be very careful with it.

"Lily?"

"It's my name. My real name."

Right. Shit. He should have known that. "I like it."

"I don't. I hate it. I always hated it. My sister's name was cool. Amaranth. I called her Amara. But Lily? I mean, come on, you've got Water Lily, some stupid little plant. And it's so girly."

Mac tried not to grin. Rogue was all girl, but definitely not girly.

"My sister named me Rogue. She found it in a book. I loved it right away. It's a lot tougher than Lily. I haven't told anyone my real name in years."

"Right. Good." He hated the sadness in her voice. Mac nodded, not knowing what else to say. No one but Bruin had ever trusted him with anything before. But when he looked at her, he could tell he was doing ok. Her color was high, her face relaxed, and when their eyes met, she smiled at him, making his heart race. He smiled back.

She shifted on the bed. "Shit, I'm a little sore. Way too long since I've had sex like that."

Mac tried to grin and frown at the same time. "How long?"

She looked at him over the bit of rice she was placing delicately into her mouth, not a grain slipping off the chopsticks. She chewed slowly, making him wait for the answer, but then she grinned. "Four years."

Hell, yeah. That's what he liked to hear. "But that's not the last time you were with someone."

She watched him again as she kept eating. "You really want to know the answer to that?"

He sighed and dug around in the food, trying to find something that looked good to him. He really wanted a sandwich. "No. Tell me about your sister. It doesn't sound like she's around."

"She's not." Mac glanced up, and the pain on Rogue's face made his own chest hurt. "I haven't seen her since I was five. Don't have any idea where she is, if she's even alive."

Shit. What did he say to that? He reached out and took her hand, the one that wasn't holding the chopsticks. She gave him a sad smile, then kept eating.

When she was done, she stretched out on the bed, pulling a blanket over her. "I really am worn out. You mind if I take a nap?"

"Want me in here with you?"

"No, go pay attention to Bruin. He's lonely out there."

Mac pressed a kiss to her forehead, got dressed, and did as she'd said. She was smart, his mate.

He plopped down on the couch next to Bruin. "What are we watching?"

He looked up. "Cake Apprentice. I was thinking about ordering some food."

"Yeah, let's get subs."

"Perfect."

But before Bruin could get off the couch, he went rigid, staring straight at the wall just above the TV, his face that slack weirdness Mac had seen once before, when Bruin had told him his mate would be at the rut.

"Claim her." Bruin said. "You must claim her this day, or she dies the next."

Mac leapt to his feet, getting in front of Bruin. "What?" he all but shouted.

Bruin shook his head, his eyes narrowing as he saw Mac in his face. "What?"

Mac grabbed him by his shirt. "You just said I had to claim her or she dies."

Bruin's hands had been moving to grab Mac's fingers off of him but they froze in mid-air and he opened his eyes wide. "No."

Mac tried to shake him, but it was like shaking a brick wall. "Yes! That's what you fucking said. What does it mean?"

Bruin dropped heavily against the back of the couch, pulling out of Mac's grip, his voice sick with guilt and worry. "I don't know, Mac, I honestly have no idea."

***

Mac paced in the kitchen, Bruin standing next to him, the bear wringing his big hands.

"Mac, I think you should call someone, tell Wade. Or Trevor, tell them."

"And what are we gonna do that we're not already doing? They don't know about you anyway, so it's not like we're going to be able to convince them how serious it is. They're gonna say it doesn't mean anything, that you could be wrong." He looked at Bruin, hopeful. "You could be wrong, right?"

The big bear shook his head. "I've never been wrong, as far as I know."

"How many times have you done it?"

"Six. The first time was when I was four years old. Nobody believed me, and we all paid for it. We're all still paying for it." Bruin walked out of the room, leaving Mac to stare after him, cold fear filling his heart.

He knew one thing that had happened when Bruin had been four years old. That had been the year the females were all killed.

CHAPTER 40

Mac paced through the house, unable to concentrate on anyone or anything. They hadn't ordered more food. Neither of them had felt like eating. Bruin was sitting on the couch staring at the wall, a pile of misery. Rogue was still sleeping.

They'd gone over and over his dilemma, and he couldn't see what to do.

Claiming was special. It meant something to *shiften*. It meant everything to *shiften*, they had no greater ritual. Even a mating ceremony paled in comparison to putting your teeth in your mate. In the old days, they hadn't even done the ceremony, just the claiming was enough. You never claimed a female without her consent. But if he told Roe what it was, he was almost certain she would say she wasn't ready for it, tell him no, Mac, don't do that to me, not yet.

And then what? Bruin said if he didn't do it, she would

die, and that was completely unacceptable. He didn't know how she would die, but he wasn't going to waste time trying to figure it out. Wasn't going to let it happen, no matter what.

So if he told her and she said no, and he did it anyway, he would be claiming her without her consent. *Wolven* didn't believe in hell, but they did believe in hell on Earth, and that was one of the things that would send you there. *Shiften* males were so wired to provide for, protect, and love their mates, that doing something so important to them without their consent was completely damning to the relationship, to the male's very connection with Rhen.

So that was out. He couldn't tell her. What if he told her what Bruin had said, convinced her that Bruin had been right before, that he believed Bruin was right now. That if he didn't claim her, she would die.

He knew his mate, knew that was no guarantee that she would say, ok, do it then. She didn't like to be told what to do, hated having her hand forced, knew she was strong and capable. She might just decide she would rather fight whatever would try to kill her than submit to something like that. He could hear her argument now.

What does the claiming do?

Nothing except bind us together, as if we'd been married.

So how is that going to save my life?

I don't know.

She'd shrug and walk off. *That's stupid. We aren't doing that.*

Which meant he was left with no choice, but to claim her without even telling her what it meant. Which was its own special kind of hell.

What was he going to do?

He had no idea.

***

Rogue woke up in the dark room, listening to the quiet of the house. The guys weren't even watching TV. She didn't have any idea how long she had slept, but it had been a few hours. She felt rested, ready for more Mac. She stretched, unfurling on the bed, rubbing her limbs against the soft sheets.

She stood, pulled on some clothes, and went out in the kitchen to find her male.

He was standing by the sink, his head down, staring at the floor like he was thinking.

"Hey," she said, getting close to him. He lifted his head and snaked his arms around her waist, his mood heavy. She could fix that.

He kissed her lightly. "Hungry? We were going to order sandwiches."

She snuggled up next to him. "I'd rather have a Mac-sicle." She licked her lips, catching his eyes. They'd had rough, clawing sex half a dozen times, and she still hadn't put her mouth on that cock. She was half-starved for it.

He groaned and his fingers tightened on her back but something was still off about him. She'd fix that, make him right as rain. She pulled away from him, then lead him into the bedroom.

CHAPTER 41

*T*his time, Rogue closed the door behind them and pushed Mac down on the bed. "Clothes off," she demanded and he hurried to comply, the worry line between his eyebrows standing out in stark relief. She shed her own clothes and sat next to him on the bed for a moment, running her fingers over his forehead. "What's up?" she murmured.

"Nothing," he said, his face relaxing. He smiled at her. "Just thinking how beautiful you are." He winced slightly when he said it and she frowned, getting up off the bed, hands on her hips.

"Are you lying to me?" she said, her voice harsh. "Cuz you suck at it."

He scrambled to his feet, and even though he was still off, his cock was at full attention. It couldn't lie.

He pulled her in close. "Shit, Roe, I'm sorry. There's just a lot going on. I'm glad you're with me and I'm sorry if I seem distracted." He seemed about to say one more thing, but then he closed his mouth with a snap. His erection was between them, pushing at her.

She grabbed it. "You better not lie to me."

"No, I wouldn't." He sounded sufficiently miserable.

She twisted. "Because I'm not a sure thing, you know. You might think I'm your mate, but that doesn't mean I'm going to stick around if you turn into an ass."

He groaned, his head dropping onto her shoulder, his hips bucking forward. "I know, Roe, I know. Shit, I know that."

"Good." She pushed him up against the wall, then dropped to her knees. Her turn to have a little toy to play with. Not that it was little. She ran her hand over his erection, loving how big it was, how it had turned dark and hard from so much blood pooling there. She ran her hands over it lightly, licking her lips as just a bit of pre-cum leaked from the tip. She darted in, quick as a cat and licked it off, then looked up at her guy. His expression was intense, feral, as sexy as she'd ever seen it.

"Fuck, that's hot," he breathed.

She took him in her mouth and grinned up at him. Probably not hot, but he would still think it was. He was putty. Pudding. If she said jump, he'd do it without hesitation, and she liked that, liked pushing him to see where his limit was, and what he would do to her when she found it, caressed it, stuck a toe over it. God, he was fun, and she was falling for him, but she was almost ok with it.

For now, though—she turned her attention back to her lollipop, her plaything, tickling him, sucking at him, grabbing his balls and pulling at them until he let out a roar and jerked in her mouth. That made her smile again and it was hard to suck dick when you were smiling. *Concentrate, woman.*

Back to the matter at hand. Stroke, suck, enjoy his moans and the way his fingers tightened in her hair. He began to jerk forward like he was fucking her mouth and she held still and let him, relaxing her throat, watching him through her lashes, her eyes following the hard planes of his abs, the rounded muscles of his pecs. She curled her fingers around his thighs as he fucked her mouth with abandon, his face tight with pleasure.

But then he pulled out of her, grabbing her under the arm and slamming her on the bed. She was about to protest, but his fingers curled into her hair and pulled, and his cock rammed home, all the way up inside her, making her moan instead.

He pushed her head to the side and got up close to her ear, kissing the shell of it before he whispered to her. "I love you," he said, and before she could even think about those three words, he growled fiercely, the sound splitting the room and then he was on her, biting her neck until she knew she was bleeding, his teeth slicing through skin and muscle, clamping down on her, holding her in place while he fucked her and growled, growled and fucked her.

Rogue screamed as an orgasm the size of the planet slammed into her, making her forget herself, Mac, everything she ever was or would be. She was nothing but pleasure, rolling through space, a throbbing collection of nerves that all fired together, sending wave after wave of bliss into existence until she thought she would die and she was perfectly ok with this being her last moment.

The pleasure eased enough to let her realize she was up in the air, head brushing Mac's ceiling, the two of them in a cocoon of… some sort of wings?

Energetic wings that had erupted from her own back, wrapped around the two of them, connecting them as a unit in a way she couldn't deny, in a way that felt totally right to her.

They were deposited back onto the bed and her wings disappeared, not even pulling into her body, but just poof, gone. Her mate disengaged himself from her neck, even as his cock continued to pulse inside her. She relaxed, feeling the need for nothing more pressing than to get as close to her mate as possible, feel her skin against his, hold onto him and keep him close forever.

She drifted off to sleep again, safe and warm in his arms, not even bothering to ask him what he'd done. Because she knew, didn't she?

He'd made her his.

Forever.

CHAPTER 42

*R*ogue's eyes popped open in the dark, quiet room. She moved slightly, causing Mac, who had both an arm and a leg draped over her, to murmur in his sleep. She held still for just a moment, then eased out from under him, replacing her body with a pillow.

She stood next to the bed and stared at him, frowning and rubbing her shoulder where he'd bitten her.

I should leave him, she thought purposely. *Now, while he's sleeping.*

No resistance. Hm.

She pulled on her clothes, her boots, her knives in their holsters, and the flat pack around her waist. Nothing stopped her, not even her own mind. She opened the door and crept down the hallway, finding Bruin on the couch, sleeping sitting up, his head straight back, his closed eyes facing the ceiling, his mouth open and snoring. Lovely.

But the couch was still away from the door. She walked softly past the couch, undid the locks on the door, and pulled it open, stepping onto the porch and staring at the night beyond.

The feel of the night told her it was early morning, just before dawn and a glance at her phone told her she was right. It was cold, but not unbearably so. A lone bird chirped somewhere in the distance as if to say, "Is it time to get up yet?"

Rogue stood on Mac's porch and stared out over his neighborhood, testing her resolve. She even took a step down off his porch, before she stopped, one hand resting lightly on the railing, the other one rubbing the spot where he'd bitten her. The skin there was healed, uneven under her fingers, but flaky with her own dried blood. It had happened.

She *could* leave. Whatever he'd done the night before, it hadn't stolen herself from her. She still had her will and her mind and if she decided to go, she could go.

She curled her fingers around the cold railing and considered. Did she want to go?

No. She didn't. She wanted to be with Mac. At least for now. She wanted to change. Be a different person. See where this connection with him would take her. She'd been raised a criminal, and she was good at it, maybe the best, but that didn't mean that was the only thing she would be good at. Maybe she could be good at being someone's mate. Someone's sister. Someone's mother.

Tears stung at her eyelids and she blinked them back. Really? Mother? Shit. Maybe. She didn't have to decide right now, but, yeah, it could be on the table someday. Especially with Mac. She could see it. Adorable smart-mouth smart-ass kids who got into trouble all day long, but adored their mother as much as their father did. Shit. She'd never seen that one coming. Maybe he had scrambled her brain after all. But that could have been the sex, not the bite.

Whatever. She turned around and made her way back up the one step she'd gone down, then put her hand on the doorknob, when a fiery smell filled her nose and eyes landed on her from right behind her. She bobbed and ducked at the same time but whoever it was had anticipated that, grabbing her from behind, twisting her arm one way and her hand the other, as a ton of weight came down on her wrist. It snapped and she tried to cry out, tried to call for Mac, but a hand clapped to her mouth.

And she disappeared.

CHAPTER 43

*M*ac blinked in the darkness, wondering what had woken him. He smiled and reached out in the bed for his mate. She hadn't yelled at him or rejected him after he'd claimed her. The act had been like a drug for both of them, curling them together, him whispering to her and her making soft noises of acceptance and, dare-he-think-it, love, while he had run his fingers through her hair until she fell asleep, and then he'd let himself drift off.

His reaching hands found only pillow, and he sat up, knowing as soon as he was fully awake that she wasn't in the room.

Mother*fuck*! He shot to his feet, praying that she was out in the kitchen getting something to eat. That she hadn't left him. He wouldn't survive it if she had. He could see himself already, chasing her around the city or the country, begging her to come back to him, making a complete fool out of himself over a woman, something he'd sworn he'd never do. But she wasn't just any woman, she was his mate, his life. And he loved her. And she was supposed to love him back.

He grabbed his pants off the floor and shoved his legs into them, trying not to fall on his face as he ran out into the main part of the house to the tune of Bruin's snoring. "Rogue," he called as he went. "Where are you?"

He passed the kitchen. Empty. Only Bruin was in the living room, his head jerking up as he tried to figure out what was going on. Mac ripped the door open, looked outside, then stared at the couch they'd never moved back in front of the door. His heart compressed as he realized it didn't matter that they hadn't. Once he'd claimed her, he wouldn't have been able to keep her here against her will anymore. Even though losing her would kill him, hurting her would kill him more.

He looked at his friend. "She left me."

Bruin stood up, his face despondent. "Blast it all," he whispered. "I didn't think she would. I really thought she was gonna stick around, Mac. You deserved her and she needed you."

Mac stared out at the dark night, knowing that wasn't true. If it had been, she would still be there.

A dark form moved on the sidewalk in front of his house and he almost shouted before he realized it was a wolf. Trent, to be exact. Trent, Troy, and Harlan had been outside his house since he'd brought her home, a hedge against Khain as well as a guard to keep her from escaping. Not that it had done any good, but it didn't matter. If she wanted to go… well, she was gone.

Trent came up to the steps, sniffing furiously, then stared hard at Mac. Mac couldn't speak *ruhi*, never could, but Bruin came up behind him. "Trent says, 'Don't you smell that?'"

Mac pushed out the door. He did smell it. The *pravus.* Khain had his female? His heart soared and withered at the same time. It would mean she hadn't left him, but it also might make her dead. He couldn't live with either.

Trent whined, and ran around the side of the house, then came back with Troy and Harlan. Harlan had a phone to his ear. "Got it." He hung up and looked at Mac. "The *felen* say Khain did not cross over. So either he's figured out how to do it without them knowing, or someone else that reeks like the *pravus* was in your yard.

"Get Wade on the phone, tell him what's going on. We might… shit, just hold tight."

Mac ducked inside his house and grabbed Bruin by the shirt. "Bru, I claimed her. I did what you told me to do. Now tell me how that's going to save her life."

Bruin put his hands over Mac's and very gently removed Mac from his shirt, shaking his head. "I don't know. I told you, the message comes *through* me. It doesn't mean anything to me."

Mac paced, frantic now. He couldn't lose his female. This was what every male dreaded, and he wasn't going to be the example that said to hold them even closer.

"So, what would the claiming do? How would it help her not to die?" The word made his chest tighten until his lungs didn't work.

They were both silent for a moment, until Harlan came up to the door and pulled it open. Mac met his eyes and finally understood the male, fully and completely. Fuck, he needed to apologize for every time he'd been an ass. Every time he'd called him Old Man River or Sir Pines-a-lot.

Harlan spoke first. "If you claimed her, you might be able to sense her. To find her. Some *shiften* with especially strong bonds have been able to do that, back when, you know."

Yeah, back when there'd been someone to be mated to. Mac held his hands up like he was grasping at nothing. "How!"

Harlan shook his head. "I don't know. I never had to try."

Shit. Mac paced some more, trying to calm himself down enough to think. He ran back to his bedroom and flipped on the light. Had she left anything behind? Only the panties he'd ripped from her, and those were in the garbage already. Her sister's book? No, that wouldn't help. He threw himself on the bed and dragged the scent of her on his sheets into his nose. *Rogue, Rogue, where are you, Rogue? I need you. I can't live without you. I have to find you.*

Nothing. He collapsed onto the bed, trying not to give way to his panic. It had always been easy for him to keep a cool head, until now. Until it was so personal…

He thought of her, pulling the image of her face, her body, her mischievous smile into his mind. He drank her scent deeper into himself, remembering what it had felt like when he'd sunk his teeth into her flesh, the sweet, overpowering taste of her tangy blood on his tongue, the rock and sway of her wings lifting them into the air.

Mac remembered, and he… felt. Felt out into the world, searching for his mate, feeling his way along, until a connection was made. Until he found her. Like a magnet, his foundering mental string, made long and thin by his grasping, connected to her mental string, which was squat and close to her body. He locked on to her, something in his brain shifting, turning over, the sound of the new groove being formed loud in his head.

She was hurt. She was underground. Oh, crap, she hated being underground!

But she was still fighting.

CHAPTER 44

*M*ac sped along the rural route toward the old airport, the light bubble on the top of the truck, but no siren going. It was o-dark-thirty, and no cars were out but them and a few tractors, easily avoided. He was going 120 miles an hour. If he could keep this speed all the way to Chicago, he wouldn't even need the fucking helicopter.

Helicopter. Tin can of death. Fuck. Don't think about it. Don't even imagine it. You can do it for Rogue. Because plummeting out of the sky to a fiery death was the only thing that was going to keep him from her. He could still feel her out there, fighting, calling for him. *I'm coming, Roe,* he sent to her, as hard as he could, even though he'd never been able to speak *ruhi. Hang in there.*

He pulled into the airfield, left the truck running, and he and Bruin jumped out, as Harlan, Trent, and Troy pulled up behind them, the two wolves out before the truck even stopped, easily beating Mac and Bruin to the hangar. But all the doors were closed.

"What the fuck?" Mac yelled, swinging around to face Harlan, who had a phone pressed to his ear.

"Around the back. There's only one pilot here and he can only take three of us. Another pilot is on his way in. We've got Chicago PD standing by, waiting to provide you backup."

Mac gave orders as he ran down the long hangar. "Me, Bruin and Troy on the first bird, Trent and Harlan on the second. I don't know exactly where she is, but I'll know when we get close. You tell your pilot to talk to our pilot."

He rounded the corner of the hangar and saw the only helicopter that had blades moving lazily overhead, as a man sat in the pilot's seat, a clipboard held up to his face. He grabbed for Bruin. "Bruin, that's a fucking baby mosquito, not a helicopter."

Harlan yelled from behind them. "That's all they've got. A Robinson R44. It'll get you to Chicago in thirty minutes!"

"Motherfuck," Mac muttered under his breath. "It's smaller than one of Beckett's drones." But he kept running.

"You got this, Mac-attack!" Bruin yelled, as they headed out over the open field. Within a minute, they were at the helicopter.

"Morning, boys," the human pilot called to them. An older guy, weather-beaten face, short-cropped hair, a hard expression that said he was in charge in his helicopter, he didn't care who they were. "You the cops, I guess."

"Yeah, we gotta get to Chicago, now," Mac yelled back, standing just outside the open door, eying the rotors above them that were turning faster and faster, making him crouch.

The pilot stared at them, taking in the three big males and two big wolf-dogs. "Who's going?"

"Me, him, and him," Mac shouted, pointing everyone out.

"How much does that him way?" the pilot yelled back, pointing to Bruin.

"Bruin, how much do you weigh?"

"I don't know Mac, 340 pounds, I guess."

"340!"

"Mmhmm, and you, how much do you weigh?"

"260."

"Well, boys, the two of you can go, or one of you can go with the dog, but not all three of you. This here bird seats four only when they aren't linebacker size. I've got too much heavy equipment back there."

Fuck. Mac looked at his choices. Harlan had to stay, because Bruin wasn't a cop, and the two wolves couldn't talk. He wanted Bruin with him, but Trent or Troy would have been a better choice. Probably. Oh, fuck it. He wanted the bear. "Bruin, get in! The rest of you catch the next helicopter!"

Mac took a deep breath and swung himself in the door, locking the harness on him tight. He could do this.

***

Mac pressed his lips together, holding on to his stomach at the same time, trying not puke all over the gadgets in front of him. The last time he'd been in a helicopter, for Trevor's wedding, the flight had been less than four minutes. This one? They'd been up for twenty-five already. And there were no doors. The wind tore at him like it wanted him.

Steve, their pilot, handed him a bag, like the one you found in the back of airplane seats. So he'd heard.

Steve spoke over the intercom, and the voice came through Mac's headset. "You gotta puke, you puke in there, or you're buying me a new helicopter. Four hundred and fifty thousand dollars."

"I won't puke," Mac said, holding on to his seat, but taking the bag anyway, wishing Steve would put his hand back on the cyclic, which was the stick between his legs that controlled the speed and altitude of the helicopter. Yeah, Steve hadn't shut up since they'd climbed in the air. Mac didn't quite dare tell him to shut his piehole, because he saw something in Steve's face that said he wouldn't be opposed to putting the damn mosquito into a dive, or maybe turning the controls over to Mac... Mac shut his eyes and took a deep breath, only to rip them open again when the mosquito jerked to the right.

Bruin hadn't said a word the entire flight, but Mac didn't dare twist in his seat to see the guy. That *would* make him puke. He was probably just as worried about Rogue as Mac was.

Mac sent out the strange feelers from his mind, hard to do in the helicopter, but he gave it everything he had, searching, searching, begging to Rhen that his Roe still be alive. And she was. They were getting close.

"There's the West edge of Chicago," Steve called. "Where are we going?"

Shit, Mac didn't know. "Just keep flying, I'll tell you when I see it."

"Where are we setting down?"

Mac had no clue. Uh. "Not sure yet. On top of a-a building."

"Seriously? You guys get clearance from the FAA already?"

Ah, crap. Sure. Harlan must have been doing something on his phone, right? "Yeah."

The city slid underneath them, Mac keeping his sights on the second beating heart inside him that was like a beacon on his mate. They were getting close, the coalescing of what was moving underneath him with the line straight inside his body coming faster and faster.

"There!" he said, pointing. "Your two o'clock. Right there, that brown brick building!"

"Yeah, and where am I landing?"

"Right on top of it, Old Hoss. Right on top of it."

Steve gave him a look that said he would be happy to do it. "Pinnacle landings are the most dangerous kinds of landings there are, Sergeant. The wind can come up unpredictably, could spill us all into the street." He came over the building and spun the helicopter almost on its side so he could get a good look at the rooftop. "And that top ain't flat. Too much shit to land on. I'm gonna have to hover, and you and your friend jump out. I'll tell you when to take off your harness. The sooner you get clear, the less chance there will be of anybody getting chopped up." Steve was practically yelling now, excitement in his voice. Mac swallowed hard, but knew once he was on the ground- no, the roof, he'd never have to get in a helicopter again. He could do it. For Rogue.

His hands hovered over the latch on his harness, as he held his breath and tried to control the helicopter with the tensing of his muscles. It didn't respond at all. "Get ready," Steve called.

"Bru?"

The bear's voice came back, totally under control. "Don't worry about me, Mac. You just get yourself down."

"Harnesses off, headsets off." Steve said, as the helicopter lowered and lowered. Mac popped his, but held on to it tightly.

"Now, go, go," Steve shouted, and Mac looked out. They were hovering only inches above the roof, the helicopter barely moving in any direction. The man was a genius. Mac untangled himself from everything and jumped to the roof. He saw Bruin hit the ground on the other side, and then the helicopter was taking off again, lifting into the air, nosing forward as it hauled ass back the way they had come from.

"Fun!" Bruin called bouncing to his feet, but Mac was already moving. He could feel Rogue, way too many stories below him, pissed as hell, but hurt and flagging. He had to get to her.

CHAPTER 45

*R*ogue played dead, not moving, barely breathing, in a heap on the floor of… somewhere. The curious psychic weight that felt like a crushing inside her skull told her they were underground, which she hated. She wasn't sure how they'd gotten there, because when she'd been pulled off of Mac's porch, it had been like she'd been pulled through some sort of different world. *Pravus*, Mac had called the place where Khain lived. Kind of like Hell was how he'd described it, and that's what she'd seen as she'd fought so hard that Rex had punched her in the side of the head until she'd gone fuzzy, then slumped her over his shoulder. A gray landscape. Barren. Lots of fire. Bad smells. Not a plant, drop of water, or slice of blue to be seen anywhere. But whatever that land had been, they weren't there anymore. No, this place smelled like home. Like Earth. Like Chicago. Like… Soren's place. She took a longer breath, and the slight movement hurt her broken wrist. Oh fucking hell shit damn. She sucked in a teeny tiny breath and tried like hell not to move again.

She took stock of her body. Head? Pounding and dizzy. Wrist? Broken, like really broken, bleeding and—shit, she didn't want to even look at it, it looked so bad. Shoulder? Sore. Other than that, she felt ok. Her knife holsters were gone completely, but her pack was still around her waist.

She wasn't sure if she had passed out or not, but thought chances were good that she had, at least a little. Who knew that you had dreams when you were passed out? She'd had one. One about Mac, promising he was coming to save her. *I'm coming, Roe.* She'd never had to be saved in her life, never had anyone willing to save her before, and she didn't know how she felt about it. Scratch that. She did know. She hated it and loved it at the same time. Every day was a barrel of laughs inside Rogue's head.

She opened her eyes just a slit, to see what there was to see. White five-gallon buckets stacked floor to ceiling against a gray wall, 'Emergency Food Supply' stamped on each bucket. Lovely. A fucking prepper's paradise. How was Mac even going to begin to find her?

She tried to push to her feet but was stayed by a wave of nausea. The room spun and she slumped, trying to make it stop.

She opened her eyes again. The only other thing in her line of sight was a table covered with junk. But no, when she looked harder, slitting her eyes and concentrating, she saw wires, pieces of twisted metal, what looked like part of a discarded suitcase, some clock faces, and a shit-ton of tools. She'd watched enough primetime TV to know what she was looking at. Someone was working on a bomb. Or something they wanted to look like a bomb.

She heard a voice and knew at once it was the evil Jeff Bridges. That fucking fucker who'd punched her in the side of the head. He was gonna regret that shit. He was far from her, in another room, but coming closer.

"Believe me, brother, there's something here that you're going to want to see. Something that's going to change your mind. Just walk right past the cops. Once you're inside, you're fine. No, you don't have any choice. Your bloodline has decided for you. Yeah. See you in five. Don't do anything stupid."

He was coming closer, right up next to her. Rogue tried to curl her broken wrist underneath her body but too late, he was there. Very deliberately, he stomped on the open part, where the bone was showing. Rogue tried not to give him the satisfaction, but she screamed. She couldn't help it.

He stepped back, grinning. "Just had to make sure you were awake."

Mac's gonna kill you for that, she thought savagely, if I don't do it first. She sucked in huge lungfuls of air and hugged her broken limb to herself, knowing that she didn't have a chance of killing him like this, unless she got awfully lucky. Mac was going to have to do it.

She sucked in a breath. "You were watching me." She'd felt him, but he must have instinctually known she could. Him disappearing and made her unable to track his interest.

Rex didn't respond. "You were in that cop's house for an awfully long time. Good thing you finally came outside. I almost gave up waiting for you. What were you doing in there?"

"Playing Scrabble. America's favorite word game. We went into quintuple overtime."

He laughed and his beer belly jiggled. Lovely. "Why don't I believe you?"

"Ok, you got me. We were really playing Dungeons and

Dragons. I'm a level 20 bard. He's a level 2 barbarian. Guess who won."

Rex put his hands on his knees and bent down to stare right in her eyes, his expression nasty. He reached for her and Rogue hated that she flinched, but all he did was pull her shirt away from her "Those marks on your neck say different, *Rogue.*"

He said her name like it was stupid. She would really kill him for *that*.

"You were getting claimed, weren't you? No wonder Soren liked you. He saw something in you I didn't. You're a promised, aren't you?"

Yeah, promised to kick your ass, dickhead. Somehow.

His eyes narrowed as if he could hear her thoughts. Then he nodded. "That's what you must be. One of the angel-born, created for the *shiften*? Soren's a *shiften*, too, you know. I wonder what he could do with you." He stood up straight and walked around a bit, picking a piece of metal up from the table, then placing it back down, deep in thought. Then he faced her again. "What I really should do is take you straight to The Father. If I needed his favor, you would be perfect, but luckily I don't right now. I'll hang on to you, use you for my own ends. The big show starts in a few hours." He looked at his watch. "Your buddies over there at the SPD are all gonna have bigger things to deal with than trying to find one wayward promised." His face tightened. "If there's any of them left."

Rogue squirmed, trying to think clearly, trying to reason her way past the fog the pain was placing over her mind. A searing, jarring knowing forced its way into her head, that she was missing something, something important, that she'd heard the first time she'd eavesdropped on Rex and Soren talking. SPD. Lombard! Oh no! The sick realization of what Rex had planned slammed into Rogue like a wrecking ball.

The sound of a door opening came to both of them and Rex scrambled to get closer to her, pulling one of her own knives out of his back pocket. He moved behind her, and she saw Soren come around a corner and into the room, his silver-white hair and oversized moustache perfect, as always. His face went ashen when he saw her. "Rex, no," he said, his voice stricken.

"Don't come any closer, Soren. She's yours. I brought her for you. But you must go to The Father. You must join us."

"Not like this, Rex, never like this." He clenched his fists tight by his side and challenged his brother. "Why doesn't The Father just come and take me, if he wants me?"

Rex's voice was low. "Don't you see? If he has to come and take you, he's going to kill you. He's planning something, something big, and he won't stand for questioning anyone's loyalty. He doesn't *need* you."

Soren shook his head. "So be it. I'd rather be killed by him, than join the fight on his side. I've told you that, Rex. Why can't you accept it?"

A hand grabbed Rogue by the hair and jerked her neck back, causing her entire arm to scream in pain and her vision to swim.

"You've forced my hand," Rex snarled. "But you'll thank me for this someday. Go to him, say the words, or I kill her."

Rogue tried not to show how much she was hurting. The weight of all of her choices fell on her at once, especially as her own knife met the skin of her neck, pressing there, slicing, exactly as she'd done to Mac, making her own blood flow in a new place. She was the villain in this story, and even though there were worse ones than her, she couldn't excuse it anymore. If she lived through this, she was done. She wanted to be the hero from now on. No more stealing, no more coercing, no more dealing with bad guys like this shithead who had ahold of her hair. She was done with it all. She tried to look Soren in the eye, maybe telegraph a little bit of that to him. Maybe he could make a few different choices, too. "No, Soren, don't do it, not for me."

Soren gave her a weak smile. "I would do anything for you. Remember me like I was." He tried to wink at her, but it fell flat.

"No!" she cried, holding out her good hand. "Especially if—Are you... going to be changed?"

Soren nodded, his voice grave, as he motioned at Rex. "I think so. My brother didn't used to be like this. So completely and totally without a conscience."

Rex laughed softly, pulling her hair as his body moved.

"Maybe not," she whispered. "I know a *foxen* who has the mark on his chest, and he's a good guy. A simple guy, not evil."

Her head was yanked backwards and she let out a part scream, part sigh through gritted teeth. Rex looked at her upside down. "Boe, you've seen Boe? Where is he?"

She stared at him, willing him to believe her. Boe didn't need to be found by the likes of him. "Dead. He aged twenty years in two weeks and died in front of me."

Rex's eyes narrowed, but he gave her hair some slack so she could face forward again. He addressed Soren. "Go in the other room. If The Father crosses over, you don't want him seeing her, or she really will be dead. Hurry. He becomes more accepting of that *wolfen* with his crazy tales every day. You must become more important to The Father than he is."

Rogue squeezed her eyes closed as Soren did as he was told. He spoke in the other room so softly she couldn't hear his words, but the weight of them was heavy. The smell of dead smoke drifted in to her, and she knew he was gone.

CHAPTER 46

*I*nside Soren Brenwyn's library, Mac flung an entire shelf of books onto the floor, then gave the next shelf the same treatment. Nothing. Just bare wood, like you would expect to see. "Anything?" he called frantically over his shoulder at Bruin, who was pulling every placard and picture and trophy off the walls.

"Nothing."

"Keep looking. She's right below us. There has got to be some way to get to her."

News from the surveillance crew watching the house was that Soren had not been home for several days, but he'd showed up only a few minutes before they had, come in the house like normal, but they couldn't find him. A small search team was upstairs, checking for him there, and they were rallying the SWAT team to come in behind them, but Mac couldn't wait for any of them. He could feel Rogue below them. The bastard was hurting her.

The library was huge, and he didn't have the time or the patience for a proper search for whatever underground lair Soren had put behind the house. He had to find it, now. He stopped what he was doing, turned in a circle, and tried to look at the room as less of a library, and more of a cover. Something legitimate pasted over the top of something Brenwyn didn't want anyone to even imagine was there. If it were his place, where would he put the secret door?

Shit. He strode to the pool table in the alcove and yanked at it. Pool tables were heavy, but not that heavy. This one was bolted to the floor. "It's under here, Bru, gotta be."

Bruin turned and stared, but he'd already ripped all the pool cues and triangle off the wall. Maybe something on the table itself triggered the thing to move? Mac started pressing buttons, flinging balls onto the floor, then realized Bruin had gone perfectly still.

"Hey," Bruin said, staring hard at the full bar on the far wall. "This guy looks like a whiskey man, yes?"

Mac glanced over. Sure. Rows of whiskey. Corn whiskey, malt whiskey, grain whiskey, more. Whatever. "So what?"

"That one bottle of wine right in the middle just seems... out of place to me."

Shit. Mac ran around the bar and tried to pick it up. It didn't move. He yanked it forward like a lever. The entire pool table lifted in a smooth hydraulic motion and swung to the left. "Go, go," Mac said, as he ran for the circular staircase that had been revealed. The two of them pounded down it, Mac in front.

"Tell me you've got Presley," Mac said.

"Of course I do." The bear produced the gun and even

held it the way Mac would have held it. Mac pulled his own gun out of his holster. The bottom was still thirty feet below them, only a landing, and a door. Their footsteps pounded, echoing in the small space, but it couldn't be helped.

"Pool table's sliding back in place, Mac. Chicago PD won't even know where we've gone."

Mac didn't bother to answer. If their phones worked and they got a chance to use them, they'd tell somebody where they were, otherwise, they were going to have to deal with whatever was below here themselves. He wasn't stopping for anything. The way he felt, he could take on Khain by himself. Or die trying. Bruin would save Rogue, if it came to that. Not that he thought Khain was down here. No, hopefully the most they were dealing with was two soon-to-be-dead *foxen*.

But no, that was stupid. "Bruin, can you contact anyone in *ruhi*, tell them where we are?" He was almost at the bottom.

"Ah, I can try. But it might not work because of the distance. The only *wolfen* I'm emotionally close to is you, and that connection matters when you're not in the same room."

"Try then, but don't waste time on it. We're going in the moment we hit that landing. I'm going low, you wait for a minute, then follow. You've heard the saying, shoot first and ask questions later? That's what we're doing."

They hit the bottom, Mac wrestled with the door for only a minute, then pushed it open, gun leading the way. Rex Brenwyn stood there in a large open room, well-furnished, with paintings where windows should be. His hands were at his sides, palms facing forward, his demeanor relaxed.

Mac could feel Rogue in the next room, alive, pissed as hell, thank Rhen. He kept Rex in his sights while shooting glances along the far wall until he found the door that would lead to her. He spoke to Rex. "Stay right where you are, you piece of shit. If you so much as sneeze, I'm blowing your head off."

Bruin came in behind him and Mac told him to cover Rex, as he edged around the side wall, itching to get to Rogue. He wouldn't be able to help her until he had Rex incapacitated, though. He couldn't count on Bruin to actually shoot someone. The guy was all for fighting Khain, but Mac was almost certain his soft heart would never let him shoot anyone else.

Rex disappeared.

"Motherfuck!" Mac shouted, pointing his gun at the floor and spinning in a circle.

Rex reappeared at the far wall, laughing softly. "Might as well put your guns away, boys. I guarantee you that you won't be able to put any holes in me. Put your guns away and fight me fair. Like proper *shiften*."

The air in the room became charged, heavy, and Rex took a step toward them. Mac leveled his gun between the guy's eyes. He didn't have time for any of this shit. He squeezed off a shot with no warning, but Rex disappeared, then reappeared two feet closer. The slug plowed into a painting behind where he'd been.

"I told you," Rex snarled. "But you didn't listen, and now you're going to pay." His body jerked forward, spasming, and he began to change, his eyes on Mac the entire time. Bruin stepped close to Mac, his own gun up. *Now,* Mac tried to telegraph to Bruin, and shit, somehow it seemed to work. They both fired three shots at the shifting *foxen*.

Or where the *foxen* had been. He disappeared again, somehow knowing when they were going to shoot, or just having the reaction time of a mongoose. He reappeared, and he was three steps closer, fully shifted, and the size of a motherfucking bear, with slobbering fangs that belonged in no mammal's mouth. No, they were the fangs of a monster-sized snake, or a demon.

Bruin took a step backwards as Rex stepped toward them. "What the fuck is he?" Bruin shouted.

Mac put his gun back in his holster, slowly, calculating. There were two of them, but Rex seemed to think he had the upper hand. That was bad news. That and the fact that Rex was playing with them. Having fun with them. Giving them time to get their bearings meant he was positive he'd win a fight against the two of them.

"He's been marked by Khain, that's why he doesn't look like a fox. I'm not sure what he really is, and he's the first one I've seen in my lifetime, but I've heard that *foxen* who've been marked are as big as a bear. That disappearing shit is a new one to me, though."

Bruin put his gun away, then dropped his holster to the ground. "I'm as big as a bear, Mac. Go, find your female, I've got this."

Bruin kicked off his boots, but didn't bother taking the rest of his clothes off. Smart. Pulling shirts over your head put you at a definite disadvantage in a fight.

Rex snorted and snarled and Mac wondered if he was trying to laugh. He couldn't leave the bear to fight by himself… but Bruin was already shifting. Rex waited, letting Bruin finish the transition, before the two animals began to turn in a tight circle, always facing each other.

Go!

Mac frowned. It had been Bruin's voice. But Mac had never been able to catch *ruhi* before. Didn't matter. Figure it out later. He had to find Rogue.

He sprinted to the next room, pulling his gun out again,

passing down a short, empty hallway, then clearing the room quickly, before he saw his female, his Rogue, near a couch but not on the couch, just crumpled on the floor in a heap.

He ran to her, knelt down, touched her softly, his heart screaming at her injuries. "Oh shit, oh baby, say something."

"Don't call me baby," she whispered, then her eyes fluttered and she looked at him. "Are you really here?"

"You're ok, Roe, shit, I thought I'd lost you." There was so much blood. One puddle under her wrist where she had a compound fracture, another under her head. Was it coming out her ear?

She tried to move, then winced. "I like Roe," she said softly.

He tried to grin but it was weak. "I know you do. It's pretty, like you."

She pulled at his clothes. He could barely hear her. "Mac, I'm not ok. I think I'm dying. I'm cold, getting colder. There's something I have to tell you."

"No, Roe, you don't have to tell me. You're gonna be ok. I'll get you out of here." He started putting his hands under her hips, trying to figure out how to lift her without hurting her.

"Just listen," she said, injecting some steel in her voice. "There's a bomb at your police station. It's going to go off at ten this morning. I overheard Rex and Soren talking about it days ago, but didn't know what they meant."

And he'd thought she was going to say she loved him. Motherfuck. "No, we got the bomb out."

Her fingers clutched at him. A great roar sounded from the other room, then a thunk like a baseball bat hitting a wooden wall. Ah shit, the bear. But Roe...

"No, Mac, that was a decoy, so you would think the

349

danger was past. There's another bomb. It's going to go off at ten. You have to…"

Her eyes slipped closed and Mac's heart seized.

Bruin's voice, in his head. Out of breath. *The pendant. Tell her to use the pendant.*

"Roe, Roe, baby, you gotta stay with me here." He couldn't even apply pressure at her wrist because of the open fracture. His fingers dug around at her neck until he found a wound there. He whipped his shirt over his head and pressed it against there, frantically whispering her name. She didn't respond.

Shit. He balled up the shirt and shoved it between her neck and the floor, then began to search her body. Nothing in her pockets. Around her waist. Her pack. He unzipped it and felt around inside, then drew out two bundles of cloth. He found the ends of the cloth and pulled and out spilled a pendant, much like the ones he knew the other mates had. He held it up to her body, passing it over her, touching her with it, not knowing what it could do, if it could do anything. "Heal her, *fix* her."

Nothing happened. Motherfuck. Tears spilled from his eyes, but he didn't notice them. He curled the pendant in his hand, getting up close to Rogue, pressing his front against her back. "Take us out of here," he whispered to it. "Please, take her to the hospital." Nothing. "Do something!" he pleaded, but nothing happened.

Mac stared at it, thinking hard, as great thuds and ripping noises came from the other room. Another roar, then a louder one.

Mac snatched up Rogue's hand, her good one, and placed the pendant in her palm, then curled her fingers around it. For good measure, he swiped a finger full of her blood from the floor and painted it across the angel's face. He bent her arm and placed the pendant against her heart, then got his mouth right up next to it. "If you don't do something, she's going to die."

The pendant began to glow. He could see the light through her fingers. "Yes, yes, that's it. Bring us help, take us out of here, something. Heal her, I don't care what you do, but do something now!"

The pendant glowed.

Nothing changed.

The glowing stopped.

Mac bent to his mate, more tears spilling from his eyes. He would have to risk moving her. Have to lift her and carry her up those stairs. He put an arm under her knees, then juggled her shoulders, trying to get his arm under her back, praying she was still breathing, but not willing to take the time to check.

A noise sounded in the room behind him, almost a popping. He jerked his head to the rear, knowing if it was Khain or another *foxen*, she was dead.

Graeme's dragon stood there, a pendant wrapped around one claw. Mac had never been so happy to see anyone in his life.

"Graeme," Mac cried out. "She's hurt. You gotta help her. But first you have to tell Wade there's a bomb at the station. Another one, set to go off soon. Everyone has to get out!"

The dragon stood stock-still for a few moments, then nodded once, then stepped forward, shrinking as he did so, until he was the size of a large dog. Or a wolf. He bit open his own front leg, then moved so he could hold the wound over Rogue's mouth, dripping dark blood inside.

When the first drop hit Rogue's tongue, her body jerked like she'd been hit with a shot of electricity.

Mac held her head, holding pressure on her neck. "Come back to me, Roe, hang in there. You've got to come back to me, baby."

Another drop, and another. Rogue's eyes shot open and she grabbed the leg so close to her mouth with her free hand, levering her body up to it, closing her mouth over the wound, sucking hard, even as her eyes stared at the dragon, clear fear settling in there.

"Oh shit," Mac breathed.

Stop!

Graeme's voice, booming. *Too much will harm you.* He pulled his front leg away from Rogue, but she came with it, unwilling to stop.

"Roe," Mac called sharply, sticking his finger in the side of her mouth to break the suction. "He said too much isn't good. Stop."

Graeme looked at him strangely. *You hear me?*

Mac shot him a look, just as surprised as he was. "Yeah, shit, I guess so. That's new."

Twin bellows came from the other room, as something slammed into the wall between the two rooms hard enough to make the wall of emergency food buckets lurch forward, before settling back again.

Who is in there?

"Bruin. He's fighting a marked *foxen.*"

We must move fast. Check her neck. It may have healed already, but you must set her arm, or it will nae close. The bone is out.

Mac pulled away his shirt and ran his fingers over Rogue's neck. Unbroken. She licked blood from her lips and her eyes rolled in her skull.

"Dragon," Rogue whispered.

"Yeah, he's a friend. Relax, we've got you."

Mac scrambled to the other side of Rogue and took her hand in his, expecting her to scream, but she didn't even look. Her big eyes were focused on the dragon.

"Rogue, I'm going to pull. You hang in there."

"Go for it." Her voice was strong, but quiet.

It may not hurt her, Mac. Do it. She has much dragon blood in her.

Mac did it. He pulled and Rogue's bone went back where it was supposed to be. Rogue didn't even whimper, like she hadn't felt a thing.

Graeme moved his front leg over the wound, while Rogue watched the two of them, something like awe on her face.

Squeeze out more blood onto her wound. Just a drop.

Mac gripped Graeme's leg and did as he'd been told. As soon as the blood landed, Rogue's wound knit before his eyes.

Something bellowed in pain in the other room, and sounds of crashing came to them.

"Bruin, he needs help," Mac said.

Graeme shot upright and ran the short hallway between the two rooms, then came back.

Bruin is holding his own. Let's get you both out of here and then I'll come back and help Bruin finish off that foxen.

He inclined his wing. *Take the pendant from me. I don't need it now and we musn't lose it.*

Mac jumped to his feet to grab the chain and pull it off Graeme's claw. Rogue pushed herself to a sitting position, still looking dazed, still staring at Graeme like she was a Belieber and he was the Beebs himself.

Is one of those hers? He motioned to the pendant on her lap and the one spilled out on the floor, still partially wrapped in cloth.

"Rogue, Graeme wants to know if that's yours."

She shook her head no, never taking her eyes off the dragon.

Tell her the ride will be bumpy, but the pendant will still take her where she wants to go. Tell her to hold it in her hand and imagine the place, then tell the pendant to take her there.

"Does she need to go to the hospital?"

Nay.

Mac repeated Graeme's instructions, then picked up the pendant and held it out to her, tucking the other two into her pack. Rogue seemed dazed. Not herself. Maybe disbelieving.

"Rogue, did you hear me? You've got to get out of here. Where do you want to go?"

Rogue licked her lips and looked down at it, nervousness flooding into her expression. "This shit is whacked, all of it," she whispered, then looked up at Mac, her face shining, her cheeks rosy with health that made him want to cry for the first time in decades. "I want to go to the happiest place on Earth, my version of Disneyland. Take me to Mac's bed."

And she was gone, winked out of existence like the *foxen*.

CHAPTER 47

Mac flopped over on his back in his bed and groaned, long and loud. "That was it, woman. I can't do it again. You took too much dragon blood and now you literally are going to kill me with sex. I gotta stretch. Fuck that, get me to a chiropractor."

Rogue pushed herself up on her elbows and eyeballed him. "Hell, yeah, that was good stuff. He should bottle it. Next time I see him, I'm gonna *bite* him. Get some more." She bared her teeth and mimed biting, tearing, and chewing.

Mac put a hand over his eyes. She *was* going to kill him. Sex, knives, biting Graeme. Something. "You do that, and I'll have to kill him. 'Cept he'll probably kill me instead. Bad scene all around."

Rogue pushed his hand off his face so she could see his eyes. "What? He was tiny. You could take him."

Mac groaned again. "He can grow."

"How big?"

"As big as he wants. Fifty fucking feet high, maybe. And he breathes fire. Just crisps shit right up. Barbecued wolf, coming up."

Rogue was quiet for a few moments. "Oh. I won't bite him."

"She sees reason."

Mac tried to pull a blanket over himself, but Rogue whipped it off, then poked his flaccid penis with her finger. "Wake up," she whispered.

"No! No more. It's been two days and I've gotten exactly three hours of sleep and we've had sex thirty-four times. I can't do it again, woman."

She bounced to her feet. "Ok, let's go outside, then. Run laps or something. Let's go to the park, climb some trees."

Mac pushed himself to his feet, praying the dragon blood got out of her system soon. Maybe he could take her to a climbing wall or something. Bruin could hang with her while he napped in the spectator bleachers.

It didn't matter, though, she could keep him up for the next week straight, demand anything she wanted from him, use his body like a whipping post, call him princess, he didn't care. He had his mate with him, and she wanted to be there. She'd asked to go to his home, and hadn't mentioned leaving since. She wasn't a big talker about serious stuff, his Roe, but she'd had a change of heart. It was in her expression, the sweetness of her touch, and the way she snuggled into him at every opportunity. She'd accepted him. She'd accepted who she was. She'd accepted how good they were together.

Rogue had already pulled on her clothes and headed out into the living room. He could hear her talking to Bruin.

"Hey, Bru, how's the head?"

"Good," the male said and Mac could imagine him thunking himself on his noggin with his fist. He and Rex both had such thick fur that neither of them had been able to use their teeth to do any damage, so they'd taken to ramming each other like mountain goats, trying to shatter each other's skulls or smash internal organs. They'd had to take Bruin to Remington when he'd been dizzy for the twelve hours after the fight and a few shifts hadn't helped. Concussion had been the diagnosis. Rest and no stimulating activities had been the treatment. He was all better after a Cake Apprentice marathon.

Mac pulled on his clothes and headed out to his living room, where Rogue was eating the rest of the cold pizza. She flopped down in a chair and faced Bruin. "I never got a chance to thank you."

Bruin shook his head. "Don't mention it. I just wish he hadn't gotten away from me."

Mac dropped onto the couch next to his friend. "With him being able to pop in and out of the *Pravus* like Khain, there wasn't shit you could do about it. You let me and Rogue get free, and that's more than I had hoped for. I was pretty terrified going down those steps."

Rogue and Bruin both stared at him, like he'd said he had grown a uterus and was going to start popping out pups. He scoffed. "What? I get scared. I can admit it. Everyone gets scared."

Rogue looked down at her pizza, her eyebrows sky-high. "Not me."

Bruin examined the wall, not meeting Mac's eyes. "Me neither. Blast, Mac, I don't know if we can still be friends."

Rogue smirked and Mac caught her, but she hid it quickly. "Right, Bru, we gotta start accepting applications or something. 'Badass wolf wanted for sidekick. Serious enquiries only.'"

Bruin pushed himself up from the couch and headed into the back room. "I'll get the laptop. Put it on Craigslist."

They were going to gang up on him? Not cool. Funny, but not cool. "You're the sidekick, big boy, not me."

"Keep telling yourself that." Bruin disappeared around the corner, then called out. "Oh, Wade's coming over."

"When?"

The doorbell rang.

"Now."

Rogue grabbed another slice of pizza off the table and disappeared into the kitchen. Mac watched her go, then opened the door.

Wade almost looked happy, a small smile on his face. Mac had never seen one pointed at him from the old male before. Then Wade surprised the hell out of him by sticking his hand out. "Mac, good to see you. You look good. You did good."

Mac let his hand be shaken, then backed into the room. "Ah, ok."

"Where's your mate? I need to talk to her."

"Ok then, I'll be right back."

Mac hit the kitchen, found Rogue leaning against the counter, eating her pizza, watching him warily. He pressed against her, his hands finding her hips, pulling her close. "Wade wants to talk to you," he whispered. "You cool with that?"

"Yeah." She threw her crust in the sink and wiped her hands on her pants. "Let's get it over with."

She wriggled out of his grasp and headed out to his living room, pulling a chair from the dining room table as she went. He followed. She placed the chair backwards in front of Wade, straddled it, and sat down, lifting her chin at him, her eyes narrowed. He was beginning to be able to decipher her moods, just a bit, and this one meant, *one wrong move and I'm out of here.*

Wade leaned forward, his hands on his knees. "First, thanks are in order. There was indeed a bomb inside the station, placed in the basement, directly under the duty room. The thing was huge, and it would have leveled the station and sent debris flying out into the entire block. At ten in the morning, the station would have been full of patrol officers, dispatchers, and our civilian staff, not to mention the people who live and work in the area. Because of you, we were able to evacuate everyone, and get the ATF in there quick enough to disarm the bomb and save the station and hundreds of lives. You're a hero."

Rogue's face slackened just a bit, her wary expression turning disbelieving. She glanced at Mac. He smiled at her, his heart overflowing. No wonder the chief was happy with him. He'd done good. His mate had done amazing. If she hadn't been who she was, if she hadn't broken a few laws, made a few mistakes, they'd all be in a world of hurt right now.

Wade nodded sharply. "We can talk about that more later. We'll want to recognize you, of course, but right now I only have a few minutes here. We need to talk about the pendants."

Rogue shot to her feet and held out a finger, then disappeared down the hall. Mac wasn't sure if he should follow her or not, because he was certain she had all three of the pendants in that flat pack around her waist, so she was heading to his room for something else. To compose herself? He knew she didn't like people to see her vulnerable, not even him most of the time. He stayed where he was.

Bruin came out and dropped onto the couch. "Chief."

Wade smiled at him and gave him a punch on the shoulder. "I heard you tangled with your first marked *foxen*. Gave yourself a concussion."

Bruin nodded, a grin on his face. "Yeah, that big son of a gun was no joke. I learned a few things, though. Next time, I'll chew him up."

Wade shot Mac a look and Mac could read it, even though no voice sounded in his head. He wondered if Wade had heard he could hear *ruhi* now. The look said, 'things are gonna get bad before they get worse, if Khain marks more *foxen* the way he marked Rex.'

Mac nodded. Didn't he know it. "What's to keep Rex from planting another bomb?"

"Ah. You know that smell? The smoke from the *pravus* Rex brings with him when he comes or goes? Canyon and Timber came up with something that they say can detect it. The station is completely wired. They are wiring Trevor's farm right now. We'll know if Rex shows up, even if no one sees him." Wade dropped his voice. "We're going to have to talk about where you and Rogue are going to live."

Shit. Rogue was going to hate this part, he knew it. He was going to have to convince her to move out to Fort Fuckall with the rest of the gang. "Yeah, I know. Just give me another couple of days."

Wade nodded. "Don't let her leave the house without you and Bruin. I know she's strong, and I know she can take care of herself, but you've got to make her realize how dangerous our enemies are."

"She knows, she learned that lesson." He hoped.

Rogue came back out, her face flushed prettily, three pendants dangling from her hands. Mac watched the wolves, the dragon, and the angels twirl below their chains. She gave them all to Wade.

He separated one. "This one's Heather's. Have you heard the story yet, how Graeme knew he was needed?"

Mac shook his head. Graeme had told him to shift, wrapped him in his wings, then did that funky sidestep through fucked-up firetown twice, and then he'd been in his own room, staring at his mate on his bed. Graeme had disappeared again while Mac and Rogue huddled together, waiting for word on Bruin.

Wade spoke. "Your voice, Mac. It came out of the pendants. All of them. Ella's, Heather's, Dahlia's. Gray or Khain has Cerise's so we don't know about hers, but we have to assume it came out of that one also. It woke up everyone in those households. Graeme transformed and went to you, allowing Heather's pendant to lead him."

"I owe Sparky a beer," Mac said under his breath. He wished he had something more to offer the male than smart words and loyalty. A talent. Something sentimental he could make with his own two hands and offer to the male's young. But no, all he had to offer was his life, which he now owed to anything the male loved. Of course, he'd always felt that way. He would give his life to protect any of them, even if he'd never shown it.

Wade curled his fingers around Heather's pendant, then offered the other two back to Rogue. "I know these aren't yours, but I think you should have one of them. Pick one and I'll give the other to Cerise. Until we can find who they belong to, they should be spread out amongst you. We have only begun to discover their powers."

Rogue picked one seemingly at random, no thought needed. He could tell she was happy to have it, tucking it back into her pack. To Mac's eyes, the two had looked the same, but maybe there was some difference she could see. He frowned, wondering why she didn't have a pendant of her own. He'd have to ask—

Wade stood. "I have to go. Big meeting. You three are wanted out at Trevor's place in two hours, and, if you don't go, they are all going to pack into the van and come over here. Rogue's sisters are dying to meet her."

Rogue's expression hardened, but in a different way. Mac studied her and decided she was nervous. He stood next to his mate and put an arm around her, waiting for Wade to leave so he could reassure her. "We'll be there."

Rogue stopped Wade just before he could step out the door. "If you knew where Boe was, what would you do to him?"

Wade turned back to her. "We'd question him."

"Would you hurt him?"

"No."

"Arrest him?"

Wade threw a look at Mac and Mac shrugged. The guy was important and who knew if he needed to be arrested or not.

Wade focused on Rogue again. "What if I say we'll try very hard not to, but he'll have to cooperate."

Rogue shook her head. "He's an old man. He's frail, and innocent, and gentle. He'd never hurt a fly."

Wade nodded. "I'll take that into consideration if you choose to tell me where he is."

Rogue stared over his head, out into the street, then focused and recited an address for Wade.

Wade gave her a reassuring nod. "Out of respect for you and your wishes, I promise you we will do our best to treat him well. If we can keep him where he's at, we will."

Rogue frowned for a moment, then nodded back. "Thank you," she said, then came quietly back in the house.

Mac watched Wade leave. The male was a diplomat for sure, and Mac liked how he had left things, especially what he had said.

Out of respect for you and your wishes...

CHAPTER 48

Rogue snuggled in closer to Mac in the back seat of Bruin's tiny car, feeling the need to poke at Mac, prod him, nip at his shoulder. He tightened his arm around her, trying to give her the stability she felt like she needed so bad. He never once admonished her or said, "Quit it," and she admired that about him. He knew her. She was nervous, and that meant her mouth was going to be worse than ever.

"I'm nervous," she whispered into his ear. "Sometimes I get mean when I'm nervous."

He looked at her, his lips curling. "No. Way."

She twisted his nipple. "Shut up or I'll make you fuck me again," she whispered.

He leaned back against the seat, looking content and happy. "You can't get steel out of a marshmallow, Roe."

She nipped his neck, then his earlobes. "You've got fingers, and a mouth."

He laughed at that, then kissed her full on the mouth. Her hand went to his dick through his jeans and she felt a little bit of a kick there. Hell, yeah, she was getting some when all this was over.

"I'm glad you came for me," she said, the words spilling out on their own.

He curled her body into his harder, tucking her against him as much as her seatbelt would allow. "I'll always come for you."

"I know that. You…" Shit. Why was this so freaking hard? "You-I… Ah, fuck it. I think you were right that we were made for each other."

His eyes met hers once, briefly, then looked away again, out onto the street. He obviously knew serious shit was easier on her when he wasn't looking at her. He smiled at the window. "I know I'm right." He found her hand and put it to his chest. "I feel it here every time I look at you, every time we touch. You're it for me, Rogue. I love you."

Fuck, why did he have to be so sensitive? So good at this shit, while she sucked at it? She did like hearing that, though. It made her feel safe and connected, like everything would be all right. She laid her head down on his chest and let the feeling wash over her, wondering if it could really be true. Could he really love her? Love was something she hadn't spent a lot of time considering in her life, had never had someone tell her they felt about her before. Like, she didn't even know if she would recognize it if she felt it for him. He was sweet as hell, constantly funny, sexier than anyone she'd ever known, and the man could fuck like a dream. But was that love? She didn't think so. She buttoned her lip, not wanting to say anything, glad he didn't seem to care that she didn't respond at all when he said that.

Bruin pulled into the driveway of a farmhouse. Rogue sat up straighter, tension flooding through her. Do or die time. Shit. Did she really believe those were her sisters in there? Butterflies fluttered in her stomach while some small part of her felt guilty, almost as if she were moving on from her first family, her first sister.

But she wasn't. No way. Now that she had access to a shit-load of cops, maybe they could figure something out that she had never been able to.

Mac helped her out of the car and she practically ran up to the house, ready to get it over with. Forty-five minutes, and then she would pull Mac back to his place. Get some *alone* time with him.

The front door opened and a woman came out. Striking black hair. A belly as big as a basketball. She smiled at Rogue and held out her arms for a hug. Rogue surprised herself by going straight into them. Bruin had told her about all her half-sisters already.

"You must be Ella," she said, cutting the hug just a little bit short. She didn't love the hugs anyway, but hugging a woman with a belly that big was double-uncomfortable. She put her hand out hesitantly and Ella nodded. "You can touch it."

"Shit," Rogue breathed. "You're like a house. When is the baby due?"

A cloud crossed over Ella's face, but only for a second. "Soon."

Rogue pushed Ella's belly with her finger, surprised how hard it was. "Is it a baby in there, or a wolf?"

"There's two of them, and every time we've seen them so far, it's been babies." She produced an ultrasound picture like a magician.

Rogue took it. "Aww, they're kind of cute, if you like really big heads."

Ella laughed. "Come inside, everyone is dying to meet you."

Rogue's nervousness eased a little. Ella was nice. Sweet. "Is the dragon in there? I want to thank him." And maybe sneak a bite when Mac wasn't looking. No! Bad Rogue. No sister's-mate biting.

Inside, everything was normal, more normal than Mac's house. Pictures on the walls, normal furniture. Boring. Tons of people. She was introduced to them one by one. Smile. Shit. Hi. Forgot your name already. Nice to meet you, too, shit, I'm not going to remember any of this in two minutes. She liked all her half-sisters, though. Ella, Heather, Dahlia, Cerise, she could remember them.

But then came Graeme. She could remember him, too. She tried to give him her most sincere smile. "Thank you. Like seriously, thank you."

"Thank yer mate and the bear," he said, in a delicious brogue. "They did all the hard work. I only did what comes naturally to *dragen.*"

He had his arm around his mate, Heather. Rogue eyed her up and down, the blonde hair, the full lips, and her own growing belly. Of course she wanted a hug, too. When they were pulling apart, Rogue said. "So, what, are you fireproof?"

Heather laughed. "Actually, I am."

Something deliciously nasty snuck through Rogue's thoughts. "So, what, you two do fire play instead of rope play or breath play? Like, does he tie you up and try to shoot fire up your cooch?"

Heather's mouth dropped open and Graeme looked equally stunned. Mac came up behind her and grabbed her by the shoulders, steering her over to the table of food, next to where Bruin was already loading up. "You gotta ease 'em in, Roe, ease 'em in. At least let them get to know you before you ask your sisters any sex questions. And maybe don't do it in front of their mates."

Rogue grabbed his hand. "Do you think they swap partners out here? They're all living together, right?"

Mac's face went rigid. "Good God, woman, don't ask them that. We'll be banned from ever coming back."

Rogue looked around. "Seriously? I thought they were gonna be fun."

Mac curled her close to him. "Well, they're *not*. I'm the only fun one. I'm probably the only one you should talk to about sex, too. I know they're your sisters, but they aren't like you."

She went to give him a kiss and ask him what that meant, when Bruin went rigid next to her, his plate of food spilling out of his hands.

He faced the wall straight ahead, and when he spoke, it sounded strange. Not like him.

"Caught between her future and her past, Amaranth calls for her sister, but denies it even to herself. Find her along the river walk, behind the purple door."

Stunned, Rogue grabbed Bruin's arm. It was like trying to move concrete. "What?"

Bruin shook his head, his eyes clearing, and looked down for his food, frowning. "What?"

Mac grabbed him, too. "Shit, bear, you did it again."

Bruin's face went white. "No." He looked around. "Did anyone hear?"

"I don't know." Mac moved in close to him and repeated what he'd said.

Rogue grabbed for Mac, pushing and pulling both males away from the table, into a corner where they could whisper fervently. "What in the hell? Somebody explain this to me."

Mac gestured at Bruin. "Bruin sees the future. He told me, just like that, all spacey and weird, that I was going to meet you at the rut, and then he told me if I didn't claim you, you were going to die."

Rogue rubbed the mark on her shoulder, the one that looked suspiciously to her like a knife, but Mac thought looked more like a sword. "That didn't sound like a future thing, but more like a present thing." Nausea swept through her as she tried to consider actually finding her sister. She'd been waiting twenty years for something like this to happen, the smallest lead, the littlest clue. Even a crazy one would do. She had to go. Tonight. Plans for how she would get out, get away, start looking for her sister, began running through her mind.

Mac grabbed her hands, tried to catch her eye, even as she tried to turn away. "It sounds like we're supposed to go look for her."

Bruin rubbed at his beard, his face pinched. "Wade's not going to like this."

Mac swore. "Who gives a shit! Rogue needs to find her sister." His eyes flashed. "You're with us, right, B? We can go without you if we have to, even if Wade won't give us anyone else, but I'd feel a lot safer having you along."

Bruin nodded. "I go where you go, Mac-attack."

Rogue's hearing dimmed as she watched the two male's lips move as they made plans. She hadn't expected this. For something so important to her to be just as important to Mac? She'd thought he would try to write it off, say it didn't mean anything, say she couldn't go, it was too dangerous, but no, he was going to defy his boss for her. He seemed to feel just as she did.

But he didn't even know Amaranth. Neither of them did.

And then it hit her. That's what love was. At that moment, she didn't question anymore whether Mac felt love for her. It was in the tense set of his shoulders, the urgency of his tone and words, the look in his eyes.

Finding Rogue's sister was important to him, because it was important to her. It was that simple.

Her heart opened. Bloomed. Love for him spilled out of it like water from an overflowing vase.

He was sweet, funny, sexy, and could fuck, but that wasn't why she loved him back.

She loved him because of who he was, and who they were together, and who they would be tomorrow and the next day and the next, as they walked through life together, always having each other's backs. Always being there for each other.

She dug her fingernails into Mac's arm until he stopped talking and looked at her.

Her voice was soft, weak, and she tried to strengthen it. "I would think Wade would want us to go find her, since she's a one true mate."

Mac's eyes popped and she smiled, wondering what her sister looked like as an adult. They weren't identical. Hadn't even looked much alike at five, in her opinion.

Mac leaned in close to her, holding her around her waist, and she was glad for his strength. "Are you telling me Amaranth is your twin?"

She nodded.

Mac pulled her close, tucking her into his side.

"Bruin, go find Wade. Shit just got real."

Rogue looked around at her other sisters, talking happily,

shooting her smiles, and wondered what Amaranth was going to make of all this.

She couldn't wait to find out.

EPILOGUE

*R*ogue gave an exaggerated sigh in Bruin's direction, then threw her leg over the side of the lawn chair she was sitting in, noting Mac's disapproving glare from across the yard as the shadows of early evening lengthened on his face. He, Wade, Trevor, Graeme, Crew, and the two wolves were clustered under a cherry tree 'dicussing' the plan to head to San Antonio the next day, which as far as she could see, meant nothing but a whole shit-ton of arguing so far. The black wolf with the white infinity symbol on its shoulder and the brush of white on the tip of its tail sat regally within the group of males, and occasionally they all quieted down and looked at him, like he was speaking. Every time that happened Mac got the goofiest look on his face, like he was proud as shit of himself. The other wolf, the one with the symbol of a bomb falling from the sky on his shoulder, mostly ran in circles around the group of males, sometimes nipping at their calves. Well, Trevor and Mac's calves. She didn't see him biting anyone else. Rogue had forgotten their names, but she'd ask Mac later. It was like coming in to a play in the middle, everyone else knew what the fuck was going on, but you're left whispering, "Who is he and why does he look so happy he just stabbed his father?" to the people around you.

Rogue caught Mac's eye again and smiled sweetly at him, opening her legs up wider. He was taking too fucking long. She didn't see how there was so much to discuss. Her, Mac, and Bruin were all they needed, in her opinion. Hit the river walk, find the purple fucking door, whatever that was, get Amara, and get out. Simple. Sure, there were other cities with river walks, but San Antonio was the right place. The pressure in her skull and the tightness in her chest told her so. Amara was alive and Rogue was going to see her for the first time in twenty years!

"Bruin," she moaned. "This is so borrriiiing."

Bruin shifted in his chair, lifting his nose. "We should go inside and help with dessert."

Rogue scoffed. "Fuck that. I don't cook."

"I meant help *eat* it."

Rogue glanced through the window. "They're still cooking, big guy."

Bruin's face fell. "Blast it all," he whispered. "I'm starving."

Rogue grinned. She liked Bruin the most, could see why Mac hung with him. Loyal, funny, uncomplicated, he was good company. And the guy was huge! Like, you always felt safe with someone like him around.

Her sisters were cool too, but talking with them was still awkward. The young one especially. Rogue frowned. They were all the same age, but Cerise seemed way younger than the rest of them, especially the way she stared at Rogue with wide eyes whenever Rogue started talking. Like Rogue to Cerise was the mental version of porn to an Amish teenager.

Her senses buzzed and she tried to ignore them; it had been happening all day. Someone nearby was talking about *her* specifically. Big surprise.

At least it was warm outside. Spring had finally arrived.

The bug zapper above them caught a particularly big bug, making her shudder with its extended *zappppp*, then its light flickered and dimmed, then turned off altogether. Rogue watched it, waiting for it to turn back on. When it didn't, she grimaced. She could fix it—she could fix anything—but that would mean getting awfully close to the electrocuted legs and wings she could already see clinging to the inside. *Yuck.*

She got up anyway. She could deal with bugs as long as they were dead, nobody hanging on to life, waving an errant antennae around. She yanked on the cord to unplug it but as soon as she touched the cord, the light flared back to life, stronger than ever, holding steady even after it was unplugged.

Ok. She plugged it back in, then pulled her hand off the cord and it still worked. Shit was getting freaky. Something similar had happened with Father Macleese's toaster when she'd gone to fix it. It had already been unplugged, but when she'd taken the cover off the toaster, she'd seen right away that the carriage was stuck in the wrong position. Just a touch from her had shot it into the correct position, without her even needing to get out her tools.

Rogue sat back down. Shit wasn't getting freaky. Shit was so far past freaky she should only get worried when shit looked normal.

She was dying of boredom! Her eyes crawled over the property looking for something to do. There was a horse in the field, munching grass. Not really her thing. Cooking was already a big fat no. She was stuffed, so no more eating. She eyed the house next to her. "Bru, see that flat part up there on the roof? If we could find some paint, we could make a huge dick up there." She smirked and stood up, looking around. There was a shed behind the guys. White paint would be perfect.

Bruin caught her elbow and when she turned to look at him his expression was horrified. "Uh, Rogue, I don't think that's a good idea."

She flopped back down in her chair and scooched it closer to Bruin's. "Come on, It'll be fun. It could be up there for years, and only people who fly over in airplanes would see it. We could laugh every time we came over. This place needs a good laugh.

Bruin's eyes were on the group of males, his face tight. "Trevor's kind of serious about his house." He turned back to her, eyes burning. "Let's do it to Mac!"

She stood. "Mac's roof is sloped all over, he'll see it. Come on, we're doing this."

She started across the yard. Mac stepped out of the group and pointed at Bruin. "You watch her!" he shouted.

She turned around, all giggles and smiles as Bruin lifted out of his chair and ran after her, face worried. "See, he told you to help me."

She ran around the side of the house to reach the front, which stood blessedly empty of people.

Bruin ran to catch up with her. "Actually, he said—"

But she had already found a way up. A porch with a built-in storage area, like a shelf. She pulled over a chair, boosted herself on top, then shimmied along it until she was close enough to the first eave of the house to climb onto it.

Bruin danced below her, arms held out. "Rogue come down. Mac's gonna kill me."

She stood and put her hands on her hips. "Bruin, I'm ten feet off the ground. I couldn't get hurt if I tried."

"Rogue, seriously, I'm young. I haven't had cubs yet, please—"

Rogue shot him a dirty look. She wasn't made of fucking porcelain! She torqued her body backwards against the pitch of the roof for leverage, then leapt out, right over the big bear, coming down in the grass behind him in a neat squat and roll.

She popped to her feet, laughing, then frowned at the look on the big guy's face. He had whirled around to see her drop, had probably seen her break both her legs in his imagination. He was clutching his chest, the air huffing in and out of his lungs like he'd run a marathon.

She twirled. "I'm fine, Bru, calm down."

He grabbed her by the elbows. "Don't do that again. My heart will never recover. I'm gonna die young and it's gonna be your fault."

The sincere fear and concern on his face got to her. "Fine. No roof. But we gotta do *something*."

She headed back over to the built in storage and cranked the doors open. Inside was a cache of toys, brand new, not even out of the packages. Someone had some serious misconceptions about what the babies would be capable of when they popped out. Sandcastle toys, ride on cars, a toddler scooter, squirt guns, water balloons.

Perfect.

"Bru, come here," she said, pulling stuff out. When he got there she loaded up his arms. "Come on, we gotta find a hose."

***

Mac rounded the side of the house. Where in the hell was the bear and his mate? Nobody had seen them for over half an hour, and Mac smelled trouble. Not evil trouble. Rogue trouble.

Bam! Something hit him in the side of the head, wet and cold, then his body was peppered with exploding bags of water. He turned the way they had come from, completely caught off guard, turned dumb by shock, and two more water balloons caught him right in the face.

With nothing to hide behind, Mac wiped his face and searched for the culprits as the wet smack of another balloon hit him in the crotch. There they were! Rogue and Bruin, with a cooler full of water balloons between them, under the budding boughs of another cherry tree. Bruin was on the ground, rolling with laughter, but Rogue was already scooping up more ammo.

Shit, so that's what was going down, huh? Mac ran around the house to find a hose. He skidded to a stop at the table full of two liter soda bottles. Even better. Grabbing three, he ran back to Rogue and Bruin.

But they had already moved. Mac was peppered in the back as they ran through the yard and fired balloons with their free hand, both of them holding a handle of the cooler between them, spilling squirt guns into the grass and yelling like warriors.

Mac turned and saw Trevor and Crew look at them like they were out of their minds. But Lillian just got excited. "I'm on your team!" she shouted, then ran behind them, scooping up water balloons and throwing them at everyone they passed. Wade backed away slowly and headed for the driveway.

Rogue and Bruin set up camp under another tree, dropping the cooler. "There's another box of balloons somewhere in the yard!" she yelled. "If you find it, maybe me and the bear and the girl won't massacre you all!" Balloons flew. Cerise and Beckett came out on the back porch to see what was going on and were immediately barraged with water balloons. Lillian had a killer arm. Crew snatched up the hose Mac had been going for, trying to reach Bruin and Rogue with it. Troy barked and ran madly, leaping in the air like a cat and snatching a balloon from its curving arc, water splashing his face as it burst. Trent sat on his haunches under the cherry tree, watching everything, his face unreadable. Smokey appeared from under the shed and ran to him, threading his way between Trent's legs, hiding behind them and watching the pandemonium in a way that mimicked Trent's serious nature.

Mac ran the other way, leaving the laughter and shrieks behind, bottles still in his hand, around the front of the house, into the forest beside. Stealthy wasn't his way, but he would make it work. His mate was gonna be wet and sticky in just a few minutes, and then he would claim champion status and never let her forget it.

Mac ran through the forest, hearing the battle ramp up. More screams and laughter, then an excited shout from Bruin. Someone must have found the other cache of water balloons.

Mac ran through the forest until he was behind where Rogue and Bruin and Lillian had set up base camp. He peeked out behind a tree to watch his mate, licking his lips at the sight of her athletic body, poured into a pair of tight jeans, a simple pink shirt on her top half, already clinging to her. Short sleeve. No knives strapped to her arms. Her hair was wet at the ends, and as she ducked to avoid a water balloon, he couldn't take his eyes off her ass. His mouth watered to bite it. Smack it. Get all up in there.

She wiggled her ass, then reached a hand behind herself to smack it. What in the hell? Shit, the little minx knew he was watching her. She was gonna get it.

He was distracted for a moment by Ella coming out on the porch, smiling, her belly leading the way, two pie plates in her hands, which she deposited on the picnic table. Trevor ran for her, grabbing her around the waist and shielding her body as a dozen water balloons hit his back. He didn't even flinch so the battle moved on to someone else.

Mac watched them for a moment, glad to feel the envy he had always felt and hated when he had seen Trevor and Ella together in the past was gone, slipped away, replaced by the warm glow of love for his own mate. Trevor was a good guy, doing the best he could, just like the rest of them. Mac felt a momentary twinge of regret for the way he had treated the male the first couple of years Trevor had been there. But Mac had apologized. Did his best to make it right. He'd always thought Trevor was an ass-kisser with a stick up his butt... right up until he'd walked into the *Pravus* to exchange himself for his mate, fully expecting to never return. Shit, you had to admire something like that. And even if the male had been a bit of a kiss-ass before, the experience had changed him. Made him harder, more wary and thoughtful. Mac could respect all of that shit.

Ella was pushing at Trevor. She wanted to play. Behind her, Heather and Graeme had come out, but water balloons that got within three feet of them just popped. Heather turned her face to the mist they made and sighed. Ella put her hands on her hips, then stuck her finger in Trevor's face. Trevor buckled at his knees and grabbed her hand, pulling it to his mouth and kissing it, his face pleading. Water balloons shot toward both of them, this time from the side. Trevor wasn't going to be fast enough to block them—

But Ella, still scolding her mate, put up a hand, very much talk-to-the-hand style, and the balloons exploded like they'd hit a glass wall no one could see. Even the water stopped, sliding down nothing to puddle on the ground.

Shit, good one. Mac searched out Dahlia to see what she was doing to the balloons. But no, she was out of the game, pressed up against the shed, her and Crew both soaked to the skin, her head thrown back, her eyes closed, as Crew angled his body against hers and whispered some shit into her ear. Probably not the recipe for a good pecan pie.

Eyes back to his mate. She and Bruin had run out of balloons. Lillian ran off to grab a squirt gun. Bruin headed for the picnic table, and sat down to wet pie, pulling a fork from a pocket and digging in.

Mac ran forward as quietly as he could, stopping long enough to drop two of the bottles of lemon-lime soda on the ground, then spin the top off the third. He bolted again, but Rogue stepped behind the tree and whirled on him. "You dump that on me and you'll be sorry."

Mac snorted, closing in on her, until he realized he could clearly see her boobs through her wet shirt. "Shit!" he dropped the bottle, whipped his own shirt over his head and handed it to her. "Put this on," he hissed. "Doesn't nobody here want to die today."

She looked down at herself, then put her hands on her hips and popped her elbows backwards, accentuating her chest.

"Woman, I am warning you." Mac advanced on her. If he couldn't make her wear his shirt, she was going to wear him.

Cerise ran by, heading for the forest at a full spring, laughing and shrieking, a white wolf with black boots pursuing her lazily.

Rogue's stance relaxed and Mac was able to grab her, pull her to him. She stared after Cerise and her wolf, who were almost to the forest. "Is that…?"

"That's Captain Cornbread, yeah," Mac breathed, sucking a bit of water off his mate's neck.

"What's he going to do to her when he catches her?"

"Mmmm, what do you think?"

Rogue looked at him, eyes serious. "It makes me think of that time in the forest at Sinissipi Park. I wanted it to end differently."

His tired but excited cock jumped in his pants as his memory went there, too. "What did you want to happen?"

She put her hands on his shoulders and licked her lips. "Everything."

He groaned. She eyed the place Beckett and Cerise had disappeared into the woods. "I want to be chased by a wolf."

Hell yeah, she did. "Wolves don't chase you if you don't run," he said, releasing his hold on her just a little bit and popping his shift in his mind. He bared his teeth at her, showing her a bit of growing fang, an uncontrollable growl starting in his throat.

She pulled away, hot excitement on her face, watching him curl his body toward the ground as his shift started and his clothing began to tear away.

Then his mate turned and ran.

And of course, he followed.

Notes from Lisa xoxoxo

This was my favorite book to date. I sincerely hope you enjoyed it. I busted my ass on it and gave it blood, sweat, tears, plus one incredibly long, shower-less week at the end, where I pulled five or six 16-hour days in a row. Something like that, it's a blur. It was both incredibly hard to write, and incredibly fun. My friend Savan Robbins and I laughed and laughed as we discussed Mac and Bruisms.

But now, I'm at a bit of a crossroads. This book was 20,000 words longer than any of the others in the series, and I'm not sure if that's the direction the rest of the books will go or not.

**** If it is, that means it's going to take me longer to get them out there. ****

So, anyway, back to the rest of the books. I've decided there will be at least 13 books in the series. There's a blog post on my website about that. Lisaladew.com

And thank you. Thank you for everything. Thank you for reading. Thank you for all your comments, and for loving this universe.

Lisa

63923328R00213

Made in the USA
Lexington, KY
22 May 2017